She watched him ride in, and immediately she lost all hope of his being someone who had come to help her.

He looked as Indian as any of them, wore only denim pants, no shirt. He was dark, big, as mean looking as the others. His black hair hung nearly to his waist and was worn loose, and he was well armed. The others gathered around him, holding guns on him.

"You will go no farther, *señor,*" Juan told him. "Speak your name."

"I am called Hawk," John Hawkins answered, deciding to use Ken's nickname for him. It sounded like something an Indian would call himself, and he sure was not about to tell them his real name.

He was hoping he'd guessed right—that none of these men knew him by sight. If he was going to get the better of this bunch, why not ride right into their nest and take them from the inside?

He gla⟶⟶ gon wheel. There she was, ⟶⟶ only knew what she'd b⟶⟶ do was figure out how in ⟶

TEXAS EMBRACE

Rosanne Bittner

Zebra Books
Kensington Publishing Corp.

http://www.zebrabooks.com

ZEBRA BOOKS are published by

Kensington Publishing Corp.
850 Third Avenue
New York, NY 10022

Zebra and the Z logo Reg. U.S. Pat. & TM Off.

First Printing: April, 1997
10 9 8 7 6 5 4 3

Printed in the United States of America

Chapter One

"Hand me that dynamite!"

"What?"

"You heard me! I'll *blow* them out of there."

"Hawk, there's six men in there. You don't know—"

"I know all I need to know." The words were spoken with obvious hatred. "They raped a twelve-year-old girl."

"She was *Indian!*"

The air hung silent for a moment, and Ken Randall regretted the statment as soon as he made it. John Hawkins was not just a fellow Texas Ranger. He was his friend, and Ken knew how the man felt about both Indians and rape. In spite of their friendship, the look in Hawk's dark eyes gave Ken the shivers and reminded him of why he was glad he was Hawk's friend and not his enemy. He closed his eyes and sighed, disgusted with his remark. "Damn it, Hawk, you know what I mean. It's not the way *I* think but you know how most men in these parts think about Indian women."

"She wasn't any woman. She was a *kid!*" John growled.

"All right. All right. But you can't tell Captain Booth you blew them up on account of them rapin' an Indian girl. It's got to be for a better reason—like them stealin' horses and cattle."

John grimaced at the statement, reloading his six-shooter. How sad but true that folks would hang a man for stealing a horse but let him go free if all he did was rape a little Indian girl. "Fine," he answered sarcastically, angrily snapping the loaded cartridge back into the revolver. "After all, we did start tracking them for stealing cattle."

Both men kept their heads lowered behind the boulder that sheltered them. Another bullet pinged against the top of the boulder, sending a spray of rock chips down on their wide-brimmed hats.

"We ain't supposed to be goin' after men for killin' or rapin' Indians," Ken reminded John. "The Apache and Comanche are the enemy, remember?"

"I've had my share of run-ins with both. You know that. I've tracked them and I've killed them, when *they* were in the wrong! This is different."

"Not in the eyes of most Texans. Now let's get this over with. You have to at least try to convince them men in there to give themselves up first."

"I'd get more satisfaction out of blowing them up."

Ken removed his hat and banged it against his knee to knock off dust and rock chips. "Damit, Hawk, will you listen to me? This is 1882. Texas is gettin' more civilized, and some folks think the Rangers is nothin' more than vigilantes. Some call us outlaws goin' after outlaws, especially the ones like you."

John removed his own hat and slowly raised his head to check out the cabin. He could hear voices. The men inside were arguing. They damn well knew that one of the Rangers out there was John Hawkins, and John Hawkins was a man of little patience and no mercy. "All we're doing is giving the people what they want—law and order. They want cattle rustlers and horse thieves caught and hanged. I prefer saving the state the cost of the hanging. Now go get the damn dynamite, Private Randall!"

Ken knew the meaning of Private Randall. John never called him that unless his patience was used up. "Yes, sir, *Sergeant* Hawkins."

John paid him no heed. He supposed he did have to give the men inside fair warning. After all, he'd been ordered by Captain Booth to tone down his ruthlessness. It would be easier if he didn't have all this hatred and frustration inside over his own sorry life, the confusion over whether his loyalty should lie with Indian or white, his feelings of worthlessness that left a constant seething anger in his soul. Besides, people never used to question how the Texas Rangers took care of their business. Now there was all this new talk about justice and law and being more humane and civilized. Bullshit! When men committed *un*civilized, *in*humane acts of crime and violence, who the hell cared how they were treated?

"Derrek Briggs!" he shouted. "You've got one last chance to give yourselves up, Briggs! I know you're one of them in there! That's your roan mare tied outside. Give it up, Briggs! The judge gave you a break last time you were arrested. Didn't four years in prison teach you anything?"

There was a moment of silence when the men inside stopped arguing.

"That you, Hawkins?"

John kept his head lowered. "You know damn well who it is!"

Another moment of silence.

"Then you come and get me, you half-breed bastard! I know what you do to your prisoners, and you ain't takin' me in again! I'll blow your guts out first and feed you to the buzzards!"

John moved to the other side of the boulder, studying the terrain, figuring how he could get closer to the cabin. "I might have given up the chase, Briggs, if you wouldn't have raped that little girl," he shouted back. "You put the noose around your neck with that one!"

"Like hell! No Texan hangs a man for rapin' an Indian, woman or child."

John closed his eyes, memories of his precious mother and her sad life only building up his hatred for men like Briggs. "Maybe not, but your problem is, it's not those people who are after you. It's *me*—John Hawkins! And I *would* hang a man for raping an Indian! The best part is, your corral over there is full of stolen cattle, and farther off you're grazing stolen horses. That's all the excuse I need to bring you in. You can make it easy or hard on yourself."

"Oh, yeah? Just how do you think you and whoever is with you are gonna' get six men out of this cabin without gettin' yourselves killed, breed? You want us? You come and get us!"

John grinned. "It'll be my pleasure!"

Ken returned, bending low as he made his way through the underbrush from where they had left their horses hidden. He handed John four sticks of dynamite. "That's all I've got," he said in a low voice. "I don't like carryin' the stuff. You know all kinds of things can happen to make this stuff blow up. Next time you carry the dynamite in your *own* saddlebags! Better yet, don't ever carry it again when I'm with you."

John shoved his six-gun into its holster. "You worry too much, you know that?"

Ken grabbed his arm. "Yeah? Well, mostly it's *you* I worry about. Seems to me you enjoy tryin' to get yourself killed."

John carefully laid the dynamite nearby and pulled a thin cigar from a pocket inside his leather vest. He could never admit openly how much he appreciated Ken Randall's sincere friendship. Sentiment was not a feeling to which he was accustomed, except when it came to his poor, dead mother. He almost wished Ken wouldn't make remarks like the one he'd just made. He lit the cigar and gave it a couple of long draws. "Well, now, Ken, just think about it. Where would be the loss if I got myself killed?"

Ken began reloading his own six-gun. "It would be a loss to the Rangers, and a personal loss for me. There ain't nobody else I'd want to serve with, and you know it."

John put on an air of being unimpressed. He laughed lightly, shaking his head. "You save a man's life once, and he thinks he owes you forever. You're too damn sentimental for this work, Ken." He stuck the cigar between his lips and picked up the dynamite.

Maybe so, Ken thought. John Hawkins could be such a bastard sometimes. The fact remained the man *had* saved his life, not just once, but twice. And he was pretty damn sure that under all that crust and pretended unconcern, John Hawkins had a heart. Why else would he care that a little Indian girl had been raped? And sometimes the man would make a remark or two about his mother, what a hard life she'd had being part Indian. The man had opened up just once about her, telling Ken the sad details, but it was obvious John and his mother had been close. Still, it was hard to imagine John Hawkins being close to anyone, even his own mother. "Why don't we just starve them out?"

"Hell, that could take two weeks or more if they've got food and water in there. I'm for getting this over with and getting back to El Paso for a drink and a bed with a woman in it." John kept the cigar in his mouth as he spoke. He held up the dynamite. "This will do the job a lot quicker."

"Well, how in hell do you figure to get close enough to throw them sticks where they'll do the most damage?"

"You just draw their fire for me." John darted away, managing to get himself behind another boulder.

The men inside began firing at them again, and Ken winced, bobbing up just long enough to get off a couple of shots, ducking back down again as several bullets chipped away more rock. When he looked over to where John had gone, his partner was no longer there. "You crazy son-of-a-bitch," he muttered. "You'll be lucky you don't blow *yourself* up!"

He began shooting at the cabin again. John had said to draw their fire, and that was what he would do. Suddenly the men inside the cabin stopped shooting.

"Where'd he go?"

"Hell, I don't know!"

Ken smiled. They were arguing—and scared, damn scared. One of them must have noticed John dart from behind the boulder. Now they were worried, rightly so.

"Watch for him! Everybody take a window!" someone ordered. It was Derrek Briggs. Ken knew the man's harsh, gritty voice. Briggs just couldn't seem to stay away from cattle rustling. It had already got him prison once. Now he'd for sure hang . . . or get himself blown up. Ken wondered what had possessed the fool to come back into territory he damn well knew John Hawkins patrolled. From El Paso east to Pecos, south to the Davis Mountains and on across the Rio Grande into Mexico, few outlaws were safe from John Hawkins. He had the tracking instincts of an animal, which most folks said was from his Indian blood. He was a big man, damn strong and tough to put down. And he had a hatred inside that fired him up and made him go up against some pretty dangerous odds sometimes, just to get his man. No one really knew the details of what drove John Hawkins, and no one asked. John was the type of man who would tell you something if he wanted, but he never answered direct questions.

"Damn it, Hawk, where are you?" Ken grumbled. There was plenty of scrubby cover several yards away from the cabin, however, all was clear for a good twenty yards or so between the brush and the cabin. How in hell did Hawk plan to get that dynamite in close? He slowly raised his head, aiming to start shooting again and draw more fire, but before he could get off another shot, John Hawkins bolted out from behind the rocks and brush at the back of the cabin, giving out a war whoop like the wildest of Indians and charging up to the cabin. Ken could see he was carrying four sticks of dynamite, all of them lit!

"Jesus, Hawk, you're crazy!" Ken swore. He started shooting again, but already bullets were being fired at John, and Ken worried the dynamite would go off before John could get rid of it. He didn't know all that much about dynamite and wondered if John himself did. The man had brought it along on a whim, another one of those crazy notions he sometimes got.

There was nothing Ken could do now but watch, sure he'd see his friend killed. It all happened in only seconds. John ducked and rolled to avoid bullets, managing to get himself to a back porch. There was only one window at the back, and whoever was shooting out of it ran out of bullets. He cussed and drew his arm back within, and before another man could take his place, John jumped up and threw the dynamite inside, then made a mad dash away from the cabin.

"It's dynamite!" Ken heard someone scream. "Get out! Get—"

Those were the last words from inside the cabin. Before even one man could make it outside, the place exploded in a fireball. Ken ducked down behind the rock, now wondering if John would be killed from the explosion. He'd surely had no time to make it to decent cover. Ken was surprised at how much damage four sticks of dynamite could do, as logs and seemingly millions of pieces of wood and debris flew overhead and showered down all around him, one big log landing just inches away. When things quieted, he slowly rose, gaping at what was left of the cabin, which was virtually nothing but a couple of logs that managed to cling to the rock foundation. In the distance he could see the dust of the stampeding cattle and horses that had been frightened off by the explosion.

"Damn it, Hawk, now we have to ride out and try to round up all them cattle!" he yelled. "What good does it do to find them for their owners if we turn around and scatter them all over Texas!"

There was no reply. Ken saw two bodies not far off, grimaced when he noticed one of them had no head. He shook his own head at John Hawkins's penchant for violence. Maybe this time that violence had caught up with him.

"Hawk?" Ken shoved his six-gun into its holster and began a search. Two more bodies lay closer to the cabin, one with an arm missing, another with both legs missing. That one he recognized as Derrek Briggs. He figured Briggs was about the same age as himself, late forties.

He shook his head at what was left of the man. Briggs had been a fine-looking man who simply drank too much and would rather steal for a living than work an honest job. Ken scratched at a three-day growth of beard and looked around.

"Hawk! Damn it, answer me!" He headed for the area behind the cabin, now littered with so much debris he had to step over things. He chastised himself for letting John use the dynamite, or even bring it along, but then nobody told John Hawkins what to do. Hell, he had a good fifteen years experience on the man himself, yet it was usually John who made the decisions. Hawkins seemed to be kind of a natural-born leader, and Ken had never really cared about being in charge of anything. He'd rather follow orders, except that was often not an easy task when working with John Hawkins. If it weren't for the fact that Hawkins was one of the most skilled men among the Texas Rangers, and the not-so-unimportant fact that the man had saved his life more than once, he'd ask to work with someone else. John Hawkins was only thirty-two, but he was looking to get himself killed before he was forty, and he'd probably take his partner with him when it happened.

Ken's heart tightened a little when he finally spotted a body several yards away lying prone amid brush and rocks and pieces of log. He knew then the real reason he remained partners with John Hawkins. He'd learned to care about the bastard, sometimes felt almost fatherly toward him. Of course he'd never tell Hawk that. He didn't like talking about anything that bordered on the sentimental, and Hawk would probably laugh his rear end off if Ken mentioned anything to him about how he felt.

He came closer, realizing he couldn't picture Hawk dead. The man was too mean to die. He saw the long, black hair then. Some of it had come loose from where Hawk had tied it behind his neck with a piece of rawhide.

"Hawk? You okay?" To Ken's relief he saw movement, but he also noticed blood on the back of Hawk's shirt, in the area between the bottom of his leather vest and the waist of his denim pants.

"I'm just lying here trying to decide if I'm dead or alive," John answered.

Ken rolled his eyes. "Damn it, Hawk, you had me scared to death! Why didn't you call out to me?" He knelt beside him. "You hurt bad? There's blood on the back of your shirt here."

John slowly moved his arms, then got to his knees. "I think it's just a cut. I felt something hit me." He rubbed at his head. "Back of the head, too. Everything went black for a while." He winced as he turned to look at the cabin, then he grinned. "I guess we got our men, huh?"

Ken rose, removing his hat and wiping at sweat on his forehead with his shirtsleeve. "I guess you could say that. You blew Briggs's legs off."

"Really?"

Ken's lips twitched in disgust. "I don't suppose you care."

John's dark eyes showed a quick return of hatred. "He raped a little girl. No, I *don't* care how he died. A man makes his bed, he's got to lie in it."

"Which means you're gonna die a violent death yourself some day."

"Probably." John looked around. "I lost my gun somehow."

Ken reached down to help him get to his feet. "I hope you ain't hurt so bad you can't help me bury these bastards. I ain't gonna do it all by myself. It's gonna be mighty miserable work in this heat."

John winced as he moved his arms around, then reached behind his neck to pull the rawhide strip from his hair. He shook his hair behind his shoulders then and retied it. "Do we really have to bury them? Why not leave them for the buzzards and coyotes?"

Ken plunked his hat back on his head. "Because we're

supposed to be civilized, Christian men. Now I know for a fact you ain't neither one, but you'll be in enough trouble for blowin' them bastards up. You'll be hanged yourself if you don't give them a decent burial! Now let's see if we can find a shovel or two in one of them sheds beyond and get to it."

John grinned, looking around again. "Help me find my gun first."

They both searched through the underbrush. "What the hell possessed you to run straight up to the cabin like that? You got a personal death wish or somethin'?" Ken kicked around at some debris.

"Well, you know how it is with the Indian. He knows when it's a good day to die." John looked up at the sky, which was overcast. "I realized this really wasn't a good day to die, so I figured their bullets wouldn't find me today."

"Oh, yeah, that makes a lot of sense. Next time some outlaw is shootin' at me, you let me know if it's a good day to die or not. If it ain't, I won't worry."

John laughed at his remark. "If you're worried about what the fine citizens of El Paso will think about this, forget it. The biggest braggart about proper law and order is Jim Caldwell, and he's nothing but hot air. I'm convinced he's up to something *un*lawful himself."

"Like what?"

"I don't know—maybe cattle rustling."

"Caldwell? He's the biggest rancher in west Texas! Why would he need to rustle cattle?"

The two men searched for more bodies as they spoke.

"I don't know. I only know I don't trust the son-of-a-bitch, and he seems real bent on getting me booted out of the Rangers, like he's afraid I might discover something he doesn't want discovered. He talks almost too passionately about justice and civilizing west Texas. I think it's all a cover."

"Yeah, well, just try proving it. Men like Caldwell keep their asses covered at all times. Either way, what you did today will give him plenty of new ammunition to get rid of you."

"I'm not afraid of that puffed-up bag of wind."

Ken spotted John's six-gun and leaned down to pick it up. "All I know right now is you could make this job a lot easier on me if you'd behave like normal men behave." He handed out the gun. "Here's your six-shooter."

John was still grinning as he came over to take the gun. "You know I'm no normal man. If you want to ride with me, you just have to face the facts. Maybe you're just getting too old for this."

"Like hell!" Ken gave him a shove and John laughed. Ken shook his head, thinking it was no wonder the whores in El Paso swooned over John Hawkins. Indian blood or not, he was probably the best-looking man around, especially when he smiled. One good thing about being his partner was there were usually plenty of women around when they were in town. The sad part was, the decent, marriageable ones wouldn't give John the time of day, not even the Mexican *señoritas,* just because he had that Indian blood. Ken had seen how some of them looked at him, though. John Hawkins was six feet of lean power, one of those mixed breeds who had inherited the best features of both Indian and white.

"Hey, here's another body," John said. "This one is in one piece, but he's dead."

"That makes five. I already seen four others."

John looked around, squinting, then pointed toward a huge oak tree in the distance. "Look over there in that tree to the front of the cabin. That look like a body to you?"

Ken turned to look, noticing something odd-looking in the tree's gnarled branches. "God Almighty, I think it is. You blew him clear up in that tree!"

John nodded. "We're going to have to remember to bring along dynamite every trip. Comes in handy, doesn't it?"

Ken frowned. "I ain't bringin' that stuff along again.

What if it had blowed up while it was still in my saddle-bags?''

John raised his eyebrows at the thought. "I wouldn't have found enough pieces to bury, I guess."

"Yeah? Well, like I said earlier, *you* can carry the stuff next time! In the meantime, we've not only got bodies to bury, we've got cattle and horses to round up, thanks to you."

"We'll get it done." John rubbed at his head again. "Let's go try to get that body out of the tree."

"You'd better let me wrap that cut," Ken told him, noticing the bloodstain on the back of John's shirt was growing. "I expect it's deeper than you think."

"Quit fussing. I said I'm . . ." John suddenly stopped walking. He turned to Ken, a strange look on his face. "Oh, shit!" With that his eyes rolled back, and dark as his skin was, he literally paled, then fell flat on his face.

Chapter Two

Tess could hardly believe what her husband had done. She had already made up her mind that Abel Carey was a coward at heart, a man who backed away from the simplest confrontation, but this was incredible. Here she was shooting at renegade outlaws to defend herself and their ranch, and Abel was in the bedroom, supposedly to find more ammunition. There was no ammunition in the bedroom. She'd screamed to him that there wasn't, but he'd gone there anyway, and he had not come back out. He'd left her alone here at the front window to fight off what she figured must be at least fifteen marauders.

Her father lay dead out by the barn, his body filled with arrows. Terror engulfed her. The barn was on fire, and some of the raiders had already made off with horses and cattle. She fired her father's repeating rifle twice more, and one of the attackers fell from his horse.

"Got you, by damn!" she cursed, fighting tears that wanted to come. She had no idea if the raiders were Comanche, Apache, or maybe Comancheros, a horrid mixture of outlaws, whites, Mexicans, and Indians, who raided outlying Texas farms and ranches and traded their loot in

Mexico, including captured white women. Whatever her attackers were, they were merciless, and her husband was cowering in the bedroom. She was alone in this fight. She'd managed to hit two of the attackers, but one had got back up, and there was no doubt in her terrified soul that there were too many of them for her to hold out much longer. She'd hoped they would leave after taking the livestock, but they continued the attack. Deep inside she knew why. They were after her.

Some had told her father he was a little crazy for settling way out here, almost a day's ride from El Paso, no neighbors; but the land had been free, and by the time they came here three years ago, free land was the only kind they could afford. At least the Army, much as her father still hated their blue Yankee uniforms, sent out patrols now and then from Fort Bliss to check on things. A lot of good that did her now. Oh, if only a patrol was somewhere nearby.

She gasped when an arrow sang past the side of her face and embedded itself in the wall behind her. One inch to the left and it would have buried itself in her eye. "Abel! Abel, where are you!"

"I—I can't find the bullets!"

"I told you there *aren't* any! Get out here with that other rifle!"

She heard it then, the sound of something on the roof. Numb with fear, she couldn't even feel her hands as she nervously reloaded her own rifle. There was no time to mourn her father, no time to go into the bedroom and argue with Abel. She wished she'd known what kind of man he really was when she'd married him, but the deed was done, and once a woman chose her man, she had to stick by him, didn't she? That was what she believed. The trouble was, a wife ought to be able to respect her husband, feel he'd protect her in times of danger.

She should have stayed in San Antonio, married Les. But how could she let her father come here alone to fight the dangers and the elements in trying to rebuild his life?

It still hurt to think of Les, leaving his offer of marriage to come here, but then he in turn had not loved her enough to come along.

She heard more footsteps above. What were they doing up there? Another arrow sailed right through the window, and this one had something burning on the end of it.

Fire! That was what they were doing on the roof! They were setting fire to the cabin! Fire was her biggest fear, the one thing that still gave her nightmares. The memory of their lovely little home back in Georgia going up in roaring flames, her mother and brother still inside, was as vivid today as if it had just happened. Would she die the same horrible death? She could still hear her mother's last scream.

"Dear God, please help me," she prayed. She turned and tried to fire the rifle again, but it jammed. "Abel!" she screamed at her husband again. "Abel, they're trying to burn down the house!" There came no reply. She grabbed up a rug and began beating at the flames that were licking at the wall where the burning arrow had landed. She managed to beat out the fire, but things were already getting hazy from the smoke it had created. She heard a crackling sound above her, and she looked up to see more flames crawling along one section of the roof.

Anger began to take over then. Life had been too unfair since the war. It had stolen her chance at a normal childhood, ruined her father's life. This was not really the fault of the vicious men outside. This was all because of the war that had devastated the South and left her once prosperous family broken and homeless. If they had not had to leave Georgia . . .

She searched for something else to use as a weapon, and she grabbed up a butcher knife still lying on the counter beside the rabbit she'd been cleaning when the Indians began their raid. The fire on the roof was getting bigger. She couldn't stay in here much longer. Which was worse? Dying by fire or dying at the hands of the renegades?

"Abel!" she screamed again. "My God, what are you

doing in there?'' She ran into the bedroom and saw no one. "Abel! Abel, where are you!''

Outside the outlaws screamed and whooped, their horses thundering closer now as they circled the cabin. She heard the thud of more arrows hitting the small wooden house, and she had no doubt they also were flaming arrows. If she didn't get out soon, she would die the way her mother had. Her choice became obvious. Maybe, just maybe, there was a chance for survival if she let the men outside take her off with them. She had no doubt what that would mean, but nothing terrified her more than fire. Nothing.

She clenched her jaw against more tears that wanted to come. There was no time for tears now. There was time only for thinking about how to survive. Pieces of roof began falling in the outer room. She headed for the bedroom window, and that was when she heard it, the sound of someone sobbing. It came from under the bed.

"Abel?'' Still clutching the butcher knife, she bent down and lifted the blanket to see her husband huddled under the bed, crying. Her stomach actually churned at the sight. "My God, Abel.''

"Don't go out there, Tess,'' the man sobbed. "Don't go out there! Kill me. Just kill me and kill yourself!''

Deep anger and a stubborn desire to live overwhelmed her. "Abel Carey, you get out from under there and face this like a man!''

"There's too many! They'll kill us, Tess. Torture us first!''

"Not *me,* they won't! They want me alive!''

The look in his eyes told her all she needed to know. He wanted her to go out there and offer herself up to the enemy. That way, maybe he would live. "Abel, if we both survive this, I'm divorcing you! You're a sniveling *coward!*'' She jerked down the blanket and went to the window, raising it. Before she could climb out, a near-naked, screaming warrior charged inside, grabbing her by the hair. Using all her strength, Tess buried her butcher knife into his side. She was not going to give up without a fight!

Another warrior came barging in from the curtained doorway, another through the window. She lashed out, and now everything seemed to be happening in a kind of unreality, as though she were just having a nightmare. She thought she cut another, but someone grabbed her arm and yanked the knife away. She heard screaming, wasn't sure if it was her own. She heard Abel now, also screaming, begging. Through the smoke that was filling the bedroom, she could see painted, dark-haired, dark-skinned men dragging Abel out the window. Then she was being shoved outside.

She fought as viciously as she could, kicking, scratching, biting. Something hit her hard on the head, and dizziness and blackness began to engulf her. She was aware of being thrown to the ground, of her clothes being ripped away. She knew then what they would do to her, yet strangely she felt nothing. Through blurred vision she saw their faces, one coming closer now.

"Well, my pretty, I will see how much you are worth, huh?"

Hands were clawing at her legs, a man's weight was on top of her.

"I am Chino. I will make you glad you are with us, no?"

Tess heard his grunting sounds, heard others talking and laughing, some in a strange Indian tongue, some in Spanish. Would the one called Chino kill her once he was through with her? She could still hear Abel screaming. What were they doing to him?

Through a haze she saw smoke and flames. Maybe it was her mother she heard screaming. Her little brother. Yes. They had died in a terrible fire. The war. Maybe this was still the war. It seemed life had been filled with hardship ever since that terrible day when she'd lost her precious mother. She had to think about that, painful as it was. She usually blocked it out of her mind, except when the horror revisited her, unwanted, in her nightmares. Now she had to deliberately think about it. That was the only way to bear what the one called Chino was doing to her now.

Finally it ended. Someone rolled her over and trussed her wrists behind her back. She was moved around more, sensed she was being wrapped in a blanket. Someone picked her up and threw her over a horse. A man mounted the horse, and she could see one of his bare legs from where her head hung over the side.

Don't think about what is happening, she told herself. *Think about something else.*

She noticed how perfect the beaded-star design was on the toe of his moccasin. How could someone work beads that perfectly? The fringes on the moccasin were quite long, hanging a couple of inches longer than the sole of the shoe.

Comanche! She'd learned enough about them to know this was the type of moccasin they wore. She remembered a soldier telling her father once about the extra long fringes of a Comanche moccasin and the unique prints such moccasins left behind. She thought about how hard it was for her father to have to be cordial to the Army units who rode through occasionally, but much as he hated to admit it—and he hated those Yankee uniforms—the fact remained they had felt safer with Fort Bliss only a day's ride away.

But that had been no help today. She was alone. Totally alone. How could she avoid the awful reality of it? She grunted with pain as the horse over which she was draped took off at a near gallop. Where were they taking her? To their camp, to rape her again? Maybe the next time they would all take turns. Maybe they would torture her. She told herself she must not panic. She had to keep her wits about her, hope to find a way to escape. Dying in Texas backcountry or maybe down in Mexico was better than being tortured and raped, maybe sold off to some sadistic person who would make a slave of her. At least alone in the wilds she would have a chance of survival.

Yes, that was what she would think about. Escape! Or

maybe someone would come along and see the ruins of her farm, find her father's body and Abel's, and figure out she'd been taken off. Maybe the Yankee soldiers would find and help her. She had to cling to any hope she could.

One thing was sure, she, by-God, was not going to show these men any fear! She would not cry in front of them. She would spit in their faces when she got the chance! She was Theresa McDowell Carey! She'd been through the Civil War, the loss of her mother and brother, a complete change in her style of living. She had gone from the moderate wealth of a family who lived on a prosperous farm in the gentle South, to struggling for survival on a ranch in the wild, rugged country of west Texas. She had fought Indians before this and helped run them off. This time it didn't work, and she had seen her father murdered. There was no doubt in her mind that Abel was dead, too. For some reason she had been spared, and she would use that to her advantage. She would damn well get herself out of this mess! No one was going to make Theresa Carey cringe and beg! The memory of Abel cowering under the bed only made her more determined never to behave that way herself.

She would start by concentrating on anything that took her away from the horror of her situation. She would start with that moccasin, that pretty, perfect star design. Such a contrast it was to the brutal savage who wore it.

"Hey, look there, Hawk. Somebody's been burned out."

John was already studying the scene below, the smoldering ruins of what appeared to have been a house and outbuildings, broken-down fences, a buckboard wagon, also partially burned. A troop of soldiers was milling about, two of them digging a grave, one farther off bent over. It looked to John as though he was vomiting.

"Comancheros, maybe?" Ken commented.

"Most likely. That's mostly who's responsible for the raiding in these parts. About the only Comanche running free are those with Quanah Parker, and lately he's been trying to show how civilized he can be, putting on a show of being a leader and a diplomat."

"The Apache are up at Bosque Redondo or over in Indian Territory," Ken said, "and the Comanche haven't been doing any raiding in these parts for a long time."

John lit a thin cigar. "Let's go down and have a look before we report in."

Ken got his horse in motion. "You're just puttin' off havin' to tell Captain Booth you blew up Briggs and his men."

John grinned, keeping the smoke between his lips. "Booth will understand."

"Long as you don't mention the real reason you wanted them dead."

John did not reply. Rape was something that set off his fuse more quickly than any other crime. He was himself the product of rape, and when he was older, yet another man had tried to rape his mother. He'd only been fourteen then, but he'd killed that man. It seemed his heart had been full of hatred and a need to kill ever since. He figured he could kill his own father if he ever found the man.

They made their way toward the burned-out ranch, having already returned the cattle and horses Briggs had stolen to two ranchers farther east. The cut on John's lower right side still pained him, and he still got headaches from the lump he'd taken in the explosion, but he'd decided that one day's rest after the incident with Briggs was enough. Briggs and his men were buried in one mass grave, and he and Ken had given away their horses and personal possessions to the ranchers from whom the livestock had been stolen. There was virtually nothing left of Briggs and his men now. It was as though they had blown away in the Texas wind. That was fine with John Hawkins. Good riddance.

As they came closer to the scene below, the stench of charred wood and burned flesh hit their nostrils with a backlash of hot wind, and Ken wrinkled his nose. "Damn.

This looks like pretty dirty business. I think this is the place where that old man lived with his daughter and her husband, ain't it? McDowell, I think his name was."

"I saw the man here once when I rode through, but I never saw the daughter out here." John paid little attention to folks who lived within a day's ride from Fort Bliss and El Paso. There was little left for them to worry about. Most Indian raids had ended, and Comancheros seldom attacked so close to bigger settlements. John's concern lay mostly with ranchers and tiny settlements much farther away, in the interior, rugged country between here and the Apache and Davis Mountains, as well as patrolling border country, where Mexican bandits did their trading along the Rio Grande.

"We seen the old man gettin' supplies once in El Paso," Ken commented. "Remember? His daughter was with him then. Pretty thing, as I remember."

John shrugged. "I think I remember." He remembered, all right. He never knew her name, but he'd noticed McDowell's redheaded daughter once in El Paso. The little snob had turned away as soon as she spotted him, like all supposedly decent white women did when they saw him. Heaven forbid they should be caught looking twice at a half-breed. "Looks like the Army didn't do too well protecting this place," he added, wanting to change the subject. He tipped his hat to one of the soldiers, who stood next to a body barely distinguishable as human.

"Damn!" Ken muttered. "That's one of the worst things I've seen in a long time." The man lay naked, most of his skin sliced off, his throat slit. "You think he was alive when they took off the skin?"

John's jaw twitched in disgust. "Most likely."

"From what I can tell, he's younger than old man McDowell. Must be the woman's husband. I ain't sure what his name was."

"Who the hell are you?" one of the soldiers asked. "You Comanche? Apache? You know something about this god-damn mess, Indian?"

John dismounted, looking down on the young man, who only stood about five and a half feet. "If I knew something about it, would I ride in here now? And I'm not Apache *or* Comanche. Is there a Lieutenant Ames here?"

"You know him?"

"I know him."

The young man looked John over derisively. "Well, maybe you're not one of the savages usually found in these parts, but Indian is Indian far as I'm concerned." He nodded toward the burned barn. "He's over there by another body. An old man shot full of arrows like a pincushion. I don't know how any man, Indian or not, can do what's been done here. Innocent ranchers, that's all they were. These men died trying to defend wife and daughter, most likely. We haven't found her yet. God help her if she's still with the ones who did this."

John did not reply. He led his horse toward the barn. Ken spit some tobacco juice at the feet of the private who'd just talked to John. "You must be new."

The young man straightened, putting his hands on his hips in a air of confidence. "Yeah. So what?"

"You just insulted one of the best men the Texas Rangers has workin' for them. He's saved my life twice, and Indian or not, he's a good man. You ought to watch your tongue when you ain't sure who you're talkin' to, soldier."

The soldier looked a little embarrassed. "Who is he?"

"That there is John Hawkins. I'll bet you've heard some of the other men talk about him."

The private turned to glance at John as he walked away. "I've heard of him." He faced Ken again. "I've heard he's the meanest, most cold-blooded son-of-a-bitch ever came to Texas. I ain't never heard him called a good man."

Ken spit another wad at the soldier's feet. "Then you ain't never talked to the people he's helped." He walked off behind John, shaking his head at the cockiness of new recruits. He walked up to John, who was watching soldiers pull arrows out of the other dead man's body. Another soldier stopped to vomit.

John tipped his hat to Lieutenant Robert Ames, a man he knew well from having to work with him. "Lieutenant."

Ames nodded to John. "Hello, Hawk. Quite a mess, isn't it?"

John looked around. "I'd say so." He turned back to the lieutenant. "No sign of the woman?"

"Oh, there's sign, all right." He pointed toward the house. "Over there. Her clothes, torn to shreds. No body, though. You know what that means."

John nodded grimly. They had taken the woman. If they'd stripped her first, they had probably also raped her. Since they took her alive, they had plans to trade her for guns, gold, whatever the Mexicans would give them for her. "Mind if I look around?"

Ames shrugged. "Be my guest. Maybe you can help us track her, unless you're already on some other mission."

John was surprised at the request. The Army and the Texas Rangers did not always get along so well. Down here they were more in competition than willing to work together. But then he'd been asked before to help with tracking. "Just finished an assignment," he answered. "Caught up with some cattle rustlers. We already returned what stolen cattle and horses we managed to round up."

The lieutenant looked around. "Where are the rustlers?"

John puffed on his cigar a moment, looking around. "Gee, I guess there weren't any left to bring back."

Ames shook his head. "Don't tell me—"

"They have to learn not to put up a fight, Lieutenant."

Ames sighed, realizing the notorious John Hawkins had apparently failed again to bring back live prisoners. "Well, be that as it may, nobody is better at tracking than you. I wish you'd agree to scout for the Army full-time instead of working for the meager pay of a Texas Ranger."

"Last I knew, a scout's pay wasn't much better."

Ames had to grin. "At least we furnish your supplies and your horse and weapons."

John nodded. "Well, I'm just not the type who likes to

ride with a lot of men and take orders. I've got more freedom as a Ranger." He left the lieutenant to look around the ruins, actually hoping to find the woman's body somewhere. She'd be better off dead and out of her misery. He found nothing. He mounted his horse, a sturdy, golden palomino gelding, and rode the perimeter, studying the tracks left from the raid. They were headed right for the Rio Grande, just like he figured. He rode back to Ames, where Ken was helping remove the last few arrows from the dead man's body. John remained mounted as he spoke. "How long ago do you figure this happened?"

"No longer than yesterday," Ames replied. "The bodies are rigid, but the embers from the fires are still plenty warm."

"McDowell was his name, wasn't it?"

Ames nodded. "A nice family. The old man was Henry McDowell. He ranched here with his daughter, Tess, a pretty, real outspoken spunk of a woman with bright red hair. She was a small thing, but from the couple of times we patrolled here and talked to her, I figured her to have a lot of sass. The one over there was Abel Carey, her husband. He was kind of a meek, quiet sort. I got the impression his wife bossed him around pretty good. They didn't seem to be much alike." He removed the bandana at his neck and wiped at sweat on his face and nape. "At any rate, if the renegades still have the woman, my bet is she'll give them a hard time of it. She'll put up a fight. Trouble is, she'll just get beat all the worse for it."

"You sending men after her?"

"I have to report back to the fort first, get reorganized. I don't have enough men with me right now for something like that."

"That will take another day or two. That could be too long for the woman. Once she gets sold off, she'll be harder to track."

"Well, I don't have any choice, Hawk. And you know how it is. Once they get her across the border, I'm not allowed to go into Mexico. I have no authority there."

John looked to the south. "Neither do I, but that's never stopped me before."

"You goin' after her, Hawk?" Ken asked.

John thought about it a minute. He had always remembered the young woman with sunset-colored hair he'd seen in El Paso. She'd been in the mercantile buying flour and sugar and such. He'd been buying tobacco. He had only glanced at her, and she had glanced at him, then looked away real quick-like. She was probably a stuck-up prude who didn't deserve being rescued by a man she'd rather spit on, but she for *sure* didn't deserve being treated the way he knew she was being treated now. Nobody deserved that. "Well," he said aloud, "she is a citizen of Texas, and we're supposed to do what we can for Texans, aren't we?"

"You're gonna' be in enough trouble explainin' about what we done to Briggs," Ken reminded him. "You know we ain't supposed to go over the border any more than the Army is."

"I know." John faced his friend. "I won't be the one telling Captain Booth what happened to Briggs. I'll let you do that."

Ken walked over and mounted his horse, riding up closer to John. "How is it I knew you'd do this to me? You're just lookin' for an excuse not to have to tell Booth yourself, and you're usin' that redheaded woman for your excuse." He scratched at his cheek, still needing a shave. "You plannin' to get that gal away all by yourself? Hell, there could be twenty men in on this. You know what big packs Comancheros run in."

John watched the horizon. "One man or ten. Makes no difference to me." He drew deeply on the cigar he still smoked.

" 'Course not, crazy fool that you are. Damn it, Hawk, let's go report to Booth together, and then you can let me go with you to Mexico."

John shook his head. "No. You go on to camp and report in. Somebody has to tell Booth what's been going on. I'll go to Mexico on my own. That way you won't get in any trouble. Besides, there are some jobs I can handle better alone."

"Maybe so. But can you *take* them by yourself?"

"Well, we'll just see, won't we?" John looked down at Lieutenant Ames. "I'm heading for Mexico."

Ames shook his head. "I never meant to make you think you should follow up on this yourself, Hawk."

"This can be handled by either the Army or the Rangers. You're welcome to go ahead and send a patrol on their trail, but I aim to get a head start. You could get there too late. You have some supplies along I could take with me? A little tobacco, some coffee, beans, whatever. I don't need much. I can always shoot what I need for meat."

Ames shook his head. John Hawkins never ceased to amaze him. He seemed not the least bit worried about going after a gang of Comancheros alone. He turned to one of the soldiers beside him. "See what you can rustle up for Hawkins," he told the man. He looked back up at John, thinking that if John were stripped half naked like a Comanche or Apache, a person who didn't know better would think he was just one of them. "You're actually looking forward to this, aren't you? You're a warrior yourself at heart, Hawk."

John grinned. "Maybe so."

"Damn it, Hawk, you're still wounded from that last run-in," Ken reminded him.

"Wounded? You hurt, Hawk?" Ames asked.

"Just a bump on the head and a little cut on my back. I'm mending all right. I heal better when I'm up and about. Don't like lying around, unless it's in some friendly woman's bed."

The lieutenant laughed. "I can't argue with that one. How did you get hurt?"

"This damn crazy fool—"

"We just had a little encounter with some cattle thieves," John interrupted before Ken could finish the statement. He cast Ken a look of warning. "We took care of them."

Ames nodded. "I expect you did."

John stuck the cigar between his lips again and nodded to Ken. "Might see you again. Might not." He motioned for Ken to follow and rode over to where the soldier who'd gone for supplies was rummaging through a pack horse's load. "Soften up that dynamite story the best you can," he told Ken while he waited. "Blame me for all of it if you want. Booth knows I don't listen to anybody once I've made up my mind."

"Yeah. Sure. I just wish you'd wait and let me go with you."

"There you go, worrying again."

The private held up a gunnysack. "A few potatoes, a can of beans, small sack of coffee, some tobacco, and flour," he told John. "Good luck, Mr. Hawkins."

"Thanks." John tied the sack around his saddle horn. He turned to Ken. "See you in a few days, or a few weeks."

"Or never," Ken scowled.

John grinned. "Depends if it's a good day to die when I reach those Comancheros."

"Maybe it will be overcast," Ken answered.

John sobered. "Maybe." He put out his hand. "See you later, my friend."

Ken nodded, squeezing his hand. "Hope so."

John turned his horse and rode south, thinking maybe he *was* a little bit crazy. He was headed toward the distinct possibility of death, just to get another look at some little redheaded woman who probably wasn't worth her weight in salt.

Chapter Three

The land held a breathless quiet, so still it almost hurt a man's ears. But John's own keen ears were picking up a sound. He squinted, straining to listen. This was a land of tortuous canyons and grotesque rocks, and in between was nothing but a barren loneliness. Sometimes the only noise was the white-hot sun that seemed to scream down on a man's head and shoulders.

He removed his cracked-leather hat and wiped sweat from his brow, then replaced the hat and dismounted, tying his horse to a scrubby bush that seemed rooted solid enough to hold the animal for a time. The golden palomino bent its head to graze on a meager stand of grass long dried up.

John was proud of his horse. Palominos were rare in these parts, and this fine specimen had cost him plenty. He had paid for it with reward money a wealthy railroad man had given him for being saved from Apaches a couple years back. Too bad, he thought, that the whole state of Texas couldn't even come up with enough money to provide their Rangers with horses and guns. A Ranger had to pay for all his own supplies. Still, with that reward money, he had more than he needed, since he had no family to provide for, owned no property other than his horse and gear. He had a good amount still in the bank in El Paso.

Sometimes he wondered why in hell he didn't settle, why he kept at this rather thankless and very dangerous job. For the satisfaction of killing men who deserve it, he answered himself. This work gave him a way to vent all the anger that kept boiling up inside. Besides, being a Texas Ranger was something that brought him some little bit of respect, and at the same time it left him with almost total freedom. That was what he needed more than anything. He wasn't going to work for some other man, having to be in one place every day, all day, taking orders. With the rangers he still had to take orders, but once he was out on his own, he seldom obeyed them. And he didn't work for just one man. He worked for the whole state of Texas.

Trouble was, not everything he did was something he would normally be assigned . . . like riding across the border into Mexico to track a little redheaded woman. Rangers weren't supposed to go into Mexico, but they did it all the time, and he was probably the worst offender. He felt lucky that so far he had not had a run-in with Apache renegades, who were scattered all over this desolate country. They could be anywhere. Sometimes they seemed to just rise up out of the ground unexpectedly.

He crouched to listen, noticing how worn and battered his leather boots were. He supposed he should get himself another pair sometime, but old, beat-up boots were so much more comfortable than stiff new ones. His denim pants were caked with dust, and he reckoned a bath would feel damn good right now, but a man didn't bother to bathe when he had to be out in this kind of sun.

There it was again, very faint, but he definitely heard voices. They were probably in a canyon somewhere to the south, down where he couldn't see them. He had followed tracks for four days now, angry with himself for making a wrong choice when the tracks split up a few miles south of the McDowell ranch, six or eight men going in one direction, several more in another with the stolen cattle and horses. It was the oldest trick in the book, and even experienced trackers like himself had to simply make a wild guess which way to go when led in two directions. He'd followed the tracks of those who had taken the cattle and horses. Eventually those tracks circled around until he came to a place where they split up yet again. It looked as though someone had met this second group and had taken the cattle and horses off with them.

They had set this up good. Already they had unloaded most of the stolen stock, but to whom? It irked him that he didn't have time to follow that trail and find out. It could lead to whoever had been behind a rash of cattle thefts over the past several months. Again he thought about Jim Caldwell, but just like Ken had said, it seemed preposterous that such a man would be involved in something like rustling. For now, there was no hope of finding out. By the time he was able to follow, those tracks would be washed or blown away. It was more important now to find Tess Carey, and the only way to do that was to stick with the original tracks, which had gone on south. That was the direction, he was sure, they would take the woman— to Mexico.

So far this second set of tracks had not met up with the original group, but he was betting they would. He was angry with himself for not following the tracks of the first group after they split up. Now if he could just catch up with this second bunch, maybe he could get some valuable information that would help him rescue the woman; and if he could keep them apart, that meant fewer men to contend with once he did reach the woman.

He waited, making sure from which direction the voices came, then untied his horse and remounted and kicked his horse into a gentle lope. He had to keep this a surprise. If he rode too hard, someone up ahead might feel the approaching hooves. Comanche could see and feel and smell man or horse for miles sometimes; but, by God, so could he, and that was how he usually managed to outsmart them.

He realized he enjoyed the challenge. Maybe it was the warrior blood that flowed in his veins. After all, his grandmother was sister to Red Eagle, a respected and often feared Lakota warrior. And a true warrior liked nothing better than to prove himself in battle. He supposed if he'd been raised among the Sioux, he would be riding with them right now against the thousands of soldiers who'd been sent West to "clean up" those who still refused to go live on reservations. He supposed he ought to go try to find some of his relatives, but he was far removed from that world. Texas was mostly all he'd known since he was fourteen and had fled here from Missouri with his mother after killing the man who'd tried to rape her.

God knew there sure weren't any Sioux in Texas, just Comanche and Apache, and it was hard to tell which was the meanest. He went another mile or so, then dismounted again, taking his canteen from the saddle horn and removing his hat. "I promise you, boy, that I'll find you some good stream water soon as I'm finished with what I have to do." He poured some water into his hat and held it out for his horse to drink. This was miserable country for man and animal alike. The only things that really belonged out here were the snakes and lizards. "Won't be long now, boy." He thought how easily a man could go crazy in these parts if he didn't at least have his horse to talk to. He took a glance behind him, wondering if Ken intended to try to follow him. It wouldn't surprise him any.

He poured a little water on top of his head, then took a short swallow and recapped the canteen and hooked it back on his gear. He led his horse to a sorry-looking mesquite tree, the only thing that might give the animal a little shade. There was some scrubby grass underneath, certainly not enough to feed a horse for even part of a day, but it would have to do. He would simply have to get this done with as fast as possible. No warning. No mercy.

He tied his horse, using a rope instead of the reins so

the animal would have freedom to move around. He took an ammunition belt from where it hung around his saddle horn and slung it around his shoulder, then did the same with a second ammunition belt, so that they draped cross-wise over his chest. A man couldn't take any chances. If he got himself pinned down, he would need all the ammunition he could manage to bring along. He checked his six-gun to be sure it was fully loaded, then took his Winchester lever-action 44.40 rifle from its boot and checked it, too. He left a sawed-off shotgun in its leather case on the horse and made off in the direction, he was sure, of the voices. He could actually smell horse dung now, knew he was close.

He made his way over crusted, rock-strewn ground, sent a lizard scurrying, felt the sun's heat on his shoulders. He thought about that red-haired woman as he followed tracks and scent. This would have to be miserable country for someone with such fair skin. The area back where her ranch was wasn't any easier on skin like that. In fact, there were few places in all of Texas where someone with red hair and freckles ought to go without something to shade them from the sun. Why in hell people like that came to places like this he would never understand. Didn't they ever wonder why God put the Indians and Mexicans here and not the white man? But the whites kept coming, risking their lives against the elements and the Indians who lived on this land, just to say that *they* owned it instead.

He heard laughter now. He crouched behind a boulder, listened intently. He heard no sound of a woman. He could tell now that the voices came from some kind of canyon, since the louder voices echoed. He peered around the boulder, and all that lay ahead was wide-open, flat desert—deceiving. Out here the land could just drop off in a sheer wall with no notice. Sometimes a man could not even see the drop-off until he was right on its edge. He made a quick dash for some scraggly brush up ahead, lay flat behind it when he reached it, then wriggled past it.

Now, finally, he could see the gap, could see the other

side. He wondered how the land had got this way. Maybe an earthquake had simply split the earth here, leaving both sides in their original flat state. He removed his hat and slithered to the edge, peering down to see men camped below. There was a stream down there, and the shadows of the canyon walls provided enough shelter from the sun to keep water and grass from drying up. These men knew the country well—must have known about this place.

He studied the camp—saw no woman, just as he suspected. This bunch would ride to catch up with the first ones who had gone on ahead. The woman would be with them. If he could get rid of these men, the job ahead would be easier.

He was surprised at the apparent total confidence of the men below that no one would find them here, or perhaps just that no one would even follow them into Mexico. They damn well knew the United States Army wouldn't come here. They evidently figured there was nothing to worry about, since they had posted no lookouts and were casually eating and drinking as though they had not a care in the world.

"You'll find out different," he whispered.

They were sitting targets. Unbelievable. God must want him to find that redheaded woman with no trouble, or He wouldn't be making this so easy for him. But then maybe it was simple luck. After all, if there *was* a God, He sure wouldn't be paying any attention to John Hawkins.

He pulled away from the edge. There were four of them down there. His aim had to be just right. After the first shot they would scatter and it would be harder to hit them. He couldn't let even one of them get away, or whoever escaped would ride ahead and warn the others. They might kill the woman before he reached them, just to be mean. God only knew what they were doing to her now. Maybe by the time he did reach her she'd be better off dead anyway.

He used his elbows to pull himself, on his belly, back to the edge of the canyon. He could see the pathway down,

just to his left. It was nothing more than a precarious,
rocky trail over which only one horse could fit at a time.
It was their only way out, and if they tried it, he could pick
them off easily. Fate and their own stupidity were both on
his side today!

He rested his left elbow on a flat rock, took a look at
the sun. He had to be careful it didn't throw a flash of
light on his rifle barrel, creating a glint they might see.
He took careful aim, slow, steady. He squeezed the trigger,
and as soon as he heard the sharp report near his ear, one
of the men went down. It was then he heard a scream to
his right.

He rolled to his left side just in time to avoid a hatchet
landing between his shoulder blades. Instead, it rang
against the flat rock, and he got off a second shot, opening
a hole in the Comanche's throat. His would-be assailant
staggered sideways and went hurtling down the canyon
wall.

Damn! There was a lookout! John hurriedly scrambled back
to the edge of the wall. The other three men below had
scattered, naturally. If not for the one who had attacked
him, he could have shot at least one more before they had
a chance to realize what was happening. Now he would
have to go down after them. If he tried to wait them out,
it could take a week or two. Just as with the rustlers he
and Ken had taken with the dynamite, he didn't like waiting. Men like that didn't deserve a chance anyway.

Rocks and gravel slid and scattered ahead of him as he
deftly zigzagged down the narrow pathway, realizing that
now he would be a target. He heard the ping of bullets
landing against rocks all around him, but he figured if he
moved swiftly and ducked and darted around enough, he
would be a difficult target. He wondered where in hell the
lookout had been hiding. Apparently the man had not
even noticed him until he heard that first rifle shot.

He felt a hot sting across his left arm. Piss on it. If he
was hit, he was hit. That wasn't going to stop him! He was

going after that redheaded woman, and he was not about to have to worry about one or more of these men following.

It seemed to take forever to get at least halfway down the rocky ledge. He took cover behind the plentiful supply of boulders, spotted one man behind a small tent. That tent would never stop a bullet. He took aim, fired. Someone on the other side of the tent cried out. Good. If that one wasn't already dead, he'd finish him off later. Now there were only two left. He turned and pressed against the boulder, taking a minute to get his breath, and looked down at his arm. There was blood on the sleeve, but he could tell by the feel of it when he moved the arm it was just a crease. There was no bullet in there. What the hell? It was too damn hot today to die, so he had nothing to fear.

"Who is there?" someone called out in Spanish.

"Texas Ranger!" he answered. "Give yourselves up! There are more of my men coming," he lied. "Give up now and we'll go easy on you!" He heard a string of expletives then, about Texas Rangers.

"Why do you kill us?" the Mexican asked. "We have done nothing wrong. You can see we were only camped peacefully here."

"You raided a ranch up in Texas, took horses and cattle, took a woman!"

"Oh, no, *señor,*" the man answered. "We have done no such thing."

"Tell me where they took the woman and I'll go away and leave you alone!" John told them. "I just want to find the woman! I know you already sold some of the cattle and horses. Who did you sell them to?"

"*Señor,* truly we did not do this."

"I don't have time for your goddamn lies!" John began firing a flurry of shots at the spot where the voice came from, behind a pile of brush and rocks. He saw a movement to the right of that. A man was running toward the tent. He fired, and the man dropped without a sound.

"There's just you now, Mexican!" he shouted. "You're

all alone! Come on out and I'll go easy on you. I just want to know where the woman is."

"Who . . . who are you, Ranger?"

John kept his rifle aimed steadily at the place where the man hid. "John Hawkins!"

There was a moment of silence. "Holy Virgin Mary!" the Mexican finally said. He put up his hands, came slowly from behind the rocks. "They are taking the woman to a meeting place on the coast, *señor,*" he shouted. "Truly I tell you the truth. If you hurry, you can catch up with them before they get there. Once they do, there is a whole village of traders and Comancheros. You will never be able to help her then. There would be too many of them."

"Throw down your gun," John demanded.

The Mexican obeyed, and John slowly came out from behind the boulders. He heard someone groan—probably the one behind the tent, he thought. He scuttled down the rest of the narrow pathway and approached the Mexican, who stood very still, his eyes wide with fright. Apparently he had heard about John Hawkins. "How many are there with the woman now?" John asked.

The Mexican swallowed. "Only six more, *señor.*"

"Did they rape her?"

The Mexican began to tremble. "Only one, *señor.*"

"Did *you* rape her?"

The Mexican quickly shook his head, so hard that his chubby cheeks jiggled. "No, *señor!* I did not do this."

"Is there a special place where they'll hole up?"

"Sí, Señor Hawkins. We were going to meet them there. It is only another day's ride, on the Rio de Bavisque. There is some shade there, and the river, she is a good water supply."

"Who did you sell the cattle to?"

"I do not know, *señor.* A man, he just met us. We were not supposed to know his name. He was tall and dark, *señor,* with a big, hook nose. Very thin. That is all I can tell you."

John nodded, then fired the rifle. The startled Mexican

stumbled backward, his eyes wide with disbelief. *"Señor, I
. . . helped . . . you!"*

"You watched those men rape a helpless woman. Besides
that, I can't afford to have you along when I meet up with
your friends on the Rio de Bavisque."

He turned away. The man would be dead shortly. He
walked over to the tent, where a Comanche renegade lay
writhing in pain from a bullet in his belly. The man looked
at him as though to beg him to put him out of his misery.
John just shook his head. "I need the ammunition," he
said. "Why waste it on the likes of you? You'll die eventually,
anyway.

He turned away and climbed back up the precarious
pathway out of the canyon. He had to get his horse and
get going. Maybe he could reach the woman by tomorrow
noon if he hurried.

Tess wondered who she hated more, the men who had
abducted and raped her or her own husband. It was not
likely Abel could have done anything to help her in the
end, but the memory of his cowering under the bed burned
in her heart and made her head ache. She had married
him partly for his kindness and gentleness, but little did
she know he was gentle to the point of being a coward.
She felt guilty over her feelings toward him, considering
how horribly he must have died, yet she could not help
the disappointment and literal shock over how he had
behaved. Maybe someday, when this was over, she could
find a way to forgive him, and to forgive herself for hating
him.

She tugged at the rope that kept her wrists tied tightly
together and then was tied to a wagon wheel. These men
apparently had planned everything well, for not far back
they had come upon two wagons full of supplies, which
she had no doubt were stolen. The men driving the wagons
had been waiting for those who had abducted her, and
now they were already across the border in Mexico. She

had given up all hope of being rescued when the first bunch of renegades had split up not long after taking her, the others taking the stolen livestock with them. She knew the fact that they had divided themselves would make it more difficult for someone to follow.

And who *would* follow? The Army was not allowed to come into Mexico, not even the Texas Rangers were supposed to come here. What man would bother to risk his neck in such desolate country for one woman?

Her abductors had forced her to walk naked in the sun, just long enough to burn her skin to painful irritation. They obviously wanted her to be uncomfortable, out of pure meanness, maybe to keep her hurting too much to try to escape.

She longed for water, had asked for it several times and had received none. And so far they had fed her nothing. They were deliberately keeping her in a weakened state so she would have little fight left in her. But so far she had fooled them. She had kicked and spit and bitten and defied them in every way possible. If she had a knife she would gladly cut their throats! She refused to think about what they had done to her. She didn't dare fully acknowledge the reality of it. Not right now. Survival came first.

So far neither Chino nor the others had raped her again. They seemed to be saving her, and she didn't even want to guess for what, nor had they told her. They spoke mostly in Spanish, three of them in the clipped tongue of the Comanche. Those three she was almost sure were full-blood Indian. Three others, including Chino, were Mexican, but Chino looked as though he also had Indian blood. It was hard to tell. The two men who had met them with the wagons brought to eight their number, all mean and well armed. How she was going to get out of this, she was not sure, but she would damn well keep thinking about it. It was the only way she could keep her sanity.

"Hey, pretty one, how you doing?" One of the Mexicans approached her with a canteen. "The boss, he say you can have water now. You want a bath?" He grinned, licking his lips. "I help you take a bath."

She sat there, wrapped in a blanket, and he opened it to have a look at her. His grin grew wider. "You will bring a good price when we sell you." He poured a little water over her head and face, and she licked at it desperately. He laughed. "Put your head back and I give you a drink."

Tess obeyed, but he poured only a little bit into her mouth, making her feel wild with a desire for more. "Please," she asked, hating to have to beg. "Just a little more."

The man grunted in laughter, and Tess fought tears, refusing to cry in front of any of them. They would love that, she was sure ... but oh, how she *needed* to cry. "Please," she asked again.

He trickled a little more into her mouth. "Someday maybe you will beg Juan to give you more in bed, like you beg for the water now, no?"

She held her chin defiantly. "You're a stinking coward, abusing a woman this way! I want no coward in my bed!"

He lost his grin, slowly corking the canteen. "Juan is no coward," he told her. "Your husband, *he* was a coward! And *you*—where you are going, you will soon learn not to have such a sharp tongue! You will wish you *were* with Juan Rodriguez!"

She spit on him, and Juan clamped a strong hand around her throat. "Where you are going, someone will cut out your tongue to shut you up!"

"Juan! Leave her alone!" The order came from Chino, the obvious leader of the bunch of renegades. He was powerfully built, of medium height, and there was pure cruelty in his eyes. One of those eyes had apparently been injured once in a fight. There was an ugly scar beneath it, and the eye kept wandering off to the left as though he could not control its movement. That eye made him grotesquely ugly, which Tess supposed was why he was the way he was; but then he had probably always been mean. His voice reminded her of gravel, it was so rough, and he seemed not to have a spark of kindness or respect for a woman.

Chino grabbed Juan's arm and gave him a shove. "Get away!"

Juan shrugged him off and left, and Chino leaned closer. Tess's stomach turned at the sight of him. It was Chino she hated most, Chino who had raped her. She would probably never get over the shame and humiliation of it; she had never thought it could be possible to hate this much, or possible for men to be such animals. From what she had heard about Indians, these men were worse. Indians supposedly tortured and killed as a kind of religion, taking strength from the bravest captives, doing what they could to keep the white man out of their territory. These men cared little about the land. They did what they did out of greed and out of pure meanness.

"The quieter you are and the more you obey, the kinder we will be to you," Chino told her.

"You don't know the *meaning* of the word 'kind,'" she sneered.

Chino just snickered. "Believe me, my fire-haired beauty, the way I have treated you so far *is* kind, compared to what I have done to some. You be careful with your tongue. I might soon tire of listening to your sass, and perhaps I *will* cut it out! Those who buy you would not mind having a woman who cannot speak. Your fair skin and red hair will bring much money, and your inability to speak could bring even more. I will consider it."

He rose, and Tess wanted to scream. She already knew the man well enough to believe he would do exactly what he threatened to do. She began to pray she would die before she suffered any more of this horror.

"Someone comes, Chino!" The shout came from one of the Comanche renegades keeping watch. They were camped near a shallow river, and Tess longed to jump into the water and feel its coolness. Her stomach cramped at the realization someone else was joining them, for she was sure it was probably just another of the outlaws own fetid kind.

She watched him ride in, and immediately she lost all hope of his being someone who had come to help her. He looked as Indian as any of them, wore only denim pants, no shirt. He was dark, big, as mean looking as the others. His black hair hung nearly to his waist and was worn loose, and he was well armed. The others gathered around him, holding guns on him.

"You will go no farther, *señor*," Juan told him. "Speak your name."

"I am called Hawk," John Hawkins answered, deciding to use Ken's nickname for him. It sounded like something an Indian would call himself, and he sure was not about to tell them his real name.

He was hoping he'd guessed right—that none of these men knew him by sight. If he was going to get the better of this bunch, why not ride right into their nest and take them from the inside?

He glanced at the woman tied to a wagon wheel. There she was, red hair and all, Tess Carey. God only knew what she'd been through. Now all he had to do was figure out how in hell to get her out of here.

Chapter Four

Tess watched the newcomer, convinced by his appearance that he was as wicked and cruel as the others.

"What is it you want?" Chino asked. "I have little patience, and I do not like new faces."

John looked around the camp, studied the wagons, every man there, his gaze finally falling on Tess. She shivered and looked away.

"I was only curious," John answered Chino. "I have left the Comanche reservation in Oklahoma. I am only part Comanche," he lied. He figured he could pass for Comanche, if that was what he needed to be for the moment. "I do not belong there where men live and farm like women. I heard many stories about how a man can come down here and make money the easy way. Now that I am forced to survive by white man's money, I am looking for work. Do you know where I can find work?"

Chino grinned, and he began strutting haughtily around John's horse. "There is the kind of work where a man must truly work, if you know what I mean." He patted the horse's rump, came back around to face the man who called himself Hawk, gauging his size, trying to read his eyes. "And there is easy work. We do easy work, work that brings great pleasure and excitement, work that keeps us free. The only thing you need for this work is to be good with a gun." He eyed John's many weapons. "You look like a man who is good with guns."

He boldly reached out and yanked John's rifle from its boot. He looked it over approvingly, while John waited quietly, hoping Chino would not suspect anything. He had hidden all supplies that might link him to the Army or the Rangers, and he was dressed like any other half-breed drifter might be. One benefit to looking so Indian was that it often helped him in his work. He could easily pass himself off as a common, poor Indian—or as a ruthless renegade—whatever the job called for.

"This is a fine rifle, Hawk," Chino said. The others continued to watch and hold guns on John. "*Are* you good with a gun?" He came back around to look up at him.

John studied the apparent leader of this sorry group. It was obvious what had happened to the redheaded woman. Part of her blanket had fallen away, revealing a naked breast. Because her hands were tied, she could not pull the blanket back over herself. He struggled with his anger, telling himself to be patient. "I hunted game for others on the reservation," he answered. "I was known for my skill with rifle and handgun. And I did my share of raiding and killing before I was confined to the reservation."

Chino nodded. "And where did a poor Indian from the reservation get such a fine weapon?" He walked closer, patting the horse's rump again. "And such a fine golden horse?"

"I stole them," John answered. "From a white man who is dead now, somewhere on a lonely road in Texas."

Chino laughed, and the others joined in. "This I like to hear," Chino said, coming around to face John again. "The trouble is, my friend, we, too, steal horses, and you have a very fine horse there. I would not mind owning him for myself. Nor would I mind owning this fine rifle of yours."

Tess watched the one called Hawk straighten, the look in his dark eyes as evil and threatening as any she'd seen in Chino's eyes. "It would be better for you if you didn't try to take what is mine. I did not come here for trouble or to lose my horse and rifle. I came here to find work. If your work involves stealing horses and . . ." He looked over at Tess again. "Women," he continued, "that is fine with me. I've heard about renegades in these parts who sell such things for great profit. I have been watching you from a distance, saw the woman. I would like to be a part of this easy work, as you call it. If you want a man good with a gun, who doesn't mind killing whoever needs killing to get what he wants, I can be of service to you. Otherwise, I will take that rifle and be on my way."

Chino's eyebrows rose in surprise at the man's boldness. He laughed again. "I like your courage, Hawk. Something tells me that if I tried to keep this rifle and take your horse, you would shoot me, even knowing it would mean my men would fill your belly with their bullets."

"You're exactly right."

For the first time Tess sensed a hint of fear in Chino's countenance. He laughed again, this time the laughter of a nervous man trying to pretend he was not impressed. He handed the rifle back to Hawk. "I think maybe we can use you after all. You stay with us, watch what we do. We in turn will watch you, make sure you are not lying to us about something."

Juan spoke up. "I do not trust him, Chino." He walked up to stand beside Chino, eyeing John. "Perhaps he is an Army scout."

"The United States Army does not come into Mexico," Chino reminded him.

"I think we should search his gear."

Chino rubbed his chin. "Perhaps we should."

"Search all you want," John told Chino. He moved his gaze to the Mexican beside him. "But this man will not touch anything of mine. I have no use for a man who is brave only because he is among many. I think perhaps this one here would be afraid to challenge me if he were facing me alone."

The air hung silent for a moment, as rage began to make itself evident in Juan's eyes. "Are you calling me a coward, *señor?*"

John swung a leg over his saddle horn and dismounted in front of Juan. "I am. I think you are one who talks big only when he thinks others will do his job for him." He held out the rifle. "If you want to search my gear, then take this rifle from me first."

Tess wondered if the man called Hawk was truly as brave and daring as he appeared at this moment, or if he was just plain crazy. Chino grinned, stepping away.

"Go ahead, Juan. Take his rifle," he teased.

The rest of them seemed to relax a little, a few putting their guns back in their holsters to just stand and watch.

Good, John thought. He was winning them over.

Juan's look of anger and arrogance began to melt into one of great trepidation. "I . . . I cannot just reach out and take the rifle," he said.

John shrugged. "Sure you can."

Juan looked helplessly at Chino. "He is trying to trick us, Chino. He does not want us to look into his gear."

Tess gasped when, in a flash, the man called Hawk raised the rifle and landed the butt of it across the side of Juan's face, literally caving it in. Juan went down with blood oozing from his eyes, nose, and mouth. Tess had to look away. The smiles of the other men faded as they stared in shock, and when Tess dared to look out of the corner of her eye, she could see Hawk had moved his horse back a little and was waving the rifle at the rest of them.

"Now," he said, "anyone who wishes may look through my gear—whoever Chino says should do it. If I find anything missing, that man will die, even if I have to die myself. I can't take all of you on at once, but I won't be talked down to, and I won't allow another man to steal from me. What's mine is *mine!* I am here to work with you, use my skills to help you, and I will expect a share of the profits, however Chino here normally splits them." He looked at Chino. "Can I ride with you?"

Even Chino seemed surprised and somewhat intimidated. He slowly nodded. "There is no doubt we can use you, Hawk." He looked down at Juan, knelt down and grimaced as he put fingers against the man's throat. After a moment he looked up at one of the others. "Bury him," he ordered.

Good, John thought. One down. Seven left.

The Mexican he had killed farther back had been wrong. There were eight here, not six. Apparently they had met up with two more men, probably those who had driven the supply wagons.

My God, Tess thought. The new man had killed Juan with no more effort than swatting a fly, and apparently he thought no more of Juan than if the Mexican *had* been a fly! She felt sick inside. This man called Hawk was as ruthless as Chino, perhaps even more so.

Chino ordered another man to search John's gear, and John turned his attention to Tess again. He shoved his rifle back into its boot and walked closer. Chino came along.

"She will bring a good price," he told John, "even though she is not a virgin. She is still tight. I think she has never had children. There were none at the ranch from which we took her."

Tess looked away, embarrassed, totally humiliated at being talked about as though she were a prize cow.

"Where will you sell her?" John asked.

"We go to the coast. There are those who come there in ships to take white women to southern Mexico, sometimes South America, sometimes even across the ocean to China. I will sell her to whoever gives the best price."

Tess thought she might vomit. She tried to hide her breast as best she could, but the position of her arms made it impossible.

"You can have a turn at her if you would like," Chino told John. "Just do not injure or kill her. She is worth too much, except for her sharp tongue. I am thinking of cutting it out. Where she is going, she will have no need to speak, only to obey. Only her light skin and full breasts and slender thighs matter. Without a tongue, a man can find other uses for her mouth, no?"

With horror Tess realized what the man was saying.

"I expect he can," John answered. "The trouble is, she would still have her teeth. Maybe you should yank those out, too."

Both men laughed wickedly. Tess felt someone grabbing her wrists, looked up to see the one called Hawk had taken a huge knife from its sheath at his waist. At first she thought perhaps he had decided to go along with Chino's idea of cutting out her tongue, and her soul filled with terror. But instead he used the knife to cut the rope that held her to the wagon wheel, although her wrists remained tied. He jerked her to her feet, and the blanket fell away. Hawk held her arms over her head, and she could feel his power. He was bigger than Chino, and God only knew what he might do to her if Chino let him have his way.

Immediately all her defenses and stubborn pride rose to the surface again. She was not going to be any more submissive to this man than she had been with Chino. She pulled at his powerful grip, but to no avail. "Let me go, you half-breed bastard!" she growled.

Just as I thought, John noted. This woman was the kind who would never give him a second glance under normal circumstances. What was he doing risking his life for her? Oh, hell, he knew why. No woman deserved to be treated this way, not even a stuck-up white ball of fire like this one. "I see what you mean about her tongue," he told Chino.

"I tell you, my friend, we could have quite a time holding her down and putting a stick in her mouth to keep it open. She would have no fight left in her if we cut out that tongue, but then, some men like the fight. Maybe I will wait and let the one who buys her take care of her tongue."

Tess kicked at John, but her aim was off just enough to do little harm to the spot she'd aimed at. John brought her arms down and jerked her around so her back was to him, then wrapped a strong arm around her in a viselike grip so that she could do nothing but kick at his legs with her bare heels and pound at his chest with the back of her head. The others laughed at the spectacle as John tried to hang on to her.

"She can fight, that one!" one of them said. "It took many to hold her down when Chino got a piece of her."

"Go ahead and take her into the wagon," Chino told John. "It is my welcoming gift to you. But be careful, Hawk. You are a big man. I do not want her ruined for the one who might want to buy her, huh?"

His laughter rang in Tess's ears as her stomach tightened painfully at the realization that yet another strange, dark, cruel man was going to rape her, maybe give her some horrible disease. She felt so filthy and disgraced, she hoped now they would just kill her. Death was better than this.

"I'll go easy on her," the man who held her replied. "The question is, how easy will she go on me?"

They all laughed again, and Tess struggled wildly as she was carried to the back of one of the wagons. John threw her inside and was quickly in there with her, his brawny body on top of her, his weight making it impossible for her to move, especially since her wrists were still tied.

"Get off me, you stinking half-breed coward!" she screamed. She spit at him several times, until finally a big hand came around her throat, just tight enough to cut off most of her air and quickly bring her struggles to a halt.

"Now, you listen to me," he said through gritted teeth, keeping his voice low. "You've got to do exactly as I say!"

She lay there with her eyes wide from terror and lack of air. John kept one hand on her throat and used the other to carefully lift the canvas at the side of the wagon to look out. Chino and his men were gathered around Juan's body, talking and laughing. He looked back down at Tess, trying to keep his mind off the fact that she lay naked beneath him, although she was so bruised and burned it was not so difficult to ignore her nakedness. He noticed teeth marks around her breasts, and his hatred for the men outside burned deep. He leaned close, talking into her ear so it would seem he was making love to her if someone looked.

"I'm a Texas Ranger," he told her. "I'm going to get you out of here."

If not for the horror of her situation, Tess thought she would actually laugh. Surely the man was joking. He finally lightened his grip on her throat, and she took a few deep breaths before spitting in his face again. "No Texas Ranger ever looked like you!" she whispered, sneering.

"You've seen me in El Paso, and you don't even know it. Women like you don't give my kind much attention. Either way, if I wasn't a Ranger, how would I know your name is Tess Carey, and that you were abducted from your ranch five days ago? Everything was burned and your pa and husband were killed."

Tess gasped at the sudden reality of it. Her beloved father was dead. Abel was dead. Everything was gone, and now she'd been so abused and shamed she could never again hold her head up in society, never find a decent man. But then, after what she had been through, she never wanted a man in her life again. Her eyes began to tear. "A Ranger wouldn't come clear down here after one woman," she said, her lips beginning to quiver.

"This one would. And don't go all soft on me. I'm supposed to be raping you, and you're supposed to be fighting it. Make some noise."

She managed to pull her arms out from under him, and all the horror and frustration surged out of her then in a fit of screaming and pummeling. She punched at John over and over, needing to hit, wanting to hurt, aching to cry but still unwilling to completely break down.

John was amazed that a woman her size could be so strong, especially after what she had already been through. He admired her grit and had to literally struggle with her to make her calm down. "All right! All right!" he growled, forcing her hands back underneath him again.

Tess kept struggling, seeing only a dark-skinned, long-haired Indian on top of her, remembering all the horror. Finally he wrapped his arms around her in an embrace that surprised her in its sudden gentleness.

"I swear to you I'm here to help you," he said quietly, his mouth near her ear again. "All I want you to do is go along with me in whatever I do. I have to wait until they all settle down for the night. Do you understand?"

He raised up just enough to look into her blue eyes. They looked back at him with doubt, curiosity, surprise. "Yes," she finally said.

"And whatever you see happen tonight, you can't cry out. You can't make any noise. I could have picked these men off from hiding, but one of them would have deliberately killed you before I got them all."

"I would have been better off," she whispered. "Chino . . . Chino . . ."

John could see the horror building into hysteria. He clamped a hand over her mouth. "You were just an object. They didn't touch your soul," he said.

Tess thought the statement odd, coming from this man who seemed to be someone who knew nothing about soul, nothing about how a woman would feel in a situation like this. And how was he, one man, going to save her from seven of the most ruthless characters who ever walked the face of the earth? He could only if he was even more ruthless, so how was she supposed to trust him? She thought hard about his statement that she had seen him in El Paso. She didn't remember it at all. Maybe that was a lie. Still, he seemed to know all about her. She couldn't believe, though, that a lawman would do what he'd done to Juan, no warning, no feeling. She had no choice but to believe him for now, pray that he was not lying about any of this. Maybe he was just trying to steal her for his own profit. Maybe he really had stolen his horse and rifle and wasn't a Texas Ranger at all.

"Hey, it is getting too quiet in there, Chino," someone outside said. "Maybe the woman likes that man. Maybe she is enjoying him instead of fighting him like she did you, no? Maybe you should go and see."

Someone cussed, and John peeked out of the wagon again. "Shit," he swore. "Chino is coming. Spread your legs!"

Tess's mouth dropped open.

"Damn it, I told you to go along with me on whatever I do!" He rose up and grasped her thighs, sorry about the bruises already there. He forced her legs apart, and she began hitting at him again. He fumbled with the buttons at the front of his pants, pulling himself out of them; then grasping her tied wrists and forcing her arms over her head with both hands, he began making movements as though he was having sex with her. She arched against him, butting at him with her head. He was finally forced to let go of her arms with one hand and hit her. "Shut up, bitch!" he shouted, wanting the others to hear. God, he hated this. He'd never hit a woman in his life—except once, a Mexican girl who had tried to knife him when he was arresting her boyfriend.

He heard laughter near the tailgate of the wagon then, knew Chino had looked inside. "She likes him no better than the rest of us!" Chino shouted. "But he is having a good time anyway, just like I did!"

The others laughed and hooted and shouted dirty suggestions for things John could do to her. John looked through a crack in the canvas to see Chino had rejoined them. He glanced down at Tess then, realizing she had quieted again. She was just staring at him in stunned silence, and it hit him that his privates had reacted to the stimulation of moving between a woman's legs, his hardness being pressed against her soft flesh. Her full white breasts brushed against his own bare chest. How easy it would be to go ahead and take her, pretending he had to do it to make things look good.

He bolted away from her, turning around and shoving himself back into his pants, angry that for that brief moment he had allowed himself to be no better than those sitting outside. God knew he wasn't much different when it came to killing men, but he'd never mistreated a woman, and he wasn't going to start now. "I'm sorry for hitting you," he told her. "I had to make it look good." He turned to see her curled up on her side.

"You wanted me, too," she said in a stony voice. "You're just like them."

"Yeah, maybe I am in a lot of ways." He threw a blanket over her. "I'll tell them it's probably best to leave you in here for a while, that you should rest or you could die. Maybe they'll buy it. You lay here and take it easy." God, his privates ached to be satisfied. Even in her sorry state Tess Carey was quite some beauty, and her courage and vinegar only made her more beautiful. He'd never come across a white woman quite like her. Most would be sniffling and begging and pleading by now.

"If you do get me out of here, I'll have no place to go," she told him.

"I know a woman in El Paso who would take you in."

She turned her head to face him. "What kind of woman would a man like you know except a whore?"

John couldn't decide whether to feel sorry for her or hit her again. "No other kind," he sneered. He leaned over her. "Insult me all you want. I'm still getting you out of here. I don't give a damn if you're grateful for it or not. I just expect you to cooperate so I don't get my ass killed. Will you do that much?"

She thought about that quick embrace, that brief moment when he seemed to actually be human. And now that she took a truly long, hard look at him, she realized he was really not a bad-looking man, for a half-breed Indian. He even had nice teeth, a rarity for most men she'd seen out here, and a lot of the women. Besides, he had thrown himself right into the lions' den for her, if he truly was not lying about why he had come.

"I'll cooperate," she answered. "If you need help and I'm able, I'll help you."

He moved his gaze along the form beneath the blanket. He would not soon forget how she looked.

"Why did you come down here from Texas just for me?" she asked.

He shrugged. "Even I don't understand half the things I do," he answered. He climbed out of the wagon, and Tess lay there quietly, realizing she suddenly felt nothing, physically or emotionally. Just nothing.

Chapter Five

Tess heard voices. She stirred awake from the only real sleep she had enjoyed since being abducted, and she realized she was still inside the wagon, where the man called Hawk had taken her. She realized he had not even told her his full name, and she still could not remember ever seeing him in town.

She sat up, managing to wrap the blanket Hawk had thrown over her around herself. She rubbed her aching jaw, remembering why it hurt. Hawk had hit her. It was difficult to believe that he could really be a Texas Ranger, not a man who looked no different from the Indian renegades who had stolen her away, not a man who could apparently be as ruthless as those he went after . . . not a man who could do such a good job of pretending to abuse a woman. Even hitting her was supposedly for show, but there had been nothing pretended about the force of the blow. Maybe hitting a woman was not something unfamiliar to him.

She reasoned he'd had to do a good job of proving himself to the others. After all, if he really was a Ranger, he didn't dare let any man out there figure it out. He was one against seven.

She turned to lift the canvas and look toward the camp-fire in the distance, thinking how every bone and muscle in her body seemed to ache. Her wrists stung painfully from rope burns. Her throat hurt from so much screaming the past few days. Now her jaw ached fiercely, and she yearned for water, water to drink, water to bathe herself, to wash her hair. How wonderful it would feel to be soapy clean, to be dressed in something comfortable . . . to be back home, baking bread for her father and . . . and Abel. Abel! The memory of his cowardliness would haunt her forever.

Through the crack where she lifted the canvas she could see two men sitting by the fire and sharing a bottle of whiskey. From what she could tell in the darkness, they were Chino and Hawk. Five other men were sleeping in bedrolls nearby. She wondered by what miracle she had been left alone since the incident with Hawk, worried the whiskey would put new ideas in Chino's head about her. Hawk handed over the bottle, as though he was urging Chino to drink even more, and she silently cursed him for doing so. If he was here to help her, why was he getting Chino drunk? When the man was drunk, he was even more violent.

And then there was Hawk himself. How in the world could he complete the task of getting the better of seven men if he was too drunk to aim at a barn? He was surely the most worthless excuse for a Texas Ranger who ever rode north of the Rio Grande! He seemed to have no plan at all.

She watched him stand up then and walk around the fire. Both men were laughing about something. Hawk sat down beside Chino and slapped him on the back. He moved his right hand to his side, and then in the eerie firelight she saw him raise that hand, saw what was in it, the huge knife he wore at his waist. In an instant that knife plunged. Tess gasped when she heard Chino grunt. Hawk continued to sit there beside him, laughed again, as though to continue the conversation. She could tell by his movements then that he was jerking the knife out of Chino, wiping the blade on the man's shirt. He put the weapon back in its sheath, laughed again.

Tess lowered the canvas and sat back for a moment. Ranger Hawk had just killed Chino with the same ease he'd killed Juan, and apparently with the same total unconcern for what he'd just done. It was not that either man did not deserve to die, but she'd always thought indiscriminate, unfeeling murder was only for the likes of such men, not a man who was supposed to be on the side of the law.

"He's passed out," she heard Hawk yelling to someone—probably the seventh man, who would be standing watch. She peeked back out again, saw Hawk laying Chino down and covering him with a blanket. "I'm going to have another turn at the woman," he continued, giving a wave to someone off in the darkness. Tess moved back into a corner, still not sure what to think of the man. Maybe he did intend to kill all these men, but maybe his reasons were not what she thought. How could she trust someone who could so easily ram a knife into a man's heart and immediately act as though it never happened? A moment later he stood at the back of the wagon.

"You awake?" he asked quietly.

Tess swallowed. "Yes."

He climbed inside. "Hold out your hands."

Hesitantly she did so. Using the same knife with which he had just killed Chino, he quickly sliced through the ropes. Then he shoved a gun into her hand. "That's Chino's. You see me in trouble, you use it. Don't hesitate."

Tess nodded. "Are you . . . going to kill *all* of them?"

"Do you see any other way of getting out of this?"

"I'm not sure."

"Chino told me more men are supposed to be meeting him here. We have to get this done and get the hell out of here. When the bodies are found, whoever is meeting them might try coming after us. I think once we get over the border, we'll be all right."

She nodded. "Who are you . . . really?"

"My name is John Hawkins. Come to the back of the wagon and be ready to help."

He climbed back out, and Tess thought a moment. John Hawkins. She remembered a woman talking about a Ranger Hawkins when she attended a meeting in El Paso for women interested in bringing a Protestant preacher to the area, where there were plenty of Catholic churches and missions but nothing for Protestants. Somehow the gossip after the meeting had ended up involving the Texas Rangers, and the woman had said that some men were a disgrace to the Rangers. It had been Harriet Caldwell, the wife of one of the wealthiest ranchers in the area. She'd said a heathen man like John Hawkins should not be representing the Rangers. Later that day, when shopping, her father had nodded toward a mean-looking man with long, black hair who'd been standing outside a saloon talking to the town's most notorious prostitute. Her father had said, "There's that John Hawkins. He's a real loner, they say." Tess had seen him again in the mercantile, but she'd looked away as soon as he'd noticed her, so she never had got a thoroughly good look at him.

She looked out the back of the wagon, heard more voices, this time in the darkness. John Hawkins was talking to the man on watch. She saw one of those sleeping by the fire stir. He sat up and rubbed his eyes, looked at Chino. She could tell he thought something did not seem right. She quickly climbed out of the wagon, her mouth so dry from lack of water she struggled not to make a choking sound. She nervously clutched the six-gun John had put in her hand, not sure she could truly shoot a man point-blank if necessary.

The test came quickly. She heard a grunt in the darkness, and only a moment later the man at the fire darted over to Chino, probably noticing blood on the man's shirt. "Chino!" he cried out. "He is dead! Chino is dead!"

Now the other four were awake and scrambling for their guns. Tess saw the flash of fire from the barrel of John's six-gun, jumped at the report. The man who had discov-

ered Chino fell into the fire. He began screaming, too
wounded to get himself back up. Tess's eyes widened as
he just lay there burning and screaming. Another shot
rang out, and a second man went down. By then the other
three were shooting in the direction from which the shots
had come and had run out of the light of the fire so they
could not be seen.

Tess stood there, feeling helpless. Where was John
Hawkins? The first man had finally stopped screaming,
and there was suddenly only silence. She was sure John
had killed the lookout, but now nothing was happening.
Had John been shot? What in God's name would she do
way out here in the middle of nowhere without him, even
if she did get out of this?

She jumped when she suddenly heard one of the three
remaining men call to the other two in Spanish, and she
backed up close to the wagon, waiting, watching. The night
air seemed heavy now, close, thick. One of the others
answered in Spanish, and it was difficult to tell how close
they were. She could not understand them, but she supposed they were checking with each other to see if they
were all right, planning what they should do next.

". . . *Señora* . . ." she heard. They were talking about her!
Perhaps they thought if they could get hold of her they
could use her for some kind of bait. "John Hawkins, where
are you?" she whispered. She clutched the blanket around
her with one hand, held out the gun in the other, aiming
into the darkness, turning this way and that.

Suddenly she was grabbed from behind, and she
screamed when a strong arm was wrapped around both
her arms so tightly she could not move them. She felt
something warm and hard pressed against her cheekbone,
and she knew instinctively it was the end of a recently fired
handgun.

"Come out where we can see you, Hawk, or I will kill
the woman!"

It was the Mexican Tess knew was called Henrique. The
remaining two men, a Comanche called Estano and

another Mexican, stepped up beside Henrique. They exchanged some words in Spanish, and then Estano walked around and yanked the gun from Tess's hand. He grabbed her from Henrique and held a huge blade to her throat.

"You must have come for the woman, whoever you are!" Estano called out with his strong Spanish accent. "Perhaps you would like to see her head cut off! Her neck is slender. My knife would cut through it easily!"

Tess's blanket fell away, and she stood there trembling with terror, knowing these were men who would do exactly as they promised. The iron blade of the knife was pressed to her throat and she could feel it nicking her skin. Her heart pounded harder when she heard the now-familiar deep voice behind Estano.

"Go ahead," John said. "The minute she goes down, you'll be headless, too."

Tess was astounded at how quietly the man had snuck up on the remaining three men. Henrique was breathing hard now, obviously afraid.

"Who are you?" Estano asked carefully.

Tess felt the knife at her throat drop away just slightly.

"I am John Hawkins, Texas Ranger. Now, you decide whether or not you want your head blown off!"

"No Ranger would come all the way down here," Henrique said, standing frozen in place.

"*This* one did."

Suddenly Estano yanked Tess sideways, literally tossing her away. Tess heard a gunshot. She stumbled and fell, as there came yet another shot, then a third report, a fourth, all in rapid succession. By the time she turned and got up, Estano lay on the ground, the knife still in his hand. The Mexican sprawled near him. Henrique was also down. He was grasping his belly and writhing in pain. She could not see John Hawkins.

Had he been hit this time? Carefully she crawled over to Estano and pulled his six-gun from its holster. She darted into the darkness then, listening. She heard someone breathing. "Mr. Hawkins?"

She waited, until finally his dark silhouette stumbled back into the light and stood over Henrique. To her surprise, he leveled his six-gun at the man's head and fired, then went to his knees, putting a hand to the side of Henrique's head.

Tess stepped closer. "Mr. Hawkins? Are you hurt?"

He did not answer right away. He rocked back to rest on his heels. "Just a little dizzy," he finally told her. "I think a bullet just creased my skull."

Never had Tess suffered such a maze of feelings—shock, horror, gratitude, revulsion. John Hawkins had ruthlessly killed every man here, as far as she could tell in the darkness. One of the bodies still lay over the fire, and the air was filled with the sickening stench of burning flesh. In her wildest imagination she never could have imagined the terrible things she'd seen and experienced since these renegades first attacked her ranch. Now she was desperately in need of help, yet perhaps John Hawkins needed her to help *him* at the moment. "I'll look for some gauze or something," she told him. "You stay right there. I . . . I have to find water first. I can't go on much longer without water."

She started past him but was stopped by a man who seemed to step out of nowhere. She recognized yet another one of Chino's men, called Dade. He was holding a six-gun, and blood covered the front of his shirt. Apparently he'd been hurt in the first gunfight, but had recovered enough to try to get to Hawk. Tess saw him raise his six-gun and point it at John Hawkins, who was still holding his head, not even aware the man was there! Tess knew instantly what she had to do. She raised the gun she was holding and fired point-blank into the man's chest.

John looked up to see the man fall. He turned and through blurred vision saw a naked Tess Carey stood nearby with a six-gun held in both hands, still pointed outward. The woman had just saved his life. He'd managed to down all seven men, but one had apparently survived long enough to try to come back at him. If not for this redheaded woman . . .

Their gazes held, both feeling a gratitude toward the other that was left unspoken for the moment. "We have to get out of here," John finally told Tess. He groaned, feeling warm blood trickle through his fingers as he still held his hand to his head.

"I don't think you can ride, Mr. Hawkins."

"Yes, I can. Find something in the wagon to put on. I'll get my horse and get another one for you. Can you ride?"

"Does anyone live in Texas without knowing how to ride a horse?"

Damn, you're something, John thought. "I suppose not." He reached back and used the wagon to pull himself up. "This is the second damn head wound I've had in less than a week."

"Both bullets? You're a lucky man, Mr. Hawkins."

He leaned over for a moment with his eyes closed. "First one was just a lump from . . . Never mind. Just do what I said and let's get out of here."

Tess felt entirely removed from her real self as she obeyed his orders. She took a lantern that hung at the side of the wagon and carried it inside, rummaging through the various supplies meant for trade on the coast. Inside a trunk she found women's clothing. Warm as it was, dirty as she was, it still felt wonderful to pull on a calico dress and cover her nakedness. She even found a pair of drawers. She pulled those on, moving a little more quickly now. She grabbed another dress and another pair of drawers, found a pair of high-button shoes. She tried one on. It was a good enough fit, but it hurt to pull them over her sore, cut feet. She would save them for later.

She wrapped the clothes and Estano's six-gun into a blanket and tied it into a bundle, wondering where on earth she found any strength at all. She wanted to collapse, but she couldn't—not yet. She searched through the trunk a little more to find a lacy slip. She ripped it up, thinking to use it for bandages.

By the time she climbed back out of the wagon, John Hawkins was standing there with two horses. "I had left mine saddled," he said. "Figured I might need it to get out of here fast if something went wrong." He led the other horse, a roan gelding, closer to her. "I found this one still saddled. Must have belonged to the lookout." He handed out a canteen. "Don't drink too much at first."

Blood poured down the side of his face from the deep cut the stray bullet had dug into the side of his head.

Tess took the canteen. "How can you possibly ride?" she asked, uncorking the container.

"A man does what he has to. I know a place where we can go to rest up a couple of days and get our strength back. I saw it on my way here. If we ride in the river itself, it will make it harder for anyone to follow if they decide to try. Where we're going, there is pure rock leading up to a cave. It might be . . ." He grimaced. "It might be big enough to put the horses inside where they can't be seen. I stashed some of my gear there so they wouldn't find any of my things that show that I'm a Ranger. There are even a few Army supplies there, a little food. We'll be all right."

Tess gulped some of the blessed water as he spoke. She wanted to guzzle it all, but he'd warned her not to drink too much at first, and if anyone knew about those things, John Hawkins would. She handed back the canteen, and he took a swallow himself and corked it. He hung it over his saddle horn. "Let's go."

"Not until you let me tie something around your head to slow the bleeding."

"Don't worry about me."

"I'm not—not personally, anyway. I need you to show me the way home. What would I do out here if you passed out on me or died from loss of blood? I wouldn't even know how to find that cave you were talking about."

His eyebrows arched in surprise at her authoritative attitude. The average white woman would probably have fainted dead away by now, or would certainly be crying and blubbering. He suspected this was one of those women who under normal circumstances took the bull by the horns and quickly informed a man who was boss. The little viper probably would have found a way out of this eventually even without his help.

"I don't think I need to guess that you might have some whiskey in your supplies, so get some out," she ordered, "and I'll pour some over that wound and wrap it."

John sighed and turned to fish around in one of his saddlebags, pulling out a small flask. He handed it to her grudgingly. "I really don't need—"

"Bend down, Mr. Hawkins. You're too tall for me to reach."

John knelt, noticing the dress she had found to put on was too big for her. He suspected a lot of things were too big for her, she was such a small thing. "Jesus!" He shouted when the whiskey hit the wound.

"Don't use the Lord's name in vain, Mr. Hawkins. I don't mind cussing of other sorts. I know men do it. But there is no excuse for using the Son of God as a curse."

John was beginning to wonder what he'd gotten himself into. Was it going to be like this all the way back to Texas? "That depends on what God you believe in. I don't believe in any, so it doesn't matter what I say."

Tess began wrapping a strip of cotton slip around his head. "It does if you are in the presence of a Christian. Believe me, Mr. Hawkins, I have not even considered the possibility that *you* could be Christian." She tied the strip, noticed it was already bloodstained. "I hope that helps slow the bleeding."

Sure, John thought. Heaven forbid something should happen to me before I get you back. After that, if I dropped dead at your perfect little feet a woman like you could not care less.

"Thanks for your concern," he said with a note of sarcasm. He grabbed hold of her shoulder to help himself up, and Tess noticed it took great effort for him to mount his horse. She picked up her bundle of clothes and plopped it on the rump of the horse she would ride, then tied it with rawhide cording that already held a few supplies still on that horse. It took all her own strength to also mount up, and she wondered what had come over her, this sudden necessity to pretend she was just fine. She was not fine at all. She wanted to just sit and scream until she had no voice left.

What an ungodly situation. Now she would be in the hands of this puzzling stranger who had already shown he was hardly any different from the men he'd just killed. She was going home to nothing . . . nothing. There was no home left, no father, no husband, nothing. Again it struck her that she also *felt* nothing, except for one thing, an awakening of gratitude for what John Hawkins had just done. "I, uh, I suppose I should thank you," she said. She saw the quick hurt and anger in his dark eyes before he just shook his head and turned his horse.

"I suppose you should."

"Really, Mr. Hawkins. I am very grateful. I'm just—"

"Quit talking. From here on don't talk. Voices carry on the night wind." He rode away, leaving the bodies behind for the buzzards and wild animals. It seemed sinful to Tess to do that, but what choice did they have? And she knew without asking that John Hawkins wouldn't bury these men even under the best of circumstances. He probably figured they didn't deserve it.

She urged her own horse into motion and followed the man on the golden horse. She had no choice now but to trust him.

Chapter Six

They rode through the shallow riverbed for close to a mile, using bright moonlight that reflected on the water to guide them. No one spoke, until John finally said they would have to wait until sunrise to go any farther.

"It's dangerous riding at night. We can't afford to have one of these animals break a leg stepping into a hole. I just wanted to get a little distance between us and the mess we left back there."

We? Tess thought how she had at least wanted to bury the men. She guided her horse up the bank behind John.

"We won't make a fire," he said as he dismounted. "We're in a lot more danger around here from renegade Apache than outlaws."

"Doesn't matter much where I am concerned," Tess answered wearily. Everything that had happened was beginning to set in now, weighing on her like cement. "Nothing much worse could happen to me than what has already happened."

"You don't know the Apache."

She sat down in some grass. "Thank you. I needed to hear that."

John handed her a blanket. "Sorry. I wasn't thinking. I never even asked if you were hurt. I mean, do you need any kind of medical attention?"

She was glad for the darkness, embarrassed at the question. "All I need is to be left alone."

He turned away. "Fine." He took the horses off to tie them, then returned with a blanket of his own.

He'd put on a shirt, and Tess was grateful. After her ordeal, it upset her to have to look at his bare chest.

"We'll have to make do tonight. We won't get any real rest until we reach that cave." John spread out his blanket and lay down on it. "Try to sleep."

Tess lay down on her own blanket, not sure just how to behave around him. This man had saved her from being taken off to something worse than death, yet overall she saw hardly any difference between him and those who had taken her, not even in looks, except that John Hawkins did not seem gritty dirty like the others. What made all this so hard was that this man knew everything that had happened to her. He'd seen her stark naked himself, had lain on top of her, touched her intimate parts with his own, yet he was still this mysterious stranger. How humiliating! From now on, every time she saw John Hawkins in town, she would feel like he was seeing her naked. "Will you please do something for me?" she asked aloud.

John stretched out, looking up at the darkening sky, thinking if he took one more blow to the head anytime soon, it would probably kill him. "What's that?"

"Please don't . . . don't tell any of your friends or any Rangers or whoever that . . . how you found me . . . that you've seen me . . . you know. Maybe you could even convince people I wasn't raped. The thought of everyone knowing . . . I just don't know how I'll face people."

"You didn't do anything wrong. I told you that. As far as I go, I never say anything. But I'm afraid people will draw their own conclusions about the rest of it. Sometimes people can be pretty damn cruel about things like that. At first you ought to be around women who would really understand. I told you before, I know a lady who would be glad to take you in for a while.

"*Lady?*"

"In *my* book she's a lady."

Tess sat up. "Just because I've been raped, it doesn't make me a whore!" she said defensively.

"I never said that, and keep your voice down!"

"You think I should be *around* whores! Isn't that what you're saying? That's the same as saying I'm not worthy to reenter decent society!" She spoke in a rough whisper.

John sighed. "I never said anything of the kind. You're inventing things in your own mind, already sure about what people will think of you. Most will understand. I was only saying that *some* won't, and if you need to talk about it, which you damn well *will* need to do, no common woman who's never been through it will be able to help you. Women like Jenny Simms—"

"Jenny Simms! She's the most notorious prostitute in west Texas!"

"How would you know?"

"Well, I just . . . I know, that's all! Everybody says—"

"Everybody *says!*" John sat up. "You see? You're worried about what people will say about you, making up things that aren't true, coming to wrong conclusions. Yet you're doing the same thing about Jenny, without knowing a damn thing about her. She just runs a saloon, that's all. And she's never taken money from a man for sleeping with him."

"Oh, she just sleeps with them for *free?* How nice for the men!"

"You don't know anything about her background."

"And people don't know anything about *my* background! They don't know what I went through in the war! They don't know what hell I've just been through . . . the . . . horror . . ." She sensed the tears finally wanting to come, and it made her angry. "They don't know . . . about my husband . . . how much it hurt to see him . . . see him . . ." She broke down then, realizing Abel's cowardliness actually pained her more than his actual death or anything else that had happened. She wept bitterly, not even aware John had come over to kneel beside her.

John just watched her, suspecting this was a woman who did not cry easily. He felt sorry for her, knew himself how hard it was to have to show true feelings. God knew he did his best never to show his. "Hey, I didn't mean to yell at you," he said, feeling awkward. He never did quite know what to do with a crying woman, always wished he'd known how to help his own mother when she'd cried. "I was just trying to tell you I know people who can help you. I'm sorry about your husband and your father."

"Don't be . . . sorry for my . . . husband," she sobbed. "He . . . he hid under the bed! He hid under the bed!" She curled up, keeping her face covered. "I kept . . . calling for him to come . . . help me fight . . . but he just hid . . . in the bedroom! He was too much of a coward . . . to risk his life for . . . his own wife! My pa . . . died for me. But my husband . . . just hid under that . . . damn bed!"

"My God," John muttered, raging inside that a man would do such a thing. He thought how if this brave, redheaded beauty were *his* wife, he'd risk everything for her. Oddly enough, he'd already done just that, and he didn't even know her. He'd been around this woman hardly a full day, and already there were things about her he greatly admired, even if she was basically a bossy, stuck-up little thing who under normal circumstances probably drove a man nuts with orders and demands.

"Do you know . . . how hard that makes it . . . for me to mourn him?" she sobbed. "I should . . . be mourning him. I *should* be! But I can't."

John started to reach out to touch her, then decided it was best if he didn't. "I expect that's a natural feeling," he told her. "God wouldn't blame you for that. Now it's your husband who has to face God with what he's done, but you have nothing to be ashamed of or to answer for."

She sniffed, forced to wipe her nose with the sleeve of her dress. "I need . . . a handkerchief."

John left her and came back with a clean bandana. "Here." He knelt down and handed it to her, and she blew her nose.

"I thought . . . you didn't believe in God," she said.

"What?"

"You said my husband . . . had to answer to God."

Lord. He'd slipped up. Damn the woman! She had brought out all his sympathy, made him talk about God like he actually believed in such things. "I was only . . . Well, I know *you* believe in Him. I'm just saying that if there *is* a God, your husband has more to answer for than you ever will."

Tess wiped at her eyes, trying to remember how this whole conversation got started. She'd asked him not to tell anyone he'd seen her naked. How in the world had they gone from that to this?"Just go lay back down," she told him. "You don't know anything about God or me or feelings or anything. Now you've made me cry. I *hate* crying! I hate any kind of weakness!"

John rose, shaking his head. And to think a moment ago he'd felt sorry for her. "My mother cried a lot," he said bitterly, "and she was the strongest woman I ever knew."

He walked back to his blanket, and Tess thought about the words. Maybe John Hawkins *did* understand some things. Why couldn't she bring herself to say anything kind to him? She sat up on one elbow and looked over at him. He was turned away from her, lying on his side. "Are you . . . are you all right, Mr. Hawkins? Has your head wound stopped bleeding?"

"Forget it," he said coolly. "Just try to get a little sleep. We have some riding to do tomorrow."

She watched him a moment, wondering about his mother. She realized she truly knew absolutely nothing about this man. What drove him to risk his life for a total stranger? Suddenly she wanted to ask him about such things, but it was obvious he would not want to talk about them. And what did it matter, anyway? Once he got her to El Paso, he would go on about his duties and she would probably never even see him again. She had enough of a dilemma of her own in deciding what she was going to do with herself now. There was no sense worrying about this total stranger on top of all that. She meant nothing more to him than someone he'd helped as part of his duty as a Ranger.

She lay back down, and it hit her then that she felt no fear, in spite of lying out here in this wild land so full of danger. John Hawkins lay nearby.

"We'll stop here and you can bathe in the river," John told Tess. "I'm going to do some circling around, keep an eye out for Apache or Comancheros. Soon as you're cleaned up I'll do the same, and we'll reach that cave by nightfall. We'll both take a day or two of rest there." He dismounted and reached into his saddlebags, taking out a bar of soap and a towel. "Here." He set them down in the grass and got back on his horse, then hesitated, noticing she just sat on her own horse looking doubtful. "Hurry it up. We can't waste too much time getting to that cave."

"I can't just take off my clothes and take a bath out in the open like this!"

John rolled his eyes and cast her a smirk of disgust. "Lady, there's nobody to watch but maybe a few frogs and coyotes. If you think *I'm* going to watch, why should I? If I wanted to take advantage of you, I'd have done it yesterday in that wagon. If that doesn't prove you can trust me, I don't know what does."

Tess felt her cheeks going crimson. He was right about that, but his remark only told her he had not forgotten what he'd seen, after promising her he had. Would she ever get over this humiliation?

"Like I said, hurry it up."

Tess had to admit nothing sounded more wonderful right now than a bath, not just to get rid of the dirt and perspiration, but to wash away the filth of the men who had touched her. She untied her bundle of clothes and picked up the towel and soap and ran to the river, hurriedly stripping down and splashing into the shallow water, thinking how much better it would feel to take a hot bath, but this would have to do. She glanced in the direction in which John had ridden. His back was to her as he rode his horse up an incline. She told herself she had no choice but to trust him, and she quickly lathered up, her body, her privates, her hair, scrubbing vigorously, experiencing a sudden near-insane need to wash and wash and wash, as though she couldn't get clean enough.

Get rid of it! Get rid of the dirt! Get rid of the ugly filth Chino had left on her and inside of her. She almost wished she could scrub off her freckles, scrub off her very skin, somehow totally get rid of the old self that had been touched by those men and bring out someone new. What if Chino had given her some kind of disease?

She scrubbed harder, in spite of her sunburn. More tears came, and she let them. It was all right, as long as no one was close by to see. She washed her hair, still sobbing. She had to let it all out before John Hawkins came back. She had a feeling he expected her to be weak, to cry and carry on, to be totally broken by this. That, by God, was not going to happen! She would get the crying done with and go on from here. Where she would go and what she would do would be decided a day at a time, but one thing was certain. She was not going to stay with a prostitute!

She dried off and dressed, looked around. She saw Hawkins nowhere. Fine. That gave her time to get over the tears and splash some of the cold water on her face again, wash away the tears and get rid of the puffy eyes they always created. She ran her hands through her hair, and realized then she didn't have a brush. She would have to do the best she could with her fingers, but her thick hair was still going to be an unholy, tangled mess. She couldn't even put it up into a bun because she had no pins for it. She so wanted to come back to El Paso looking as prim and proper as possible. How else would anyone believe her story that those men had not raped her? It was bad enough that she probably still had bruises on her face.

Finally the golden horse appeared at the rise over which Hawkins had first ridden. She watched him approach, thinking for one flickering moment what a grand specimen of a man he was, what a beautiful horse he rode. She turned away, refusing to recognize anything good about any man right then. And this one had the same dark, sinister, Indian looks of most of those who had abducted her. Not only that, but she had a feeling the line of difference between John Hawkins and men like Chino was very thin.

"You can lay down in the grass and rest a few minutes," she heard him saying. "I'm going to clean up myself now."

Tess did not answer. She sat down in the grass, her back to the river. She wondered for a moment how he had known exactly when to come back. Had he been watching from somewhere after all? She sighed, rubbing at her eyes. What difference did it make? He'd certainly seen everything there was to see. And, after all, he had to make sure she was safe. That was what was so damn irritating, having to admit that she felt totally safe as long as John Hawkins was nearby. Right now she hated to have to give any man any credit for anything.

She waited quietly, heard his splashing in the river. A little while later his voice was behind her again. "Let's get going." She turned to see him shoving dirty clothes into one of the saddlebags. He wore clean denim pants and a blue calico shirt with a leather vest over it. "We'll eat tonight at the cave. My better supplies are there." He mounted up and turned to face her. "We'll follow the river again for a while. Saves leaving tracks for anybody that might find those men back there, and we don't want any Apache picking up our tracks either."

Tess again was struck by a small flash of attraction. His shirt was open at the neck, revealing a striking necklace made up of a simple rawhide cord on which hung what looked like quills, or maybe some kind of claws. She wasn't sure. They were painted in bright red and blue. It was the first time she had truly looked at him as just another human being since he'd come for her yesterday.

Had it really only been that long? How could so much have happened in one day? This man had walked right into a den of thieves and murderers and had taken her out of there. Now, cleaned up and dressed normally, he wasn't quite so intimidating as he'd looked riding into that camp. She realized now he'd deliberately made himself as unkempt and half naked as the rest of them so he would fit in. She noticed he'd removed the bandage from around his head, and his wet, black hair was pulled straight back into a tail that hung nearly to his waist. With his hair that way, his face was much more noticeable, and again she was struck by how handsome he was. He had dark, deep-set eyes, high cheekbones, a nicely shaped nose, full lips and a square jawline. Everything about him spoke of a man of courage and skill in a land where those things were requirements for survival.

She turned and mounted her horse, ashamed and even angry that she had noticed him as just a man, had even considered him handsome. "How is that head wound?" she asked.

John headed for the river. "Hurts," he called back to her. "I couldn't brush my hair there or even wash it good. I'll have to wait until the scabbing is gone." He thought to ask if she felt a little better now that she'd had a good cry, but he suspected she would be angry that he knew. She was a woman who preferred to cry alone, and he respected that. Besides, if he told her he'd seen her crying, she'd know he'd been watching her, not for lustful reasons, but simply because he couldn't let a woman bathe out here without being watched. She thought he hadn't looked, so let her think it. His only problem was he'd had a real yearning to go down there and hold her, especially when he saw her scrubbing herself so hard he thought she might actually hurt herself.

He took his own floppy, leather hat from where it hung over his saddle horn and handed it over to her. "Wear that. It will be too big, and it's been used to water my horse at times, but you've got to protect that fair skin or your nose will be burned right off by the end of the day."

She took it hesitantly, not sure she wanted to plop the gritty-looking thing on her head. "What about you? Don't you need it?"

He grinned, and she felt silly for even asking.

"Men like me are made for the sun," he answered. "I only wear it to keep the heat off the top of my head, not for my skin. I'll get by for a couple of days without it."

She put the hat on, and it fell to just above her eyebrows. John couldn't help grinning at the sight, and Tess was struck by his smile. He looked completely changed when he smiled, like a regular human being. She couldn't help smiling herself, knowing how silly she must look. It felt good to smile. It was something she'd thought she would never do again.

A shiver of doubt shot through her then, at the way he looked at her. She reminded herself this man had seen all there was to see. She shouldn't be smiling at him now. Maybe it would give him ideas. She looked away. "I think you're the one who said we had to hurry," she reminded him.

John's own smile faded. It was going to be very hard for this woman to ever be her natural self again, and he was sorry for that. One thing was sure, though. She was godawful beautiful, brave and feisty to boot. He'd never actually met anyone quite like her.

"I'll fix us something to eat." Tess rummaged through the extra supplies in the cave, grateful for the cool retreat from the sun, which had pummeled them all day.

"You don't have to do that." John sat down on a blanket near the supplies. "You need to rest. I'll—"

"I'm fine! I don't want to rest. I want to eat. I need to

keep busy." She pulled a can of beans from the supplies, found a few potatoes. "Do you have coffee?"

"First we have to have a fire. I'll have to light a match and check the draft in here. If it isn't right, we'll smoke ourselves right out of this cave. If things seem right, I'll go scrounge up as much dry wood and weeds as I can. At least there are a few pine trees around here. Dry pine burns good, and the sap in pine makes it burn slower." He dug into a pocket of his denim pants and pulled out a match, striking it on a rock. A draft blew it out almost immediately. "Looks like the smoke would trail deeper into the cave. Let's hope that by the time it comes out someplace else, it's dwindled some and won't be too noticeable. I don't like making fires and advertising our presence, but we both need to eat." He nodded toward his supplies. "There is a little black fry-pan in that gear somewhere. Go ahead and slice some potatoes if you're so bent on keeping busy."

He left, and Tess found the pan and a small knife. Her head ached with indecision over what she was going to do with herself now, but she forced herself to think only about the moment, fixing something to eat. John had hobbled the horses somewhere outside. The animals had already had plenty to drink for the day, since they'd ridden through the middle of the shallow river for several miles. At last she could truly rest for a while, somewhere out of the miserable sun.

She took several deep breaths to keep her hands from shaking as she sliced the potatoes. Just the sight of the knife, even a small one, brought back ugly memories . . . She'd been threatened so many times with knives the last few days. The vision of John Hawkins ramming his own big blade into Chino flashed before her eyes, and she had to stop for a moment. She was traveling alone with a man who killed as easily as he breathed. How strange to not be afraid of him, yet sometimes she still was. She had never been so unsure of how she felt about another human being.

John finally returned, carrying an armful of wood. He said nothing as he made a circle of rocks and got a fire going, then took out a pocket knife and opened it. He plunged it into a tin can of beans and carefully cut around the lid. He caught Tess watching tentatively. "What's wrong?"

She swallowed. "I just . . . I hope you haven't used that smaller knife on a person." She sensed a hint of anger in his eyes. She had apparently insulted him again.

"This little thing?" He peeled back the lid, then set the can aside and poured a little water over the knife to rinse it. "I only use my *hunting* knife to cut out a man's heart." He snapped the pocket knife closed. "And sometimes I even eat the heart raw after I cut it out!"

He turned and walked out, and Tess sighed, feeling like crying again. She didn't understand men like John Hawkins. One minute he took something as a joke, the next he was angry at something she said. How could she understand a man who was as ruthless as Ranger Hawkins? Her father was kind and gentle, strong and demanding sometimes, but someone with whom a person could reason, and he was a Christian, forgiving man. Then there had been Abel, a meek, cowardly man. Neither of them compared to someone like Hawkins.

"Let him be angry," she muttered. How could she not wonder about the knife after what she'd seen? How could she eat beans that had been touched with a knife used to kill someone? Apparently that was not the case, so she poured the beans into the smaller of the only two pans in his gear and set it on the fire. She added more wood, then finished slicing the potatoes. She found some lard to put in with them, then also set those on the fire. She filled a cloth bag with crushed coffee beans from Army rations, then poured cold water from a filled Army canteen into a tin coffee pot. The three pots barely fit together over the fire. She wished she had some kind of grate, but there was nothing to do but set the food right on top of the flames.

She sat back to watch everything cook, thought about home, how she would be making supper now for her father and Abel if they were still alive. All that was gone now, her little house, her kitchen, all her clothes, her father and husband, everything that mattered.

John finally came back inside, a cheroot between his lips. He sat down near the fire, smoked quietly for a moment while Tess turned the potatoes. "I'm sorry," he finally told her "Believe it or not, I'm not an animal. Sometimes I'm as normal as everybody else, but on the job I do what I have to do to get my man."

"That's what it's all about, isn't it?"

"What do you mean?

"Getting your man. You didn't come after me out of any gallant plan to rescue a damsel in distress. You came for the challenge, to see if you could outsmart and outgun men who were as ruthless as you are. You enjoy the chase, the fight."

He did not answer right away. When she finally met his dark eyes they bored into her as though he could read her very thoughts. "Believe what you want. You're here and alive, aren't you?"

Tess stared at the spatula in her hand. "Yes. I already thanked you for that. I don't know why I . . . I am just so full of anger. I need to hurt someone. I'm just taking it out on you."

"I know. I've seen it before."

She frowned. "Don't patronize me."

"Patronize you? Hell, I don't even know what the word means."

"It means . . ." She met his eyes again, finally saw a little humor in his own again. "You *really* don't know?"

A hint of a grin crossed his lips. "I'm not exactly the best educated man who ever walked. My education has mostly just been real life, survival. That's one thing I know all about, and that's why we're sitting here now. If you don't like my methods, I'm sorry."

She stirred the beans. "No. *I'm* sorry. I had no right insulting you after what you've done."

He leaned back against a rock wall, the cheroot still between his teeth. "Yeah, well, a man gets tired of being judged because of his looks. I look like the ones who attacked your ranch, so you're thinking I *am* like them."

She studied him—dark, brawny, his legs stretched out, his big frame seeming to fill the small cave. "*Aren't* you, Mr. Hawkins?"

He held her gaze. "I don't know," he finally answered. "I guess in a lot of ways I am. But I've never stolen. I've never killed an innocent man, and I've never raped a woman."

Tess sensed the color coming to her cheeks, and she looked away. "You are a very unusual man, Mr. Hawkins."

He laughed lightly. "I've been called worse."

"I'm sure you have."

"Well, you can call me whatever you want. Once I get you to El Paso, we won't see much of each other anymore, so it really doesn't matter to me."

She sat back herself, holding his gaze. "I think it does matter to you, Mr. Hawkins, more than you let on."

He leaned forward. "Let's make a pact. You don't nose in and try to analyze my behavior, and you don't *criticize* my behavior. You just be glad I got you out of that mess. In return, I won't patronize you, once I figure out what that means."

Tess bristled. "It means don't treat me like a fainting ninny who needs to be pampered and pitied, and don't act as though you know how I feel about all of this. You can't even *begin* to know how I feel. You're a man." She saw a strange hurt in his eyes and almost regretted the remark.

"Lady, you might be surprised at what I know about these things. I'm the *result* of rape, and I've seen plenty of it in my own lifetime. So just drop all the pride and pretense. Like I said, we'll just make a pact and I won't treat you any more special than anybody else. You in turn will quit looking at me like you think I'm going to pounce on you any second. Believe it or not, I actually know how to treat a respectable woman, and any offers I make for how you can get some help are made because it's a plain fact you'll *need* help. I'm not patronizing you, so quit getting all defensive. End of conversation!'' He put his head back and closed his eyes. "Let me know when that food is ready."

Tess turned the potatoes again, hating herself for being so judgmental and ornery. She was being a complete ass toward a man who probably did not deserve it. "I'm sorry. I don't know what's wrong with me. I'm just . . . angry. I'm so angry inside."

He kept his eyes closed. "Well, I'd say I understand, but you'd say I was patronizing you again, so why don't we just not say anything the rest of the evening? We'll just eat and sleep. Trying to talk about something so serious when you're so tired and it's all fresh in your mind isn't a good idea. I did a lot of killing last night, and believe it or not, that doesn't always set good with me. But *I* don't want to talk about *that* any more than you're ready to talk about what happened to you. And by the way, thanks for saving *my* ass back there when you shot that man. I didn't even know he was standing there."

Tess stared at the flames. She'd actually killed a man point-blank! Suddenly she understood men like John Hawkins a little better. Survival was what it was all about. It sometimes made people do things completely against their nature. She shivered, wondering just how ruthless all people could be when necessary. "You're welcome," she answered quietly.

Chapter Seven

Tess could see it all over again, hear it all over again . . . the fire, the war whoops, the gunfire, her father's screams . . . Abel cowering under the bed . . . the fire . . . the fire. Was it the ranch house burning? Or was it her home back in Georgia? Were those really her father's screams . . . or her mother's and little brother's?

She started awake, realized she was bathed in sweat. She looked around the almost-dark cave, taking a moment to remember where she was. The fire had dwindled down to embers. She heard a horse whinny, remembered John Hawkins had brought the animals inside and left them farther back in the cave so he would not have to worry about coyotes or cougars . . . mostly so their manure would not build up to the point where the odor might waft on the wind and attract the attention of any Apache who might be nearby.

"They can smell a horse a mile or more away if the wind is right," he'd told her.

She could understand why. Now the whole cave smelled like a horse barn. It didn't bother her so much. She had cleaned out the horse stalls on the farm plenty of times. She lay back down.

"You all right?"

Tess started at the words spoken by John. "I was dreaming." She sat up again. She could hardly see him where he sat, closer to the cave entrance. "Haven't you slept?"

"Too many things to watch for."

"You have to sleep *some*time."

"Catnaps are enough for me. Out here it's dangerous to sleep too hard. I might try to sleep a little tomorrow after daylight. You'll be more rested, and you can keep watch for a while."

It struck Tess how alone they were, actually dependent on each other. This man who dearly needed his rest because of his head wound was staying awake to keep watch over her. She actually felt a little sorry for him sitting there all alone. "How did you get to be a Ranger?"

She sensed him looking over at her, but she could not see his eyes well. She reached over and picked up a piece of wood and laid it on the coals.

"Had nothing else to do. When you have Indian blood, most regular folks won't hire you. I had a mean temper and was good with a gun and knew how to track, so somebody suggested I try joining the Rangers. I figured maybe I'd get a little . . ." He hesitated.

"Respect?"

"Something like that."

"You strike me as man who doesn't care if he's respected or not."

"Every man cares about that."

The words surprised her. "Surely you also joined the Rangers just for the adventure." She heard scraping sounds. He was shifting his position.

"Some. It sure wasn't for the money. There's not much of that, and we have to furnish our own horse and gear and weapons." He sighed. "What were you dreaming?" he asked, as though he preferred to change the subject.

"Can't you guess? A nightmare is the better description."

"I've had plenty of those myself."

Tess thought how low but soft his voice was right now. "About your mother?"

There was a long pause. "Why do you ask that?"

"I don't know. You mentioned her once or twice, something about her suffering like I have."

Another long pause.

"My mother was a good woman, treated poorly because of her Indian blood. She was part Lakota Indian. My grandfather was French—married a Sioux woman. He brought her to St. Louis and settled there, got himself killed in a tavern brawl after my mother was born. My Sioux grandmother died when my mother was sixteen, and she was on her own then, got a job cooking on a riverboat. The captain of the boat took advantage of her, and I'm the result."

Tess added one more piece of wood to the fire. "I'm sorry."

"About my mother being raped, or me being born?"

Tess couldn't help smiling inwardly at the remark. "About your mother, of course. How did she manage to raise you after that? How did she support you?" She heard him sigh before continuing.

"She went to work for a laundry house in St. Louis, worked herself nearly to death. I started working myself by the time I was ten, to help her out. When I was fourteen I caught another man trying to force himself on her, and I killed him with a knife. That was in Missouri. I figured the law would come after me, so my mother and I fled— landed in Texas and ended up both working for a rancher in northern Texas. I caught a few cattle rustlers for the man. He's the one who suggested that with my nose for finding men like that and my skill with a gun, I ought to join the Rangers. After my mother died, I figured that was what I would do."

Tess was surprised he'd offered so much information about himself. The quiet night and some rest had apparently calmed his normally defensive, ornery nature. Now he was easier to talk to. She suspected, though, that the hurt of things that had happened to his mother, the things he had suffered for having Indian blood and being a bastard, ran much deeper than he was letting on. He liked pretending it didn't bother him . . . just like she was pretending she was not bothered by what had happened to her.

"What about your own mother?" he asked. "She dead?"

Pain shot through Tess's heart at the memory. "For fifteen years now. She was killed by Southern rabble who set fire to our house a couple of years after the war ended. I was only seven then. My father was off trying to find work so we could hang on to what was left of our place. My mother and I were in the barn when they came." She shivered at the memory. "Things were terrible after the war. Lawless. We all hated the Yankees for what they had done to the South, but it was outlaws from our own kind who were committing most of the crimes, men gone mad from losing everything in the war—land, homes, families. Those who had nothing plundered those who had anything good enough for the taking. They came to our farm, stole food from our fields, stole our livestock, clothes, anything of value in the house, then set fire to the house while they held me and my mother back. My little brother was in the house. When the raiders finally left, my mother told me to stay put. She ran to the house to try to save my little brother. Neither one of them ever came back out." She saw a quick little flame, and John's face lit up as he put a match to a thin cigar. She watched the end of it glow.

"I'm sorry," he said. "That must have been an awful thing for you."

"It has given me nightmares for years since then. I stayed hidden in the barn until the raiders finally left. My father came back, buried my mother and young Terence. He was never the same after that. We lived in the barn for a while, ate what was left in the fields."

So, that's what made you so tough, he thought. It took a lot of strength and grit for a seven-year-old girl to endure what she had. And what a small thing she must have been then. "I admire your guts, lady."

Tess actually smiled a little, realizing that from a man like John Hawkins, that was probably a high compliment. He wasn't a man to tell a woman how beautiful she was. Such things probably didn't matter much to him. Strength was more important. How different he was from Abel Carey. "You do what you have to do to survive. Now I guess I'll have to do it again."

"I'm sure you will."

"You've done the same."

"I guess."

Tess watched the glow of the cheroot as he took a deep drag from it. "Thank you for talking to me, Mr. Hawkins. It helps shake the nightmare out of my head."

"Just call me John. Or Hawk. My partner calls me Hawk."

"Partner?"

"Most Rangers have one. I came on down here alone because we'd just finished an assignment." He wondered what she would think of him blowing up those men back in Texas. "He had to go on to El Paso and report in. I figured there wasn't any time to waste coming after you, so . . . here I am . . . and here we are."

Tess wondered when she was going to say something to make him angry again. She spoke the next words carefully. "So, you really did come down here just for me? Not for the chase? The challenge?"

Again he waited to answer. "I have a need to kill men who abuse a woman. There's no greater crime in my book."

Tess was actually beginning to like him a little. "Because of your mother?"

"I guess."

Well, well, well. The man actually had a conscience, a heart. At least he'd loved and respected his mother. It was obvious they had been very close. "Have you ever been married, Mr.—John?"

He snickered. "No, ma'am. I've been too busy to look, and no decent woman will give me the time of day. People have a certain opinion of me because they don't really know me."

I can understand why, Tess mused. "I have to admit I remember my father saying something about you once, said he'd seen you in town," she told him. "He said he'd heard you were the meanest son-of—well, you know—that ever rode as a Ranger."

He laughed lightly. "See what I mean?"

She was actually enjoying this talk. "I suspect he wasn't far wrong."

"He wasn't."

She poked at the logs, which were just beginning to flare up a little. "I think I remember seeing you in town."

"You did. Or at least I saw you. You glanced my way, but not long enough to really *look* at me and remember me. You looked away again right away—like all decent white women do."

"They do?"

"Of course they do. You did it yourself."

She lay back down. "I am sure, Mr. Hawkins . . . I mean, John . . . that I did not do it out of rudeness. I am not like that. Perhaps I was preoccupied about something else. Besides, you are quite a handsome man. Surely you know that." Why in God's name had she told him that? *Now* what would he think of her? She was glad he probably could not see how red her face was.

"I've been told a time or two."

By Jenny Simms, I'll bet, she thought.

"Never by a proper lady," he added, as though to read her thoughts. "Most women think it's a sin to even look twice at a man who obviously has Indian blood. When you're a bastard, that makes it all worse."

Bastard. That had to sit hard on a man, especially one with his pride. "I am sure most women don't even know that part of your background. How could they?"

"Oh, word gets around, believe me."

She was almost surprised that it appeared to really bother him. He seemed like a man who could not care less what anyone thought of him. This was a side of John Hawkins she suspected few people saw. "What kind of Indian did you say you were?"

He shifted again. "Lakota. Most whites call them Sioux. Hard to tell, isn't it? We all look alike to whites. Sioux, Apache, Comanche, Shoshoni, Crow—they can't tell the difference. But there *is* a difference among the Nations, if people would really take the time to notice."

Tess decided to end the conversation before she delved a little too deeply and he got mad about something she said. She could already tell he was getting defensive about his Indian blood. "Thank you for talking to me, John. And you may call me Tess. It's short for Theresa."

He thought a moment. "Seems a little too personal the other way around. You're a lady and a widow. I'll call you Mrs. Carey—or just ma'am. And when we get back to El Paso, I'll do what I can to convince people you were never raped, if that's how you want it."

She felt her cheeks going crimson again. "Yes. Thank you, John. And in front of others I will call you Mr. Hawkins. It would probably be better that way—bring *you* a little more respect."

"Don't worry about me. I've got pretty tough skin. None of those things bother me much anymore."

The heck they don't, John Hawkins. "Just the same, I'll call you Mr. Hawkins." She turned over, pulling a blanket over herself. The cave was cool and damp. "I'll try to sleep again so *you* can get some sleep tomorrow."

"Fine." John smoked quietly, thinking what a fine woman she was at that. Maybe she wasn't the stuck-up snob he'd thought she was. Feisty, though. He was surprised he hadn't said something to set her off.

Thank goodness I didn't make him angry about something, Tess was thinking at the same time.

Tess watched the lovely morning from the cave entrance. They were high enough that the view was quite magnificent, and she wondered at how this land could be so dan-

gerous, the elements so unbearable at times, yet it was all
so beautiful. The sun shone down on a wide scattering of
colorful boulders, rising cliffs in the distance. Patches of
blue and green grass woke the otherwise flat and pale
ground, and the entire panorama spoke of wrenching isola-
tion that stretched to far-off, jagged lines which in turn
stretched into nowhere.

She wondered sometimes why God even put people in
a land like this. Surely it was meant only for the rocks and
the few animals that could subsist here. She looked over
at John Hawkins, realizing God *had* thought wisely about
who he put in this land—people like John. It was people
like herself who did not belong here, but her father had
wanted to get as far from Georgia as possible. He'd wanted
to leave the horror behind them, and he had taken advantage of the free land Texas had offered to Confederate
veterans, although most of Texas could not compare to
Georgia for rich soil and easy farming.

She watched John Hawkins, thinking what a big, wild
man he was, yet he lay there sleeping so quietly. It was
hard to imagine him as a little boy, suffering the insults
he must have suffered for having no legitimate father.
She suspected he'd gotten himself into plenty of scrapes
defending his Indian mother, which was probably what
had made him so mean and tough as a man. Having to
kill a man at fourteen certainly didn't help.

She looked back outside, and that was when she noticed
him, a lone rider in the distance. "Oh, dear!" She got up
and walked over to John, kneeling down and touching
him. "John." She shook his arm, then jumped back when
he bolted upright, coming fully awake much quicker than
she thought he would. He looked around.

"Something wrong?"

"There is a lone rider out there in the distance."

Immediately he leaped up, grabbing his rifle and darting
to the cave entrance. He watched for a moment, then
stepped outside and yelled something akin to a war cry.

Tess moved to the entrance to see him standing there with the rifle in the air. "What on earth—?"

"It's my partner!" he answered, still watching. "His name is Ken Randall. He's a tough old crust and we argue a lot, but you couldn't ask for anybody more dependable. We've got some help now if we run into more trouble."

Tess doubted a man like John Hawkins ever needed help, but she was still glad a second man would be along.

John let out another shout. Ken had halted his horse on the first yell, and now he headed for the cave. It took him several minutes to reach them, and Tess watched the two men embrace after Ken dismounted, a gesture that surprised her.

"You all right?" Ken asked. "What the hell is that on your scalp?"

"Dried blood. One of the bastards decided to put a new part in my hair. I'm all right, and so is the woman. She's inside."

"You got her out of there by yourself?"

John laughed. "Don't tell me you're surprised."

Ken scowled. "Hell, no, I guess not. You didn't use dynamite on them, too, did you?"

Tess wondered at the words. Dynamite? John Hawkins sometimes blew men up?

"Hell, no. Didn't have any left, and I had to watch out for the woman. I just dirtied myself up, took off my shirt, and rode in as just another renegade looking for someone to ride with. They bought my story all the way. I waited till they were asleep, got their leader drunk, and landed my knife in his heart. That's when the shooting began." He turned to Tess. "This little lady here shot one of them herself. Saved my life, I expect."

Tess was embarrassed. She'd shot at the outlaw out of pure reflex, hardly aware of what she was doing. The man called Ken sobered as he approached her. She noticed this Ranger was all white, a short, stocky man compared to John. He was older, and he needed a shave, but he was otherwise decent looking, wearing a flannel shirt and leather vest, six-guns on his hips. His boots were caked with dust, to be expected out here. He removed his floppy, leather hat. "Ma'am? I'm Ken Randall, Hawk's partner. I'm damn glad he got you out of there, sorry for what you've most likely been through. How are you doing?"

She folded her arms. "I'm fine, Mr. Randall," she lied. "Thank you for coming along to help."

Ken glanced at John, and he could tell by John's eyes the worst had happened, but this woman was not the shriveling, weeping thing he'd expected to find.

"Mrs. Carey is a tough lady," John told him, setting his rifle aside. "She'll be okay. She uses her wits and knows how to shoot."

Ken nodded, turning back to Tess. "I'm sorry about your loss, ma'am. You got folks back East you can go to?"

"No." Tess turned to the fire. It hurt to think about it . . . Abel . . . her father. She didn't want to talk about it or face reality yet. "Would you like some coffee, Mr. Randall?"

"Yes, ma'am, I'd appreciate that." Ken glanced at John again, still surprised at Tess's calm nature.

"My mother and brother were killed in raiding after the Civil War," she told Ken as she used her skirt as padding to grab the handle of the coffee pot. She poured some of the liquid into a tin cup. "I have an aunt and uncle somewhere in Georgia, but I haven't seen them in so many years I wouldn't feel comfortable going to them. I don't even know them." She handed out the coffee. "I'll figure something out," she told Ken. "I still own the land my father farmed. I can sell it if I have to, sell whatever is salvageable, maybe find work in town. I don't want to just up and leave Texas right away. I've been here ten years now, long enough to call Texas home. My father brought me here when I was twelve. We lived near San Antonio for a while, came to west Texas three years ago to farm free land given to us by a Colonel Hewlett Bass. That's who we worked for near San Antonio. My father rode with Colonel Bass in the Confederate Army during the war."

"Bass! I remember that old codger. He gave a lot of land away to Confederate friends before he died." Ken turned to John. "Say, I think that's how Jim Caldwell got all that land he ranches. He was friends with Bass."

Tess noticed a look of disgust in John's eyes. "Caldwell likes to brag he built that ranch all on his own."

"Well, he didn't," Tess verified. "Colonel Bass told us about Mr. Caldwell, who was a lieutenant who served under him. He once owned a huge plantation in Virginia, lost everything in the war and moved to Texas with Colonel Bass. Bass gave him most of the land he owns now, asked him to go there and work it for him, as well as take care of the surrounding land, including what is now our farm." She poured herself some coffee. "The trouble is, Jim Caldwell thinks he ought to own every bit of the colonel's land, resents those of us who also were given some of it. He's already bought out several other veterans—forced them out is more like it. But he couldn't make us leave." She stared at the coffee, her heart aching for her father again. "Lord knows he'll certainly try to get the farm again, now that I'm alone, thinking I won't be able to take care of the place."

"You never mentioned Caldwell last night," John told her.

She looked across the fire at him. "I really hadn't given it much thought until we started talking about Colonel Bass." She couldn't hold back a wry grin then. "I might add that although I've never known you before now, I had heard about you through gossip from Caldwell's wife, Harriet. She doesn't think too highly of Ranger John Hawkins."

Ken laughed. "That ain't exactly news to Hawk!"

John scowled at his friend. "I don't care what his wife thinks." He looked back at Tess. "It's Caldwell himself that concerns me. I don't like the man, and I don't trust him."

"Nor do I, but I may have to deal with him now."

"Well, little lady, the first thing you have to do is get

back to El Paso safely, and me and Hawk will see that you do. After that we'll help however we can." Ken raised his coffee cup. "And by the way, I gotta say this is sure better coffee than the black pitch Hawk makes!"

John waved him off. "I keep telling you to make it yourself. Coffee is a white man's drink."

"Well, you're more than half white, so you ought to at least be able to make decent coffee." Ken handed an empty cup to Tess. "You figurin' on gettin' some miles behind you yet today?" he asked John.

John shrugged. "I was going to let Mrs. Carey rest one more day before making her travel."

"I don't need to. The longer we hang around here, the more likely it is the Apache will find us, or maybe whoever was supposed to meet those men you left lying dead south of here," Tess answered. "I don't need pampering, Mr. Hawkins," she added, preferring to use his formal name in front of someone else. "I've told you that."

Ken looked at John with raised eyebrows. This was some woman. He expected John was quite impressed with this one. He turned back to Tess, seeing determined fire in her blue eyes—pretty eyes, they were. And that hair, red as Texas clay. And it was amazing such a little thing could have suffered the horror she surely had and not be completely broken.

John just shook his head. "I think you *should* rest, but since you're so bent on showing us there isn't a weak bone in your body, I'll pack up our things and saddle the horses and we'll go." He walked to the back of the cave to get the horses, and Ken turned to Tess.

"Well, I'm right honored to meet you, Mrs. Carey. I admire your courage and stamina. Hawk and I will get you back to El Paso, and we'll help you however we can once you get there. You just tell us what you need."

Tess liked him right away. "Thank you, Mr. Randall."

He leaned closer. "Ole Hawk there is an ornery cuss, ain't he? I expect you saw some pretty rough things once he made his move. He's mean and sometimes downright vicious, but he gets the job done. He was so bent on reachin' you that he just took off alone to go after you. That was a dangerous thing to do."

"I know. I appreciate it very much." She folded her arms. "And yes, he *is* an ornery cuss. It's hard to carry on a conversation with him without making him angry about something. A person doesn't even have to try."

Ken laughed. "You've got that right. I've been pissin' him off for a couple of years!" He covered his mouth. "Oh, excuse my language, ma'am."

"Quit talking about me, and get over here and saddle this other horse," John ordered his partner.

Ken rose. "You clean up here and we'll be on our way in no time," he told Tess.

Tess poured what little coffee was left into the fire, and the liquid hissed against hot coals. She wondered why she felt suddenly a little sad about leaving the cave. More than that, she was a little sad that once they got back to El Paso, it was unlikely she would see much of John Hawkins again. How silly to care.

Chapter Eight

They seemed to rise right out of the earth, totally invisible one moment, appearing from behind rocks and brush the next. Their screams and war whoops were chilling, and Tess watched in terror as one of them headed for her. His black hair looked dusty, and a red scarf was tied around his forehead. His hand was raised, a hatchet in it. She heard a boom beside her as John quickly whisked out his six-gun and shot.

The Indian's face exploded in blood, and Tess felt helpless as more of them came on. John shoved his six-gun into her hand.

"Use it!" he ordered. He yanked his rifle out of its boot. Ken's horse was turning in circles, and Ken was shooting at the Indians with both his six-guns, downing them right and left. John aimed for a few farther away, dropping several of them before they could get closer.

Tess screamed when someone grabbed her leg, and she fired point-blank into the forehead of a another marauder. She noticed they were much shorter than the Comanche renegades she had seen, and their faces were flatter. Apache! She damn well *did* know the difference between some Indian tribes. The Indian she'd shot fell away from her, and then her horse began to go down. She realized only then that her attacker had buried a hatchet into the animal's rump. "Mr. Hawkins!" she yelled as the horse fell. It rolled onto her left ankle, and she cried out with pain, the hard saddle crushing her ankle bone against the hard ground.

Another Indian came at her, and she shot him in the belly. He fell over the horse, and Tess frantically began trying to get her leg out from under the animal. Quickly John Hawkins was beside her, shooting at more Indians. He turned then and shot her horse in the head before grabbing her about the shoulders and pulling while kicking at the horse at the same time until finally her ankle came loose. He dragged her away, shooting one more Indian, then rose and picked her up as though she were light as a feather. He plopped her on his horse and quickly pulled the saddlebags off the dead horse and threw them over her lap.

"You okay, Ken?"

"I'm fine. Let's ride hard before more come. We can make the Rio Grande in a few hours."

John mounted up behind Tess, putting his arms around her to grab hold of the reins. "Hang on!" he told her. "We downed this bunch, but there are probably more." He kicked his horse into a hard run, and Tess clung to the saddle horn, realizing that even if she held on to nothing, John's strong grip on her would keep her from falling.

They had been traveling for two days, putting in long hours in the saddle, trying to get out of Mexico. This was the first trouble they had had. Tess had avoided any more personal questions, afraid that if she got too nosy, Ken would think she was actually interested in John Hawkins as something more than just a Ranger who had rescued her. Besides that, they were all too worn out for much conversation.

She truly wondered how much more she could take. The sudden attack had rekindled all the horror of her abduction. In only ten days she had seen so much death and violence, had known so much personal suffering. She was now far removed from the Tess Carey who'd been casually preparing lunch the day the Comancheros had come to the ranch, and she wondered if true law and order would ever really come to this land.

She was not sure how far they had traveled at the aching pace before John finally slowed his horse because he feared he'd ride it to death. The palomino was breathing in panting snorts, and lather was beginning to appear on its neck.

"We'd better get off and walk the horses for a while," John told Ken.

His hand casually gripped Tess's stomach as he dismounted, and she felt a stirring that disarmed her. She had shared an odd intimacy with the man that left her at a loss over how she should feel about him. His strong hands gripped her about the waist then, and he lifted her down with the same ease he'd put her on the horse to begin with.

"Glad you were along, Ken," he told his partner. "I don't think I could have handled that one alone."

"The bastards came out of nowhere. Typical Apache."

Both men took their horses by the reins and began walking, Tess between them. Tess realized they must have forgotten about her ankle. In fact, she had nearly forgotten herself, until she began walking. She'd been so concerned about getting away and hanging on to John's saddle that she had ignored the pain. Now that was impossible. She put up with it as long as possible, hating to have a fuss made over her, but finally she had to grab John's arm. "My ankle," she said. "It must be broken or sprained. The horse fell on it."

He stopped walking and looked down at her. "Well, since you weigh hardly anything at all, I expect you could ride on Sundance while we walk." He frowned. "Unless you think I would be *patronizing* you by the offer."

Tess scowled. "Please. It really hurts."

"Oh, I believe that." He picked her up and set her back

on his horse. "Let's have a look." He unlaced her shoe and easily pulled it off, since it was too big. These had been the only shoes she'd found in the trunk of stolen goods at the outlaw camp. She didn't wear any stockings because she had none.

A wave of embarrassment and uneasy memories moved through Tess as John pushed up the hem of her dress a little and studied her swollen, bruised ankle. Normally it wouldn't seem right, letting a near stranger see her bare foot and part of her leg . . . but this man had seen much more than that. She winced when he plied the ankle with fingers surprisingly gentle.

"I don't think it's broken, but it's going to give you a lot of pain for quite a few days. I can wrap it with something to secure it and maybe keep some of the swelling down if you want."

"I'll be all right until we make camp. We have to keep going. I want to get across the river."

John met her eyes, still admiring her spunk. Those blue eyes looked back at him with pride, and a hint of indignation. He suspected she could not quite get over the embarrassment of knowing he'd seen much more of her than an ankle . . . and *he* could not get over the memory of it himself. He almost hated the thought of leaving her in El Paso, or wherever she wanted him to take her, probably to see her seldom, if ever again. He handed her the shoe and took up his horse's reins.

"Say, you did right good back there, Mrs. Carey," Ken told her. "You got two of 'em. Maybe you ought to join the Rangers. You think they'd take a woman, Hawk?"

John snickered. "That will be the day."

"Don't be so condescending, Mr. Hawkins," Tess told him. "Women can do a lot of things men can do. I believe I saved your own hide more than once the last four days."

Ken laughed. "She's got you there, Hawk."

"The only thing she's got me on is when she uses those damn big words. I've just started figuring out what patronizing means. Now she says I'm condescending. I don't know what that means either."

"It means—"

"I don't *want* to know!" John bit out at her. Why did these sudden feelings he kept getting for Tess Carey make him so angry? Lord, her leg was pretty. Even her feet were pretty. Most people had ugly feet. He needed a reason to dislike her, simply because she'd probably never give him an ounce of credit or a moment of her time once they got back. Of that he was sure. She'd probably laugh her head off if she knew she gave him fancy thoughts about wanting to hold her, comfort her. If he needed a reason to be irritated with her, and to be sure he could never be interested in a woman like that, those damn words she used were a good enough reason. How could a man be around a woman whose conversation he didn't even understand half the time?

"Oh, go ahead and tell us what it means," Ken put in, figuring Tess needed something to talk about. Surely she'd been shaken by the run-in with the Apache, even though she was trying not to show it.

Tess pulled some hair behind her ear. The day had grown cloudy, and at last they were not being pummeled with hot sun. Still she felt filthy again, longed for another bath. She would have to stay this way until they reached El Paso, for she had no clean clothes to put on. She hated the thought of riding in looking like this, dusty, sweaty, her hair a tangled mess.

"It means almost the same thing as patronizing," she answered. "It means arrogant, snobbish. You were being condescending to say women cannot be Rangers, as though only men like you can do such things."

"Well, then I *meant* to be condescending," John answered, "because women *can't* be Rangers."

"I am sure there are some who could be," Tess answered.

"I have to agree with her, John."

"Now *you're* being patronizing," John told him.

Ken laughed. "You're gettin' pretty good at rememberin' them words. Next thing you know, you'll be learnin' to read.''

John gave him a scowl.

"You must know how to read, Mrs. Carey, if you know all them words," Ken told her.

"I learned mostly on my own by studying books, asking my father to read to me and then reading as much as I could on my own. I have . . ." She remembered the farmhouse had been burned by the Comancheros. Her books, all gone! "I *had* a lot of books at home. I suppose I will have to find a way to replace them."

"Well, there's the railroad comes through El Paso now, and wagon trains of trade goods. I expect you'll find somebody sellin' books or who knows how to get them. If we had a schoolteacher around there . . . Say, there's somethin' you could do to make a livin'. You could teach folks around town how to read. Maybe even John here would like to learn."

"Shut up, Ken," John warned. "I've got no need to learn how to read. All I need in this life is a horse and my guns. I don't want to hear any more about big words and reading."

Ken pursed his lips in thought, and Tess wondered if it embarrassed John to have her know he couldn't read.

"Where would you like us to take you once we reach El Paso?" Ken asked, figuring he'd better change the subject.

Tess rubbed at her gritty neck. "I'd like to visit my father's and husband's graves first," she answered. "Mr. Hawkins told me the Army found what was left and buried them."

"Yes, ma'am. We'll take you there. What will you do after that?"

Tess sighed. "I don't know, Mr. Randall."

"I figured Jenny would gladly give her a room for a while," John told Ken.

"Jenny? She'd be livin' over a saloon. A lady like Mrs. Carey can't live over a saloon."

"Well then, we'll have to find somebody else, won't we?"

"I'll find my own accommodations, thank you!" Tess told them. "I am perfectly capable of taking care of myself."

John just rolled his eyes. "Whatever you say, but you'll need help for a few days while you let that ankle rest. There isn't even a doctor in El Paso."

"I'll manage."

"I'm sure you will." The words carried a ring of sarcasm. *And you will probably go straight to Jenny Simms's bed,* Tess thought with disgust. She looked around, still worried about more Apache. She would be glad when all this tension was overwith, when they were back to civilization and she could leave the company of one John Hawkins. She didn't like the feelings he stirred in her, didn't like his attitude, didn't like his vicious nature, or the way he sometimes snapped at her. Most of all she didn't like being around a man who had practically known her intimately when at the same time they hardly knew each other at all. Would he tell others about that? It sickened her to think that he might. Maybe he would tell that Jenny Simms and that evil woman would laugh about it!

She watched him walk ahead of her, all broad shoulders, sometimes such a silent man. She remembered their conversation about his mother. Maybe he *did* understand what she'd been through. If he did, he surely would not tell others and make light of it. He'd promised to keep it a secret. He already even had Ken convinced she'd not been touched, but she suspected a man like Ken knew better. The biggest problem would be convincing the general public she'd not been touched wrongly. People could be so cruel about those things.

"I have a little money in the bank in El Paso," she told them. "I'll use it to rent a room for a while until I decide what to do or if I'll even stay."

"If that's what you want," John answered.

"That's what I want. And I would somehow like to repay you both for what you've done for me, especially you, Mr. Hawkins."

"No need. It's just what we do for a living."

So, now he was back to pretending he didn't have an ounce of pity or concern in his blood. She suspected the closer they got to civilization, the more quiet and callous he would become. God forbid anyone should know he had feelings. "I wouldn't feel right if I didn't give the two of you some small reward," she told them. "It's only right. A person has to do the decent thing."

John just shook his head. "By all means, let's be decent."

Ken just laughed again. "John Hawkins, you don't know the meanin' of the word," he teased.

"Right now not slugging you in the mouth is being pretty decent, as far as I'm concerned." John stopped and watched the horizon. "The Rio Grande is only a few miles ahead. I can almost smell the water. We'll keep going until we get across, then make camp on the other side."

"Fine with me."

John looked up at Tess. "You able to ride that far?"

She scowled at him. "Of course I am."

He closed his eyes and turned away. "I should have known better than to ask."

"Do you think we're out of danger, Ken?" Tess asked the question softly. The night was so still, except for the singing of nocturnal insects, it just didn't seem right to talk loudly. Besides, John had said voices carry far in the night, and Indians had ears that could pick up the tiniest sound a mile away. She suspected his own hearing was just as keen. He was out there somewhere in the darkness right now, keeping watch. They had made no fire, afraid some enemy out there might see its glow.

"Hard to say," Ken answered. "But if somethin' is out there, you can bet Hawk will know it."

She stared up at a nearly full moon and millions of stars. "Well, he didn't do a very good job of detecting those Apache who attacked us this morning."

Ken chuckled. "I'll give you that one. But it was daylight,

and we didn't see no tracks of any kind. They must have come up on us from another direction, got there long before we did. At any rate, we was all talkin' and not payin' attention. That's not like Hawk. Normally he scouts way ahead of me. He's damn good at it, and he's mad that he didn't know them Apache was up ahead waitin' for us. That's why he had you ride with me the rest of the day and went on ahead with his horse after we started ridin' again. He wasn't gonna let that happen again. And that's why he's out there somewhere now, although most Indians don't go out raidin' at night. They don't like the dark. They figure evil spirits lurk about in it."

Tess turned on her side to face the man. "Just how Indian is John Hawkins?" she asked quietly. "Does he practice their customs, pray to some strange God?"

"Hawk don't pray to *no* God that I know of. Mostly what's Indian about him besides his looks is that wildness about him, his keen senses and such. But he don't practice no special customs that I know of. His ma never really had the chance to get involved with Indian ways herself. It was *her* ma that was all Indian. She married a white trapper, a Frenchman. He brought her to St. Louis to live, and then he was killed in a tavern brawl."

"I know. He told me about his mother and grandfather."

"He did? That ain't like him to tell no stranger about them. He only just told me a few weeks ago. You ought to feel real privileged."

Tess shrugged. "We were alone, and I needed to forget a nightmare I'd just had. I guess he figured telling me would help."

"Well, generally ole Hawk has to know you good before he'll open up to you. He's basically a good man, believe it or not, but he's carryin' a lot of hurt and anger inside because of things that happened to his ma and abuse he took as a boy for lookin' so Indian."

They both kept their voices to a near whisper. Tess was glad Ken was along. Unlike John, he liked to talk, and she welcomed the conversation, as well as the opportunity to learn more about John Hawkins. "How old is he?" she asked.

"I ain't sure. Thirty-one or-two, I think." Ken was not surprised she was asking questions about Hawk. He was the kind of man who spurred questions from a lot of people.

"Where do Rangers live?" Tess asked, eager to talk about something that kept her mind off herself. "I mean, you surely don't just ride all over the place and never settle anywhere."

"Actually we *do* travel most of the time. When we get a break we sometimes stay in tent camps with other Rangers, and sometimes we just go to a town and stay in a broth— well, we find a room for a couple of days."

Tess rolled onto her back. "Like with Jenny Simms?"

He grinned. "Sometimes. But not me. Just Hawk."

I'll bet, Tess thought. "He thinks I should go there and stay at first. I can't do that. It would look bad."

"Oh, Jenny ain't so bad. She's really a pretty nice woman. It's just that folks judge her without knowin' her. And listen, you can tell her anything, anything at all that bothers you, and she'll talk to you about it. You remember that. You might like her better than you think you would."

"I will get a room and a job. Maybe I *could* teach reading. Maybe people would pay me for that."

"It's worth a try."

"What will you and Mr. Hawkins do next?"

"Depends what the captain has waitin' for us."

"Well, I don't like the way I had to meet you, but I am glad to know both of you. I don't exactly approve of some of your methods, but someone has to do something about the lawlessness out here. Sometimes I wonder if things will ever be truly civilized."

"It's women like you who will do that. The women bring the preachers and the teachers and the doctors and such. Basically most men ain't civilized at all."

Especially the ones like John Hawkins. Tess looked around, saw no sign of him. "Do you think Mr. Hawkins is all right?"

Ken snickered. "Sure he is. He's just bein' extra quiet. He could be anyplace. He can sneak up on a bird. I seen him grab one once."

"Really? He didn't hurt it, did he?"

"Hell no. He let it go. Hawk only kills men, not animals."

Tess rolled her eyes. "How kind of him."

Chapter Nine

Tess stared at the shell of what had been her home the past three years. Everything was gone, but she reminded herself that no fire could burn away memories. The fire in Georgia hadn't taken them away, and neither could this one.

"You want to get down?" Ken asked her. She sat in front of him on his horse, and before she could answer John rode up beside them.

"There are two wooden crosses and fresh graves behind the barn. The crosses have your husband's and father's names on them." Without asking if it mattered, he reached over and wrapped an arm around Tess, pulling her onto his own horse. "I'll take you over."

Ken looked at him in surprise, then grinned. That one simple gesture told him Tess Carey meant something to John Hawkins. He knew this was a tough moment for her, and he wanted to be with her. "Well, well, well," he muttered, watching John ride off with Tess.

"Mr. Randall could have brought me over here just as well," Tess told John.

"I know. I just wanted to do it myself. Don't ask me why,

because I don't know." He stopped at the graves and dismounted, lifting her down. She winced with the pain in her ankle, and he handed her a long piece of wood he had torn away from the unburned parts of the barn. "Here. Use this to lean on. Try to keep your weight off that ankle."

Their gazes held for a moment, both realizing they would soon go their separate ways, both unsure how to feel about it. "Thank you. I would like to be alone, if you don't mind."

John glanced at the graves, then took hold of his horse's reins and led it away.

Tess stared at the graves, which had rocks piled on top of them. A crude cross marked each one simply with a name. Abel Carey. Henry McDowell. It seemed it should be normal to mourn a husband more than a father, but try as she might, she could dig up little feeling for Abel. She had thought him so kind and good, and truly he was. But she had discovered he was also very timid. She had ached sometimes to have him make love to her, but often he had made excuses as to why they could not make love. He had never given her the true spiritual, physical, and mental support—and love—a woman craved.

It almost startled her to realize that the one embrace John Hawkins had given her in the wagon had been the first truly manly, genuine, compassionate embrace she'd ever experienced. That was the hell of it. Ornery and vicious and uncivilized as he was sometimes, let alone part Indian, John Hawkins was all man, a real man. He feared nothing, challenged everything; and she suspected that any woman he loved would never have to worry about being fulfilled as a woman, or being protected from all harm.

She could not forget the way Abel had cowered under the bed. All feelings for him had gone out of her then, and when Chino raped her, she'd seen that vision again, and she'd actually hated her own husband as much as she'd hated Chino.

"God forgive me," she groaned. She used the board for

support as she bent down beside her father's grave and reached out to gently touch the rocks. "I'm so sorry you had to die such a terrible death, Daddy," she said. "Everything has been hell for you ever since the war and Mama's and Terence's deaths. I tried to give you all the love I could, tried to take good care of you. I know you were never really happy."

It was only over the loss of her father that the tears finally came. She had no choice now but to let the sobs come forth again, only the second time she had truly cried since her abduction. It was so hard to let go like this, but sometimes it just had to be done. Her father was gone. She had no one, nothing but memories. She realized then that she had never really been able to enjoy a normal life as a child. The war, her mother's death, had forced her to grow up overnight. She had spent the next few years devoting all her attention to her father, the last three helping him build this farm, such as it was. She'd had little chance to meet other young women of her age. In fact, for the first two years since coming here, there had been no other women of her age in the area. She had known nothing but work and her father. In her whole life she had never even been to a dance. She had lived out such things through reading wonderful stories about other young women, pretending she was the heroines in the books. Now she could not even do that. The books were gone.

She'd gone from seven to twenty-two hardly noticing there was a difference. She was a widow, homeless, and for the moment had no means of support. Now others would brand her as "that woman who had been abducted by Comancheros." Everyone would probably think they had all raped her, that she was somehow soiled.

And she was. Much as she pretended it did not bother her, she wanted to scream and pull out her hair. She wanted to dig inside herself and scrape out anything that had to do with the horrifying Chino. She wanted desperately to wipe away everything that had happened, but it had, and that was the hell of it. The only one who understood how she felt, strange as it might seem, was John Hawkins.

Why did all thoughts keep coming back to John? It seemed ridiculous. And for the moment she should be thinking only of her father. She lay across his grave, hardly aware of the stones poking at her. If only she could hug him once more. If only there had never been a war, they would all still be back in Georgia, enjoying the rich earth, mother, father, brother, sister. Life would have been so different. She would not be alone in west Texas lying across her father's grave, a man who'd been viciously and sense-lessly murdered. She would not be a "soiled" woman, a widow, a—

"Stop it!" she whispered. She was Henry McDowell's daughter, and the McDowells were a proud people not easily broken. That was what her father always said. He would hate seeing her this way, wanting to give up, to let someone like Chino take away her pride. Men like Chino were *nothing,* and now he was dead. She was glad John Hawkins had plunged his knife into the man's heart! She hoped Chino had suffered some before he died.

She sat up, using the skirt of her dress to wipe at her nose and eyes. It was then she realized just how dusty and sweaty she was, how dirty her dress was, how awful she must look in a dress too big for her, one shoe on, one shoe off, her hair a nightmarish mess, her face probably dirty. If she was going to convince others she had not been raped, she couldn't be seen like this. But she had no clothes to change into. How on earth . . . ?

She wiped at her face more, then used the board to get back to her feet. She drew in several deep breaths for self-control. The crying was done. She had to get control of herself, had to go on from here, like any proud McDowell. She had to face her situation and do something about it. "Mr. Hawkins," she called out. She could see John and Ken talking in the distance. John turned at his name, then said something to Ken and mounted Sundance, riding over to her.

"You ready to go into town now?"

She held her chin proudly. "Yes. But I have a request."

John's heart ached at the sight of her, such a small thing acting so brave, standing there in that dirty dress that was too big for her, that red hair tumbled around her face like a broken bird's nest, those blue eyes showing such pride and fire yet swollen and bloodshot from crying. "Whatever you want."

"I must clean up and put on decent clothes before I face anyone. The problem, of course, is that I don't *have* any clean clothes to put on. The second problem is that if you take me to the home of any decent woman, she might help me with clothing, but she won't know how to keep a secret. Most women love gossip, and if I am presented to any respectable woman looking like this, heaven only knows how I will be described to someone else."

John frowned in confusion. "I'm not sure what you're getting at."

Tess closed her eyes for a moment, hating to ask. It was like giving in to what he had already suggested and admitting defeat. "What I am getting at, Mr. Hawkins, is . . ." She put one hand on her hip authoritatively, while still clinging to the board. "I want to know if your Jenny Simms is a woman who would keep quiet if I asked her, or I should say if *you* asked her."

John forced back a grin, knowing it would only irritate her. At last she was beginning to see why Jenny was the one she should go to first. "Let's get one thing straight. She's not *my* Jenny Simms. She's just a friend, like she is to a lot of people. And yes, women like Jenny understand a lot better than others would. If you want her to keep her mouth shut, she'll do it. What I'll do is send Ken into town first. He can go straight to Jenny and describe you and have Jenny bring out some clothes in her carriage. You still have a water pump here that works. Jenny can bring a washtub and soap and creams, anything you need. We'll build a fire while we're waiting and heat some water. I'm sure we can at least find a bucket or something around here. Ken and I can hold up some blankets and you can take a bath and change right here, then ride into town."

She raised her eyebrows. "You two will hold up blankets while I take a bath? Facing which way?"

Now he had no choice but to grin. "Whichever way you say."

Tess could not help a smile of her own then. "You will keep your backs to me at all times, or I will have you hanged when we get to El Paso." A look came into his eyes that made her want to hit him as those dark eyes moved over her.

"Yes, ma'am," he answered. God, he suddenly realized he wanted her. He wanted to remind her how good making love could be, take away the ugliness for her. Surely she had some good memories of things like that with her husband. But then if he'd been a man who would cower under a bed while Indians made off with his wife, what kind of man had he been *in* that bed?

Good God, he had to get rid of these thoughts. Not only was making love probably the last thing Tess Carey would want to do for a long time, but even when she was ready, she sure wouldn't settle for a man like himself. "I'll go talk to Ken. I'll tell him to go up to Jenny's the back way so no one knows he sent for her."

He rode off, and Tess watched him talking to Ken and she wondered how many times John Hawkins had gone up the "back way" to see Jenny Simms himself. She hated having to do this, but there seemed to be no other choice.

Tess hated admitting it, even to herself, but she liked Jenny. She felt a little guilty for having prejudged the woman and having joined other "decent" women in the area in having no association with her at all. She could not begin to imagine running a saloon for a living, and whether Jenny slept with men for money or not, everyone knew that's what the woman did. It made Tess shiver to think of it . . . of being with any man anytime soon, even if she loved him. There were so many things about Jenny Simms to make her someone no proper woman should associate with, and yet she was one of the friendliest women she'd ever met. Jenny couldn't be more than a few years older than Tess, yet she treated her almost like a daughter.

"I can't believe how wonderful this soap smells," she told Jenny.

The woman helped her wash her hair. "Honey, I get my soaps and lotions from only the best places back East, have them shipped out here to me. Every lady ought to pamper herself the best she can, and Lord knows out here a woman needs to put on plenty of cream and wear nice, big hats, keep the damn sun off her face. 'Course my face looks a lot older than I really am on account of kind of hard living, if you know what I mean. I think it's all the smoke inside the saloon that does something to a person's skin. I don't know."

The woman rattled on, as though she knew Tess needed to hear lots of nonsense talk, things to keep her mind off the fact that she wanted this hot bath in order to wash away more of the filth of the man called Chino. Tess was glad the woman seemed to realize she wouldn't want to talk about what had happened in front of John Hawkins or Ken Randall, who both stood holding the blankets out, their backs to her, just as they had promised.

"How much longer do we have to stand here goin' crazy knowin' a pretty woman is takin' a bath right behind our backs?" Ken teased.

"Either one of you looks, I'll find a way to make you pay," Jenny told them. "You both know I can do it."

"You can be meaner than any outlaw or renegade I ever went after," John told her.

"Ha! No one meaner than John Hawkins ever walked the face of the earth," she shot back at him.

"You've got ways of being mean that are worse than anything I've done."

Jenny laughed, and Tess struggled with the same strange emotion she'd felt when Jenny first arrived and greeted

John Hawkins with a quick hug. Why did the man's friendship with a woman like Jenny disturb her? She had no desire to think of any man sexually now, and yet it bothered her to think of John Hawkins sharing such things with someone like Jenny.

She tried to let the thought rinse away with the clean water Jenny poured over her head. She decided she was having these silly little feelings of affection and even jealousy over Hawkins because he had literally rescued her from hell. Now she felt somewhat obligated to the man, and perhaps because he had come for her when she was so vulnerable and hurting and shamed, it had made her feel dependent on him.

She stood up, and Jenny wrapped a towel around her. "Give me one of those blankets, then you two can go have a smoke or something," Jenny ordered John.

"Can I turn around?"

"Soon as you hand me the blanket."

Tess studied the woman's face, trying to guess her age. She was right about her skin. It was showing some wrinkles, and her makeup was too heavy and looked caked from perspiration. She thought the woman would actually look younger and prettier without so much powder and rouge. She thought about suggesting it, but she did not want to seem insulting or to embarrass her. Jenny was plump but not fat, and she had a pretty smile. Her hair was a sandy color, her eyes green, and she looked like she might have been quite pretty as a girl. Her bosom was no larger than average, but the cut of her dress revealed a great deal of flesh, and she suspected the woman wore some kind of special undergarment that pushed her breasts higher.

John let go of the blanket, and Jenny wrapped it around Tess as she stepped out of the washtub. Ken dropped the blanket he was holding.

"My arms was gettin' tired," he said, glancing at Tess. "Say, that hair looks even redder now that it's clean," he told her. "You feelin' better now, ma'am?"

Tess held the blanket tightly around her. "A little."

Jenny turned to John, and she raised her eyebrows in surprise at the way he was looking at Tess Carey. One thing she knew well was men, and this one had an ache for the woman he was looking at. "You go occupy your time someplace else. This lady has some dresses to try on," she told him with a scolding look.

John felt he'd been jolted out of some kind of spell. He glanced at Jenny, realizing he'd allowed his feelings to be seen in his eyes, and he was glad Tess herself had not been looking. "Sure," he answered, walking off after Ken.

Jenny picked up the carpetbag she'd brought along and put an arm around Tess, leading her over to the small carriage she'd driven out herself. "Both those men can be meaner than skunks, but they won't look while you dress," she said, rummaging through the carpetbag while Tess leaned on the carriage to keep the weight off her sore ankle. "Still, you might feel better at least keeping the carriage between you and them. I'll help support you while you put on some drawers and the corsette I brought along. I hope I chose well, Mrs. Carey. Ken said you were small, but you're even smaller than I pictured. I brought three different dresses. They're in the carriage there. I made sure to bring something real proper, not something *I'd* wear." She laughed lightly, handing out a pair of white, ruffled drawers.

"You're being very kind," Tess told her. She wrapped the towel around her hair and managed to pull on the drawers, embarrassed that Jenny, too, had seen her naked. It was probably nothing to a woman like her, but Tess felt she'd lost all her dignity the last few days, wondered how she would ever get it back.

"You've been through hell, Mrs. Carey, and you've lost a husband and a father. You need help. Besides that, John asked me to do this. I figure if he thinks it's important, I'll do it." She handed out the corsette. "I'll put this around you and lace it up while you hold on to the carriage. And don't be embarrassed. I've seen everything there is to see in this life, and I *am* a woman, you know. I know what you've been through, honey, so if you need to talk about it, I'm here."

"No, I . . . I don't want to talk about it. I'll be just fine."

Jenny began yanking at the corsette strings to tighten the undergarment. "No you won't. Not that easy. You can be proud and stubborn about it if you want, but the hurt is down there somewhere. I'll help make it a little better." She stopped lacing for a moment and met Tess's eyes. "Maybe it will help to tell you that what happened to you is at least better than being raped at twelve years old by your own uncle, who then steals you away and begins selling you to men and then abandons you out in the middle of nowhere at sixteen."

Tess's eyes widened at the shocking story. Jenny began lacing the corsette again. "At least you've had a good life," she continued, "a normal life, a family, a father, and a husband. The man who raped you is dead, and rightly so, but you still have your dignity and honor. By the time I was sixteen, I had neither one. I was a well-used woman, so I just kept on doing the only thing I knew how to do to survive. My saloon is the first respectable business I've ever had, and I'm proud of it." She tied the string. "There. You're a very beautiful woman, Mrs. Carey. We'll fix you up so pretty, folks won't ever believe any of those bastards touched you. Those that do and treat you bad for it can go to hell, right?"

Tess blinked back tears. She'd been so wrong about this woman. "I'm sorry," she said, "for what happened to you."

Jenny shrugged. "You learn to just keep going. Don't feel sorry for me. You just concentrate on yourself. Let's try on a couple of dresses." She pulled out two slips and helped Tess put them on, then took a dress from the carriage. It was a plain, short-sleeved blue calico that buttoned up the front clear to the neck. "This should do. It matches your eyes."

Tess let the woman slip the dress over her head, and Jenny buttoned it for her. "A little big, but it looks just fine. Now let's hope the shoes fit. Sit down on the running board there, and I'll put a pair on. I brought a couple different sizes."

Tess obeyed, and the woman slipped a pair of stockings over her feet, being careful of her swollen ankle. "I don't know how to thank you, Jenny."

"You don't need to. And if you don't want to be seen talking to me in town, that's okay. I'll know how you really feel." She carefully slipped on a high-button shoe. "I'll lace this one real lightly."

Jenny finished with the shoes, and Tess realized her ankle actually felt better with the shoe on because of the support it gave her. Jenny brushed her tangled hair as best she could, then twisted it into a bun at the nape of her neck and pinned it.

"There. You look like a perfect lady, which, of course, you are. Anyone who tries to say different ought to get knocked up the side of the head." She stood back and looked Tess over. "Where will you go once John takes you into town and reports in?"

Tess sighed in weary confusion. "I don't know. I have a little money in the bank. I'll get a room and find some kind of work, I guess."

Jenny nodded. "You'll do fine. You're a strong, stubborn woman. I can see that. And I also know it from the simple fact that I could see how much John Hawkins respects you. His respect doesn't come easy. Sending for me to bring you some decent clothes and let you clean up and all tells me what he thinks of you. You let him do the talking when he reports in. He'll cover for you as best he can, honey. You just keep holding your head proud, and folks will think nothing about it after a while. Before long some nice man will come along and will see what a good wife you'd make, and you'll have a new home."

Tess pushed a stray piece of hair behind her ear. "The last thing I care about right now is finding another man. I can get by just fine on my own."

"Sure you can." Jenny leaned closer. "You just remember you can come talk to me anytime. Talking about things sometimes helps make it all better." She looked up at a sun that was beginning to lower in the western horizon. "We'd better get moving. We have three or four hours of daylight left. We can probably make town by then. You don't want to be spending another night sleeping on the ground, and you sure don't want to spend it here where it hurts to look at what's left." She yelled for John to come over. "I'll take her in the carriage till we get closer to town," she said when he rode up to her. "You take her in from there and I'll go around and come in from another direction. Nobody really cares where I've been so they won't ask."

Tess looked up at John Hawkins, realizing this was the most normal she had looked since he had first come for her. Their eyes held in an unspoken understanding. If only he hadn't held her the way he had for that one brief moment, she would not be so confused. "Thank you, Mr. Hawkins, for everything."

John nodded, thinking she was as pretty as a bluebird, and so hurt and lonely. He wanted to hold her again, but once he got her to town, that would be the end of it— and that was the way it should be. She had already gone back to calling him Mr. Hawkins, so formal and proper. "You're welcome, Mrs. Carey." He looked at Jenny, who was smiling. The damn woman knew he was having feelings for Tess Carey. "Let's get going." The sooner I get Tess Carey back, the sooner I can get the hell out of her life, he thought.

Chapter Ten

"Sí, es Señora Carey."

Tess heard one Mexican woman say the words to another who stood nearby, both women nodding to her as she rode by on John Hawkins's horse. A few others were gathering, staring, whispering, white and Mexican alike, certainly all wondering what had happened to the poor captive woman. She knew what they were thinking. She would probably never convince all of them she was untouched, but she would damn well try.

It just seemed so important. She'd been robbed of everything else. She couldn't bear to also lose her dignity.

"Someone should go and tell the priest," she heard from nearby. "Perhaps she will need to talk to him."

She needed no priest! Her father had been a Catholic, but not a practicing one, mostly because of her mother, who was a Protestant. The woman had taken her to the local Methodist church when she was young, but that church had been burned in the war, and ever since those war years Tess had attended no church at all. She believed in God, though, had no doubt He was out there . . . somewhere.

They rode up to a little building with a sign that read

Sheriff across the front. A man with a badge sat on a chair
out front, his feet up on a hitching post. El Paso was still
a rather quiet little Spanish town, most trouble taking place
in the outer wild country; but apparently they had decided
a sheriff was necessary. This was the first time Tess had
been to town in several weeks. The sheriff was Sam Higgins,
who formerly drove freight wagons into Mexico for Jim
Caldwell, the rancher who also owned a supply store in
town. She wondered if Caldwell had rigged the election.
He'd backed Higgins all the way, and since the man was
elected, Caldwell seemed to have a lot of say in whatever
went on in El Paso. She had never liked Jim Caldwell,
whose sprawling ranch nearly surrounded her farm. Now
she would have to contend with the man. She would have
to find a way to hang on to her father's land.

Higgins rose and nodded to John, and Tess could immediately see the two men disliked each other.

"Hawkins!" The shout came from their right as John
dismounted and helped Tess down. "You murdering bastard! What the hell gives you the right to blow cattle thieves
to smithereens! You're supposed to bring men back to
be judged and hanged, not execute them for your own
enjoyment! And where are the men who abducted this
poor woman here? All dead, I suppose!"

The words came from Jim Caldwell, who had apparently
spotted them and come running over from his store.

John took Tess's arm and led her up the steps. He faced
Caldwell squarely, calmly folding his arms with a note of
authority. "All dead," he answered. "It was them or Mrs.
Carey here. Would you rather I took a couple of them
alive and let them slit this woman's throat?"

Tess suspected Caldwell probably would not have
minded. That would have left him free to take over her
land.

"Of course not!" the man answered, reddening a little.
"But what is your excuse for blowing up the cabin where
you found cattle thieves a while back? The Army discovered
the truth a few days ago. It's all over town!"

This was the first time Tess had heard the story, although she remembered Ken had mentioned something about dynamite in one of their conversations.

"Them men got what they deserved," Ken spoke up, walking up beside John. "They was holed up in there and fixin' to make us waste our time—days, maybe weeks—waitin' for them to come out."

"One of you could have gone for help!" Caldwell insisted.

"And leave the other one there alone? No, sir," Ken retorted. "Sometimes we ride out on assignment alone, but once we're together, we stay together."

John thought it a little strange that Caldwell should care so much about what happened to a bunch of cattle thieves . . . and rapists. He decided to do as Ken had advised—not mention his real reason for blowing up the rustlers, because they had raped a little Apache girl. Caldwell would have a fit over that one. Maybe even Captain Booth would be outraged.

"I've talked to your captain, told him citizens like ourselves are not going to continue putting up with such behavior from the Texas Rangers!" Caldwell demanded. "No bloody half-Indian bastard should even *be* a Ranger!"

"John Hawkins is the best man for the job in Texas!" Ken retorted. "He's probably saved your own ass, or at least your property a few times, without you even knowin' it!"

"Shut up, Ken," John said, still remaining calm. However, Tess could feel his tension, his quiet anger. He looked down on Caldwell, a rather burly man, rugged and leather-faced, as any Texas rancher would be, but he was much shorter than John. "You might think to ask about Mrs. Carey here, how she is, what she's been through. You might ask if he needs any help, if she has any place to go. You might tell her you're sorry about her husband and her father, or maybe be glad I found her and got her back here in one piece before those men could violate her and sell her. It seems to me, Mr. Caldwell, that you are more concerned about a bunch of worthless cattle rustlers than you are about a fine lady who has lived and struggled in these parts for years, one of the fine citizens you say deserves our protection!''

Caldwell pressed his lips together in chagrin, embarrassment obvious on his red face. He glanced at Tess and tipped his hat. "I'm sorry, Tess. I've been stewing the last few days about this other thing. I didn't think——''

"It's all right, Mr. Caldwell," she answered, not believing for one second the man really cared. "I am fine. It was a horrible experience, but Mr. Hawkins came along before they . . .'' She began to blush herself. "Before the worst could happen. He took me to a farm where a kind woman lent me some clothes. I am back safe and sound, and the awful Comancheros who did this are dead, something for which Mr. Hawkins should be praised, I might add.''

Caldwell scowled with irritation that she would defend John.

"He and Mr. Randall also saved me from an attack by Apache Indians," Tess added, "and he would do the same for any one of you. He does not deserve to be insulted or reprimanded for doing what was simply his duty. You might note the still-bloody scar across the side of his head. He also suffered an arm wound, but that is mostly healed. You surely know this is not the first time he has been wounded protecting Texas citizens, so save your criticism for the true murderers and thieves, Mr. Caldwell!''

Tess was surprised at her sudden desire to defend John. She had herself thought him not much different from those he hunted, but the fact remained he'd risked his life for her, and he'd been nothing but respectable and kind ever since.

John wanted to smile, moved by Tess's defense, as well as curious. Was she actually beginning to like and respect him? He glanced at Ken, who *was* grinning.

"All right, all right," Caldwell said, waving them off. "Make a report here to the sheriff," he told John.

"I'll make my report to Captain Booth and no one else,"

John answered. "I've brought Mrs. Carey back untouched, except for some bruises and humiliation. She was treated pretty bad, so give her your respect. You've got no need to ask her any questions. I'll answer all questions. This is Ranger responsibility. Higgins has no hand in this. I'd like you to help Mrs. Carey find a room, maybe at Mrs. Baker's boarding house. She needs a few days to decide what she'll do next."

Higgins scowled at John, irritated at John's snubbing him. Caldwell sighed, nodding to Tess again, whom he knew through dealings with her father. "I'll be glad to help you. I truly am sorry about your father and your husband. I had a great deal of respect for both of them. Someday Texas will put a stop to such horrors and be rid of its outlaws and renegades."

"Then you don't really mind *how* we get rid of them?" Ken asked mockingly.

Caldwell's thick eyebrows came together in a scowl. "We're supposed to be trying to civilize Texas, Mr. Randall. That means even those who go after the thieves and murderers must be halfway civilized in how they apprehend these men."

"If the men I'm after would just as soon gut me out as look at me, then that's exactly how *they'll* get treated!" John put in. "Now, since apparently you recently talked to my captain, maybe you could tell me where he is."

"He was at Fort Bliss, the last I saw him, trying to explain your last escapade to Lieutenant Ames, who found the mess you left behind." Caldwell took Tess's arm. "Come on, Tess. I'll take you to the boarding house. I'm sure several of the ladies in town will offer their help however they can, and I'll let my wife know you're back. Maybe there is something she can do."

Tess doubted the haughty Harriet Caldwell would offer much help. "I'll be fine, Mr. Caldwell." She looked up at John, suddenly feeling too rushed. There was so much to say. After all they had been through, it didn't seem right to just leave and end it so quickly. "I . . . what can I say,

Mr. Hawkins?" She turned to Ken. "Mr. Randall? There is no way to thank you."

John knew by her eyes she was really thanking him for convincing people she'd been left untouched. "Thanks aren't necessary. Good luck with whatever decisions you make, ma'am," Ken told her.

"I hope you don't go back out there and get yourself wounded or killed." She looked up at John. "Please do be more careful, Mr. Hawkins."

He could not help a grin. "I don't much think about being careful when there is only time for saving my hide. I've been honored to know you, Mrs. Carey." He turned away and told Ken to mount up. "Let's ride to Fort Bliss," he said.

Without a glance back, the two men rode off. Tess stood there feeling suddenly abandoned, lonely. She wanted to call out to John to wait, but she knew it would look bad, just as he did if he stayed and lingered over goodbyes. She was sure he had more to say, as she did, but then a man like John Hawkins would never allow himself feelings for a woman like her . . . and she should never allow herself feelings for a man like John Hawkins.

"He'll be back," Caldwell was saying to Higgins, "to pay a visit to Jenny Simms, no doubt."

A sharp pang of jealousy stabbed at Tess's heart, something she thought silly and sinful. She reminded herself that her own husband was fresh in his grave. John Hawkins was untamed, uncivilized, a wandering nomad who didn't even know how to read. Again she reasoned that her odd attachment to the man was only due to his having been the one to rescue her, as well as her only hope and salvation for the last few days. She would forget him soon enough.

"That there Jim Caldwell's got some kind of burr in his butt over you, and I can't quite figure out why," Ken told John. "You two ain't never had any real run-ins that I know of. Is there somethin' you ain't tellin' me?"

John rode silently for a moment, sure he could still smell that fancy soap Tess Carey had washed her hair with. He pulled a thin cigar from a pocket on the underside of his leather vest. "What?" He put the cigar between his teeth while Ken let off a string of expletives over the fact that he had not heard a word that had been said.

"Get your mind back on matters at hand, Hawk," he scolded. "Where in hell are you driftin' off?" He halted his horse. "It's *her*, ain't it? It's Tess Carey!"

John just kept Sundance moving at a slow walk. "What are you talking about?"

Ken trotted his horse up beside John's. "You know damn well what I'm talkin' about. You're thinkin' so hard on that there Mrs. Carey you didn't even hear a word I said just now."

John shrugged. "She went through a hell nobody even knows about, and she's going to try to keep it all inside. Now she's alone and not sure what to do. You don't know how I found her, but I expect you can imagine. It's hard to help someone in a situation like that and then just leave them off somewhere and forget about them."

"Ha!" Ken raised up in his stirrups and took a plug of tobacco from his pants pocket and bit off a piece. "That ain't *never* bothered you before! You're sweet on that woman. You, John Hawkins, the man of no feelin's, sweet on that little bitty, redheaded, stubborn, back-talkin', independent widow woman who, I might remind you, would never look twice at you under normal circumstances."

John halted his own horse and lit the cigar. "I never said I was sweet on her."

"Just bein' *concerned* about her makes you sweet on her. That's sayin' a lot for a man like you. You forget how well I know you, John Hawkins. I also know you said once you'd never have any association with any white woman unless she was a whore like Jenny."

"Jenny isn't really a whore."

"Well, she *used* to be one, and she still *is* whenever *you're* around."

John puffed the cigar and got his horse into motion again. "Jenny and I are good friends."

"Yeah, and you'll pay her a friendly visit after we report in, I'm sure."

"Probably."

"And don't think she don't know you're havin' thoughts about that there Mrs. Carey. Jenny's a smart woman when it comes to things like that. There's no foolin' her."

"Probably not."

"So, your *admittin'* you're havin' thoughts about Mrs. Carey!"

"I'm not admitting anything. She's just different from any other white woman I've had occasion to help out or associate with. I admire her courage, that's all. And you know how I feel about rape. I'll get over it after a couple of hours."

Ken spit some tobacco juice into the dirt. "Why is it I don't believe you?"

"I have no idea."

"You ain't gonna forget this one. This one is different, ain't she?"

"No." John cast him a look that said he'd better not take the conversation any further. "I'm no fool when it comes to things like that, and you know it. I simply admire the woman's courage and spunk. It's nice to know there are a few white women out there who have those qualities, and I've never had a lady like that stick up for me like she did."

"Which brings us back to what I was askin' you about in the first place. She defended you against Jim Caldwell, and I was askin' why Caldwell seems to have it in for you. Why do you think that is? You've never done nothin' against him."

John shook his head. "I'm not sure. I guess he figures I'm not respectable enough to be representing Texas."

"No, it's somethin' more. Almost seems like he wants you out of the way. Hell, the way he carried on about you blowin' up them rustlers, you'd think he knew them himself.''

John considered the remark as he rode on silently, taking a couple of drags on the cigar. He looked over at Ken. "You know, for somebody as ignorant as you can be, sometimes you have damn good insight.''

Ken grinned. "I was just jokin'. How would a man like Caldwell know men like Derrek Briggs?''

"I don't know. Maybe he *didn't* know him. It's just interesting that he would care about what I did to some cattle thieves. He knows rustling's been getting worse in this part of Texas. A lot of ranchers have been complaining, and we probably solved a good share of the problem when we took care of Briggs and his bunch. Caldwell should be glad about that, being a rancher himself.''

"I'd say so.''

The strange thing is, John thought, Caldwell himself has had no complaints of cattle being stolen. "Seems strange that Caldwell's the biggest landowner and cattle rancher in these parts, but he's had no trouble with rustlers. Yet other ranchers in the area *do* have problems. What do you make of that?''

Ken spit again and scratched at the ever-present batch of whiskers on his chin. "Don't know.'' He frowned. "You still thinkin' Caldwell might have somethin' to do with the rustlin'? Jesus, Hawk, you're talkin' about Jim Caldwell, one of the most important men in this area. He'd have no need to get caught up in somethin' like that.''

John shrugged. "Well, how did he *get* so big? It's a known fact he's tried to badger a few neighboring ranchers into selling out to him, including Henry McDowell, Tess Carey's father. He has a lot of gall doing that, seeing as how most of his own ranch was given to him free and clear by Colonel Bass.''

Ken shook his head. "You thinkin' he could have had somethin' to do with them bastards that burned out Tess Carey's ranch and made off with her?'' He removed his hat and wiped sweat from his brow. "I can't believe that. Caldwell is the one who has been screamin' for more law and order around here. He's talked about bringin' in a preacher for the white Protestants, and a schoolteacher. His wife runs a quiltin' bee, and they both go to barn raisin's for neighbors and all. He wouldn't be mixed up with rustlin' cattle!''

He would if it meant adding to his own wealth, John thought. "Probably not," he answered aloud. "But I'll tell you one thing, if I ever discover he *did* have anything to do with what happened to Tess Carey, Jim Caldwell will be one sorry man.''

"One *dead* man, you mean.''

"Most likely.''

"You'd never get away with that one, Hawk. You'd have to have some awful good proof. If you went and killed a man like that, they'd hang you for sure. And now we're back to the subject of Mrs. Carey. You just admitted if Caldwell had anything to do with what happened to her you'd kill him. That tells me you do have special feelin's for the woman.''

"I've killed for others before, people who meant nothing to me.''

"You're avoidin' the facts here.''

John stopped again, facing Ken with the cigar still between his teeth as he spoke. "The only facts here are that you talk too much and you make too much out of nothing. Another fact is, if you don't quit trying to make me admit I have feelings for Tess Carey, I'm going to knock you right off that horse. She's just a woman I helped, like a few others. I admire her guts, and that's the end of it. We're as different as the sun and the moon. She's the kind of woman I'd never associate with if she was the last female in Texas, and she's the kind of woman who probably drives a man to drink after a time. I have no doubt Tess Carey is glad to be rid of both of us, so shut up about it and let's go make our report to Booth and see what he's got for us to do.'' He turned and rode off.

Ken shook his head. "I'll be damned," he muttered. "She got to you, Hawk. She got to you real good.''

Chapter Eleven

"Why don't you just sell your place to me?" Jim Caldwell leaned back in the leather chair behind his desk, and Tess hated the sound of squeaking leather, as though the expensive chair announced that the man who sat in it was some kind of royalty. "You must realize, my dear, that Colonel Bass always meant for me to have all of it. He only gave your father that piece because he knew your father needed something of his own, and because Henry had worked for Bass for so long back in San Antonio. Bass told me himself if it weren't for that, he'd have given me that land."

"I have no way of knowing that, Mr. Caldwell. Maybe it's true, but the fact remains the land is mine now, and I am not ready to decide just what I will do with it." Tess could hardly believe she'd come to Caldwell's office at his supply store, but what choice did she have if she was going to survive here? She sat straight and proud, facing the man squarely. "All I am asking is that you allow me to work for you in some capacity in return for your taking care of my ranch, keeping the fences mended, feeding the chickens that were left behind, having someone help me harvest the corn, clean up the debris, things like that. Whether I sell or not, I have to keep the place in order, and I can't do it alone. Nor can I pay someone cash to help me do it. Although I do have some money in the bank, I have to be careful how I spend it, so I am willing to return labor for labor.''

The man shrugged. "What kind of labor?"

Tess refused to shift under his scrutinizing gaze. This man was thinking what everyone in town was—that she had probably been raped by the men who'd abducted her, which in their eyes somehow left her tainted. She had tried to get work from other businesses in town, but they had given her that same look, a couple of women pulling their children away as though she were something to be shunned. The last thing she wanted to do was come to Jim Caldwell for help, but she was not sure where else to turn.

"Whatever needs doing," she answered. "Perhaps Harriet could use some help in the house—cleaning, cooking, mending. I happen to be an excellent seamstress. I used to make most of Mrs. Bass's clothing. I learned on her sewing machine when we lived at the Bass ranch at San Antonio. Or I can help clean stalls, feed horses, pitch hay. I am quite capable of any number of jobs. I could even teach reading to some of your ranch hands if they are so inclined, or to their children. I enjoy reading, but I lost all my books in the fire. I intend to collect more. For now I simply need the work, and I need a place to stay. I can't afford to keep paying for my room at the boarding house. Besides that, I need time away from some of the stares I get in town. Some people haven't been very understanding about what happened to me. At any rate, there seems to be no work for me here, and like I said, I can't afford the boarding house.''

Caldwell rubbed his chin, studying her intently. The woman had spunk. Maybe if he let her work for him for a while, he could win her friendship and convince her to sell the ranch to him. "It's human nature, Tess, for people to be curious. They wonder what it's like to be taken off like you were, but they're afraid to ask. Some wonder if . . . well, you know. Let's face it, woman. Nobody in this town thinks you were left untouched by those men, and people's imaginations can conjure up all kinds of things to where some actually blame you for it, figure if you didn't come back half-crazed and covered with bruises and your clothes all ripped and dirty . . . well, they wonder, that's all.''

Tess rose, her fury so great she felt sick. "I preferred to keep my dignity, Mr. Caldwell! I preferred not to let those men destroy me! Anyone who wants to think I did not fight hard enough has no idea what I suffered, no idea how hard I *did* fight, no grasp of the horrors I saw and experienced! And for those who might think I actually *enjoyed* whatever happened to me, they, and you, Jim Caldwell, can go to hell!'' She turned and headed for the door.

"Wait up there!'' Caldwell spit out the command in his gruff voice, spouting off the order as though she were one of his ranch hands. "Don't go blaming it all on me. I was just trying to explain—''

"I know what you were trying to explain. What's done is done, and I cannot change it. I am now a widow without family, and I need work. If I have to leave El Paso to find it, then that is what I will do, but right now I will not sell my father's land. Are you willing to help me take care of it and to let me work for you or not?'' She turned and faced him, her hand on the doorknob.

Caldwell sighed and stood up, folding his arms across his big belly. "All right. I'm not sure what my wife will think of it, but I'll talk her into it. If she doesn't want you in the house, I'll find farm work for you.''

"Fine. Where will I stay if not in the house?'' How she hated having to work for this man! She should have left the area entirely, but something held her here—something too silly to even admit . . . a man named John Hawkins . . . a man who had become so important for those brief days . . . then had ridden away and she'd heard nothing from him since and probably never would. So, why did she stay? What on earth did she want or expect from John Hawkins?

Caldwell ran a hand through his hair. "Well, the house is certainly plenty big enough. You've seen it. We've got six bedrooms, but four sons live in Virginia. Two are off in college, one is a doctor, the other is married and has built his own house on our old property, so it's just me and the Mrs. Harriet complains the house is too big and rambling for her to take care of. We have a couple of Mexican women who help, but she can't communicate with them too well—has never tried to learn Spanish. I'm sure she could use your help keeping the place up. I don't see why you couldn't stay in one of the guest bedrooms upstairs. Ours is on the main floor, so you wouldn't have to mix with Harriet except when you're cleaning or cooking. She's beginning to develop a lot of aches and pains, has trouble going up and down the stairs, and frets that she can't keep the upstairs clean enough. I think I can talk her into letting you stay there just for that if nothing more."

Tess had to be grateful for his efforts, even though she suspected it was only because he hoped to take over her ranch someday. "Thank you, Mr. Caldwell."

"You gather your things and I'll pick you up in a wagon tomorrow morning around nine and drive you out to the ranch."

"Fine. I will be ready."

He nodded, his eyes moving over her in a way that made her uncomfortable. Suddenly she was not so sure this was a good idea, but what else could she do for now? She turned and walked out, half-tempted to go to Jenny and ask if she had heard from John Hawkins since he'd left six days ago. She had not noticed him anywhere since then. She felt she should go and thank Jenny once more for what she did for her, but she did not want to be seen walking into the woman's saloon. People already thought ill enough of her without seeing her associating with Jenny, although now that she knew Jenny as she did, she would have no personal qualms about visiting with the woman. The situation left her conscience in a dilemma.

She glanced up the street toward the saloon when she went outside, and part of her questions were answered. John Hawkins's golden horse was tied in front of Jenny's place. Again she felt the sharp stab of jealousy, that ridiculous feeling she'd felt before when she'd seen the friendship between those two.

So, he had come back . . . to see Jenny, not to see Tess Carey. That was the way it should be. She turned and headed for the boarding house to pack her things.

"What was *that* all about, as if I need too ask?" Jenny got up and walked to her washstand, feeling no embarrassment over her naked body.

"What was *what* all about?" John studied her fleshy bottom, damned himself for thinking what a small, firm bottom Tess Carey had.

"You've never been quite so violent in bed." She poured some water into a bowl. "I'd almost think you were mad at me about something, but I know what you're really mad about."

John scooted up in bed, pulling a sheet over his privates and reaching to the table beside him to pick up a cigarette paper and tobacco pouch. "Well, since you already think you know the answer, why'd you ask?"

"Just to see if you would admit the truth."

He scowled as he tapped some tobacco onto the paper. "And what is the truth?"

"You were thinking about Tess Carey."

"That so?" He set the pouch aside and licked the paper to seal it. "How in hell did you come to that conclusion?"

"Simple." Jenny wet a rag and washed herself. "I saw how you looked at her that day I went out to help her take that bath. And don't tell me you weren't dying to turn around and have a look. She's the first white woman you've ever had serious thoughts about, and when you remembered what those men did to her, it made you mad. You're thinking how you'd like to make love to her yourself, the right way, maybe help take away all her bad memories.

John lit the cigarette and took a long drag. "For one thing, if I had turned around while she was taking that bath, I wouldn't have seen anything I hadn't already seen. And sure, it pisses me off what they did to her, but something like that always pisses me off. She's no different from any other woman. Hell, I blew up those cattle rustlers because they raped an Indian girl, not because they stole cattle. Nobody else but Ken knows that, by the way."

Jenny pulled on a feathered robe and picked up a perfume decanter, squeezing the rubber dispenser and spraying some of the lavender scent on herself. She turned and sauntered back to the bed, grinning. "You can protest your feelings for Tess Carey all you want to anybody else, including yourself, but don't try it with me, John Hawkins. This is Jenny Simms, and I know men." She crawled onto the bed, nuzzling up next to him. "So, what are you going to do about it?"

He snickered, giving her a sarcastic grin. "In case you haven't noticed, Tess Carey is white, with red hair, no less. She's a proper lady, a widow on top of that. And after what she's been through, if I was the most wonderful man who ever walked and could offer her the world, she wouldn't be ready to think about another man. But even under the best conditions, the fact remains I am far from the best man, and I am Indian. I have a reputation that makes most proper women embarrassed to be associated with me in any way. I know when there is no sense giving certain women a second thought, so I'm not going to do *any*thing about any feelings I might have."

"Mmmm-hmmm. So, you *do* have feelings for her?"

He took another drag on the cigarette and leaned forward. "I'm getting tired of answering the same questions from you and Ken Randall. Just shut up about it, Jenny. There's nothing to talk about anyway."

"You don't know that without paying Mrs. Carey a visit.

Maybe she feels kind of bad that you just rode off and left it like that."

"I said I don't want to talk about it. If you want me to stay the night here, you'd better make up your mind not to bring up Tess Carey's name anymore. I'm not going to sit here and argue about it all night. She's a closed subject. I found her, I got her back here—did my duty—and that's the end of it."

Jenny studied his muscled back, the long, black hair that hung down it nearly to his waist. He was the most beautiful specimen of man she'd ever come upon, powerful, broad shoulders, a slender waist, firm hips, muscled thighs. He was the perfect combination of Indian and white, with a square jaw, dark, deep-set eyes, a proud nose, full lips. She knew damn well his feelings ran a lot deeper than he ever let on, about a lot of things besides Mrs. Tess Carey. Somewhere behind all that rough exterior lay a good man who had never been allowed to reveal that goodness, whose defense was thick and fierce because of all the hurt he'd suffered in his life. She had a way of getting men to talk, and John had talked plenty about his life, his mother. This was the first time he had absolutely refused to continue a conversation, and that told her one thing. He had more serious feelings for Tess Carey than he'd had for anyone in his life, except maybe his mother.

"Well, far be it from me to do anything that would make you leave this bed," she said aloud. "Lord knows you don't end up here often enough." She began running a hand over his back. "So don't you go running off, John Hawkins. I plan to keep you busy all night."

He drew on the cigarette, then took it from his lips and set it aside in an astray. "What if I told you I was tired?" he asked, exhaling smoke as he spoke.

"I'd say that's too bad." Jenny let her robe fall open, and she reached out to him.

John pulled her into his arms, bending down to savor a nipple. "You're a mean woman, Jenny Simms." He moved to her other breast, licking it as he probed secret places with his fingers.

"No meaner than you, John Hawkins." She wrapped her fingers in his hair, liked the way it hung down and tickled at her shoulders and breasts.

"I'll try to be a little more gentle this time," he said, moving his lips to her throat, then planting his mouth over hers.

Jenny relished the deep, delicious kiss, the feel of his hard body moving on top of her, the excitement of his growing hardness probing for a nesting place. The man could be ready for a woman on a moment's notice, and when John Hawkins got inside a woman, she hated for it to ever be over.

She gladly parted her legs and welcomed him, and this time he moved a little slower, using a gentle rhythm and circular motions that made her feel wild with desire. She could tell he was trying to make it nicer for her this time, letting her take more pleasure than she did from his first rough, quick, fierce ramming. This time his mating was almost sweet, and she felt a little jealous of Tess Carey, for she had no doubt that was who he was wishing lay beneath him. She tried picturing the two of them together this way, this big, dark, strong man hovering over that woman's small, lily-white body, and she laughed lightly, returning his kisses with eager passion.

John raised up and grasped her hips, pushing harder and faster, knowing that with a woman like Jenny Simms, a man had to give it everything he had to keep her pleased. Visions of Tess Carey flashed into his mind again, and he wondered if he could get inside her without hurting her. Maybe Chino had hurt her that way. Again he felt angry at the thought, but he forced back the emotions, feeling sorry he'd been rough with Jenny the first time because of it.

Tess. Tess. God, he'd sure like to make love to that woman. The thought of it brought another release sooner than he would normally allow. He felt like an idiot allowing such thoughts, knew how useless they were. He collapsed on top of Jenny, holding her against himself. "Shit," he swore.

Jenny grinned. "I believe you told me not to mention a certain name," she answered. "So I won't. All I'll say is you just remember who to come to if you need to talk about a woman. Ken is useless in that department, and you know I'll understand anything you want to say."

He rolled away from her. "There's nothing to talk about."

Jenny closed her eyes and sighed. "I said *if* you need to talk. You just remember that."

John lay facing away from her, and the room hung silent for several minutes before he spoke again. "I can't forget about her, Jenny. That's never happened to me before."

She moved against his back and ran a hand over his muscled arm. "Maybe you should go talk to her—at least let her know you think about her, that you're concerned about her."

"I don't think so. I'm better off not seeing her again. It's easier that way."

Jenny realized she actually felt sorry for him. "If that's how you want it. I can't make those decisions for you, honey. I can only make suggestions. She kissed his back. "You going out on another assignment soon?"

"Tomorrow. The captain thinks some men who robbed a bank in Las Cruces and then attacked a train and killed the men guarding the mail car might be hiding out in the Hueco Mountains. He wants us to try to find them before they get rested up and head for Mexico. The Army is already on it, and you know how the Army hates to be shown up by the Texas Rangers, so we've stayed out of it so far. I'm going in on my own without Ken so as not to draw much attention. If I happen to find them, I'm supposed to let the Army take care of it."

"Sure you will. By the time the Army gets there, there won't been enough left for them to bother with."

John stretched his arm over his head. "I'll try to be a

good boy this time and do it the right way. This is a pretty bad bunch, Holt Puckett and his gang. They wreaked havoc all over Indian Territory, then northern Texas, then New Mexico. Even *I* might not be mean enough for his bunch."

Jenny laughed as she curled up against him. "John Hawkins always gets his man. They'll shake in their boots when they find out who's after them."

"Yeah, well, I won't be in any condition to get anybody if I don't get some sleep."

Jenny kissed at his chest. "Don't plan on sleeping too hard."

He took a deep breath, closing his eyes. "She still at the boarding house?"

Jenny smiled. "Far as I know. People haven't been real kind to her. She's trying to find work. I hoped maybe she'd come talk to me about things she needs to talk about, but she hasn't. You going to see her before you leave tomorrow?"

"I don't know. Maybe."

"You in love with her?"

There was a long pause before he replied. "I don't know . . . maybe."

Tess studied herself in the mirror. She had used some of her money to buy a new wardrobe, two rather plain dresses and this one dress that was a little fancier. It was blue, which her father and Abel had always told her was her best color. She felt a stab of grief over both of them, but she figured over the last six days she had cried so much there was no tears left. Finally alone, she'd been able to vent her emotions with no one to see.

That was done now. She had swallowed her pride enough to find a way to hang onto the farm, and she would at least be away from town for a while, someplace where she would not have to suffer the stares of others; but she feared Harriet Caldwell would be no kinder than anyone else had been.

She smoothed the draped apron-front skirt of her dress, thinking how in spite of all her alterations the dress was still a little big on her. It was impossible to find store-bought dresses that fit her right. She had purchased some material she would use to make more clothes for herself once she got settled in at the ranch. She turned in the mirror, studying the way this dress was gathered in the back and topped with a silk bow. The fitted bodice accented her tiny waist, and the elbow-length sleeves were trimmed with white ruffle. She had asked the clerk at Cooper's store to please order for her a book of patterns showing the latest styles that she could use to make more dresses for herself.

She put a lightweight black scarf around her shoulders, as she had done whenever she had gone out in public, a sign of mourning. She picked up the one and only hat she had purchased so far, a black straw bonnet with black netting she could pull over her face. She pinned it into her hair, which she had piled into curls at the crown of her head. She wanted to look her most respectable when she left El Paso. She was not going to go slinking out of town in shame, nor was she going to face Harriet Caldwell with anything but pride and an air of respectability. Eventually people would understand she was the same honorable woman she'd been before her abduction.

She finished pinning the hat and picked up her purse and a large suitcase that held all she owned in the world now. With one last glance she wondered what John Hawkins would think if he saw her. The only time she had even come close to looking this decent since his rescue was when Jenny brought her that one plain dress to wear into town. Even then she had looked nothing like this, her hair finally done up nicely, a little powder and color on her face. The only trouble was, her face was peeling from getting sunburned during her ordeal, all the more reason to wear the veil.

"And what does it matter what John Hawkins might think?" she asked herself. She started for the door when someone knocked. Thinking it must be Jim Caldwell, she opened it to see John standing there. His presence startled her, especially since she'd just been thinking about him. And she was somewhat taken by the sight of him, cleaned up, his black hair shiny and clean and tied at the side of his head so that it hung down in front over his shoulder. He wore clean denim pants, a black shirt and vest, and had a six-gun strapped to his slim hips. He held a black felt hat in his hand, which he held up.

"New hat," he said. "I figured I'd let my horse drink out of the other one too many times to keep putting it back on my head."

Tess sensed he was a little nervous. Why? She stepped back, raising her veil. "As you can see, I've had to buy a few new clothes myself."

"You look nice." My God, you're beautiful! he wanted to say. "I'm getting ready to head out on a new assignment. I just thought I ought to come and tell you I'm glad you seem to be doing okay. I wanted you to know I didn't just ride off and forget about you."

She felt her cheeks getting warmer. "Well, I . . . I'm glad you took the time to stop by. I needed to thank you once more for what you did. I'm leaving El Paso for a while. I have found a way to work and hang onto my farm until I decide what to do."

"Oh? Where are you going?"

"I will be living at the Caldwell ranch." She saw him bristle. "I don't like the man one whit, as you well know. But he has promised to take care of my farm in return for my doing some work for his wife at the house. I have little choice at the present time. I'm hoping that after a time people will realize I am no different than I ever was. Perhaps I'll be able to come back to town and teach reading, something like that."

John nodded, hating the thought of her having to put up with the very snobbish Harriet Caldwell. The woman had insulted him in public a time or two, just as Jim Caldwell seemed to enjoy doing. "Don't let Mrs. Caldwell break you."

She raised her chin with a hint of arrogance. *"No* one can break me, John. I've been through the worst, and I came out just fine."

Let me hold you, Tess. "Looks like it. I'm glad you're all right."

"And so, apparently, are you. I see the scabbing over your head wound is gone."

He put a hand to the left side of his head. "There's a scar there, under all the hair.

"And did Jenny Simms help you wash it?" Why had she asked that! She had actually allowed a ring of jealousy to the words. He looked surprised at the question, and he smiled a little but also looked embarrassed.

"No. I went to the public bathhouse."

She closed her eyes in exasperation with herself. "I happened to notice your horse tied in front of the saloon late yesterday. I . . . I would like you to thank Jenny again for me. I think . . . I hope she understands why I haven't come over to talk to her. I'm having enough trouble overcoming people's judgments without—"

"Jenny understands. When I left her this morning she told me to come over here and tell you she thinks about you, too, and wishes the best for you."

When I left her this morning. So, he had spent the night with Jenny Simms. "Well, thank you for coming over. I hope you don't have any problems on your next assignment. I will pray for your safety."

He nodded. "I'm not so sure any God exists who would care about me, but I appreciate the gesture. I wish only the best for you, too. I just thought it only right to come and see you once more."

He put out his hand, and hesitantly Tess took it. He squeezed her hand gently, and she felt the same warmth and true compassion she had that moment when he'd held her in the wagon. She looked up at him. What was that in his dark eyes? He truly cared! "Well, I'm . . . I'm glad you did. I was hoping you would." She pulled her hand away, stunned by the comfort she'd taken in his touch. "Mr. Caldwell will be pulling up at any moment to pick me up. I had better go outside and wait for him." She turned to pick up her bag, but John picked it up for her. She met his eyes again. What was this strange feeling he gave her? And what was he trying to tell her with those eyes? "Thank you," she said. She pulled down her veil and hurried out the door.

John followed. "Damn," he muttered. *I don't want to leave you, Tess Carey.* He watched her walk, studied the slender figure he knew lay beneath all the layers of material and under that silk bow. "Tess," he said when they reached the porch outside the door.

She turned, obviously surprised by the way he had gently spoken her first name. "Yes?"

Why had he done that? Now what was he going to say? "Everything will work out for you. You're a beautiful, educated, respectable lady. They'll all see that. Good luck to you."

Why did she suspect he wanted to say more? "And good luck to you. Please don't keep taking such chances when you go after murderers and the like. You really should be more careful, John."

The only thing I have to be careful about are my feelings for you. "I'll try."

She smiled. "You'll do no such thing. But thank you for telling me you will."

John laughed and set down her suitcase. He plunked the new hat on his head. "Goodbye, Tess."

He spoke the words with surprising gentleness. "Goodbye . . . John." She watched him mount up, thinking how grand he looked on that golden horse. He nodded to her and rode off, and for a brief moment she almost wished she were riding with him. Her thoughts were interrupted when a wagon clattered up to the front of the boarding house and Jim Caldwell jumped down to take her bag and throw it in the back.

"You ready, Tess?"

"I'm ready." Why did she feel like crying again? She climbed onto the wagon seat, and Caldwell snapped the reins to the two horses pulling the wagon. The vehicle lurched forward. After a few minutes Tess looked back in the direction in which John had ridden, surely headed for more danger. She could no longer see him.

Chapter Twelve

"I would like you to bake some cookies. I am having some ladies and gentlemen here for a meeting about hiring a teacher for the white children in the area, so I would like you to prepare sufficient cookies and sandwiches."

Tess hid her contempt for Harriet Caldwell. Before her abduction she had been a part of some of the women's circles that met occasionally in town, friendly with many who attended them. Now most of the women treated her as though they hardly knew her, and Harriet was as bad as the others. She wanted to ask her what was wrong with also teaching the Mexican children, but she decided to keep her usually tart tongue in its place as long as she had to work for the woman. Harriet obviously had no use for Negro, Mexican, or Indian other than as a servant, and now she was treating her no better.

Tess had come to appreciate the Mexican women with whom she had to work. They had been far friendlier and kinder than the women she had known and called friends before her abduction. Several Mexicans worked on the Caldwell ranch, but Harriet did not associate with them, except to give them orders.

Tess had resigned herself to doing what she must. She was not afraid of hard work, and she was not going to go back on her word to Jim Caldwell that she would do whatever was necessary in return for his taking care of her father's land. He had in turn kept his word to do just that. Some of his men were harvesting her corn this very day.

"How many will there be?" she asked Harriet, who had turned away to chide a Mexican woman for putting too much sugar in her tea.

"Oh, I am guessing perhaps twenty. I'll see that Jim brings plenty of stores from town. We'll be getting some fresh ham from Al Plenty's hog farm in just a couple of days. The meeting is Saturday." The woman stepped closer, frowning. "You look pale, and tired. Are you ill?"

Tess hated admitting she was down in any way, but she had been sick lately, usually in the mornings. She attributed it to overwork. "In Texas, anyone with skin as light as mine and red hair looks pale," she answered. "I am fine, Harriet. I'll have the things ready that you want." She wished the woman might be truly concerned, but she knew she'd only been asked because Harriet did not want anything to go wrong at her meeting. The woman's pale brown eyes had never shown any true sympathy. Her pudgy, wrinkling face always had a rather stern look to it, her thin lips usually pressed tight, her nose high. The woman was so "proper" she was always rather rigid, and her stocky build made one wonder how she managed to even bend over and lace her shoes. She and her husband did not seem to have a very warm relationship, each one going about his or her busy, separate life, crossing paths only at suppertime.

A trace of a smile passed over Harriet's lips at Tess's attempt at humor about her pale skin, and Tess decided to take advantage of the brief display of human emotion. "Harriet, I would like to remind you that I read very well. I would be glad to teach other children. I need a job where I can be more independent, and—"

"Oh, dear, you must realize that after your abduction you couldn't possibly teach little children."

Tess frowned. "Why!"

The woman reddened a little. "Well, dear, you know. Everyone knows about your misfortune, and some people hold the ridiculous belief that once something like that has happened to a woman she is . . . well . . . rather tainted. You would cause talk among the children, perhaps make them ask embarrassing questions their parents cannot answer. Schoolteachers are required to hold a most honorable reputation. A woman who has been, well, you know . . ." She leaned closer and whispered the word. " 'Raped' . . ." She shivered. "It puts a stain on her character."

Tess wanted to scream. "I did nothing wrong! How can people blame me for what happened. If it had happened to you—"

"I am sure I would have to kill myself," the woman interrupted.

Maria Juarez, who always worked only in the kitchen, glanced at both of them, and Tess could feel the woman's sympathy. Tess faced Harriet squarely. "And I am sure I am much stronger than that. I repeat that I have done nothing wrong, Harriet, that I was not raped by any of those men. I am perfectly capable—and worthy—of teaching little children. And I will not tolerate being treated no better than a woman of the streets or as though I am somehow tainted. All I have done is survive. That is something you could never understand without having to go through it yourself!"

Harriet drew in her breath, pulling in her chin at the same time so that it tripled at her neck, reminding Tess of a turkey. "Well!" she sniffed. "I did not mean to say you had done something wrong. I was only trying to explain how some people look at the matter."

"Including you."

"Well, I . . ." Harriet sniffed again and turned away. "You might be a little more grateful you have work here, Tess. It is not proper or necessary that you lose your temper with me. I will remind you that my husband has men harvesting your corn this very day. What would you do without us?''

Tess returned to polishing silver, hardly able to believe the gall of the woman. "That does not give you the right to treat me like something lowly," she answered. "I think we agree that we both deserve some respect. I know you once owned slaves, but I am not one of them!"

Harriet did not answer right away. She glanced at Maria, irritated by the mocking look on the woman's face. "We lost what took generations of hard work to build back in Virginia," she finally said to Tess. "And *you* would not know what *that* is like."

"Do you truly think I don't understand loss, Harriet? My God, look at what has just happened to me! Before this *my* family also lost everything back in Georgia. And my mother and little brother were killed in a fire after a raid by Southern outlaws. We have *all* suffered losses, Harriet. That's the reason eighty percent of the whites here in Texas *came* here to start over." She could tell by Harriet's eyes that the woman wanted to say more, but she was stubborn and proud and arrogant. She was not about to share her feelings with anyone.

"I know good and well why most of us came here," she answered, looking rather shaken. "The war ruined a lot of things for a lot of people, Tess. It totally changed my husband."

She walked out, and Tess wondered at the remark, realizing Harriet's feelings ran deeper than she let on. Still, she was not sure how much longer she could tolerate Harriet's aloofness and the way she seemed to look down on her now. She, too, had pride, and she was not going to let someone like Harriet squash that pride, even if she had to quit her employ here after all.

"You tell her good, Señora Carey," Maria said. "I wish I had your courage. Please know that I do not feel as she does about what happened to you. I am very sorry for it."

Tess blinked back angry tears. "Thank you, Maria. Will you help me prepare the food for the meeting?"

"Certainly. And I must say, *señora*, that you *have* looked a little ill lately. Is there anything I can do? Perhaps you are just working too hard. Señora Caldwell treats you like a slave. I think she enjoys having a white woman working for her. It makes her feel even more important."

"I don't mind, Maria. I am used to hard work." She put the back of her hand to her forehead. "It's just that lately I've been feeling sick to my stomach, in the mornings. I have always been quite healthy, so I don't know quite what to think of it."

Maria frowned, wiping her hands on her apron and stepping closer. "Excuse me, *señora*, but . . . perhaps you are with child."

The words made Tess's blood run cold. "What!"

"Oh, I know it would be difficult, now that you are widowed. But at least you would have something of your dead husband to keep forever, no?"

No! Tess wanted to scream. She and Abel had not had sex for over a month before her abduction, certainly not since her last period. She turned away, trying to think. That had been about a week before the farm was attacked. She grabbed hold of a chair, suddenly feeling faint.

"*Señora!* Are you all right? Did I say something wrong?" Maria put a hand to her waist. "I am sorry if what I said upset you. Perhaps I am wrong."

"I . . . It's all right." Tess fought a building panic. "Tell me, Maria. You have had several children. Is being sick in the morning a sign?"

"*Sí, señora.* You should be happy if you are with child."

Tess was amazed she had not thought about that herself. Yes, she *would* be, if the child were Abel's. But that was impossible! That left only one other possibility. Chino! Who else could be the father? How could she possibly carry the child of such a man? How could she love such a baby? Bastard! That was the only thing one could call it! She was trying so hard to prove she had lost no honor, even trying to make people believe she had not even been raped. How was she going to deny it as her belly got bigger, a single woman with a big belly! She could claim it was Abel's, that she was already pregnant when she was abducted, but when the baby was born . . . God only knew what it would look like! If it came out with dark skin and straight, black hair, how could she deny its father?

"Holy Mary, Mother of God," Maria said softly. "Are you thinking the child could be . . . from one of the Comancheros?"

Tess took a deep breath and straightened. "Of course not. That is impossible, Maria. Those men never touched me. You're right. If I am carrying, it's Abel's child, but I might not be carrying at all. It's just . . . such a shock to think I might be pregnant, now that I have no husband. Please don't say anything about this to anyone right now."

"*Sí, señora.* I am so sorry to upset you."

"It's all right. You were only trying to help." Tess half stumbled out the kitchen door, then began running. She had to go somewhere, anywhere, be alone, think about what she should do. Pregnant! She might be pregnant! She had never even considered such an outcome.

John waited for Lieutenant Ames and his troops to move in behind him. He would much rather fix his sights on the men below and shoot down as many of them as possible before they could scatter. That always seemed the easiest way to rid Texas of its outlaws. But he'd been ordered to "be reasonable" this time and bring some men back alive, or he could lose his job . . . maybe even be hanged, if Jim Caldwell could have his way. Texas had to show how "civilized" it was through law and order, and those who dispensed that law and order had to show they also were civilized.

Besides all that, there was a new decree in Texas that the Rangers should try to get along with the Army a little better. There had been hard feelings for a long time, since most Rangers were Confederates at heart, and most of the Army men down here had fought for the North during the war. Texas had not even wanted any troops here right after the war, but the Army had been shoved down their throats anyway. With constant Indian trouble, the government had decided it was time Texas cooperated with the troops, although as far as John could see, the Rangers still did a better job handling Indians and outlaws alike than the Army did. As far as North and South, he'd never cared much about which side was right or wrong. Men were going to find something to fight about no matter what, and he had no cause to get involved in the war either way. He'd been too busy taking care of his mother back then.

He scooted back from the ridge where he'd been watching Holt Puckett and his bunch. He'd tracked them here, and like a good boy he'd gone to get the lieutenant so the Army could take the credit for capturing the outlaws, unless they botched the job. He ran back toward the approaching troops, telling them not to get any closer or their horses and gear would make too much noise and alert the outlaws. "You'll have to go in the rest of the way on foot, Lieutenant," he told Ames. "Keep a few men out here on horseback; have some of them circle around and be ready to go after any who manage to escape."

Ames nodded. "How many are there?"

"About ten that I could count. They're well armed and they *think* they're well hidden."

Ames turned and signaled his men to dismount. "Thanks for finding them for us, John. You can help us with the capture or not. It's totally up to you."

John glanced at Ken, who had ridden in with Ames. "I say we help," Ken told him with a grin. "And try to take one alive, Hawk. Show Captain Booth and that there Jim Caldwell you can actually do that."

John rolled his eyes and headed back up the ridge with troopers who were on foot. Ken left with those who would watch the escape routes for the camp in the canyon below. John thought again abut his conversation with Ken about Jim Caldwell—the possible reasons the man could have for wanting him removed from the Rangers . . . and why the man was so upset that he'd blown up Derrek Briggs and his bunch.

Maybe the reason Caldwell himself had not had any trouble with cattle rustlers was because he knew them, maybe paid them to leave his cattle alone and to bring him cattle they stole from other ranchers. Others would say he was crazy. He didn't dare even suggest such a thing without some good proof, and he was not likely to come by that. Caldwell would be too smart. Maybe he *was* crazy to even think it, but Caldwell seemed a little worried about something, and all too eager to end his career with the Rangers. There had never been anything personal between them, except that Caldwell hated all Indians and anyone with Indian blood. He'd had to fight them over the years to build his little Texas empire, and John could understand how both sides felt about that. Again he didn't care to get involved in such issues. Life was hard enough without getting into other peoples' problems, and that included allowing any interest in Tess Carey. The woman was out of the question, out of his life, out of his heart. She'd made it very clear she was going on with her life in her own way and needed no help from anyone, least of all John Hawkins.

All thoughts were interrupted when Lieutenant Ames stood up and shouted to the men below. "Holt Puckett! Give up your weapons! You are surrounded by the United States Army! We are arresting you on behalf of the citizens of Texas, New Mexico, and Oklahoma for murder and robbery!"

"Puckett won't give up that easy, Lieutenant," John warned. "I wouldn't stand right out in the open like that if I were—"

A shot rang out, and Ames's hat flew off. The man was instantly on the ground, his eyes wide with surprise. Two more shots were fired, and a couple of the soldiers went down.

"The man is crazy!" Ames told John. "He's surrounded by the Army!"

"You don't announce yourself to men like Holt Puckett," John shouted above a barrage of gunfire. "That's what I keep trying to tell people like you and men like Jim Caldwell. You might as well get off the first shots by surprise and bring a few of them down right away."

Ames scrambled away to get his hat, then crawled back to John. "But if he had any common sense—"

"If he had any common sense he wouldn't be robbing banks and killing innocent people everyplace he goes," John shot back. "Now you've gone and got a couple of your men hurt or killed, and those outlaws down there are going to dig in for a fight." He took careful aim with his own rifle and fired twice, hitting one man but missing another who dived into the cabin, as did most of the others. "Too bad they've got so many boulders and that sagging little cabin down there to use for shelter." He fired again. "God only knows how many supplies they've got in there. You might have to camp out here for a few days."

Lieutenant Ames positioned his rifle and aimed at a window. "We'll roust them out of there."

John grinned. "A few sticks of dynamite would do a better job."

"No! We are not going to blow them up like you did Briggs and his men."

John rolled onto his back and pulled a cheroot from his shirt pocket. "Suit yourself." He lit the cheroot. "I've done my part helping you find them. I don't aim to stay here for a week or more waiting them out."

Ames closed his eyes in exasperation. "Well, what else can we do?" he yelled.

John calmly puffed on the thin smoke while the noisy exchange of gunfire continued, made more deafening by the fact that most shots echoed agaist canyon walls. Finally things quieted when Ames ordered his men to desist firing for a few minutes and just watch the cabin.

"Well?" Ames asked John.

"Well, what?"

"Do you have any ideas?"

John looked at Ames, a handsome enough man, probably about his own age, but too inexperienced with men like Puckett to be going after him—as well as too inexperienced to be fighting Indians. And he couldn't help wondering how the man managed to stay so tidy looking in a place like Texas. "I told you what I'd do."

"Damn it, John, you know we can't do that! Don't you have any other ideas?"

John shrugged. "I thought the Army wanted us Rangers to stay out of their business."

"I believe it's the Rangers who want the Army to stay out of *their* business, but this bunch of outlaws has been committing crimes in several states and territories. That is why this *is* Army business. Now, do you have any ideas, or not?"

John turned back over and carefully raised his head up enough to look at the camp below, the cheroot between his teeth. "Well, Lieutenant, you know how men like Jim Caldwell feel about me. If I get involved in this and do it my way, I could get my head sliced off. Caldwell would love to bring me up on some kind of charges, better yet, see me hang. I agreed to let the Army handle this one. I just hate to break promises."

"John, you are testing my patience," Ames said with a sigh of irritation. "I believe I gave you some supplies a few weeks back before you went to search for Mrs. Carey. You owe the Army."

Damn! Why did the man have to mention Tess? "Hell, I'll pay you in cash for the supplies if that's what you want."

"What I want is to get those men out of there. Now, I know you have an idea. Just spill it, will you?"

John grinned, turning to look at the man. "All right." He took another puff on the cheroot before taking it from his mouth. "I warn you, it's not exactly a tactic the Army would usually use."

"Just say it out."

John scooted down farther so he could sit up straight. "Rattlesnakes."

Ames frowned. *"Rattle*snakes? What the hell are you talking about?"

John nodded toward a distant ridge. "I happen to know that they abound over there, hundreds of them. It's called Snake Hollow. The Apache call it Place Where Men Die. He studied the cheroot as he spoke. "I figure I could go in there, bag a few rattlers, sneak down to that cabin tonight, climb up on the roof and wait till morning light. I'll dump the snakes down the chimney. There won't be a fire in the hearth this time of year. You just watch how fast those men run out of there."

Ames stared at him in dismay. "You're crazy!"

John stuck the cheroot back between his lips. "Everybody knows that. Who better to do the job?"

"You can't just go walking into a nest of rattlers! You'll get yourself killed. If they don't do it, those outlaws will. Do you really think you can climb up on the roof of that cabin without them knowing it?"

John nodded. "I can. I've done it before. I'm part Indian, remember? Us redskins can sneak around quiet as the air."

Ames removed his hat and ran a hand through his hair. "It will be my ass if I let you go collect snakes and you die because of it—or if you get killed going down to that cabin. The Rangers would love to be able to accuse the Army of being inept or making a poor decision."

"Don't sweat it, Lieutenant. I'll get them out of there and you can take those men in and get all the glory."

"I don't want the glory. I just want to get these men. They've killed a lot of innocent people. I want to take them back alive so the relatives of those killed can watch them hang."

John got up and walked down the hill to his horse. "You keep them busy and holed up. I'll go get the snakes. Empty a couple of potato sacks from your supplies. I'll take them with me and be back by nightfall."

Ames gave the order to his sergeant, who ran back to a pack mule and untied two sacks of potatoes. Ames shook his head as John took the sacks and rode away. The man truly was crazy.

Tess could not sleep. It had been six weeks since her abduction, and she now had no doubt that she was carrying a child ... Chino's child. How could she love a baby fathered by a man like that? What was she to do about her situation? She had no idea where to turn. She could not stay here at Caldwell's once she started showing, unless she lied and said the baby was Abel's. But once it was born, everyone would know the truth ... the awful truth.

The house was dark and quiet, and she was wide awake. She got up and pulled on a robe, deciding to go downstairs and quietly prepare herself some tea. She had to think. There was one person she could talk to who might be able to help her decide what to do, but she hated the thought of crawling to Jenny Simms with such an embarrassing problem. Still, women like Jenny probably knew how to get rid of babies. She might have to consider doing that, but it gave her chills to think about having that done to her, and, after all, the baby inside her was innocent of its conception. Abortion seemed so wrong, let alone dangerous. But what were her options if she kept the child?

She quietly went down the stairs, then frowned when she thought she heard voices. It was two o'clock in the morning. Who would be up talking at this hour? She listened closer. The Caldwell home was very big, several bedrooms on the second floor, a parlor, study, library, kitchen, and another bedroom on the ground floor. The voices seemed to be coming from the study, which she had to pass to get to the kitchen. When she reached the study door, it was closed, and light shone from underneath it.

Now the voices were more clear ... men, speaking softly, as though sharing some kind of secret. There was no mistaking Jim Caldwell's gravelly voice, and her curiosity made it impossible not to try to listen. She leaned closer to the door.

". . . have to be careful," she heard Caldwell say. "That damn John Hawkins is too good at what he does. I'm worried someday he'll track somebody's stolen cattle right to my ranch. I hope the son-of-a-bitch gets himself killed one of these times, and if I can find a way to get him hanged, I'll do it."

Tess's eyes widened in surprise. Stolen cattle? Was Jim Caldwell dealing in stolen cattle? Others in the area had had trouble with rustlers, but to think that Caldwell . . . She knelt down to peek through the keyhole, and she saw Sheriff Sam Higgins! The man had surely sneaked here after dark and been let in, since he had been nowhere around at bedtime. Another man stood beside him whom she did not recognize, but he wore snakeskin boots. The only boots she'd seen like that were worn by Caldwell's top man, Casey Dunlap. She recognized him even though his back was to her. Dunlap was tall and thin, and no one else wore boots like that. She didn't like the man, who always looked at her as though she were a prostitute.

"I've got to get some new men together now that Briggs is out of the picture," Dunlap said. "Goddamn Hawkins blew him up with dynamite."

"I am well aware of that, Dunlap. His ass is on the line for that one."

"I can take care of Hawkins for you anytime, boss. You know the kind of aim I have. I could hunt him down—"

"No! None of that. Not unless it seems we have no other choice. Shooting a Texas Ranger will only cause the rest of them to investigate even deeper, maybe lead them to places we don't want them. We'll just have to reorganize. Maybe you can go up to Indian Territory and find some new men. We'll lay low for a while, let the rustling matter die down. I've collected plenty of extra beef. Just do a damn good job of altering the brands before you bring them in."

Tess quickly turned away, afraid she would be spotted. She'd heard all she needed to hear. Now she understood why Jim Caldwell had put up such a fuss about John

Hawkins killing Derrek Briggs. He had *known* the man!
Briggs had been stealing cattle for him! Jim Caldwell had
built his sprawling empire partly from stealing other
ranchers' cattle, and yet he passed for being one of El
Paso's leading citizens!

Did Harriet know about this? She suspected not. The
woman would be mortified and devastated if she knew,
especially if the public found out. How tempting it was to
tell her, after the snobbish, cruel way the woman had been
treating her.

She quietly slipped back up to her room. Now there was
even more to think about. Should she tell John what she
had heard? It could be dangerous for him. Caldwell had
probably already sold what stolen cattle he had, and John
would look like a fool if he accused the man of a hanging
offense without any real proof. His only proof was her
word about what she'd seen and heard. As respected as
Jim Caldwell was, no one would believe her, and John
could get himself hurt, or discharged. Besides, if he tried
snooping around Caldwell's ranch to find evidence, he
could get himself killed.

Her dilemma was great, but one thing was certain. Now
that she knew what she knew, on top of being pregnant,
she had to leave the Caldwell ranch. She would find an
excuse, perhaps just that she wanted a more independent
job. She had talents. She could cook. She was a good
seamstress. She would go back to El Paso, earn her own
way. Caldwell had cleaned up the debris at her farm, and
if it sat there and became overgrown, that just left more
grass for grazing horses and cattle if she sold it or got
things going again herself. The corn was harvested, so
now she'd have some money to help her get started in
something new. She could go back to town, maybe talk to
Jenny Simms. Jenny had money, it seemed. Maybe she
would back her in some kind of small business . . . and
help her decide what to do about the baby she was carrying.
For the time being she would say nothing about what she'd

overheard downstairs. She had to give that a lot of thought, too.

She heard a door close below and went to her bedroom window, which was at the front of the house, and in the bright moonlight she could see a man getting on a horse. That would be Higgins. He quietly rode away. Another man walked across the lawn toward the bunkhouse in the distance. That would be Casey Dunlap.

She moved away from the window, stunned by the revelation of the kind of man Jim Caldwell really was. John really should know about this, but it could bring him far more trouble than it was worth. Maybe he would stumble across something on his own, find proof in his own way. Besides, an idea was forming in her mind, one that involved John. She could not risk something happening to him. The idea seemed outrageous, but she wondered if she had any other choice.

She shivered, struck by the most horrible indecision she had ever grappled with. What an ungodly turn her life had taken since that day Abel shivered in hiding under the bed while she fought alone against Chino and his men.

Chapter Thirteen

Tess looked around the ostentatious bedroom upstairs from Jenny's Place. The wallpaper was red with gold velvet flowers, the carpeting also red. Lace curtains hung over gold window shades, and the spread on the brass bed was red satin. Although gaudy, the room was surprisingly neat. For some reason she had expected a mess, since Jenny Simm's life itself seemed a wild mess. On a dresser sat a variety of perfumes and powders, neatly lined up, and a rack in the corner held a number of fancy ruffled and feathered robes. If Jenny Simms was not an all-out prostitute, one certainly would not believe it on seeing this room.

She stared at the bed, which sat high because of what Tess guessed to be several mattresses. She couldn't be sure, and she did not want to go over and look. She could not help picturing John in that bed with Jenny, could not help wondering what that would be like. She imagined John as wild and untamed and passionate about making love, much as he was outside the bedroom, and she chastised herself for even wondering.

Why? Why did she care? She told herself she really didn't. If not for what she had in mind, it would not matter to

4 BESTSELLING HISTORICAL ROMANCES BY YOUR FAVORITE AUTHORS CAN BE YOURS, FREE!

Kensington Choice brings you historical romances by your favorite bestselling authors including Janelle Taylor, Shannon Drake, Rosanne Bittner, Jo Beverley, and Georgina Gentry, just to name a few! Each book is filled with passion, adventure and the excitement of bygone times!

To introduce you to this great club which is part of Zebra Home Subscription Service, we'd like to send you your first 4 bestselling historical romances, absolutely free! And once you get these 4 free books to savor at home, we'll rush you the next 4 brand-new books at the lowest prices available, as soon as they are published.

The way the club works is that after your initial FREE shipment, you will get our 4 newest bestselling historical romances delivered to your doorstep each month at the preferred subscriber's rate of only $4.20 per book, a savings of up to $8.16 per month (since these titles sell in bookstores for $4.99-$6.99)! All books are sent on a 10-day free examination basis and there is no minimum number of books to buy. (And no charge for shipping.) Plus as a regular subscriber, you'll receive our FREE monthly newsletter, *Zebra/Pinnacle Romance News*, which features author profiles, subscriber benefits, book previews and more!

So start today by returning the FREE BOOK CERTIFICATE provided. We'll send you 4 FREE BOOKS with no further obligation: A FREE gift offering you hours of reading pleasure with no obligation...how can you lose?

AFFIX
STAMP
HERE

KENSINGTON CHOICE
Zebra Home Subscription Service, Inc.
120 Brighton Road
P.O.Box 5214
Clifton, NJ 07015-5214

IF YOU LOVE READING MORE OF TODAY'S BESTSELLING HISTORICAL ROMANCES.... WE HAVE AN OFFER FOR YOU!

*L*OOK INSIDE TO SEE HOW YOU CAN GET 4 FREE HISTORICAL ROMANCES BY TODAY'S LEADING ROMANCE AUTHORS!

4 BOOKS WORTH UP TO $24.96, ABSOLUTELY FREE!

4 BESTSELLING HISTORICAL ROMANCES BY YOUR FAVORITE AUTHORS CAN BE YOURS, FREE!

Kensington Choice brings you historical romances by your favorite bestselling authors including Janelle Taylor, Shannon Drake, Rosanne Bittner, Jo Beverley, and Georgina Gentry, just to name a few! Each book is filled with passion, adventure and the excitement of bygone times!

To introduce you to this great club which is part of Zebra Home Subscription Service, we'd like to send you your first 4 bestselling historical romances, absolutely free! And once you get these 4 free books to savor at home, we'll rush you the next 4 brand-new books at the lowest prices available, as soon as they are published.

The way the club works is that after your initial FREE shipment, you will get our 4 newest bestselling historical romances delivered to your doorstep each month at the preferred subscriber's rate of only $4.20 per book, a savings of up to $8.16 per month (since these titles sell in bookstores for $4.99-$6.99)! All books are sent on a 10-day free examination basis and there is no minimum number of books to buy. (And no charge for shipping.) Plus as a regular subscriber, you'll receive our FREE monthly newsletter, *Zebra/Pinnacle Romance News*, which features author profiles, subscriber benefits, book previews and more!

So start today by returning the FREE BOOK CERTIFICATE provided. We'll send you 4 FREE BOOKS with no further obligation: A FREE gift offering you hours of reading pleasure with no obligation...how can you lose?

We have 4 FREE BOOKS for you
as your introduction to
KENSINGTON CHOICE!
To get your FREE BOOKS, worth
up to $24.96, mail the card below.

FREE BOOK CERTIFICATE

Yes! Please send me 4 Kensington Choice (the best of Zebra and Pinnacle Books) Historical Romances without cost or obligation (worth up to $24.96). As a Kensington Choice subscriber, I will then receive 4 brand-new romances to preview each month for 10 days FREE. I can return any books I decide not to keep and owe nothing. The publisher's prices for Kensington Choice romances range from $4.99-$6.99, but as a preferred subscriber I will get these books for only $4.20 per book or $16.80 for all four titles. There is no minimum number of books to buy and I may cancel my subscription at any time, plus there is no additional charge for postage and handling. No matter what I decide to do, my first 4 books are mine to keep, absolutely FREE!

KF0398

Name _____

Address _____ Apt. _____

City _____ State _____ Zip _____

Telephone (___) _____

Signature _____

(If under 18, parent or guardian must sign)

Subscription subject to acceptance. Terms and prices subject to change.

4 FREE
Historical
Romances
are waiting
for you to
claim them!

(worth up to
$24.96)

*See details
inside....*

KENSINGTON CHOICE
Zebra Home Subscription Service, Inc.
120 Brighton Road
P.O.Box 5214
Clifton, NJ 07015-5214

her if he slept with six different women a day. In fact, he would probably have a good laugh once he discovered her plan. It was a daring, probably foolish idea, but she was not going to allow herself any more humiliation than what she was already in for. Jenny had told her to come talk to her anytime, so here she was . . . in the notorious bedroom of Jenny Simms. She had come to the back door asking to talk to her, and the bartender had led her up some back stairs to this room and had gone to get Jenny.

Surely she had lost her mind. Yes, that was it. Her abduction had caused some kind of mental relapse so that she didn't even know what she as doing. Desperation had driven her over the edge . . . and to this place. She prayed Maria had believed her when she'd told the woman she was not with child after all. For her plan to work, people had to believe this baby was sired by . . . John Hawkins.

"Well, for heaven's sake."

Tess gasped in startled surprise when Jenny spoke up behind her, and she felt her face turning red at the realization the woman had caught her staring at the bed.

"I never really thought I'd see you again, not like this anyway," Jenny said. She closed the door and glanced from Tess to the bed. "You wondering what it's like to be bedded by John Hawkins?"

Tess held her chin high and walked to a window. "Certainly not!" She took a couple of deep breaths for self-control. She had to be very businesslike about this. "However, John Hawkins is part of the reason I am here."

"Okay." Jenny sauntered over and sat down on the bed, her breasts billowing over the low neckline of her blue velvet dress. "Talk away. I'm a good listener, and God knows you must need to talk to someone. I heard you'd gone out to work for Harriet Caldwell. I have a feeling that won't last long. Who could bear to live with that woman more than ten minutes?"

Tess sighed, walking over to a rocker near the bed and sitting down in it. "I have to agree with you there. Harriet has treated me dreadfully. I came into town with her today to shop. She doesn't know I am here."

"Humph," Jenny grunted. "That's no surprise. So, you're back in town, thinking to find work, I presume, hoping to leave Mrs. Caldwell's employ. But what is this about John, who, by the way, I've heard pulled another one of his famous stunts in capturing a gang of outlaws led by Holt Puckett. Puckett is a bad one, but John helped capture him, they say—helped the *Army* capture him, I should say. You won't believe how he did it. Jim Caldwell will probably try to make something out of it again."

Tess leaned back in the rocker. "What happened? And how do you know about it? Is Mr. Hawkins in town?"

"Not yet. I heard it from Ken Randall. He's back, but John went to Fort Bliss first with a Lieutenant Ames, to report to his own commander, a Captain Booth. I don't doubt what he did will be the talk of the town soon enough." She chuckled. "John sure does know how to create gossip." The woman got up and walked over to her dresser, surprising Tess when she picked up a thin cigar and lit it. "Do you mind?"

"No. Please tell me what happened."

Jenny puffed the cigar for a moment. "Well, apparently Puckett and his men holed up in an old cabin and the Army couldn't root them out. So, John went to a place the Apache call Place Where Men Die, better known to white men as Rattlesnake Hollow. With his bare hands and the skill only an Indian could possess, he collected several rattlers and put them in burlap bags. Then, after dark, he snuck down to the cabin. Nobody knows how to take chances like John Hawkins. Who else would do a thing like that? A cabin full of ten desperate men with guns and a need to kill, and John walks right down there and climbs up on their roof. Not many men could do that without being detected. At any rate, come morning light, he dumped a bagful of rattlers down the chimney. During all the screaming and gunfire, he climbed down and dumped another bag of snakes through a window, and in no time those men were running out of there. A few got shot. The rest gave themselves up. I guess John shot Puckett himself, only this time he was a good boy. He aimed for the man's legs so Puckett couldn't run away. At least he didn't kill him. That's a step in the right direction for a man like John. The Army arrested all of them and took them to Fort Bliss.''

Tess put her head back and closed her eyes. ''Rattlesnakes.'' John Hawkins was indeed a man of unusual talents and tactics. She could not help smiling. ''Who else would think of something like that and be daring enough to do it?''

Jenny laughed. ''Actually, Ken said John would probably rather have put dynamite down that chimney, but he's already used that idea, and it got him in trouble. When it comes to getting his man, John will stop at nothing. Most of the time a man just gives up because John Hawkins is after him.''

The story made Tess even more apprehensive about what she was considering. ''Could he ever be dangerous around a woman?''

Jenny lost her smile. ''John? He's the most considerate, gentlest man I've ever . . .'' She hesitated when she noticed a sudden flash of what looked like jealousy in Tess's eyes. ''Slept with,'' she finished. ''John would never force a woman or hurt a woman. In fact, he hates that sort of thing. His mother was raped twice, you know. He killed the man who raped her the last time. That's why he had to flee Missouri and come to Texas. From the way he talks, he was always very protective of his mother. She was often mistreated because she was part Indian and had a bastard son.'' She puffed on the cigar again. ''Now there is something else that runs deep with hurt in John. He's not a man to let on that he has any emotions at all, but I've seen that deeper side of him a time or two. I know it bothers him that he never knew his father, that he was himself a product of rape. But his mother loved him dearly. He still speaks fondly of her. And to this day he hates rape. Between you and me, he blew up Derrek Briggs and his men because they raped a little Apache girl, not because they stole cattle. Nobody knows that, so don't spread it around. Others would think nothing of it because the girl was Indian, but John can't tolerate such things. I'm sure that's part of the reason he took a chance with his life going after you like he did." She leaned closer, resting her elbows on her knees. "What in God's name made you ask a question like that? You should know better, after being rescued by the man and after all the trouble he went to to let you clean up before you came into town. He even tried to convince the authorities you weren't touched. Why would you think he could be dangerous around a woman?"

Tess rubbed at her eyes. "He's so violent in other ways, that's all. I just wondered if you thought he—well, you must know him about as well as anyone. I wondered if he was actually married to a woman, sort of owned her . . . you know . . . had legal claims to her . . . if he might not be so considerate."

Jenny was astounded at the question. She studied Tess intently, hardly able to believe the woman must be suggesting she wanted to marry John Hawkins! Surely the last thing Tess would want was to go to bed with *any* man, and a more opposite match couldn't possibly exist. "What in God's name are you talking about, Tess?"

Tess leaned forward and put her head in her hands. "I'm pregnant, Jenny."

The room remained silent for several long seconds. "My God," Jenny finally said softly. "It's not your husband's?"

"It isn't possible. We hadn't . . . It just isn't possible. It can't be anyone's but that brutal Chino's. I'm going to have a baby, and it's going to look Indian, or Mexican, whatever Chino was. It will need a father who looks similar so it will be believable that man *could* be the father. That way the child won't be called a bastard. I am sure I could not possible truly love such a baby, but I would never be cruel or unkind to him or her. I can't get rid of it because the thought of such a procedure frightens me, so don't even suggest it. Besides, I think it's wrong. I have to find a way to suffer through this with some kind of dignity, and a way to keep my baby from being called a bastard. John Hawkins would understand that. If I am to marry to make things look proper for this child, then I must marry a man who would look like the father of a dark-skinned, dark-haired child. Since I can't marry just any stranger, John was the only one I could think of. I wanted to know how you think he would react to such a proposition. I couldn't bear for him to laugh at me. And I wondered if you thought he would stay out of my bed once I was his legal wife."

Jenny could hardly believe what she was hearing. She got up from the bed and walked over to look out a window. "Good Lord," she muttered. She puffed on the cigar again. "Honey, I have no idea how he would react to such a proposition, except that he'd hate for any baby to be called a bastard. He knows what it's like to grow up with that label, never knowing a real father. He might marry you just for that reason. As far as him forcing his husbandly rights—no, John Hawkins would never do that."

He has you for that, Tess thought. That was a part of the bargain John Hawkins might not go for. She couldn't have her husband be seen visiting prostitutes. "Do you think I'm crazy for even thinking of doing this?"

Jenny came back over to kneel in front of her, setting the cigar aside in an ashtray. "Well, considering the circumstances, I guess not. And I don't think John would laugh at you. He would understand your dilemma. I just can't say for sure if he would agree to it, but he wouldn't laugh. I'm sure of that."

Tess kept her head in her hands. "I have never been at such a loss. My life has been turned completely upside down, Jenny. Six weeks ago I was just a busy farm wife, cooking, cleaning, taking care of my own home, my husband, my father. Everything was so . . . normal." She sighed and rose. "People are going to talk about this, wonder about it, about me. I'm supposed to be a grieving widow. I won't go into details about my relationship with my husband, and I do grieve for him, Jenny, but not quite in the way most wives would. It's a personal thing. The fact remains people will be shocked that I would marry so soon, let alone someone like John Hawkins. I am just trying to avoid something worse, which would be me walking around with a big belly and people wondering . . . who the father is. Most don't believe I wasn't raped. Once the baby is born, they will know for certain it's a bastard. I am hoping most will at least believe it's John Hawkins's child, and if he is my husband, after a while they will accept the marriage and the talk will die down."

She faced Jenny.

"I will offer to let Mr. Hawkins take over my farm, build a ranch out of it if he wishes. Until he decides, I know a Texas Ranger makes very little money, so I need another source of income. I am thinking of starting some kind of business, perhaps as a seamstress. I was wondering if you would consider backing me on building a little place near town. Mr. Hawkins could live there with me when he's not on assignment. And when he's gone I could help support me and the baby by earning my own money. I would pay you back as quickly as I could. In fact, I have some money. I just don't want to use it up all at once. Of course, I would not want others to know you gave me the money." She felt guilty for the look of hurt in Jenny's eyes.

"Of course." Jenny stood up and put on a quick smile. "I understand. And sure, I'll back you. I like you, Tess Carey. And I happen to know something that might make you feel a little better about all of this."

"Oh? What's that?"

Jenny sauntered closer. "John Hawkins is already in love with you."

Tess's eyes widened. "What!"

"The man opened up to me the last time he was here, just enough to let the feelings show through. You were just about all he could talk about. He greatly admires your strength . . . and you *are* a beautiful woman. I'm sure you know that."

Tess turned away, flabbergasted at the revelation. Surely Jenny was imagining things. Was John Hawkins even capable of truly loving someone in that sense? He was such a wild, violent man. She had never considered . . . "Thank you for the compliment, but you must be wrong about Mr. Hawkins."

"Honey, I'm never wrong when it comes to men. And you had better quit with the Mr. Hawkins stuff. If he's going to be your husband, I'd start calling him John. People will wonder if you keep being so formal about him."

Tess felt stunned at the thought John might actually love her. How could he? He'd known her such a short time. And it irked her that he already knew how she looked naked. Would he somehow hold that over her? She met Jenny's eyes. "I'll be returning with Harriet today. I'll have to tell her my plans. I'll come back to town in three days, get a temporary room at the hotel, hire someone to build a small house for me. You can talk about this with John, have him get a message to me about where we can meet alone to discuss this."

Should she tell anyone about what she had overheard between Caldwell and Sheriff Higgins and Casey Dunlap? Not now. There were too many other things to think about, things to settle. "I hate to keep imposing on you, Jenny, but someone has to tell John, and you're the only one who can help me with this."

Jenny shrugged. "Sure, I'll tell him. Might be kind of fun to watch his reaction."

Tess cringed at the thought of how he might react. "I just thought it would make it easier if he is forewarned, rather than me springing something like this on him point-blank. It will give him a little time to think about it before he talks to me."

"I suppose that might be better." Jenny put a hand on her shoulder. "I'm sorry for the way things have worked out, Tess. But you're a strong woman. You'll survive. You're the kind of woman Texas needs."

Tess put a hand to her stomach. "Maybe. I don't know

anymore. I feel . . . numb . . . like the world is just revolving around me and I'm not really in it." She blinked back tears. "Thank you for helping, Jenny. I had no idea you were such a good person."

Jenny laughed. "Well, that makes two of us."

Tess smiled through her tears. "I am keeping you from your work. I will go talk to Mr. Jeffers at the feed supply. He and his son do fine carpenter work, I am told. I will find out the cost and let you know."

Jenny looked her over, thinking what a stark contrast she was to John Hawkins, so prim and proper, organized, a woman who should be married to a man ready to settle, a man who truly wanted home and family. Maybe John was ready for such things, but she couldn't picture him living that kind of life. "Just tell Peter Blake over at the bank. He's . . . sort of a good friend, if you know what I mean. He would be discreet if you tell him he has to be. Tell him the amount you need, and I'll go over in a day or two and tell him it's okay. That way you won't have to risk being seen coming here."

Tess walked to where she'd left a parasol she used to keep the sun off her skin. She picked it up and turned. "Thank you for understanding I can't be seen coming here. I do hope you realize it has nothing to do with you personally. I just . . . I will have a difficult enough time overcoming how people will react to my marrying John. To have to try to explain—"

"I've said before I understand."

Tess's mind raced with indecision. She wanted to talk more, but their conversation was interrupted by a commotion downstairs. Several men were talking loudly, hooting and laughing.

"Nobody can say John Hawkins don't get his man!" someone hollered. The statement was followed by more laughter. It sounded to Tess like Ken's voice. "Come have a drink, Hawk!"

Tess's heart beat a little faster. Had John come to town while she spoke to Jenny? She had thought it would be a few more days yet. But then Jenny had said Ken had already been back for three days.

Jenny read the look in Tess's eyes, knew she was nervous as a trapped mountain lion over what she wanted to ask of John Hawkins. "Wait right here," she said. She went to the door and out onto a walkway above the saloon. The door to her room was slightly hidden from the area downstairs, and Tess had come up a back stairway that led off in the other direction. She could leave right now without being seen. She gripped the parasol, thinking at the last minute that maybe she should tell Jenny to call the whole thing off and not say a word to John Hawkins. Was he down there?

"Hey, you bunch of rabble, what's this mob doing in my saloon?" Jenny called down to them.

"We're celebratin' another Ranger victory," Ken called up. "We've got a man here who can catch rattlers with his bare hands and walk right into a nest of killers without them even knowin' it. Only a Texas Ranger can do things like that."

"John Hawkins, you devil!" Jenny glanced over at the door to her room to see Tess standing there. She nodded slightly. "Looks like you'll have an answer sooner than you think. Go on down the back way," she said quietly.

"Come on down and have a drink with me, Jenny," John himself called up to her.

When Jenny turned and sauntered down the stairway. Tess moved out of the doorway and stood against a wall around the corner of which a person could see the entire saloon. She moved her head just enough to peek downstairs, and her heart filled with doubt. John embraced Jenny and planted a kiss on her mouth. In one hand he held a whiskey bottle.

Tess rolled her eyes and pulled back, leaning against the wall, wanting to die from a feeling of hopelessness. Maybe her idea was simply too ridiculous. How could she marry a man like John Hawkins? He drank whiskey, slept with prostitutes, killed men with the ease of breathing, took chances that would surely lead to his death at an early age. She could hear all the men below, Mexican and white alike, talking and laughing about the snake story.

"I wonder what ole Jim Caldwell will think of this one," Ken told the others. "At least Hawk didn't kill Puckett. People are gonna get to see him and his bunch hang."

Someone else spoke up. "There will be a hanging all right. Probably the whole gang at the same time. You think it will be in Texas, Randall?"

"Who knows? There's a lot of folks in a lot of states who want to see their necks stretched."

"Why don't you find something else to talk about?" Tess heard John say. "You'll end up getting me in more trouble, friend. I did what I had to do and that's the end of it. You know I never talk about what we do when we're out there on assignment."

"Oh, but this one's a corker," Ken answered. "How many men can walk into Rattlesnake Hollow and bag a dozen or so of them slithery bastards without gettin' himself bit to death? How many men can crawl up top a cabin full of outlaws and not be detected? And what would the United States Army do without the Texas Rangers?" He half yelled the last words, and a cheer went up inside the saloon.

Tess peeked around the wall again and noticed Jenny lean close to John and say something to him. He turned to look up toward her room, and Tess quickly ducked back so he would not see her. Jenny must have told him she'd been there. Anytime soon she would probably bring him upstairs and explain all of it. Tess hurried away, darting down the back stairs.

What had she done? The only way to change her mind was to stay and tell Jenny to forget about it, but now John's curiosity was already aroused. He'd have to know the truth even if she didn't want to go through with this. She found it hard to believe he would not laugh at her. But then, Jenny had told her John Hawkins loved her. It seemed incredible. How could he know already that he loved her?

And how should she react to such feelings? She felt like such a fool, so lost and alone.

"John Hawkins!"

John turned to see Jenny standing at the bottom of the stairs.

"Quit your bragging and get up here before you're so drunk you can't think straight."

"Don't you mean before he's so drunk he can't do somethin' else?" Ken shouted. Most of the men in the room laughed at the insinuation.

"Better get up there, Hawk. The lady looks mighty anxious," someone teased.

John joined the others in more laughter, slugging down a quick shot of whiskey before turning to go upstairs amid whistles and lewd suggestions about what it was Jenny wanted. John put an arm around Jenny and walked her into her room, promptly closing the door and grabbing her close. He planted a long, groaning kiss on her mouth, surprised she did not seem to be returning it as warmly as usual. She gave him a gentle shove.

"I didn't ask you here for that," she told him.

John grinned. "Since when?"

Jenny planted her hands on her hips. "Since Tess Carey told me she wants to marry you."

John straightened, his grin quickly fading. Jenny smiled at the look of sudden shock on his face, and his dark eyes showed his disbelief. Flickers of indecision moved across his face.

"What the hell kind of joke are you trying to pull?" he finally asked.

Jenny folded her arms. "It's no joke. Tess just left this room a few minutes ago. She had come here to ask me what to do about the fact that she is carrying a child—*Chino's* child!"

John blinked, and now it was anger that showed in his eyes. "That sonofabitch got her *pregnant?*"

Jenny nodded. "You know she's been trying to convince people she wasn't raped. She thinks if she hurries up and gets married, people will think the baby belongs to her new husband. And since the baby is very likely to be dark and look Indian or Mexican . . ."

John waved her off, turning away, a barrage of emotions tumbling inside. Should he hate Tess for the spot she was putting him in? Or should he be glad for the chance to claim her for his own? "She wants a husband who would fit a baby like Chino's," he finished for Jenny. "She doesn't give a damn about me personally. She just wants me to help her retain her honor."

"Something like that."

He shook his head, walking farther away. "Jesus," he said softly.

"What the hell? You *do* love her, don't you?"

He let out an exasperated sigh. "So what? That doesn't erase the fact that she couldn't care less if I dropped dead, as long as she can claim it's my baby. And what will marrying me help? People in this town don't consider me any more honorable than a man like Chino. I'm half Indian, and that's all they need to know."

"You're a Texas Ranger. And you aren't Comanche or Apache. Those are a couple of things in your favor."

He laughed, more a sarcastic grunt than true laughter. "Well, I guess that makes me a first-class citizen, huh?"

Jenny shook her head. "In Tess's estimation, you carry enough respect to call you the father of her child. That's all that matters to her. She's devastated over this, John, and getting desperate. She doesn't exactly have time to search all of Texas for the right man. She at least knows you, and I think she is secretly attracted to you, no matter how much she might deny it."

"Not likely." John rubbed at his eyes. "Why did she come to you about this instead of just asking me?"

Jenny walked to her dresser and poured herself a drink. "Isn't it obvious? She is very embarrassed, for one thing, and she wasn't sure how you would react. She figures I know you as good as anybody can, wanted me to break the news first so you'd have time to think about it before you talk to her about it. She also wondered if I thought you would agree to being a husband in name only, or if you might try to force your husbandly rights on her."

John rolled his eyes. "My husbandly rights?"

Jenny shrugged. "She isn't exactly ready for anything like that, you know."

John stepped closer, looking down at her sternly. "That will be *my* decision."

"Will it?"

He frowned with irritation. "Does she expect me to be a husband in name only forever? I'm supposed to go without a woman the rest of my life, if she happens to decide she never wants to be with a man again?"

"That's between you and her. I'm just delivering the message."

"And what did you tell her about being able to trust me?"

Jenny raised her chin. "I told her you would never force a woman to do anything." She ran her gaze over his enticing physique. "Not that any average woman would have to be forced by the likes of you."

"Tess Carey isn't the average woman."

Jenny smiled. "Oh, she's as much woman as any other. You be good to her, she'll come around. I'm betting you won't have to go without all that long."

He shook his head. "You talk like I'm going to be crazy enough to marry her."

"Like Tess said, I probably know you better than anyone."

"Maybe not as good as you think."

"Well, it's up to you. Make whatever arrangements you want with Tess. She did ask me to loan her some money. She intends to allow you to go on with your Ranger work. She'll open a seamstress shop here in town. Apparently she's very good at such things. She'll build a small house here, and maybe some day when things are more settled between you and her, you'll settle on her farm and work the place yourself."

"So, she has it all worked out, has she?" John spoke the words in a sneer.

"John, she's just trying to allow you to do whatever you want to do—Ranger work, or start your own ranch. Whatever you want."

"I'll plan my own life, thank you."

"And you love Tess Carey. Don't tell me you don't."

"Love has nothing to do with this. Besides, what the hell do I really know about love?"

"Enough to do the right thing by Tess Carey."

He sighed. "I don't know *what* the right thing is. She was right about one thing—I need time to think about this." He walked to the door. "This day sure as hell turned out different than I thought it would. I figured on staying downstairs and celebrating, playing a little poker." He turned and looked Jenny over. "Spending the night with you."

She smiled seductively. "You still can."

He opened the door. "Not tonight. Too much to think about."

He walked out, and Jenny shook her head. "Poor John." She couldn't help a chuckle. "You can lick the best of them, John Hawkins, but one little lady has you whipped already."

Chapter Fourteen

Five days passed. Tess left Harriet's employ, amid the woman's tirade that she had backed out on her promise to work for her and that she would never succeed on her own. Tess wondered how Harriet herself would survive if and when her husband was found out for what he really was. She still said nothing about what she knew to anyone. She couldn't prove a thing, and now that she had left the Caldwell ranch, people would probably say she was lying out of spite over Harriet's anger with her.

The only message Tess had received so far was from Peter Blake, telling her he was prepared to loan her whatever amount of money was necessary to build a house in town. She had not gone for the loan yet. First she had to know John's decision, and now she was beginning to wonder if she would ever hear from him. Didn't he understand that time was of the essence? The longer they waited, the less believable it would be that her baby belonged to him and there would be no reason to marry at all.

She felt crazy from the waiting, had gone shopping to stay busy. She sorted through a variety of material at a dry-goods store, deciding to begin stocking up on supplies for her new seamstress work, but it was difficult to think positively. If John would not marry her, she would have to leave El Paso, maybe find a mission or convent, someplace that would take her in and put her baby in an orphanage after it was born. She certainly could not keep it, knowing it surely would look Indian and that she could not possibly love it.

She chose a bolt of blue calico, one of green velvet, and another of yellow cotton, as well as a roll of lace trim. She purchased some thread and a few patterns, and while her things were wrapped, she looked through a catalog from which she would order a sewing machine.

She turned when a little bell that hung over the door jingled, and several women strolled inside, led by Harriet Caldwell. "Well, Tess Carey," the woman said, looking down her nose. "Have you decided how you will support yourself now that you have left my employ?"

Tess picked up her wrapped items. There was no sense ordering a sewing machine until she knew what John intended to do. "Yes," she answered. "I believe I will open a seamstress business. I have enough money to back a loan to build a small house here in town, and I happen to be very good at making clothes." She faced the other women with an air of confidence. "If any of you needs any kind of seamstress work done or a dress made for a special occasion, be sure to come to me. I can also make men's suits. I learned on Mrs. Bass's sewing machine when father worked for the colonel back in San Antonio."

She could read the women's thoughts as they looked her over. What was it like to be captured by Comancheros? What was it like to be raped? Did she enjoy it? She felt like spitting at all of them.

"You don't have to socialize with me. I am simply offering to do your seamstress work for you. I know it takes a long time to receive clothes ordered from back East. Show me a picture or a pattern, and I can make the same dress, cheaper and quicker."

"Well, we didn't know you had such a talent," Harriet said, putting on a fake smile.

"I never had the time to devote just to sewing. I was always too busy helping on the farm. I made all my own clothes, as well as most of my husband's and father's. If I'd had the time to sew for others, I would have offered, and if you had not kept me so busy with mundane chores, I could have sewn for you, Harriet."

"My goodness. All the times we've seen and talked with you at socials, we never knew." The words came from Mrs. Carla Sanders, the wife of the livery owner, Ben Sanders, Joe Sanders's brother.

Harriet spoke up. "I am surprised you have enough money saved to build a house and buy material and such. And you will need a sewing machine."

"I will manage. I am getting a small loan from the bank."

"Oh? What on earth are you using for collateral?"

The last thing Tess wanted was for the woman to know her money was coming from Jenny. "I do still own my land, Harriet. That is enough collateral."

"You could have sold that land to my husband and had cash money and no land to worry about taking care of. Why on earth—"

"I don't want to sell my land. Father would want me to keep it, and I intend to do just that for as long as possible, maybe even move back and farm it again someday. I might . . . marry."

"Marry! You have only been a widow for six or seven weeks!"

Some of the other women gasped, and they all stared at her.

"A woman does what she has to do to survive out here. All of you know that," Tess told them. "We've known other women who lost husbands and remarried rather quickly. I've even heard that some women who came West in earlier years and lost their husbands married total strangers, just to have a man's support, especially if they had children to care for. I need a man to take care of my farm, and I can't afford to pay one. Perhaps if I marry I can have my business *and* the farm.''

"My goodness!" one woman commented. "Who would—?" She stopped, turning away.

"Who would marry me, now that I've been the victim of Comancheros? I was not violated, Mrs. Cook. There is no reason why a man should not want to marry me.'' Tess walked past them. ''Please do remember me when you need some sewing done. I hope to have a place of my own very soon.'' She walked out the door, aching with the need for one good friend, realizing that her only true friend at the moment was a woman these others thought was unworthy of their attention. She was beginning to see Jenny Simms in a different light.

Anger filled her as she walked toward the hotel, but she halted her rushed footsteps when she heard someone call her name. She turned to see John standing in an alley. He was leaning against a building.

"Rent a buggy," he told her. "Tomorrow morning. Nine o'clock. Meet me under the old mesquite tree out beyond the graveyard.''

She could not quite read his eyes. Was it a yes or a no? Was he serious or laughing? She felt the heat rising in her cheeks at the thought of Jenny's remark that he already loved her, and she swallowed. "All right. I'll be there.''

He stepped up onto the boardwalk next to her, glanced down at her belly, which for now looked no different; but his gaze embarrassed her. He knew she was pregnant . . . pregnant by Chino.

"We have a hell of a lot to talk about," he told her. "And I won't be lied to or used. Understand?"

She raised her chin. "Of course. I am not a liar. Nor do I use people.'' She held his gaze, again struck by his dark handsomeness. She had not seen him up close in weeks.

He turned away. "See you in the morning." He walked off, and she studied his long stride, his slim hips, broad shoulders, the black hair that hung long and loose down his back today. He wore a six-gun on each hip, a leather vest. She saw his golden horse then . . . tied in front of Jenny's Place.

"Damn you, John Hawkins," she whispered.

He was standing under the tree as Tess approached, his horse calmly grazing a few feet away. Tess's stomach went into a tight knot. Her hands felt clammy, and her face felt flushed. What was she getting herself into? Maybe her experience with the Comancheros had left her demented.

One thing was certain. Never in a million years would she have done something like this before the attack. Never in a million years would she borrow money from a prostitute, offer herself in marriage to a wild heathen like John Hawkins. The only thing admirable about him was that he would never hide under a bed just when she needed him most. He would have walked right outside and fought the Comancheros hand to hand.

John approached her as she drove up close, and he took hold of the horse that pulled her buggy. He could see how nervous Tess was, wished she would just let him hold her and reassure her he wasn't the wild animal she thought him. He'd thought he had proved that when he'd rescued her, but then he wasn't to be her husband. This would be a whole different situation. He could hardly believe what Jenny had told him, for he knew Tess Carey didn't truly give a damn about him. Still if this was the only way to lay claim to her . . .

He reached up to help her down, but she waved him off. "I'm not a weakling who needs help every time she climbs into or out of a buggy," she told him.

John threw up his hands and stepped back. "Pardon me for wanting to help a woman who's carrying." He watched her stiffen, saw the quick shame in her eyes. Damn, she could be stubborn. What was he getting himself into? He quickly made up his mind that no matter what happened between them sexually, this woman was never going to run his life like some wives did. He was his own man, and he would stay that way.

"Well?" she asked, facing him squarely. "Have you made up your mind?"

He let out a little hiss of exasperation. The woman's defenses were up, that was sure. "You remind me of a hissing bobcat that's been cornered, its back arched, the hairs standing up, all poised to pounce if necessary. Why don't you relax, Tess?"

She climbed down and walked to stand under the shade of the tree. "That is impossible. I have asked you to marry me, probably the most ridiculous thing I have ever done, but I am desperate, as you already know. I weigh one hundred ten pounds, and you must weigh double that—well, close to it, anyway. You would be my legal husband. I think you know what I am getting at."

John snickered, walking over beside her and bracing himself with one hand against the tree. "Look, I haven't even said yet that I would marry you. But either way, I'm no rapist, Tess. You damn well already know that. Now why would I turn around and force my own wife to submit to me? I don't want any woman who doesn't want me."

Tess felt she would die of embarrassment at such an intimate discussion. "My God," she muttered, turning away. "You are a healthy, vital man. I am not foolish enough to expect you to go without, but I cannot have my husband be seen sneaking over to Jenny's Place every night." She waited during a strained pause.

"Let me get this straight," he finally said. "You want me to marry you, but you don't love me and you don't intend to allow me into your bed. However, I am supposed to remain . . . What's the word for it?"

"Celibate."

"Yeah, something like that." He grunted a laugh. "Lady, you expect a lot for nothing. What do I get out of this besides having to go without sex and then having to support a wife and a child?"

Tess faced him. "Is that it? You're worried about being paid somehow?"

He slowly shook his head. "I don't give a damn about being paid. I happen to love you, Tess Carey. And I wouldn't mind being loved in return. How's that for surprises?"

The words knocked some of her defenses away. It sounded different coming from the man himself. She had not really believed it until now. There was a deep sincerity in his dark eyes, and she was suddenly at a loss for words. "I . . . don't quite know . . . what to say."

John sighed and sat down in the grass under the tree. "How about restarting this conversation and putting aside all your stubborn defenses? How about helping me understand all of this, like how you can be so sure the baby is Chino's."

Tess closed her eyes. Abel. Why had she ever married him? "Believe me, I know. Abel and I hadn't . . . Abel was a very passive man."

John wondered if she had ever experienced true pleasure in a man's bed. God, how he'd love to show her how it should be. "Why don't you tell me more about him, your marriage? I have a right to know a little more about you personally."

Tess glanced at him, then sat down a few feet away from him, smoothing the skirt of her blue dress around her. She had dressed simply today, had not wanted John Hawkins to think she was spiffing up just for him, did not want to look in any way enticing. He in turn wore his usual denim pants and leather vest, a red calico shirt. He wore no hat today, but rather had a red bandana tied around his forehead.

"I suppose you do have a right to know a few things." She looked down at the flower design in her skirt. "When Abel came to work for my father, he'd lost his whole family to cholera, parents and siblings. I felt sorry for him. He was very kind, didn't believe in fighting. I admired that in him. But after a while . . . he . . . was a bit too passive in the marriage itself. We didn't . . . we were not often . . .

intimate." She could hardly believe she was telling a man like John Hawkins such embarrassing details. "He was good in his own way, but he was a poor husband. We had not . . . been together that way since my last . . . before the attack. The baby can be no one else's but Chino's."

My God, John thought, how can a man be married to a beautiful, fiesty woman like you and not want to bed her every night? "How long were you married?"

"Two years." She still looked down at her skirt. "Before we came here, there was someone else. Les Peters. He owned a hardware store in San Antonio. He wanted to marry me, but I turned him down to come here with my father. I realize now Les never truly loved me, wasn't willing to make any sacrifices for me. Of course, I suppose it was unfair of me to expect him to come with me, but I knew Father would be happier here, having his own land again. He needed that. We had always been so close after losing Mother. I was all he had, and I couldn't bear to let him come here alone." She sighed. "Now I realize I married Abel out of pity . . . and living out here where there is little chance to socialize . . . I don't know. I guess I thought if I didn't marry Abel, I might never get married and have a family at all. Now here I am pregnant by—" She shivered. "Fate can be very cruel."

There was a long pause in the conversation before John spoke again. "And how do you feel about that baby in your belly?"

The question startled Tess. He could be so abrupt with words, right to the point. A hot flush rushed to her face, and she put a hand to her stomach. "I really don't know. Right now I cannot imagine loving it. I thought about getting rid of it, but that goes against my conscience. I thought if I could not find a husband, I would go to a convent somewhere and have the baby and give it away."

"And you need a husband who looks Indian because you figure the baby will be dark."

She quietly nodded.

John sighed, taking a thin cigar from his vest pocket.

"Let me explain something to you," he said. He struck a match and lit the cigar, puffing on it quietly for a moment. *"I* was that baby once. I was the product of rape, a bastard child. But my mother, by-God, loved me, because I was all she had in the world and she realized I was innocent of how I'd been conceived. Besides that, I had come from her own flesh. You don't carry a baby inside you for nine months without beginning to feel some kind of attachment, at least that's the way my mother told it."

He smoked quietly for a moment, and Tess waited for him to finish.

"I grew up learning to always have to defend myself against those who called me a bastard, and I wouldn't wish that kind of life on any kid."

He leaned back against the tree. "At any rate, I guess part of my meanness is my own anger from what I went through. It made me determined not to be outdone or abused in any way again."

He puffed on the cigar again, stood up and walked a few feet away from her, then turned to face her. "I figured you'd better know what you're getting yourself into. In general I am considered a worthless bastard who can't go by rules and who would kill a man as easy as looking at him. I have no education, but neither am I stupid. Maybe you could even teach me to read. That could be part of our bargain."

Tess felt a sudden glimmer of hope. "Of course."

He walked over and smashed the cigar against the tree to put it out, then stuck it back into his vest pocket. "My original point was to tell you I will not marry a woman who thinks she couldn't love her own baby. That child in your belly is innocent. He or she deserves to be loved and deserves to grow up with a father. I always wished I had a real father." He came closer, kneeling near her. "My deal is this kid is going to believe *I* am his father. He will never, never know who his real father was or how he . . . or she . . . was conceived. If you're going to marry me to keep this kid from being a bastard, you're going to let me really *be* a father to him. No matter what happens between us, you will never let on I'm not the father, and I will always be allowed to *be* a father. Agreed?''

Tess was surprised he truly cared. "I . . . yes. But are you . . . are you *ready* to be a father?''

"Hell, no! I never figured I'd *ever* be one. The farthest I ever got picturing such a thing was getting some Mexican girl or Indian girl pregnant and having to marry her because of it. I never figured on marrying someone like you, which brings us to more problems. Nobody is going to accept this, you know. They're going to think you're nuts.''

Tess looked him over, raw power, mostly untamed, wild as the wind. "I probably am." She looked away. "I have already hinted that I might remarry soon. Let them think I *am* nuts. I was abducted by Comancheros. They will probably think it affected my mind, and they're probably right. But at least I will be legally married, and when I start showing, they won't think so much about it.''

"Why don't you just leave El Paso, go someplace else, and tell people the baby is your dead husband's?''

"Because you know that dark prevails. This child is about ninety-five percent sure to look Indian.''

"Another problem is how we will live, *where* we will live. We have to live together, you know. And a Texas Ranger makes hardly enough to support himself, let alone a family.''

She met his gaze again. "Didn't Jenny tell you I will open my own seamstress business? On your time off, you could go out to my land and begin rebuilding. As we can afford it, we will buy cattle, lumber, build a house there. Gradually you could settle there with me. Have you ever gone out and caught wild horses?''

"Does the sun rise every morning?''

She rolled her eyes at her own stupid question. "Well, you can begin building a herd. Put up a fence. Get into ranching. I would think that would fit you, working outdoors, raising horses and such.''

John shook his head. "I've never been that domesticated in my life."

She faced him. "You said you worked on a ranch once. You must know all you need to know."

He shrugged. "True. I'm just saying . . . you're expecting me to settle, live like a normal husband and father, stay in one place."

"Can you do it? Don't you want to settle someday, have a home and a family? Those are things you never had. Wouldn't you like to have them? You just said you'd be a real father to my baby. That means living a normal family life."

John leaned closer, grasping her arms. "Do you intend for this to be for good?"

His touch sent shivers through her in spite of the hot day, and she could not be sure if it was from fear or desire. "I do not take wedding vows lightly," she answered.

"You haven't said a thing about what I told you earlier . . . that I already love you."

Why was it so hard for her to admit she needed to be held? She dropped her gaze, staring at his vest. "I am . . . surprised. You hardly know me."

"I know enough. I'm not a man for a lot of fancy words, so that's all I'll say. You've already made me spill my guts to you. That has to mean something. And something tells me there's a whole different woman inside you that you've never let go of. Abel Carey couldn't find her, and neither could that Les Peters, and as far as I'm concerned, they were both fools. I intend to find her and show her how a woman ought to be loved."

Tess pulled away and stood up. "I've told you how it must be. As far as the living arrangements you mentioned, we'll . . . I suppose we'll have to stay in one hotel room together . . . for looks. As soon as my house is built, we'll live there. Eventually we will rebuild at my farm, and you can start a ranch, make a living doing something that is your own. You would have to quit the Rangers."

John was angry over the way she'd pulled away from

him, as well as the way she was setting all the conditions, taking on that bossy attitude again. "I don't intend to take nothing but orders from you. I'd like to make a *few* decisions of my own, if you don't mind, and a kind word or two from you wouldn't hurt. I'm doing you a hell of a favor here, and you're asking an awful lot from me in return."

"I know that." Tess fought a sudden urge to cry. "I am sorry that's how it has to be for now. Perhaps in time . . . perhaps I can be a true wife to you. I know it isn't fair to ask you to go without . . . to abstain."

"Jesus," John muttered, turning to get his horse. "Don't do me any favors in return, *Mrs.* Carey. When will this farce of a wedding take place?"

"I . . . tomorrow . . . if that is all right. It must be done quickly."

She said it as though she were getting herself ready to stand in front of a firing squad. Something wrenched in John's gut as he mounted Sundance. "The only man of the cloth around here is Father Miguel Hermosa at the Catholic mission. That all right with you?"

She nodded. "My father was a Catholic."

John sniffed. "At least you had some religion. I had none. Now your baby will also be born to a faith. I should say *our* baby." He rode closer. "What time?"

Tess looked up at him, her sight blurry from tears. "Ten A.M.?"

"Fine. I'll stay with you the first couple of nights to make things look good. Then I have some patrolling to do for the Rangers. I don't intend to quit them right away. There is still a lot of rustling going on that hasn't been solved, and I'm curious about why Jim Caldwell was so upset over me killing Derrek Briggs, why the man is so against me. Most ranchers appreciate my work." He took the cigar back out of his vest pocket. "You lived at Caldwell's for a while. You got any ideas?"

Tess thought about what she had seen and heard late that night at Caldwell's. Such news might only get John

Hawkins killed or in a lot of trouble. It was unlikely Caldwell had left any proof around, and he was a powerful man who hated John. She could not afford to have something happen to him now. "No," she lied. "And Mr. Caldwell has a lot of power around here. He probably just hates Indians. Who knows? I wish you would stay away from there."

He raised his eyebrows in surprise. "Are you saying you care what happens to me?"

"Of course I care! You're supposed to marry me, be a father to my child."

"Oh, I see. You don't care about me *personally,* just about the role I am to play in your life." He lit the cigar. "Lady, I think you're perfectly sane. *I'm* the one who is nuts." He puffed on the cigar. "Don't worry. I'll watch my back. You saying I need to?"

She met his eyes. "I don't know. I just don't like the way Jim Caldwell talks about you. And I . . . I *do* care about you personally. Please know that I don't take the fact that you think you love me lightly. Surely you know how confused I am right now, afraid and . . . and desperate."

He kept the cigar between his teeth. "Yeah, well, you *must* be desperate to be marrying the likes of me. And by the way, don't be borrowing money from Jenny. Believe it or not, I have money, plenty to help you build a house and help get the ranch started. It's reward money, hard earned. I've never had need of it. Now I do. We'll do this together without borrowing from a bank or anyone else. Understand?"

"Yes. I appreciate your generosity, John."

His smile had a hint of sarcasm. "You'll be my wife. It isn't just a matter of generosity. It's a matter of what is the right thing to do." He turned his horse. "I'll see you at ten at the mission. I'll bring Ken and Jenny along for witnesses. The Father won't mind. He doesn't look down on people like me and Jenny—like some others do." He started to ride away.

"John," she called out.

He stopped and turned Sundance. "Now what?"

"You . . . you will keep your promise? I mean . . . you won't go see Jenny anymore, will you?"

John studied her closely. Was that a flicker of jealousy in those pretty blue eyes? Maybe that was what she needed to feel. "I'll keep my promise . . . for as long as I can stand it. Maybe it will help if I get a few things out of my system tonight." He grinned, taking hope from the more obvious flash of jealousy he saw this time. He tipped his hat to her. "See you tomorrow, Tess. Sleep tight."

Tess watched him ride off, her emotions tumbling in on her. Love, hate, confusion, desire, horror, excitement, dread. She ached for him to hold her the way he had that night in the wagon. Why couldn't she bring herself to tell him? She thought to call out to him, but she decided that if she asked him to hold her, he might get ideas. He might try something else. She could not encourage him in any way. After all, they would have to stay in the same room together the next couple of nights. She might have her work cut out for her in denying his husbandly rights. Much as she felt uneasy about his snooping around the Caldwell ranch, it would be best if he did leave again for a while and get away from here—and from her.

Chapter Fifteen

Tess waited with Father Hermosa, an old man accustomed to marrying people in this wild country without the usual Catholic requirements. She only hoped others would accept this marriage with the same understanding shrug as Father Hermosa.

She wore a simple yellow dress and a straw hat decorated with silk flowers. Anxious to make herself more clothes, as well as glad to think she would have a respectable business, she had ordered a sewing machine. Soon she would also have a legitimate marriage to explain her growing belly. She had to think positively about all of this. John would build himself a ranch. Maybe, after a time, she could learn to truly think of him as her husband in the fullest sense, but that seemed impossible right now.

Finally she saw Ken and John coming, a buggy ahead of them. That would be Jenny. She suddenly wondered if she looked all right. She had worn her hair pulled back at the sides and long in the back. Her dress was quite plain, and as with all store-bought dresses, it was a little big on her. It was gathered at the back into a moderate bustle, and as was the style, an extra skirt was draped apronlike at the front. The sleeves were short and puffed, the bodice cut in a square and trimmed with lace.

She noticed both Ken and Jenny were grinning from ear to ear. Ken Randall must have been flabbergasted to learn about this—his partner, John Hawkins, of all people, marrying a woman who would give him a family in only a few months.

"My, don't you look pretty!" Jenny said, climbing down from the buggy.

Tess felt embarrassed. She'd wanted to look nice, yet now she worried that John would get the wrong idea. She self-consciously put a gloved hand to her breast while Jenny greeted Father Hermosa in a way that told Tess the woman had been out here before. She was surprised. Did women like Jenny Simms actually believe in God and come to church? The only reason Tess could think of that the woman would come here was for confession.

She sensed John walking close to her. She had not even been able to meet his eyes. She felt awkward, embarrassed, unsure, nervous, foolish. A strange sensation shot through her when he touched her arm, something she could not even explain. My God, this man is going to be my husband, she thought. There was still time to get out of this. Still time. But what else could she do?

"Well, I never would have believed this one!" Ken was saying. "My wild, no-good partner marryin' a sweet lady like you." He leaned closer. "Don't you be worried about nothin', Mrs. Carey. Hawk's a good man, better than you know."

John still had hold of Tess's arm, and she finally looked at him, noticing he wore dark gray cotton pants, a white shirt, and a black suit coat. She was startled to realize she had not even noticed at first how he was dressed. He must have bought these clothes just for this occasion . . . as though it really was special to him. What startled her even more was how handsome he looked, probably the best-looking man in El Paso, Indian, Mexican, or white. "You didn't change your mind," she said.

"Why should I?" His gaze dropped to look her over, a strange tingle went through Tess, one she'd never felt before under any man's gaze. "You're carrying a baby that needs a father, and I aim to do the job."

She nodded, feeling stiff, tense. "I thank you for this." She blinked back tears. "I . . . let's try not to say anything today to make each other angry. I suppose we should . . . make the best of this and . . . try to be happy about it."

Try? That remark made John angry. She acted as though she was being led to a hangman's noose, and he could feel her trembling. He noticed a tear slip down her cheek, realized she was scared stiff, and why shouldn't she be? After the ceremony, she would belong to John Hawkins . . . to do with as he pleased. Why couldn't she trust that he would never force anything on her? He brushed at the tear with his fingers. "I already *am* happy. I wish you could be."

Tess was surprised at the gentleness of his touch. "I . . . I've just never been so confused and afraid," she admitted. More tears started to come, and she struggled to keep them back.

"You folks hang on," John said. "We'll be right with you."

Tess felt herself being led away, found herself in a cool, shady area of the mission, felt strong arms come around her. What was this? The embrace! It was very much like the one he'd given her in the wagon that awful night, so full of compassion. She clung to him, wept against the new suit coat he wore. She needed to do this, needed to cry and get it over with. But she never dreamed a man like John Hawkins would understand that. "I'm sorry . . . I always say things to . . . make you angry," she sobbed. "I'll try . . . not to do that anymore. We . . . have to find a way . . . to get along . . . to be civil to each other."

"We'll find a way," he told her. "It will be easier for me. I already love you, Tess."

She stood there letting him hold her, thinking about what he'd said. It finally began to sink in that he really meant it. She could tell by the way he held her. Could this be such a terrible thing after all? He *was* a man of strength and daring, a man who would always protect her. She'd never find John Hawkins hiding under a bed! And he was certainly very handsome. His Indian blood made him unacceptable to some, but she was beginning to see him as just a man like any other, surprisingly capable of feelings. He did not seem like a man who knew anything about responsibility, yet look at the responsibility he was taking on now, willingly. "I . . . can't say . . . the same words in return," she admitted. "But I . . . respect you for what you are doing."

John figured maybe, if he was lucky, that respect would turn to love someday. "That's enough for now. Let's go get married."

Tess pulled away, and John pulled a clean handkerchief from his pants pocket and handed it to her. "Here."

She took the handkerchief, brushing it over his suit coat first. "I'm sorry. You look . . . very nice today." She wiped at her eyes. "I didn't think you would care enough . . . to dress like this." She blew her nose.

"Hell, this is my wedding day. I had to look nice for my bride, didn't I? I didn't even wear my guns today."

She smiled through tears. "I just realized why you look so different. It isn't the clothes. It's the absence of those guns."

John grinned. "Actually I feel kind of naked without them." He put a hand to her waist. "You ready to get married?"

Tess was astounded at how understanding he was being. She took a deep breath and nodded. "Yes." For the next several minutes she felt as though she was standing aside watching the events. Jenny, dressed demurely today, watched with honest joy on her face. Ken grinned through the whole ceremony, and Tess was sure the man was astounded by the whole thing. John must have told him the truth about it all, but Ken was a man who would understand. She heard herself repeating the wedding vows, heard

John saying them. He sounded so sincere. All too soon it was over. She was Mrs. John Hawkins. Tess Hawkins.

"You may kiss your bride," Father Hermosa told John.

Kiss the bride? How strange that this man had already lain, near-naked, against her own nakedness, yet they had never kissed. She had never even thought about kissing, had forgotten that most newlyweds did so after the ceremony. She felt a gentle hand at her chin, felt her face lifted, sensed him coming closer. Full, gentle lips parted her mouth slightly in a kiss that astounded her with its sweetness, even more by the way it awakened an ache inside her for something . . . something she'd never known. What was it? His tongue flicked over her lips lightly. No one had ever kissed her this way before. Abel's kisses had been quick and urgent, his lips always a little cool. Sometimes he'd pressed to tight and hurt her lips. Chino had not bothered to kiss her at all. His lips had been hot and vicious, all over her, every place but her mouth. This was entirely different.

John pulled away, and she met his eyes, suddenly thinking about the fact that he had probably spent last night with Jenny Simms "getting things out of his system," as he had put it yesterday. She almost wanted to hit him for it, but she had, after all, made it very clear he would not enjoy any sexual husbandly rights. Now she felt tiny little spasms of desire, wondering in the back of her mind what it might be like to afford this man those rights.

Chino flashed into her mind then. No, she could not bear it! She looked away, but his kiss remained sweet on her lips.

"Well, Mr. and Mrs. Hawkins, you make one hell of a beautiful couple," Jenny told them. She hugged Tess, turned to John. "Boy, am I gonna miss you, you wild heathen." Tess had to look away, and she touched her own lips again. In the next moment Ken was vigorously shaking her hand.

"He's a good man," he repeated. "No woman was ever mistreated by John Hawkins. He'll do good by you, Tess."

Tess nodded, and she thought about telling Ken what she knew about Jim Caldwell, but this was not the right time or place. "He doesn't know it, but he needs you to watch out for him, Ken."

Ken nodded. "I already know that."

John went to get his horse and tied it to the back of the buggy Tess had driven to the mission.

Jenny embraced Tess. "You'll be all right, honey. You might even get to like the idea of being married to John Hawkins . . . after a time. Don't be too short with him. He's done a good thing for you, you know." She patted Tess's arm and walked off with Ken, who helped her into her carriage and mounted his horse. He waved his hat to John.

"I'll meet up with you at the livery tomorrow mornin' around nine," he called out. "Too bad Captain Booth is sending us off so quick after you're married."

John waved back, then came over to shake the priest's hand. "Thanks for agreeing to marry us," he told the man.

"God bless both of you," the priest replied. *"Vaya con Dios, amigo."*

"Vaya con Dios, Father Hermosa."

Tess thanked the priest herself and walked with John to her carriage. "I take it you're riding in the carriage with me."

"Seems only proper, being newlyweds, doesn't it? I think we'd better go let ourselves be seen about town. I'll buy us some lunch. Until we get into a house, I guess we'll have to eat all our meals at Ruby Watson's place. She's got the best food around, unless you want only Mexican. Something tells me you prefer Southern fried chicken to hot peppers."

Tess climbed into the carriage. "Yes, but there is some Mexican food I like. How can a person live in Texas and not like Mexican food?"

John grinned, climbing onto the seat beside her and taking up the reins. "Can't argue with that one."

"Do you speak Spanish?"

He snapped the reins. "Well, it's like with the food—how can a Texas Ranger do his job without knowing Spanish, as well as a little of the Comanche and Apache tongue? Most of the men we go after are either Mexican or Indian. You have to be able to converse with them."

"In your case, what does it matter? They're usually dead before they get a chance to argue the point."

John grinned. "Not always."

Tess thought how intelligent he had to be to be able to pick up those languages the way he had. "I know some Spanish, just what is necessary to get by. You would think that after ten years here, I would know more than I do. But most of my socializing has been with other white . . ." She hesitated, realizing she might be offending him. "Well, you know."

"Oh, I know, all right. What you have to get straight in your own head is that I am more white than Indian, if that helps any. Maybe not in looks, but by blood I'm only one-quarter Indian, I think. It was my grandmother who was full-blooded, my mother only half."

Tess studied the hands that held the reins, strong, dark. To look at John Hawkins, one would think he was certainly more than one-quarter Indian.

"What do you suppose people will think of this, Mrs. Hawkins?"

The words almost startled her. Mrs. Hawkins. She was Mrs. John Hawkins. "I'm not sure I want to know what they're thinking. Let them draw whatever conclusions they want. I'm not showing yet, so I hope to fool all of them. That's the most I can hope for. Women like Harriet Caldwell and her friends will look down their noses at me, but they'll get used to it."

"How about you? Will *you* get used to it?"

"I have no choice, do I?"

They rode on in silence for a few minutes. "I hope you don't look at this like some kind of jail sentence. It's for life, you know, so why not relax and let yourself think of me at least as a friend, Tess. It's all right to touch me, you know. We're supposed to be newlyweds. And since you are my wife, I can't exactly look at your touching me as being forward or brazen now, can I? We're coming into town. You'd better look the happy wife.''

He glanced at her with a smirk on his face, and Tess wanted to hit him. Instead, she placed a hand through his arm, holding her chin proudly as a few people began to stare at them. A couple of men called out to John, obvious curiosity in their eyes.

"Who you got with you there, Hawkins?" one man yelled.

"*Mrs.* Hawkins. I just got married, Hank."

"Married! *You?* Ain't no wild man like John Hawkins gets to marry a pretty little thing like Mrs. Carey there."

"Well, she's not Mrs. Carey anymore."

"I'll be damned!" The man ran to tell someone else, and Tess began to feel embarrassment as she could tell the talk and whispers were moving down the street almost as fast as their carriage. Mexican and white women alike stared, talked low to each other. The men were more outspoken, some congratulating John, some giving out whistles and hoots. Tess noticed Ken's horse was tied in front of Jenny's Place, and she decided she would remind John later that she had better never see *his* horse tied there anymore.

Several people congratulated them when they stopped in front of Ruby's and climbed down. Tess knew some of them, but not all. Most were men. The women hung back, wives of the men who ran businesses in El Paso. Tess knew they were probably in complete shock over what they were hearing.

Beside John she walked inside Ruby Watson's restaurant and sat down, and Ruby was rather terse as she poured their coffee. She was a stout woman of normally gracious manners, a hardworking woman who ran this restaurant as well as tending to three children while her husband helped out at the feed store. It was obvious she disapproved of John as a husband for Tess.

"Well, I am told congratulations are in order," she said, standing there with the coffee pitcher in her hand. She looked at Tess. "Whatever has gotten into you, Mrs. Carey? You always seemed so sensible, at least before . . ."

"Before my farm was raided and I was carried off?"

"Well . . . you have to admit this marriage is rather odd. Your first husband has only been dead—"

"You know most women don't stay single long in this land," Tess interrupted. "And my decisions are my business. Mr. Hawkins here is a fine man, and I will remind you *my* name is Hawkins now, not Mrs. Carey. If not for Mr. Hawkins, I would probably be dead now, or wishing I was. I owe him a great deal, but that is not the reason I married him. He has expressed feelings for me, and he is certainly deserving of home and family. I intend to provide both for him, so you can tell that to the other ladies in town. I care a great deal for John, and I would appreciate the respect of others for my marriage. Now, may we please have some chicken and potatoes? And is there cream for the coffee?"

Ruby Watson stood there looking rather chagrined, scowling first at John, then at Tess. "Certainly." She walked away in a huff, but others continued to stare. John looked at Tess with a mixture of pride and curiosity.

"Quite a little speech, Mrs. Hawkins."

"It needed saying. Ruby is quite the gossip. Let her tell it around town. Maybe then I won't have to repeat the same explanation to every lady I meet."

"Did you mean that—about caring a great deal for me?"

She dropped her gaze to her coffee cup and picked it up. "I suppose. Either way, it certainly doesn't hurt to make sure others believe it."

He leaned back in his chair. "I wish *I* could believe it."

Tess glanced sidelong at some of the others. "Be careful what you say," she answered softly. She finally met his eyes, such dark, sometimes unreadable eyes they were, sometimes gentle, sometimes showing a viciousness that could turn a person's blood to ice. Right now they actually looked sad, and it surprised her. "Believe it," she answered.

Their gazes held as he slowly nodded. "All right. I'll settle for that much."

Tess felt a quick flash of desire over the way he looked at her, then chastised herself for it. Not only did the thought of a man touching her right now make her feel sick, but it seemed so wrong to care this soon for anyone else . . . And here she sat married to the last man on earth she would ever have considered even looking at a few weeks ago! What was she going to do when she recovered from this insanity? The deed was done. What if she lost her baby or it died? Then what would she do about this marriage?

Ruby brought their food, but Tess could hardly eat because of the stares and her own nervousness.

"You should eat more," John urged.

"I can't."

He sighed, wondering when she was ever going to stop behaving like a scared kitten while putting on a brave, uncaring front for others. He leaned close to her. "We'll go back to the room from here," he said quietly. "People will expect it. Since we won't be doing what they'll *think* we're doing, maybe you can teach me something about reading. Do you have any paper, ink, a pen? Something to write with?"

She nodded.

"I'll get a newspaper from the desk clerk and take it up with us. Teaching me to read is part of the deal, remember?"

"Yes." She met his eyes. "We'll . . . I suppose we'll have to stay in that room the rest of the evening . . . the rest of the night."

He wanted to laugh at the look on her face. "I suppose we will," he answered. "Don't worry. Come morning I'll be out of El Paso, maybe for days or weeks. You'll be safe. You can have that house built so I'll have a place to come home to."

She nodded. "All right."

They finished eating, except that Tess left most of her chicken. John paid for the food, ignoring a very cold Ruby Watson. A couple of men in the restaurant congratulated him, but the women only silently stared. They left, and John told Tess to go to the hotel. "I'll take the horse and carriage and my own horse to the livery. I'll get my things from Jenny's later tonight, after dark so no one sees me. I'll go up the back way."

Jealousy again struck her. He'd left his clothes and gear at Jenny's last night. She met his eyes. "You . . . won't stay there, will you? I mean . . . you'll just get your things and come right back?"

He grinned. "Would it matter?"

"Of course! The desk clerk has to know you're up in our room all night."

"That the only reason it matters?"

She reddened a little. "Of course it is. If you could get away with it, I wouldn't care if you slept in Jenny Simms's bed every night!"

He just shook his head. "The hell you wouldn't." He untied the carriage horse and led it away.

Tess stood there feeling ridiculous, embarrassed that he'd apparently read her jealous thoughts. It angered her that he would think he mattered to her that way. She simply had to be more careful. She couldn't give him any ideas. She headed for the hotel. This was going to be the longest night of her life.

Chapter Sixteen

Tess scanned the newspaper John brought back with his gear. "I see Harriet Caldwell has convinced a Baptist minister to come here, and her husband will head a commission to raise money to build a church for him." She turned a page of the paper. "Harriet might try practicing the Christian religion herself before worrying about bringing a preacher here."

John removed his jacket. "You never told me how things went at the Caldwells. Would you have stayed if not for the baby?"

Tess lowered the paper. "I couldn't have. The woman treated me like a slave, always at her beck and call. I had to get out on my own, and I would have, even without the baby. I only went there in the first place in return for Jim Caldwell's taking care of the farm. Now I suppose it will grow into a tangled mess before I can do anything with it."

"That's my job, remember?" John untied a black string tie and loosened the buttons of his shirt. "I'm taking this thing off. These clothes aren't exactly comfortable for a man like me."

He removed his shirt, and Tess could not help noticing his muscled chest and shoulders. She quickly looked away. "Jim Caldwell has been trying to get my land almost since we moved there. If not for old Colonel Bass promising it to us, we never would have got it. I think Caldwell thought if he took care of it he could eventually talk me into selling out to him. I might consider it if I thought he was a decent man, but I don't like him at all."

"Well, that makes two of us. Personally I think it's a little mysterious that other ranchers in west Texas have had so much trouble with rustlers while Caldwell hasn't had any problem at all. He says it's because he has a lot of men and thieves are afraid to mess with him. I don't believe it. Rustlers, Indians, Comancheros . . . whoever . . . when they steal, they steal. They don't give a damn how big a rancher is."

He pulled on a blue calico shirt, but left it open as he sat down on the bed beside Tess to pull off his shoes. "In the meantime, Caldwell just keeps building his herd, claims he sends men into New Mexico and northern Texas to buy more cattle." He grunted as a new shoe came off. "My beat-up, dusty old boots are a hell of a lot more comfortable than these." He pulled off the other shoe. "At any rate, I suspect Caldwell is somehow involved in the rustling. I haven't even told anyone else about it except Ken . . ." He looked at her. "And you."

Tess only then realized they were sitting together on the bed. She scooted over a little, and John just grinned and shook his head. "At any rate, I only started thinking about it the last few months, and I got even more interested when Caldwell put up such a fuss about me killing Derrek Briggs. Now I wish I'd have kept Briggs alive. I've got ways of making a man talk. He might have given me some very interesting information." He got up and began rummaging through his gear. "Mind if I smoke?"

"Go ahead." How tempting it was to tell him what she knew. "I am sure that if Caldwell is into something like that, he will be found out. You should stay away from there,

John. If he really is involved in rustling, he . . . well, he has so many men. And no one would believe he would be a part of something like that. He's already come close to turning people against you. Heaven only knows what he might do if he would catch you alone on his property."

Proof. He needed proof, and if he made trouble for Caldwell without it, the entire public might turn against him.

John snickered. "You know yourself I've gone up against a lot worse than Jim Caldwell." He rolled himself a cigarette. "When I started with the Rangers in seventy-five I walked right into the Las Cuevas war—Rangers against Mexicans, on Mexican soil. It was a hell of a big battle, over Mexican cattle thieves. I also had a part in the Mason County war, and the El Paso Salt War. Ever hear about that?"

"Plenty of talk after we moved here in seventy-nine."

"Well, most of those confrontations came down to Rangers against Mexicans. Most Mexicans still figure Texas belongs to them, you know. I don't much care either way. I'm just doing my job. At any rate, that one was over the rights to claim and market the salt from Guadalupe Lakes, or Salt Lakes, whichever you want to call them. We lost three good Rangers in that mess, executed and butchered by a Mexican mob." He lit the cigarette and took a deep drag from it, exhaling smoke as he continued. "Then, of course, we have always had Indians to contend with. I guess our biggest battle involving Indians was when we had to go after the Mescalero Apache leader, Victorio, after he escaped from the reservation in seventy-nine."

"That I do remember. My father kept a constant watch. All farmers and ranchers were afraid of being raided and murdered."

He walked to a window and looked out. "Well, our main problem continues to be Comancheros, horse and cattle thieves. Things have actually calmed down a lot over the last couple of years, since the railroads came, more settlers. The more civilized it gets around here, the less use they have for Rangers like me, ones who go in and shoot first, not bothering with questions. I guess the timing is right after all, me marrying you." He looked at her. "I'll quit the Rangers, probably by the time that baby is born, but not until I can find proof of what Jim Caldwell is up to. Between other assignments, Caldwell is my primary target now. I intend to do some private scouting."

Tess swallowed, suddenly realizing she would truly grieve if something happened to him. "John, why don't you just quit and let someone else find out the truth . . . if it's true at all."

He stuck the cigarette between his lips. "It's true, all right. And after the way Caldwell insulted me, I want to be the one to show him up for what he really is. I have a suspicion Sheriff Higgins is in on things and probably keeps Caldwell informed on Ranger activity. He usually knows what we're up to. That's why I have to do this myself, not tell Captain Booth what I'm doing."

His intelligence when it came to scouting and deciphering human nature was astounding to Tess. He had mentioned Sheriff Higgins without her saying a word about seeing him at Caldwell's ranch. It also dawned on her he had been talking steadily since he'd got back to the room. Was he as nervous as she was? Trying to find a way to pass the time?

"Would you . . . would you like to do a little reading?" she asked, hoping to take his thoughts away from Jim Caldwell. "You must know how to read some, don't you? Do you know letters?"

He still stood at the window. He smoked quietly for a moment before answering. "I know letters. I've learned what some say when they're put together by having to know what certain WANTED posters say, and from signs, like down there at Jenny's Place. I know that's what the sign says, and I know how those letters sound, so when I put them together I can understand why that sign says Jenny's Place."

And are you wishing you were over there? "Well, then you have mastered most of the battle. Come over here and see what you can read from one of these articles. I'll help you through the words you can't read—help you sound them out. We have a rather long night ahead of us. We might as well use it to some good."

I can think of a hell of a lot better way to spend my wedding night, he wanted to shout at her. He *would* claim Tess Hawkins one of these days, or nights, but he'd made her a promise, and he would honor it. She wasn't ready yet, but he was determined that someday she would not only allow him his husbandly rights, she would actually love him.

"Might as well," he answered aloud. He walked over and smashed out what was left of his cigarette. "I will rebuild out at your farm, Tess. That's a promise. I'll start raising some of my own horses and cattle once I quit the Rangers. For now I might as well stay with them. The assignments take me away for weeks at a time." He sat down beside her again. "Considering our situation, that's probably best right now."

Tess felt heat rising into her face. "Yes, I suppose it is. She stared down at the newspaper, thinking about the way he had held her earlier, such a wonderfully comforting embrace. She would not mind another embrace like that . . . but she couldn't let him do that here . . . not when they were both sitting on a bed. What was harder to forget was the way he had kissed her. This man sitting next to her had kissed her as a husband kisses a wife. He *was* her husband! Her *husband*. For life. "This is all so strange."

He sighed. "Hey, look, I'm as nervous as you are. I'd rather go over to Jenny's and play poker and drink whiskey all night, but that wouldn't look too good, considering I'm supposed to be a new husband. We're stuck here, so we'll have to make the best of it. It would be easier for me to face a bunch of outlaws right now than face spending all night in this room with a woman I love and can't have." He got up from the bed.

Tess couldn't bring herself to look at him. "I'm sorry. I've gotten you into a mess."

He walked back to the window. "The only mess I'm in is waiting for you to care about me as much as I care about you, Tess Hawkins. I don't mind having to marry you. I don't even look at it that way. I *wanted* to marry you. It's you who didn't want to marry, and I know you never would have given thought to such a thing with me if not for the baby. I can even live with that, as long as there is some hope you'll look at me with love in those pretty blue eyes someday." He faced her. "I'm really not so bad if you give me a chance. I won't run out on you and I won't break any other promises. You've already figured out that in spite of my ornery nature I have a soft spot for good women because of my mother. Just don't expect me to sit back and wait for months for you to come to me. I expect you to at least try to like me a little, and to quit acting afraid of me."

Tess closed her eyes and shook her head. "I do like you, John . . . more than a little. Surely you understand . . . after Chino—"

"I'm not Chino. And you're still young and beautiful. You're going to want a man again in the way every woman wants a man. I'm just telling you not to be afraid of your own emotions and to quit comparing me to a bastard like Chino—or even to your own first husband. I have a feeling he didn't know the first thing about . . . how to treat a woman. Tell me something, did you really *love* the man?"

Tess met his dark eyes. "Love?"

"Yes. Do you even know what the hell love is, Tess? Have you *ever* really loved a man?"

She looked away. "I—I respected him. And I guess I did love him, in a special way."

"A special way? How?"

"Well . . . as a husband, the man I promised to love, honor and obey. I truly felt I loved him until . . ." She got up from the bed, hating to talk about such intimate things with someone like John Hawkins.

"Until you found out he wasn't a real man?" he asked.

"Until you found out he didn't know the first thing about loving a woman?"

She folded her arms and paced. "Something like that. But who am I to say how a woman should be loved? I had no experience with such things. Maybe I expected too much from him."

"You expected what every woman expects—for a man to be a man, to take charge, not just in decision-making and work, but in bed, too."

She sensed herself reddening deeply. The statement left her speechless, and she felt jittery and much too warm.

"You've never known real love or real love *making* since you were old enough for such things," John told her.

"Stop it," she asked, still unable to look at him. She heard his footsteps behind her, gasped when he grasped her arms and turned her around.

"How did he kiss you?"

Her eyes widened in surprise as she looked up at him. "What?"

"Did he ever kiss you like I kissed you today?"

Now tears were wanting to come again. "You're going to break your promise, aren't you? And I can't do a thing about it without embarrassing myself to the whole town! You know I don't dare scream!"

He rolled his eyes in exasperation. "Jesus God Almighty." He let go of her and began buttoning his shirt as he walked over to where his boots stood in a corner. He pulled a pair of denim pants from his gear, and Tess's terror grew when he unbuttoned the new pants he'd worn for the wedding and yanked them off.

"What . . . what are you doing?"

"I'm changing. You're my wife. You can see me in my underwear without fainting." He pulled on the denim pants and stuffed his shirttail into them.

"Are you . . . are you leaving?"

"I guess I have to. I told you to trust me, but apparently you don't. I'll think of some excuse." He buttoned the denim pants and pulled on his boots. "I'll come back later, after you've changed and gone to bed. I'll rig up some kind of bed on the floor. Come morning I'll be gone, maybe for quite a while. Then you can relax, Mrs. Hawkins. I won't attack you in the night."

She wanted to protest. It would look bad if he left now. "Where . . . where will you go? You won't go to Jenny's, will you?"

He strapped on his gun. "Do you care? Do you *really* care?"

God, how she hated admitting it. "Well . . . I . . . yes."

"Why?"

"Because you're supposed to be my husband now."

"Is that the only reason?"

Their gazes held for several silent seconds. "No."

His angry look softened a little. "What's the other reason?"

A tear slipped down her cheek. "Because . . . because you're right. No man has ever kissed me like you did today. And because . . ." She turned away. "And because I . . . I need you to hold me. Just hold me." She shook on a sob. "Just hold me."

Almost instantly she felt his arms come around her. She turned and wept against his chest, getting the blue calico wet. "I didn't know . . . what you would think of me," she sobbed. "It doesn't seem right . . . to care for any man . . . in any way . . . after losing my husband not even two months ago . . . and after what . . . what Chino did. I don't know what's right or . . . wrong anymore."

He wrapped a hand into her hair, causing some of the hairpins to fall out. "Letting go of your feelings is always right. And I've got more feelings for you than you could know. Away from you I'm a worthless, mean bastard who doesn't give a damn about anything. But you—you make me . . . feel so deeply it hurts down deep in my guts, Tess Hawkins."

She half smiled through tears at the remark. Only John Hawkins would use such a crude expression to say something so beautiful. She clung to his shirt. "I can't . . .

honestly say that I love you, John. But I ... I admire you more than you know. I respect what you're doing. And I ... Sometimes you make me ... feel things I never felt before. I'm just so ... confused ... and scared about the future. Mostly I'm afraid to care. I've always lost every person I ever cared about, and always in a violent way. And you ... you lead such a violent life."

He buried his face in her hair. "You won't lose me. Ken says I'm too mean to die."

"I think he's probably right."

He held her for several more minutes, enjoying the feel of her body against his own. Suddenly unsure, he was afraid if he made one wrong move she would be terrorized, hate him again, accuse him of going back on his promise. She turned her tearstained face up to meet his gaze. What was that he saw in those big, blue eyes? He leaned closer, and she did not pull away. He met her lips, gently, so gently, being so careful to keep from sending her running. To his near shock, she was returning the kiss. He crushed her against himself, kissing her more deeply.

Tess had no idea why she wanted this kiss, why she had allowed it. She reasoned it was more out of curiosity than anything else, and she had no idea what was happening to her then as some kind of powerful emotional need shot through her with such force she could not control it. She cried more when he left her mouth, and through her tears the words spilled out.

"Make love to me, John Hawkins," she said as she wept.

Chapter Seventeen

This was not supposed to be. Tess felt she was on a wild spiral, falling down and down into a new phase of life she never would have thought possible two months ago. Lost in a swirl of deep, warm kisses, she was being carried to the bed.

Why was she doing this? Why could she not stop John Hawkins? More to the point, why didn't she *want* to stop him?

John was right. He was not Chino. He was all gentleness, in spite of his power and size, yet there was a sure, demanding way about his lovemaking. He was completely in control without being abusive, commanding her every move while at the same time she wanted him to take command; and there was a sincerity about his kisses, his touches, that told her he honestly loved her.

She was aware that her clothes were coming off, and she knew he was right about something else. Abel Carey had not known the first thing about how to please a woman.

John's hands moved over her in magical ways, while she was so smothered in kisses there was no chance to talk, to protest . . . and why should she? She was the one who had asked him to do this. Even if she changed her mind now, she had no right to stop him. She had invited him to explore her soul, and that was just what he was doing. She reminded herself this man was her legal husband. There was nothing wrong in allowing him this one thing he so wanted.

She heard the thump of his gunbelt being thrown to the floor, felt almost numb as he pulled her dress, slips, and drawers down and off her all in one movement.

"My shoes . . ." she heard herself say.

"Don't worry about it." The words were spoken softly, close to her ear. He was kissing her neck, her throat, unlacing her camisole. He kissed lightly at the swell of her breasts, moved back to her throat. Tess heard a soft groan from deep in his throat as he met her mouth in another commanding kiss. His tongue moved between her lips, and a strong hand grasped her bottom, plying her flesh. He moved to her side, and his hand came around to explore her private places. He touched a magical spot in a way that surprised her with how it brought out a wanton desire she'd never felt before. Abel had never done something like this to her. She was overtaken by an odd mixture of bold eroticism and pure shame, yet even the shame was pleasurable. As he teased her with his fingers, something happened that took her by surprise, and she found herself pressing against him, whispering his name. Something warm and wonderful had overtaken her senses. Now it was she who was kissing him aggressively, grasping at his shirt, wanting him as she had never wanted a man.

He moved between her legs, not even taking the time to undress. The back of his hand touched her private places as he unbuttoned his denim pants and underwear. She sensed his own urgency. If this was to be done, it had to be done quickly before she even realized it was happening. She agreed. She wanted this night to be the way it should be for a new husband, needed to know what real lovemaking was. It was not the fumbling, quick penetration she'd known with Abel, nor was it the vicious, brutal ramming

Chino had given her. Lovemaking was not supposed to involve pain and terror, nor should it be something almost void of emotion.

She felt it then, the deep surge inside of her. John Hawkins was a big man, and that apparently included this most private part of him. At first she experienced only deep pleasure, for whatever he had done with his fingers, it had brought forth an exploding need to have a man inside her. But when she opened her eyes . . .

Chino! There he was, with his dark skin, his long, black hair. For a moment she could even see those eyes, those ugly eyes! She gasped, pushed at him. Someone grabbed her wrists. The gentle, rhythmic penetration continued, along with kisses to her eyes.

"It's me, Tess, John Hawkins, and I love you. Do you hear me? I love you. You're my wife."

"Please . . . don't—"

"Tess!" The name was spoken more firmly. "Look at me. Open your eyes and look at me."

He held both her wrists above her head with the grip of only one strong hand, while his other hand moved to her bottom, gently pressing upward to support her as he continued his deep thrusts. Tess did as he asked, meeting his dark eyes. They were not Chino's eyes. They were so handsome, deep set, full of love. That whole face was utter perfection. Tears came to her eyes as she realized she really could love this man.

"Please . . . let go of my wrists," she asked. "I don't like it."

He let go, moved his hand to her hair, leaned down and kissed her forehead as his thrusts grew deeper, more rapid. Tess felt his life surging into her then, and he groaned with the pleasure of his release. He seemed tense for a moment, then relaxed against her, moving slightly to the side as he pulled away from her. They lay there quietly for a moment, and he kept his arms around her, kissed her hair. It was only then Tess realized he still had his shirt on, everything except the gun belt. All he had done was unbutton his pants. Even she was not fully undressed. She still had on her camisole, although it was unlaced, exposing her breasts; and she still wore her shoes and stockings! She turned away from him, pulling a flannel sheet over herself and putting her hands over her face.

"My God," she groaned. "I've just made love . . . with a man who is . . . hardly more than a stranger." Never had she experienced anything quite like this, nor did she expect it would even happen. Yes, she truly had lost her mind. "What must you think of me now?"

John frowned. "What *should* I think of you, except that you're a beautiful woman who has finally realized what being with a man is supposed to be about. I've just made love to my wife. I'm not a stranger, Tess. I'm your husband."

She felt him shifting on the bed as he adjusted his pants. "I . . . I shouldn't have . . . asked you to . . . I don't know what got into me."

He leaned over her, pulling her hands away from her face. "You listen to me, Tess Hawkins. For once in your life you were a woman, and you gave me the chance to take away some of the ugliness of Chino's attack. That's what I wanted to do. As far as I am concerned, Chino never existed. He never touched you, and he never fathered a child by you. The baby in your belly is *mine!* You are now my wife in every way, and no other man will ever touch you again but me!"

She studied his eyes. "I . . . don't know what to say . . . how to feel."

"Just be honest and tell me how you feel right now, this minute."

Her eyes teared. "I think I . . . *could* love you, John Hawkins."

He smiled. "Well, that's a start. And we *are* married, so why should there be anything wrong with what we just did?"

"I don't know. I . . . I need time, John." She pulled away from him again. "We've consummated our marriage. It's done now, right or wrong. I need to think about all of this."

"Meaning this is the end of our lovemaking?"

"I'm sorry. It has to be . . . for now." She felt him get up from the bed. Why couldn't she admit she wanted him to hold her again? Kiss her again? Make love to her again? Why couldn't she get rid of this stubborn pride? He was right to say there was nothing bad or wrong in what they had just done, but she could not quite believe it. She had just allowed this man, who only a few weeks ago was a stranger, a wild Texas Ranger come to help her . . . she had just let him do the most intimate thing a man could do to a woman . . . and she had *invited* him to do it, like some kind of harlot!

She heard him walking around, opened her eyes to see him strapping on his gun again. "Where are you going?"

"To the bathhouse. We both need to wash, and you'll feel embarrassed doing it here in the room together. I'll be back in a while. You go ahead and try to sleep. I'll make do on the floor. I've slept in worse places."

She rolled onto her back, pulling the flannel sheet up to her neck. "You may sleep in the bed."

He buttoned his shirt a little higher. "I *may*?" He shook his head, a bit of anger coming back into his eyes. "Yes, I suppose I *may* do anything I want. But you aren't ready for that, in spite of what's just happened. You still aren't ready to be a full woman." He pulled on a leather vest, rummaged through his gear and pulled out a pair of clean underwear, rolling it into a towel. "I haven't even begun to show you all the pleasures you deserve, Tess. The next time we do this, you won't turn away from me afterward. In the meantime, I can at least be glad that you think you *could* love me." He put on his hat. "I'll be up and out of your way tomorrow, and you'll have plenty of time to think about all of this. I'll give you full access to my money. You build that little house, start your business, whatever makes you happy and keeps you busy while I'm gone."

He turned and went out the door. *John, wait!* Why

couldn't she open her mouth to say the words? Wearily she got up, looked down at herself, thinking how ridiculous she must look in shoes and socks and an unlaced camisole. What kind of spell had John Hawkins cast on her to make her do what she had just done? She walked to a bowl and pitcher that sat on a stand with a bar of soap and some towels. She washed herself and pulled on clean drawers, removed her camisole and put on a light flannel night-gown, then sat down and removed her shoes and socks.

She stared at the rumpled bed. A man who was her husband had just laid claim to her in that bed. Maybe it was someone else. Maybe she had just dreamed all of it . . . but she had not dreamed the aching desire or the almost painful pleasure she had felt beneath John Hawkins's body. She could not deny the fact that he had made her experience her womanhood in ways she'd never known before.

She brushed the bed and straightened the covers, then lay back down, rubbing her stomach. *As far as I am concerned, Chino never existed. He never touched you and he never fathered a child by you. The baby in your belly is mine!* How strange that such beautiful words could be spoken by a man like John. Who would ever have thought he would care about such a thing? She stared at the ceiling, wondering how he thought she could possibly sleep now. She could only wait, wait for him to return, try to get through the night.

She sat back up and read through the paper. She had not given him the reading lesson they had talked about. This whole day was as unreal as a wild dream. She looked at the plain gold band on her finger that he'd thought to buy for her. She considered everything John Hawkins had said and done so far, and all of it pointed to a man who was truly in love. And the way he had made her feel—sparks of true desire, a willingness to surrender—the magical ways he had touched her, drawing out something no one else had ever created in her soul . . . did that mean she loved him after all?

She heard a tap at the door, heard the turn of a key.

She set the paper aside and climbed back under the blankets. John walked inside, turned, and locked the door again. He glanced at her. "Still awake?"

She looked away. He'd been inside of her. That changed everything between them. He had the advantage now. He could honestly say she had practically begged him to make love to her. That made her angry . . . not with John, but with herself. She didn't know her own mind anymore, didn't know who Tess Carey . . . Hawkins . . . really was. "How can I sleep?"

He sighed and removed his hat, hanging it on a hook. He threw a wadded-up towel in a corner and removed his gun belt. "You'd better try. You're carrying. You need to take care of yourself."

She turned on her side, saying nothing, listened to the sounds of him undressing, other noises that told her he was making up a bed on the floor. "You don't have to do that. You have a right to sleep in this bed."

There was a moment of silence.

"I guess you still don't understand how I feel about you. I thought you did."

"What do you mean?"

"I mean I can't sleep in that bed without wanting you again, plain and simple. I'll take the floor."

She waited. It would all be so much easier if she had fallen in love with him first, if they could have had a normal courtship, if he wasn't so "Indian," so wild, so different from any man she'd ever known. It would all be so different if she knew for certain she loved him, not just that she loved certain things about him, his chivalry, his courage, his willingness to be a father to her baby. She wanted to love him completely, every fiber of him, with joy and utter devotion. She didn't want to let him make love to her simply because it was the most wonderful thing she'd ever experienced or out of pure curiosity, or because she "owed" it to him. But if that was how it had to be for now, then that was how it had to be.

"It's all right. You can sleep in the bed," she repeated. "Don't make me say it any more plainly than that."

She heard a long sigh, followed by a bitter laugh. "Won't work, Tess. I told you how it will be next time. You'll want all of me, my heart, my spirit . . . all of me. It won't be some desperate act of allowing me my husbandly needs, or you just needing me to help you wipe away some other man's horror. And you won't say you *could* love me. You will know it." She heard his movements, another long sigh. "Good night, Mrs. Hawkins."

Tess raised her head to see he was on the floor, turned away from her. She picked up a pillow, suddenly angry and embarrassed that he had turned her down. She threw it at him. "Good night, Mr. Hawkins."

The stress of all the tension from the day, and a mostly sleepless night, caused Tess to fall into a deep, exhausted sleep toward dawn, so that she was not even aware her husband was awake, washed, and dressed. She started to wakefulness when she felt him press her shoulder.

"Wake up, Tess."

Tess sat up, confused for a moment until she remembered where she was or that she was married. She realized a bright sun was shining through the curtains. "What time is it?"

"Around eight, last time I looked at my pocket watch. I'm heading out."

"What!"

"I've got to get going. Ken and I got orders yesterday morning from Captain Booth to head out today for Indian Territory."

"Indian Territory! That's five or six hundred miles away!"

"We've gone that far before. They're having a lot of trouble up in the north central plains, mostly Indians coming south to raid and steal from settlements in northern Texas. They need more Rangers to help put a stop to it."

"But . . ." Tess put a hand to hair, realizing she must look a mess. "You'll be gone for weeks!"

"That's right." He strapped on his gun belt.

"Why didn't you tell me about this yesterday!"

"You had enough to think about. I didn't want it to interfere with more important things."

"More important things?" Tess got up from bed and walked to where her robe hung on a coat stand. She pulled it on. "This is entirely unfair of you. Not only do you not tell me about this, but you don't even wake me in time to bid you a decent goodbye! We could at least have gone to have breakfast somewhere. I can't even walk outside with you."

"It's all right." He finished packing his gear. "People will just think my wife is too worn out from her wedding night to get up this early."

Tess rolled her eyes at his sarcasm. "Please don't be this way."

"What way?"

She rubbed at her eyes. "Angry. I don't want you to leave angry."

John put on his hat and threw his saddlebags over his shoulder, facing her. "I'm not angry." He walked closer, touching her cheek with the back of his hand. "You have plenty of time to think about us, Tess. I hope last night helped you see how it can be between us."

She dropped her eyes, still surprised with herself for her behavior.

"It wasn't wrong, so quit acting like it was. The only wrong thing about it was you still don't love the real John Hawkins. The next time I bed you, it will because you love me the way a real wife loves her husband."

"I don't want you to go."

"It's best I *am* gone for a while. We both know it. You're a strong woman, Tess Hawkins. I figure I'll come back to find you doing just fine on your own. And by then maybe you'll be healed from your experience with the Comancheros." He leaned down and kissed her cheek. "I've made arrangements at the bank. You have full access to my money. So now I have made you my wife in every legal way. The only thing I still don't own is your heart. Maybe you'll be more ready to give that when I get back."

Tess could not help the tears. "I'm sorry."

"For what? For giving me the most pleasure I've ever had with a woman? For letting me call the prettiest woman in Texas my wife?" He squeezed her shoulder and turned to pick up his bedroll and a canvas duster and a rifle. "Don't be sorry for anything, Tess. I'll see you in two or three months."

Months! There was so much she should have said. "My God, this isn't right. What if something happens to you?"

He opened the door and faced her. "If something happens to me, use the rest of my money however you need it." He turned and left, and Tess went to the door, watched him go down the stairs. She ran to a window then, looked down on the street below. Ken was there with the horses. John tied on his gear and mounted up, shoving his rifle into its boot. Tess thought how she loved that golden horse he rode. He glanced up at the window and tipped his hat, turned his horse, and rode off with Ken.

Tess watched until she couldn't see him anymore. She let the tears come then. "I do love you, John," she sobbed. "I do."

Chapter Eighteen

"You gonna talk about it?"

"No."

Ken shrugged. "Fine. Just don't be in no sour mood this whole trip. We've been on the trail for six days, rode the train three before that, and you've hardly spoke the whole time. It ain't no fun ridin' with you when you're in a sour mood. Sometimes it's bad enough when you're in a *good* mood."

John waited several minutes before speaking again. "I'm not in a sour mood. I just have a lot to think about."

"Like wishin' you was back in El Paso with your new wife. The weddin' night must have been better than you thought it would be."

"My wedding night is none of your business."

"It is if it affects you so's you do somethin' stupid and careless when we're on the tail of a bunch of thievin' Indians."

"It won't affect my work."

Ken adjusted his hat. "I just don't want to have to go back and tell your wife she's a widow again. That woman has been through enough." He buttoned his denim jacket a little higher. "This is pretty cool weather compared to what we've been havin'."

"It's always cooler on the high plains." She was so far away now. So far away. Had he actually married Tess Carey? Actually bedded her? The whole thing seemed like a mystic dream. How would she feel about him when he got back? Would she let him make love to her again? He would have done so again that night, but he wanted to hear her say she loved him with true passion and sincerity; and he wanted to be able to wake up with her the next morning, every morning after that for a while, spend lots of time with her. But he wanted that only when she was truly ready for it, truly ready to love again. He never thought leaving would be this hard, that he would miss her this much.

"Well, it's gettin' on September, too. Pretty soon it will cool down some back in El Paso. As for as that wife of yours, she's a tough cookie. She'll do just fine while you're gone."

"I suppose." John glanced sidelong at his friend. "To solve that damn nagging question I know is in the back of your mind, yes, she's my wife in every way, legally and physically. That's all I'm going to say about it."

Ken raised his eyebrows. "Well, I ain't surprised. She cares more about you than most people suspect. And you ain't exactly the ugliest thing that ever walked."

"It didn't have anything to do with my looks or ..." John threw the stub of his cigar into the dirt. "I said I didn't want to talk about it. From now on, for the rest of this trip, the subject is closed, understood?"

Ken nodded. "Fine. At least talk to me about other things. It's a bitch ridin' all this way with a man who's so lost in thought he don't talk at all."

John drew his horse to a halt. "All right. Do you still think Jim Caldwell could be involved with some of the cattle rustling back home?"

Ken frowned, turning his horse a little to face John more squarely. "I don't think I ever said that's what I thought.

All's I said was it seemed strange to me the way he is always after your ass, the way he was all upset about Briggs.''

''That's the same as saying you think he was *involved* with Briggs.''

Ken grinned with a hint of sarcasm. ''Well, if you hadn't gone and blown Briggs clear into the next county, maybe we could have found out, couldn't we?''

John sighed. ''All right. When we get back home I promise to try to leave a few of those we go after alive. And you're right. There is nobody left to question.''

''There will be if the rustlin' starts up again. If Caldwell is into somethin' like that, he'll start again.''

John nodded. ''I'm going to find out, Ken. Before I quit the Rangers, I'm going to prove Jim Caldwell is a liar and a thief.''

''Well, you just be careful about that. For one thing, it ain't part of our mission. You're on a personal vendetta that could get you booted out of the Rangers, let alone goin' up against somebody like Caldwell. You gotta have some pretty damn good proof for somethin' like that.''

''I'll get it.'' John started riding again. ''And I'll do it on my own. I don't want you involved, since it won't be official Ranger business.''

''Where you're concerned, I'm always involved.''

John grinned. ''You're a good friend, but you stay out of this one.''

''No promises.''

''We'll leave it at that. Right now we have our work cut out for us here. Anyway, if there is going to be any more rustling done, it probably won't be till spring, but I intend to check out some of Caldwell's herds when we get back, study some of the brands and see if they've been altered.''

''Yeah, well, you just watch your back if you're gonna' mess with Caldwell.''

''That's why I want you to stay out of it.''

Ken pulled his hat farther down on his forehead as a stiff wind began to turn even cooler. ''You just remember you're a husband now, and you'll be a father soon enough. Don't go gettin' yourself killed now of all times.''

John looked over at him and grinned. "You know I'm too mean to die." He kicked Sundance into a harder run. "Let's get up to the Red River and get this job over with."

His last words were lost as he charged ahead of Ken. "Too mean to die, that's a fact," Ken muttered. "Maybe Tess Hawkins can take some of that meanness out of you." He had a feeling that whatever had happened on Hawk's wedding night, it had for the time being only made him meaner.

The quilting bee was at the home of Louise Jeffers, whose husband owned the feed store. Tess had paid him to build her house in town. Louise usually ran the store while her husband and their two sons did carpenter work, and between the two of them, they were considered moderately wealthy by El Paso standards. Their home just north of town was a large, two-story frame house with a porch that wrapped around all four sides, a place to spend hot summer days. But it was November now, and although winter was seldom severe here, it could get very cold.

Today was one of those days. Tess wrapped her velvet cape tighter around herself, wondering if it was the chill in the air that bothered her or her own chill at having to face all the most respected women in town, including Harriet Caldwell. A stiff wind whipped up sand, and she ducked her head against its sting as she went up the steps to the wide veranda, thinking how difficult it often was to keep anything really clean in this part of Texas. Louise obviously was trying, but her freshly painted, white clapboard home already showed layers of dust along the slanted edge of each board, and the slots of the green shutters at the windows showed the same.

She knocked at the fancy oak door, admiring the beveled oval glass and the lace curtain that covered it on the inside. The door opened, and Louise greeted her rather stiffly, but smiling. She was a short stout lady, who always walked straight as a stick. Her graying hair was folded up at the sides and twisted into a bun at the back, and she wore a lovely day dress, gray with a biblike insert of white lace at the bodice. Tess felt a little better about being there. She had made the dress herself, and was proud of her work.

"Well, I am glad you decided to come, Tess."

Tess wondered if she really meant it. "I appreciate the invitation." She looked the woman over. "The dress looks lovely on you."

Louise smiled, losing some of her aloofness. "Thank you. You do fine work, and I have been telling the other ladies about it. I think you will have a lot more business after today."

"Thank you, Louise." Tess stepped inside, hanging her cape on a coat rack just inside the hallway. "I need the work."

"Well, there are some who highly disapprove of your marriage, dear, including me, but what's done is done. Who of us knows what we would do in the same situation. The fact remains, you are an excellent seamstress. Why should we waste our money spending three times as much ordering dresses from New York and waiting two months to get them when you can make the same garments in two weeks?"

Tess forced back her ire over the first remark. Who were they to tell her whom she should marry? She had never been close to any of them, had always been too busy on the farm to do much socializing. Why should they suddenly take an interest in her personal life? "Well, I am glad you understand the value of using my services. The work keeps me busy, and I certainly need to, with John gone."

She followed Louise into the parlor, where a rack was set up and a quilt stretched across it. Seven women sat around the rack, each one working on a different patch. They all looked up when Tess entered the room, and she could read their thoughts. What was it like being married to a man of Indian blood, a wild, sometimes violent man who was as lawless as those he hunted? The trouble was, she couldn't really say what it was like being married to John Hawkins. She had spent only one night with him. That was over two months ago. The only thing she knew was that one night had left a hot brand on her as real as if he'd set a branding iron against her buttocks. She belonged to John Hawkins now, totally. She just wasn't sure how she felt about that.

The ladies greeted her with varied expressions—smiles, frowns, raised eyebrows, friendly greetings—some saying nothing. Harriet Caldwell returned to her stitching as though to ignore her completely. Louise showed Tess a chair, positioned at one corner of the quilt. She handed her some swatches of material, needle, and thread.

"Ladies, we should all watch how Tess Hawkins wields a needle. We might learn something. She will probably sew two patches to our one."

Tess felt a little embarrassed, and some of the women seemed to warm a little at the comment.

"Louise's dress is lovely," Rachael Patterson told her. Rachael was the young wife of the bank manager, a very pretty woman with light hair and green eyes. "I definitely want you to make some things for me."

"I would be glad to do it," Tess answered. "I need to keep busy. It helps me not to worry so much about my husband."

She shouldn't worry. She shouldn't even care. But she did, more every day that John was gone. If something happened to him, she would never forgive herself for not making his wedding night a little more memorable. She had let him make love to her—and never had she known such pleasure—but she had quickly turned her heart from him again, refusing to admit to her feelings. Why was she being so stubborn about it? Why couldn't she get over the feeling it had been wrong to enjoy having the man in her bed?

Her remark caused all of them to look at her, and she could read their questions. "You are all wondering about my marriage," she said, deciding to get the uneasy situation over with. "I had no one. When Mr. Hawkins rescued me from the Comancheros, he was very kind to me. We had a lot of time to talk, and we became good friends. He . . . expressed certain feelings for me. He is not the cruel, hardened man you all think he is. He is just a man who has a job to do, and he does it very well. He also wants the same thing all men his age want, a wife and family. In spite of the fact that I was not . . . violated . . . by the Comancheros . . ." Did they believe that? ". . . I knew the few available single men in these parts would hesitate to take me for a wife. Mr. Hawkins, however, knows the truth—that I was untouched. And he expressed a desire to marry me."

She began threading her needle, needing to look away from their curious stares. "In these parts a woman is better off not being alone. So I married Mr. Hawkins, and he is a surprisingly gentle and sincere man, in spite of what all of you have seen of him. In fact . . ." Should she tell them? Yes, this was the perfect time. They had to believe the baby was John's. "I am with child."

A round of gasps circled the quilting frame, and several of the women broke into smiles.

"Congratulations, Tess," Louise told her.

Tess ignored the cold disapproval of some, who she supposed considered her nothing more than a harlot for marrying a wild man like John Hawkins, a man only women like Jenny Simms would go to bed with.

"Thank you," she answered. She began sewing her patch.

"I will bring a tray of tea for everyone," Louise announced.

They all sewed quietly for a few tense seconds, until Harriet spoke up. "You say a woman should not be alone in these parts, yet here you are alone anyway," she told Tess. "What good did it do to marry someone like that wild Texas Ranger? Where is he now? He certainly is not at his wife's side, and Rangers make hardly enough to feed themselves, let alone a family.''

Tess struggled against a growing anger. "My husband intends to quit the Rangers," she answered calmly. *After he proves your own husband is a cattle thief!* "We are going to rebuild at my farm, and he will begin ranching."

"John Hawkins? Settle down into a normal life?" Harriet sniffed. "You will be very lucky if he even returns from this trip. He could quit the Rangers while he is someplace else and just keep on riding right out of your life."

"Harriet! There is no call for such talk. You'll upset Mrs. Hawkins, and she's carrying now." The words were spoken by Bess Johndrow, a young woman with four small children who were playing behind Louise's house. Tess could hear their squealing even with the windows closed against the chilly air.

"I am not going to faint or lose my baby over ignorant remarks," Tess told them. Her eyes, however, were on Harriet, and tenseness filled the room for a quiet moment as Harriet reddened.

"I think you owe Tess Hawkins an apology," Rachael told Harriet. "The woman has been through enough. She has married John Hawkins, and that is that."

Tess wanted to get up and leave, but she decided she would damn well stay. At least one of these women was sticking up for her, and they seemed convinced her baby was John's. "Thank you, Rachael," she said quietly.

"You are a fine seamstress," Louise added, "and one of El Paso's pioneers, just as much as any of us. I invited you here because you live in town now and certainly ought to be part of our gatherings. We have never had the chance to get to know you well, Tess. Personally I am very sorry about the tragedy with your father and first husband and the awful terror you must have suffered at the hands of those . . . Comancheros. We all fear such a thing could happen to us." She looked at Harriet. "Well, are you going to apologize?"

Harriet sighed and looked at Tess. "I will only say that

I hope I am wrong in my opinion of John Hawkins, for your sake," she answered, looking at Tess. "As far as I am concerned, the man is a discredit to the Rangers, in spite of his ability to find the thieves and killers he hunts. The Rangers must cease being considered nothing more than vigilantes. That is part of the reason for this gathering."

"Yes," Louise put in. "We have decided to do all we can to further civilize Texas, Tess. We have already written to the headquarters of two different church denominations, Methodist and Baptist. Heaven knows there are enough Catholic missions around here. The Mexican influence is everywhere, and I suppose that has its place. But it is the Americans who have been building Texas into the great state she is, since the thirties. We need churches here, and a decent school. We will also be bringing in more teachers, and hope to teach English to a larger number of the Mexican children. I hope you do convince Mr. Hawkins to go into ranching and make him settle into a normal life. As for the rest of the Rangers, they will simply have to be more law-abiding themselves."

Tess set her needle aside. "I suppose they will," she answered, facing them all. "But I assure you, the kind of men they go after would kill any of you in the blink of an eye for money. When you go after men like that, you can't give much thought to being nice about it. I've seen firsthand what they are like. They murdered my husband and father. They would have sold me off in Mexico to God knows what kind of horror. Mr. Hawkins had no choice but to kill them in order to get me out of there."

"There have been other situations in which it was unnecessary for him to kill the men he went after," Harriet put in. "The man often behaves no better than those he goes after. When stories get out about things like that, it makes Texas look bad. We intend to improve our image."

Tess could well imagine how devastated the woman would be if she knew the truth about her own husband. "I have no argument with that," she answered. "But I will not sit here and listen to my husband be insulted. He is a better man than any of you know, and it is men like John Hawkins who have made it possible for people like us to live here." More and more she was realizing that her feelings for John were growing deeper.

"We are not ungrateful for the things men like Mr. Hawkins have done for Texas," Rachael said. "We are just saying that change is in order."

Tess picked up the needle again. "I agree. I just find it very strange, Harriet, that your husband would be more concerned about the death of cattle thieves than he is about our own Texas Rangers."

The room quieted again as Harriet stiffened. "Whatever do you mean?"

Tess shrugged. If only they all knew what she'd heard. "Mr. Caldwell was furious when he heard John had killed that gang of rustlers headed by someone called Derrek Briggs. Why should he care? Texas should be glad to be rid of them. There has been a rash of rustling going on all over west Texas. Maybe now it will end, or at least not be quite so bad, thanks to John. But your husband was angry about it and insulted him. It seemed very strange to me."

Harriet held her chin defiantly. "Jim was only angry because of the vigilante-style execution your husband used. He is one of those heading the movement to give Texas a better reputation for being civilized. Blowing men up inside a cabin without giving them a chance to surrender is as *un*civilized an act as any I could think of."

Tess suddenly had to force back an urge to laugh. She could just picture John blowing those outlaws out of that cabin. Only John Hawkins would pull a stunt like that. Before her abduction she would have been entirely against such a thing herself, but now she was not so sure it was such a bad thing to do after all. Derrek Briggs had raped a little Indian girl. Why *shouldn't* he be blown to pieces? But then these women probably would not think raping an Indian child was so bad. John knew that. That was why no one knew the truth behind his deed.

"I suppose it was quite uncivilized," she answered. "But then none of us was there. Who are we to say he didn't do what needed doing?"

Louise quickly guided the conversation to another topic, sensing the animosity between Tess Hawkins and Harriet Cooper was not going to end soon. She got the women talking about selling their quilts and having a bake sale to raise money to contribute to the coffer being set up for a new church, whatever denomination it might be. Most of the women were starved for any kind of Protestant faith, to be able to go to church. The room was soon filled with so much gabbing that at first they did not even hear the knock at the door.

Someone pounded harder, and Louise left them to go to the door. She quickly returned for Tess. "It's that partner of your husband's, Ken Randall," she told her. "Oh, my dear, I'm afraid something has happened to your husband. He says you should come right away!"

Tess tucked her needle into the quilt and quickly rose, hurrying out into the hallway to see a dusty, tired-looking Ken standing just inside the door. "Somebody in town told me you'd be here," he said. "You've got to come to the house, Tess. I just took John there. He's bad hurt. The doc's with him now."

"Oh, dear!" Tess's chest tightened with dread. She had actually looked forward to John's return. There was so much she wanted to tell him. What if he died before she got the chance? She wrapped her shawl around her shoulders and turned to Louise. "I must leave. Tell the other women for me."

"Of course, dear. I hope Mr. Hawkins will be all right. I'll tell Mary Sanders her husband is at your house doctoring your husband."

"Yes, thank you. And thank you for inviting me to the quilting. Anything I can do to help with your projects, just let me know." She hurried out with Ken before Louise could answer. Why did this have to happen now? All the danger John had faced, and as far as she knew he'd never been seriously hurt. Why now? Oh, God, she loved him! She actually loved him! "How bad is it, Ken?"

"Real bad, I'm afraid. Shot in the back from far off. I couldn't see nothin'. It was like somebody was just out to execute him."

"My God," Tess whispered, tears stinging her eyes. One night. They'd had one night together, and as beautiful as it was at the time, it had turned into disaster before John left. She would never forgive herself for that if he died now.

Chapter Nineteen

Tess sat watching her husband, feeling helpless. It seemed incredible that a man like John Hawkins could be lying near death. To see him this way made her realize how she truly felt about him. There was so much to say, and she hoped she would get the chance to say it. The man had married her just to give her child a name, with no promises from her to ever truly love him. How many men would give up their freedom like that for a woman who could give them nothing in return but a child that was not even his own?

For all his ruthlessnes, there was a goodness about him she was growing to love. If only he would wake up . . . live . . . so she could tell him. He'd been shot in the back. The bullet had passed through a lung, and the doctor said there was little anyone could do but wait and hope the lung would heal, as well as the damaged muscle and broken rib around the lung. There was no bullet to remove, but there had been a lot of internal bleeding. John's chest was horribly bruised, and an ugly hole at the front of it had been stitched.

Poor Ken was beside himself. He had been near tears

several times, and Tess decided that such loyalty only proved John was a much better man than most people gave him credit for. "He's saved my hide more than once," Ken had told her. "Risked his own life doin' it. We've been in a lot of fixes, near to got our heads blown off a hundred times; but this . . . this was about as low-down and unfair as a man can get. Back-shot! We had some dangerous run-ins up in Indian Territory, got through all that, got all the way back home, and now this happens here. If I ever get hold of the son-of-a-bitch who did this, I'll slit his throat!"

What made Tess sick at heart was the fact that this had happened after John had paid a visit to Jim Caldwell's ranch, asking questions. Caldwell was behind this, no doubt about it.

The door to their small bedroom opened, and Ken looked inside. "Any change?"

Tess swallowed against a lump in her throat. "No. He just . . . lies there . . . groans once in a while, but he hasn't opened his eyes." She put her head in her hands.

"It helps, you bein' here, talkin' to him, touchin' him. He knows. He feels it. If he's gonna' pull through this, it will be for you, Tess. All he talked about comin' back was how he'd missed you and hoped you could have a real marriage when he got back. Fact is, that's a little bit the reason this happened."

Tess raised her head and looked at him with tear-filled eyes. "What do you mean?"

Ken came inside and removed his hat, hooking it on the back of a wooden chair across the bed from where Tess sat. He sat down. "Well, the one thing he wants to do before quittin' the Rangers is prove Jim Caldwell is involved in cattle rustlin'. That was why we paid the man a visit before comin' back here, just kind of lookin' around the place, seein' how Caldwell reacted to us bein' there. 'Course we didn't tell *him* why we was there. We told him we was just passin' through on our way back here and wondered if he'd had any trouble with rustlers. We'd checked with a couple other ranchers who told us the trouble seemed to be startin' up again. On our way off Caldwell's ranch, we checked the brands on some of his cattle just for the hell of it. Everything seemed fine, till we got about a mile off his place, then bam. A rifle shot from way up in the hills. I jumped down, and Hawk, he fell off his horse. I could see he was bad hurt, so there wasn't time for me to go chargin' over to where I think the shot came from. I never saw nobody, no horse, no nothin'. It all happened so fast, and for no reason."

Tess sighed with sickening guilt. "This is my fault, Ken. You should be as angry with me as you are with whoever did this." She put her head back and closed her eyes, a tear slipping down her cheek. "I have a feeling I can name exactly who shot John."

Ken frowned. "What are you talkin' about?"

She brushed at the tear. "I have never liked Jim Caldwell myself. He often harassed my father about selling out to him. And his wife is rude and arrogant." Tess rubbed at her eyes. "Anyway, my carrying is not the only reason I left Caldwell's employ. I couldn't have stayed even if I wasn't going to have a baby."

"Why is that? Because of *Mrs.* Caldwell, I expect. There's a witch if I ever saw one."

Tess shook her head. "It wasn't just because of Harriet either." She looked at John. Instead of his normally robust, sun-browned coloring, he had a sick gray look to him. She reached out and touched his hand, still astounded to see such a big, strong, daring man lying so near death. "I . . . should have told him," she said, the tears wanting to come again. She sniffed and swallowed. "I should have told both of you what I heard."

Ken leaned forward, resting his elbows on his knees. "What did you hear? What ain't you told us, Tess?"

Tess watched John as she spoke. "I didn't sleep very well after I knew about . . . the baby." She touched her stomach with her free hand. She was a little over four months along now, but her waist was just beginning to swell. "I was lying awake, trying to decide what to do. It was about two A.M.

I was so restless that I decided to go downstairs and make myself some tea, but when I got down the stairs, I heard voices, men's voices." She turned her gaze then to Ken, studying his gray eyes. "It made me curious, voices at that hour of the morning. I determined they came from Jim Caldwell's study and went down the hall, noticed the door was shut. I suppose I had no right, but I couldn't help leaning close to listen."

She closed her eyes again, rising from her chair. "I heard Mr. Caldwell say something about John Hawkins being too good at what he does. He said he was worried John would someday track someone's stolen cattle right to his ranch. He said he hoped John would . . . would get himself killed or he would find a way to get him hanged. He said John's killing Derrek Briggs had foiled some of his plans, something like that, said maybe he could find some new men in Indian Territory. He said he would have to lay low for a while, said something about someone doing a good job of altering the brands on the cattle they bring in."

"Damn!" Ken muttered. He also rose. "Why in hell didn't you *say* somethin'!"

Tess shook her head. "Who in this town or in all of Texas would believe it? Everyone knows Jim Caldwell has wanted my father's land since we first came here. They would think I was making it up. It would have been my word against Jim Caldwell's, the word of a grieving widow who people think turned a little bit crazy after being abducted by Comancheros, a woman who has had problems in the past with Jim Caldwell. And God only knows what kind of stories Caldwell would have made up about me! You can't go accusing someone like that of such a crime without good, solid proof, and I knew he would never be stupid enough to allow any kind of proof to be found anyplace in his papers or on his land. What good would it have done to say anything?"

Ken frowned, running a hand through his hair. "But . . . surely John mentioned his suspicions to you. Surely you knew he might go try to investigate Caldwell himself. He should have been warned!"

"I know that now!" Tears started coming again. "I didn't tell John because I suspected he'd go storming onto Caldwell's ranch and risk his life trying to prove it. And I knew he would find nothing. He would only anger Jim Caldwell even more against him, make unnecessary trouble for himself. You know how he is."

"He ain't that stupid, Tess. Sure, he risks his life, but he'd have known in that case to be extra careful. Now he's gone and got himself shot anyway."

Tess turned away, no longer able to stop the tears. "Damn it!" She sniffed. "He'll probably . . . never forgive me . . . if he lives through this! And neither will you, whether he lives or dies. I'll never forgive myself. I just . . . I thought it was the best thing to do. I'm so sorry!" She pulled a handkerchief from where it was stuck into the sash at the waist of her dress and used it to blow her nose and wipe her eyes. "I had so many . . . plans . . . for when he returned. So much to . . . tell him . . . about how I feel . . . how I missed him. Now this. He . . . married me to give my baby a father . . . and now he might not even live to see the baby."

"Oh, now wait a minute." Ken walked around the bed and came over to put a hand on her shoulder. "I'm sorry myself. I guess I can understand why you did it. Don't be cryin'. It ain't good you gettin' all upset." He took his hand away and paced a little. "Me and Hawk—we've both told you he's too mean to die, so quit talkin' about him dyin'. That ain't gonna' happen unless . . . well, unless he decides himself that it's a good day to die. That's what he always tells me. That's an Indian sayin', you know, decidin' when it's a good day to die."

He rested a hand on the bedpost at the head of the bed, looking down at John. "And don't think he won't forgive you. If he sees in your eyes that you really love him, want him to live and want to be a real . . . well, you know . . . a real wife to him, ain't nothin' you could do that he wouldn't forgive. It's for that same reason that he'll live, so you just concentrate on that. When he's well enough, you can tell him the rest of it. I'll do some scoutin' around myself in the meantime.''

"No!" Tess quickly wiped at her eyes again. "Please don't, Ken. If you go and get yourself killed over this, then he *surely* would never forgive me, nor could I live with it. Please promise you'll stay away from there until John is well and you can decide together what to do.''

Ken sighed, facing her. "You said earlier you could probably guess who actually shot John. You think it was Caldwell?''

She walked around to the foot of the bed. "No. I . . . embarrassing as it is to tell you how snoopy I was, I knelt down and looked through the keyhole. Believe it or not, one of the men in the study with Caldwell was our illustrious sheriff, Sam Higgins.''

"Higgins!"

Tess saw the anger rising in his eyes. "The other man in the office was Caldwell's foreman, Casey Dunlap. I could tell by the snakeskin boots he wore. I've never seen boots like that on any other man around here.'' She turned away. "He . . . I heard him offer to take care of John Hawkins. He said he could hunt him down, that he was a good aim.'' She shook her head, still riddled with guilt. "I guess I just never thought he'd really do it. Caldwell told him no, that he didn't want to get into a mess like that, bringing an investigation by Texas Rangers. It's possible, if Dunlap did do it, he didn't have Caldwell's permission. Caldwell is probably furious with him right now, if he's heard about this.''

"Oh, I expect he's heard about it, all right. And after what *you* heard, it's a good bet it *was* Dunlap who did this. One thing you're right about is tryin' to prove it. My problem is decidin' whether or not to tell Captain Booth what you heard or to just keep quiet and wait till John recovers, tell him about it first.''

Tess wiped at more tears. "I don't know the answer. I only know you need real proof."

Ken shook his head. "We don't even have a bullet for evidence, in order to tell what kind of rifle it came from. It passed right through him, and I sure as hell couldn't take the time to try to find it. All I could think of was gettin' John out of there and gettin' him some help."

Tess walked to a washbowl and wet a rag, walking around to lay it on John's fevered brow. "You did the only thing you could do, Ken. Thank God you got him here when you did, and thank God you were with him. If he'd have gone out there alone, he would have lain there and died before anyone knew what had happened."

Ken studied John quietly, thinking how strange it would be riding with the Rangers without John Hawkins at his side. Even if John lived, he'd lose him as a partner . . . to Tess Hawkins. God knew he'd quit the Rangers himself if he could find a woman like that.

"Well, it's done now. And if anybody can pull him through, it's you."

Tess wiped at perspiration on John's face. "I hope you're right, Ken."

Ken cleared his throat. "I, uh, I have to ask you. I promised Jenny I would."

Tess met his eyes. "She wants to come and see him?"

He rubbed at the back of his neck. "Yeah."

Tess experienced the sting of jealousy again. "Then by all means, tell her to come. Maybe there is something she can say that will help. Maybe the love of *two* women will help." She looked back at John. "I know she loves him in her own way. And I am beginning to understand why. After he left, I . . . I began to realize just how deep John's feelings run, in spite of that careless attitude of his, all his pretending to be so hard and unfeeling. How many men would do what he did for me? He isn't near the savage he pretends to be."

"Oh, he can be savage, all right, but not with a woman.

Never with a woman." Ken sighed and headed for the door. "I'll go talk to Jenny."

Tess turned. "I'm sorry, Ken, for not telling both of you what I heard. I thought I was protecting John."

Ken glanced from her to John. "Sure." He turned and left, and Tess sat down carefully on the edge of the bed. She leaned close, touched his face.

"Can you hear me, John? It's Tess." Her throat ached. "I love you, John Hawkins. Don't you dare die on me."

He groaned, but his eyes did not open, and she wasn't sure if he heard her at all.

Tess grimaced as she took the soiled bandages from Jenny. She dropped them into a pan. "I couldn't keep doing this without your help," she told the woman.

"You know I'm glad to do it," Jenny answered. "You do the rewrapping. I'll take the job of rolling him some way to get the bandages around him. It will require a little lifting, and you shouldn't be doing that."

Tess cut some gauze and leaned over John's naked torso.

"Here," Jenny said, grunting then as she shoved a pillow under John's hips. "We'll lift him a little this way. Then you pass the gauze under him and I'll bring it over and you take it again. We'll wrap him good and tight. Maybe that will help his rib, too."

Tess nodded. She held one end of the gauze and brought it over the wound, sick at the sight of how bruised he still was. "I hope the internal bleeding hasn't started up again. I just wish he would open his eyes and let me know he can hear me." She handed the gauze under him, and Jenny took it, bringing it around. Tess took it and pulled it over the top of the first piece to hold it in place, then passed it under him again.

"He'll come around." Jenny took the gauze again. "You sure you don't mind how this looks, me being here so much?"

"I don't care about that. I know in my heart my husband

is a far better man than Harriet Caldwell's. All her pride and arrogance and wealth doesn't make her any better than I. At least I've done nothing wrong, and neither has John. Besides, his life is all that matters right now. You were a good friend. If your presence might help, then I want you here." She took the gauze and brought it around again. "And who else could I have come over here and work over John Hawkins's naked body? Certainly not any of the other women of this town, except maybe some of the Mexican women. They would understand this. The others would faint dead away." She passed the gauze under him again. "I decided that since there is nothing here you haven't already seen, why not you?"

Jenny laughed. "Well, that's smart thinking." She met Tess's eyes as she handed the gauze over again, and her smile faded, her eyes tearing. "You know I love him too, don't you?"

Tess felt the familiar pain in her heart. "I know." She took the gauze, and the two of them continued wrapping. "We just love him in different ways, and I suppose he loves you, too, in a special way. I just don't intend for him to ever have to come to you for . . . physical satisfaction again. I will give him all he needs."

Jenny grinned again, in spite of the tear that slipped out of one eye. "Well, I'm sure he'd be glad to hear that."

Neither of them noticed a hint of a smile on John's lips. "Did you . . . I mean . . . how was the wedding night?"

Tess cut the gauze and tucked in the loose end. "I am his wife in every way, if that's what you mean." She straightened. "I decided he deserved that much. But afterward I felt . . . I don't know . . . foolish, guilty."

"Guilty?"

"I shouldn't have . . . wanted him. It seemed so wrong. I decided I had just acted out of duty. The worst part was . . . I enjoyed it. I would never tell anyone that but you. No one else would understand."

Jenny put her hands on her hips. "I can't imagine any woman being with John and *not* enjoying it."

Tess covered John. "Please don't, Jenny. It wasn't just that John was still practically a stranger. It was the fact that I'd been . . . soiled and abused by Chino. For a moment I could see him hovering over me. It just didn't seem right that I could want a man at all."

Jenny wiped at the tear and came closer. "I'm sorry. I can understand what you're saying."

Tess folded her arms nervously. "I wanted to . . . I don't know . . . it was a way of helping me pretend John really could be the father of this baby. I guess what I felt most guilty about was the fact that he told me he loved me, but I couldn't say the same, not with the same sincerity. Now I'm afraid I'll never get the chance."

"Oh, you'll get the chance, all right."

Tess pushed a piece of hair behind her ear, thinking what a tired, soiled mess she must be. "Do you think he'll be terribly angry with me for not telling him about what I heard Jim Caldwell saying?"

"Oh, he might at first. But he'll understand why you kept quiet. He'll get over it because he loves you."

Tess faced her. "Don't you say a word to anyone about it until Ken and John decide what to do."

"Honey, I'm no fool. One thing I *will* do, though, is keep my eyes and ears open. Men tend to brag and say things they shouldn't say when they're drunk. Maybe I'll hear something that could be useful, now that I know what to listen for." She turned back to the bed. "Why don't you go lie down on the lounge in your parlor? I'll give him his bath by myself this time. I can handle it."

"Are you sure?" Tess rubbed at an aching neck. It was John's fifth day here, and she had tended him nearly around the clock. The doctor had done all he could, and this was the second time Jenny had come today. She noticed the woman had dressed demurely in a simple calico with a high neckline, a sign of respect for her. "I do so much appreciate the help, Jenny. The doctor said this could go on indefinitely, and you were the only one I could think of who could probably handle this without fainting dead away."

"Like I said, it's no problem. I'm glad you asked me. I was worried sick." She came around beside Tess and led her out into the main room, which served as both parlor and sewing room. The simple home consisted of only four rooms, the main room, a kitchen, dining room and one bedroom. "You go lay down like I said," Jenny told her. "We'll work in shifts. You sleep a while, and then you can take over for me. My bartender will take care of the saloon."

"All right." Tess faced her. "What if he dies, Jenny? How will I ever forgive myself?"

"He won't die. And you only did what you thought was best."

Tess squeezed Jenny's arm. "Thank you, Jenny."

Jenny shrugged. "I'm the one who is grateful." She left Tess to go into the kitchen and take a kettle of hot water off the iron cookstove Tess had only recently received after it being on order for weeks. Carrying the kettle into the bedroom, she poured some of the hot water into a bowl, then mixed a little cool water from a pitcher into it. She pulled the blanket away and gently pulled the pillow out from under John's hips and set it aside, then gasped when she turned back to notice he had opened his eyes. She leaned closer. "John," she whispered. "Are you conscious? Do you know me?"

Pain showed in his eyes, but he managed a little grin. "Not fair . . . you giving me a . . . bath. I'm . . . a married man."

Jenny grinned. "You devil, you," she said softly. "You *do* know me. How long have you been conscious?"

He grimaced. "Long enough . . . to hear my wife say . . . she enjoyed being in my bed, and to . . . hear you both say . . . you love me. Maybe I should . . . live with . . . both of you."

Jenny smiled her familiar crooked smile. "You're such a bastard, John Hawkins. You never did play fair." She covered him again and walked to the door, calling for Tess. "Your man is awake."

Tess had barely settled down when she heard the welcome words. Her heart raced with hope as she hurried into the bedroom. She leaned over John to see his eyes were still open. "John! Thank God! How do you feel?" She turned to Jenny. "Go get the doctor, Jenny. We'll give him his bath after the doctor has seen him."

Jenny fought her own tears. "Sure. I'll get him right away." She took her shawl from where it hung over the foot of the iron bed and left, and Tess leaned closer to John again.

"You're going to be all right. God surely wouldn't take you from me now."

He gritted his teeth against pain as he managed to raise one hand to touch her face. "Missed you, Tess . . ."

She grasped his wrist and kissed his palm. "And I missed you," she whispered. "I love you, John Hawkins. I love you!"

John watched her beautiful blue eyes, and he could see she really meant it this time. He wanted to answer, had so much to say, but already he was too tired to speak. One thing was sure, just hearing those words was all he needed to get better—fast.

Chapter Twenty

Tess thumbed through one of several books she had purchased from a drummer who had come to town only days before John was shot. *"The Adventures of Tom Sawyer, by Mark Twain,"* she muttered. From what she'd read so far, it certainly seemed to be a story someone like John would appreciate, especially since he had spent part of his growing-up years on a riverboat.

Setting the book in her lap, she watched John again with deep concern, agonizing over the endless waiting. Since that first time he'd seemed lucid four days ago, he had again slipped in and out of consciousness and into deep sleeps. This morning, for the first time, he'd had no fever, and some of the bruising about his chest was beginning to fade. She reached out to touch his brow again, and he opened his eyes.

"John! I didn't know you were awake." She leaned forward in her chair. "How do you feel?"

He drew a deep breath and put a hand to his head. "A little more normal. It doesn't hurt so much to breathe."

"You were shot through the lung, you know."

He rubbed at his eyes. "I seem to remember hearing

someone say that. Everything I've heard has been like a strange dream." He glanced at the book on her lap. "You been reading?"

Tess leaned back and picked up the book. "I bought it from a traveling salesman. I thought I would read to you once you were more alert and on the mend. Maybe that will stimulate your interest in learning to read better yourself."

He closed his eyes again for a moment. "You're determined to civilize me, aren't you?"

She moved her chair closer. "Something like that. But I must say, you are more civilized than some around here who profess to be our best citizens." She swallowed, looking down at the book. "There is something I have to tell you, John, but first, is there anything you want? Something hot to drink? Another bath? Something to eat?"

He grimaced as he tried to scoot up to a sitting position. "Just help me . . . get up."

She set the book aside and hurriedly took the pillows to stack them behind him. "I don't think you should be doing this."

"I have to. I've lain here long enough, and you've been caring for me like a damn baby."

"John, you've been very sick, near to death. There were a couple of times when the doctor thought you *had* died! When you love someone you do what's necessary to keep them in your life."

The remark surprised him, and he wondered if she even realized she'd said it. He studied her, as she plumped another pillow, the scattering of freckles on her face, her eyes, so incredibly blue. She wore a blue dress that seemed to match those eyes, and this was the first time he'd noticed her waist was getting thicker. "I missed you, Tess."

She straightened, meeting his eyes. "And I missed you."

John saw the color coming to her cheeks, and she turned away. "I'll go fix you some tea."

He knew she was suddenly embarrassed. This was not the time to press her about her feelings.

Tess left, her heart pounding at realizing something had

changed between them. She loved him. She truly loved him. She fixed the coffee and cut a piece of bread, taking both into the bedroom on a tray, which she set on his lap.

"This is a lousy way to come back and impress my new wife," he said with a frown.

"Just eat," she answered. "I'm glad to take care of you. I believe you helped care for me once, and the necessity is bound to come up again. That's part of what marriage is all about, John Hawkins. The words are 'for better or worse, in sickness and in health.' You continue to love and support each other in the worst of times. Now drink some of this coffee and eat the bread. I'll make you something better in a little bit. All you've eaten up to now is broth. You'll waste away to skin and bones if you don't start getting solid food into your stomach soon. Dr. Sanders says there is no damage to your stomach or digestive tract. You should be able to eat anything you want." She sat down on a chair beside the bed. "You look better, John. Your coloring is more normal, and your fever is gone. Surely you'll be all right now."

He sipped some coffee. "Did you ever doubt it? I told you I was too mean to die." A sharp pain jabbed his ribs, and he grimaced before drinking more.

"How do you like our house?" Tess asked, feeling suddenly a little awkward, hating having to tell him what she knew about Jim Caldwell.

"Hard to say. All I've seen is this room." John studied the colorful quilt on the bed as he took a bite of bread and swallowed it. "I've never lived anyplace that had a woman's touch, at least not the touch of a woman like you."

"We'll build an even better house out at the farm someday, something bigger. We'll need the room." She dropped her gaze at the remark. If she was going to be a real wife to him, they would surely have more than one child. Besides, he deserved children of his own blood.

"I guess we will," he answered. "How's the seamstress business?"

Why did she feel so nervous? When he'd been sick, she had been in full control. Now at the first sign of his getting better she was reminded of what a powerful, sure man he could be. They were still a little bit like strangers. "It's going very well, although I haven't done anything the last few days. I've spent all my time with you, except for resting whenever Jenny could come over."

John frowned. "I meant to ask about that, but just didn't feel good enough to bother. You've been letting Jenny Simms help take care of me?"

"I decided she was the best one to ask. She knows you . . . intimately." She felt too warm. "And she's not the fainting type."

John grinned. "You're a strong, smart woman, Mrs. Hawkins."

Tess sighed, rising from the chair, still averting her gaze. "Not so smart."

"What do you mean?"

She sighed, moving to the foot of the bed. "John . . ." She finally looked at him. "I have something to tell you." She confessed what she'd heard at the Caldwell house. "It's my fault you've been through this hell," she ended. "If you had died . . ." She swallowed back tears. "I thought I was helping by not telling. I was afraid if I told, you'd go charging in there and get yourself shot. Now look at what's happened. If I had told, you probably would have been more careful."

She wished she could read his dark eyes. He took one more swallow of coffee and asked her to take the tray. When she walked around the side of the bed to do so, he gripped her arm gently.

"You were thinking of me," he told her. "That's all that matters." He let go and rubbed at his eyes as she set the tray aside. "The fact remains I did a stupid thing, whether you had told me or not," he continued. "At least now I know I was right, about Caldwell, but the man is bound to lay low for the winter, so I'll still have trouble proving anything. I'd just better not set eyes on Casey Dunlap anytime soon!''

The look in his eyes set fear in her heart. She knew that, because of the shooting, John Hawkins would not quit the Rangers until he found the man who had shot him and proved Jim Caldwell was guilty of cattle theft. "Maybe you should tell all of this to Captain Booth and let him take care of it.''

He shook his head. "No. I'll probably talk to Booth, but proving who did this is something I have to do, especially now. It was either Dunlap or Caldwell himself who shot me.'' His hands balled into fists. "I'll find out which one, and he'll damn well regret it!''

"John, if you find out, you have to let the law take care of it. Bring them in with proof. Don't try to settle it yourself. No one would believe you. You could hang. Let the *law* settle this, the right way, for once." She rose. "Harriet Caldwell is so bent on civilizing Texas, talking of bringing in more teachers, preachers, and such. Imagine if she finds out her own husband . . .'' She sighed. "Much as I dislike the woman, I actually feel a little sorry for her. I am sure she has no idea what's been going on. And poor old Colonel Bass would turn over in his grave if he knew the kind of man he was giving so much land to.''

John just shook his head. "Leave it to you to feel sorry for an old bat like Harriet Caldwell. You told me she treated you no better than a slave.''

Tess sat down on the edge of the bed. "I suppose that's the only kind of life she's ever known. I heard Jim Caldwell talking one evening about the grand plantation they once owned in the Virginias. Maybe he felt desperate after losing it all. The way we're all brought up, the things we lose in life can cause us to sometimes make rash decisions, like you . . . killing the man who hurt your mother and carrying so much hurt and hatred around inside of you.''

John frowned. "You think marrying me was also a desperate decision? A rash decision?''

She met his gaze. "Of course it was. But we don't always

have to regret such decisions. I just think Jim Caldwell is going to regret some of the decisions he's made.''

John leaned his head back. "I *know* he'll regret them.''

"John, you have to be more careful than ever. I didn't go through all this just to have you turn around and get yourself killed.''

His look of vengeance softened, and he moved a hand to press it against her belly. "How are you? All this extra work can't be good for a woman in your—''

"Don't talk about my condition as though I'm going to collapse at any moment.'' She stood up, shaken by his mere touch. "Just because I'm carrying doesn't mean I'm not as strong as ever.''

He smiled. "Heaven forbid you should show any weakness.'' He put his head back. "I'm willing to admit . . . I'm *not* feeling very strong right now; but that's going to change . . . real quick.''

Tess sat down on the edge of the bed. "I'm glad to see you looking better and talking more normally.''

He watched her eyes. There was something there he'd never seen before. Love. "You didn't answer me—about how you really are.''

She rose, tucking blankets around him. "I'm just fine. You rest now. I'll fix some homemade soup for you.'' She walked around to the foot of the bed. "I'm so sorry, John. Are you sure you aren't angry with me for not telling you what I heard?''

He watched her lovingly, already feeling tired again. "All I care about is how you feel about that baby you're carrying. He's mine, you know. You remember that. Come spring, we'll be a family.''

She touched her stomach. "I don't know yet how I feel about the baby. Maybe it will be more real for me when I actually give birth. I'll know then.''

His eyes began to droop shut. "The natural thing for a woman . . . is to love any child that comes . . . from her own body. It shouldn't matter who fathered it. That's what my mother . . . always told me.''

Tess walked to the doorway. "Your mother must have been very special," she said quietly. She realized they were more alike in their life experiences than she'd given thought to before. They both knew what it was like to lose someone dear to them. They had both seen violence and death, and prejudice. She was relieved he didn't seem to blame her for what had happened, but she would always blame herself. She would make it up to him. The best way to do that was to love him the way he wanted and needed to be loved. She turned to tell him that she loved him, but he had already drifted back to sleep.

"You stupid son-of-a-bitch! It was *you*, wasn't it?" Jim Caldwell glowered at Casey Dunlap. Caldwell could tell by the look in Dunlap's eyes that he was right. He fought an urge to pull his gun and shoot the man, and instead turned away, fists clenched. "You came riding in that day a couple of hours after Hawkins left, never said a word. Then I go into town four days ago and find out from Higgins that Hawkins was shot the same day he'd been out to my place! Higgins is so busy pretending to be working with the Rangers to find out who did it, he didn't get the chance to come out here to the ranch and let me know what was going on! You could at least have let me in on this mess, dammit, Casey!" He whirled. "What in God's name were you thinking! And where have you been all this time!"

Casey shrugged, a hard look in his eyes. "I just figured it was time to shut Hawk's mouth, so I shot him. I rode out to camp in the hills till things quieted down."

"Well, you should have at least *finished* Hawkins! The bastard is going to live! And you should have waited for a time when he was completely alone, not when he was with his partner. If you were going to shoot one, you might as well have shot *both* of them!" He threw up his hands. "You know goddamn well that when it comes to decisions like this, you let *me* make them! Here I am trying to keep Hawkins off my back, and you pull this stunt! There will be Rangers all over this ranch in no time! Thank God there aren't any stolen cattle around here."

"I shot him after he was off your property," Casey spoke up in his own defense. "They can't pin this on you or any of your men. His partner never saw me, didn't have a chance to come lookin'. I made sure my tracks led away from your place, took a long way around, rode through a stream bed for quite a ways to help cover my tracks. Besides, like I said, Ken Randall didn't have a chance to come after me. We've had a good rain since then. By now the tracks are gone."

Jim rubbed at his aching head. "Thank God the bullet went clean through him, so they say. There's no way to even be sure what kind of gun was used. But whatever gun you *did* use, you get rid of it, you hear?"

"I already did. I sold it to a trader I ran into on the Santa Fe Trail."

Jim paced, trying to think. "I don't like it. This could put an end to my deal with those Comancheros down in Mexico a few weeks ago. Now I'll have to get a message to them to lay low." He stuck his face close to Casey's. "You've cost me plenty, Dunlap! You're going to take my message to those rustlers yourself, fill them in on what's happened up here. If John Hawkins lives, the man won't rest until he's found whoever shot him! You'd better pray he never figures out it was you!" He turned away. "*Damn* you! *Damn* you!"

Anger rose in Casey Dunlap's chest. "I thought I was helping you out, Jim. I've told you before we need to get rid of Hawkins."

"And I've told *you* that those are *my* decisions to make, not yours! Hawkins is a married man now, with a kid on the way! He never had anybody's sympathy before, but he's got it now! All the damn women are fixing to get some food together and take it over to that damn Tess Hawkins." He shook his head. "That Damn woman and her pa have been a headache to me ever since Colonel Bass gave them that land. He was too damn generous. He knew what I'd lost in Virginia, knew I wanted more land here. Hell, I'd have *paid* him for it, but he insisted on giving more to other Confederates. He gave Henry McDowell one of the best pieces of grazing land around here. And they used it to *farm!* Now that damn John Hawkins will be my goddamn neighbor! What in hell possessed that woman to marry a man like that!"

Casey shrugged. "Maybe he got a piece of her after he rescued her, took advantage while she was all messed up in the head. Maybe she *had* to marry him. They've only been married a couple of months, and some say her waist is already looking thicker. That whore Maybelle at the Sagebrush Saloon says a woman almost never starts showing that quick. Maybe that's because she was already carrying when she married Hawkins."

Jim took a cigar from a box on his desk. "I never thought of that."

"Why else would she marry the man? Maybe the kid doesn't even belong to Hawkins. Maybe she was raped by those Comancheros after all. If so, she'd know that baby would have to look Indian. Who else could she marry to make it look legal besides somebody that looked Indian himself?"

Jim thought about the comment as he lit his cigar. He puffed on it for a moment, then turned to Casey. "You know, for somebody who can be so stupid, you can think pretty smart sometimes. Whether it's true of not, that kind of gossip could be just the thing to drive Mr. and Mrs. John Hawkins right out of El Paso, in which case they would want to sell that land. If that woman is carrying some Comanchero's bastard, she won't want the kid to be around here where everybody knows. And I'm married to just the woman who can make sure the rumors fly. When she gets back from town I'll suggest to Harriet the very thing you just told me. It does make sense, doesn't it?"

Casey nodded and grinned. "Sure it does." He walked to a chair and picked up his hat. "You want me to light out for a while, maybe go to Mexico?"

"No. That will just make things look more suspicious. You stay right here. If they come around asking questions, I'll testify you were with me during the time of the shooting. You let me do all the talking, understand? You've done enough damage. Get the men ready to go round up strays, see if you can determine how many pregnant cows we have. We've left the bulls free to roam long enough. The demand for beef gets higher every year since the war. The damn Yankees might have defeated us in that war, but I'll get it out of their hide in beef prices. If I have to steal more cattle to build my herds, I'll do it. Neither John Hawkins nor anybody else is going to stop me from building this place into something even bigger than what I lost back in Virginia."

He kept pacing, thinking, and Casey waited nervously.

"We have to stay on the up and up for the winter," he continued. "And come spring we have to avoid scum like the Comancheros." He faced Dunlap. "Are there stolen cattle still being held in that canyon near the Rio Grande?"

Casey nodded. "The man watching them can be trusted. They probably have all the brands changed by now."

Caldwell paced again. "All right. What I'll do is get a letter to Don Emeliano Cordera. The last person the Rangers would think would buy stolen cattle from one of the wealthiest ranchers in Texas is one of the wealthiest ranchers in Mexico. The Rangers go across the border sometimes, but they'd never go three hundred miles inland and invade the ranch of a powerful man like Cordera, let alone risk pissing off that damn dictator running Mexico now." He nodded to himself. "Yes, Cordera is our answer. He already agreed to buy some of my cattle. Maybe he'll buy them all, some of my own *and* the stolen cattle. He's done it before. That's our only chance of getting rid of the stolen beef without getting caught. Selling them to the Comancheros is too dangerous right now. In the meantime, maybe I can find a way to get rid of Hawkins by spring. I'll either force him out because of gossip, or lure him away somehow, to someplace far away where he can be killed without any fingers pointing at my ranch. You'd better be glad the wife and I have such a good reputation in this town."

Casey put on his hat. "I'll see to the bulls and the strays. Sorry I messed things up, but I'm sorrier John Hawkins didn't die."

Jim watched the smoke curl up from his cigar. "So am I, Casey, so am I. You just act the model citizen for a while. Go talk to your men down by the Rio Grande. Tell them to be mighty careful rustling more strays over the winter and to keep all of them down in that canyon—maybe move them on into Mexico. I'll get a letter to Cordera, have his men meet you at Fire Canyon down on the Conchos in April. We'll sell the stolen cattle and then lay low for a year or so. No Texas Ranger could ever find out about Fire Canyon. It's too far south into Mexico."

Casey nodded, grinning. "We'll manage it, boss. Ain't no Rangers gonna' go that deep into Mexico."

The man picked up his hat and left, and Jim listened to the jingle of the spurs he wore around his snakeskin boots. "Damn fool," he muttered. If the man didn't already know too much, he'd fire him, but he couldn't do that now, at least not until he got rid of the cattle already collected down by the Rio Grande. Cordera was his answer. A sale clear down by Camargo in Mexico would never be discovered by Texas Rangers.

Tess opened the door to Louise Jeffers and Rachael Patterson, who each stood there holding food.

"I baked an apple pie for you, dear," Louise told her. "And Rachael has brought some homemade pea soup with ham. It's fresh hot, so you can just keep it warm on your stove. It should be good for your husband, put some meat back on him. We hear he's doing much better."

Tess could not help noticing both women were glancing at her waist, as though trying to figure out how big she was getting. "My goodness! I didn't expect this," she said, stepping aside. "It really isn't necessary." She ran a hand through her hair as they came through the door, realizing the neat bun she'd worn it in earlier was coming apart. "I'm afraid I'm a bit of a mess. After helping my husband clean up and eat earlier I decided to finish some sewing before I did anything with myself. I'm backed up because of caring for John."

"Oh, we understand," Louise told her. "There are cookies and a cake and some smoked venison in the buggy. We still have to bring them in. It's food from some of the other women."

"This really isn't necessary," Tess answered, leading them through the small parlor into the kitchen.

"Oh, of course it's necessary." Rachael carted the pot of soup to the stove. "And believe me, getting this here without it spilling was no easy task." She turned and faced Tess, looking neat and lovely in a flowered dress. "There are so few of us here, Tess—white women from the South and East. We have to stick together, you know." Again she studied Tess's waistline. "I'll go get the rest of the food." She walked out, and Louise stood at the table, looking a little nervous. She also glanced at Tess's waist again.

Tess pulled out a chair. "Sit down, Louise. I have some coffee that is still fresh enough to be drinkable. Would you like some?"

"No, thank you, dear. We shouldn't stay long. We might disturb your husband. How is he doing?"

Tess sat down. "Well, things were very bad the first five or six days. He came so close to death. Since then he's improved every day. It's been over three weeks now. He even got up and walked some today."

Louise smiled, but Tess sensed there was little sincerity to it. "Well, that's good," the woman told her.

Rachael returned with a plate of cookies and set them on the table. "Harriet had Maria bake these for you. I'll go and get the cake." She glanced at Louise before leaving again, and Tess felt a need to defend herself rising in her soul.

"Why don't you tell me the real reason you came, Louise?"

Louise finally pulled out a chair and sat down, fidgeting with her handbag as she spoke. "Well, dear, we just—we want you to know we understand."

Tess frowned. "Understand what?"

"Well, it seems . . . Harriet had a talk with Maria. And Maria told her . . . something . . . about you."

Tess closed her eyes. "I made Maria promise—"

"You know how Harriet can be. Somehow she got the idea you were . . . with child . . . before you married John Hawkins. She questioned Maria to see if the woman knew anything, since you two worked together when you were there. Maria said—"

"I know what she said. I'm sorry Harriet pressured her that way." She stood up. She had promised John she would defend this baby. She faced Louise boldly as she spoke. "All right. I was already with child when I married John. I married him because . . . because it's *his* child."

Louise's mouth dropped open. "What! We thought—"

"That I had been violated by the Comancheros. I have told you all along that I was not."

Rachael came back into the kitchen, carrying a cake. She glanced at Louise. "It's his," Louise told her.

Tess studied them both, almost wanted to laugh at the look on Rachael's innocent face. Her eyes widened, and she moved to stand beside Louise. Tess faced both of them squarely. "I hate to malign my dead husband's memory, but the truth is, Abel crawled under the bed to hide the day of the attack. He left me alone to fight the Comancheros. After I was taken off, I was so beaten and terrorized that to be rescued was the most wonderful thing I could imagine. You weren't there. You didn't see John Hawkins take on that whole gang of Comancheros himself. You didn't see his heroism, his bravery. He's more man than any I can think of. And on our way back something . . . happened . . . between us."

It wasn't *all* a lie, was it? Something *had* happened between them.

"Who are you or Harriet—who is anyone?—to say what you would do in the same situation? None of us knows until the time comes. You can't say, if you haven't walked in my shoes. Afterward we both feared we had made a mistake. Mr. Hawkins is himself a very lonely man. We were going to give it some time, but then I realized I was . . . with child . . . John's child. I know it's his because . . ." She turned away. "I just know, that's all. John loves me, and since this shooting I realize I love him. People in this town are just going to have to accept that. I am not ashamed of it. We are husband and wife now, and that is that. I have my land here, and I intend to stay in El Paso. John has been in this area for years, I've come to call it home, so home it is."

Silence hung in the room for several quiet seconds, as Rachael took a chair. "My goodness," she murmured.

Tess felt better. At least she had seemed to convince them once and for all that her baby was John's, and she was beginning to believe it more herself. "If we are going to be relegated to living in west Texas, ladies, we must learn to adapt, to accept the fact that there will always be Indians and Mexicans to deal with and that they have just as much right here as anyone. I have learned through John that they are no different from us in their loves and needs. We cannot abide intolerance. Part of civilizing Texas is teaching that those who were here first, and who will always be here, must be accepted and allowed to cohabit with us. John is a good man and would defend me to his dying breath. There are other good people in this town, and if I am going to lose all of you as my friends over this, then I have plenty of friends among the Mexican women to whom I can turn. Some of them have already been asking me to sew for them, and many have already brought food. If you think you are going to shame me out of El Paso, think again, and with John Hawkins for a father, I dare anyone to insult or bring any kind of hurt to our child because of his Indian blood. Is that understood?''

Louise met her eyes. "We just . . . weren't sure what to think." The woman stood up. "No, Tess, we won't try to make you leave. I have tried to learn not to be too shocked by anything that happens out here. I never wanted to come, but we have all followed husbands and fathers to this godforsaken country, and all of us have our stories to tell. I think Harriet Caldwell has had the hardest time adjusting. I will try to explain to the other ladies, and I . . . I hope all goes well for you and your new marriage. Heaven knows you will have your hands full with a man like John Hawkins."

Tess could not help a smile. "I am sure I will, but what man is not a handful?"

The other two looked at each other, then both smiled. "We can't argue with you there," Rachael told her.

"We had better go," Louise said. "God be with you, Tess."

Tess nodded. "Thank you. And I will have that dress you wanted finished next week. I would have been done if not for having to care for John. I've had some help from Jenny Simms. I suppose you have heard that, too. I am sure you disapprove, but I simply couldn't handle it alone, and Jenny is a strong woman who has been . . . friends . . . with John for a long time."

Louise raised her eyebrows. "I hope she understands that friendship must end now."

Tess led them to the door. "Friendships never need to end, Louise, but Jenny understands John is a married man now. She respects that. Jenny is also a better person than you know, and a smart businesswoman. You really should invite her to join our circle. We have to face the fact that things are just different out here, whether we like it or not. We can't live by the same rules as in the Old South or the more civilized East."

Louise sighed, holding herself stiffly. "Yes, I suppose." She and Rachael stepped outside, then Louise turned back to Tess. "You are a very strong woman. Personally I think we need you in our circle. I will see to it that you are always welcome."

Their eyes held in mutual understanding. Tess knew that meant going over Harriet Caldwell's head. If only they knew the truth about Jim Caldwell. If John had anything to do with it, that truth would be known soon. "Thank you, Louise. And thank you both for the food. Please thank the other ladies who contributed. Who sent the cake?"

"Oh, it's from Bess Johndrow," Rachael told her.

"Well, thank her for me. I will come to another meeting as soon as I am able." She watched them leave, closed the door. "Dear God," she muttered. She hoped she'd convinced them. She put a hand to her belly and walked into the bedroom to check on John, who was standing by a window in only his long johns. "What are you doing getting out of bed by yourself?"

He turned to face her. "Getting out of bed by myself," he answered with a grin.

She rolled her eyes. "You lie back down, Mr. Hawkins."

His eyes moved over her in a way they hadn't since his return home, the look told her he most certainly was getting better. "That was quite a speech you gave those old bats," he told her. "I couldn't help hearing." His smile faded. "Thanks for convincing them the baby is mine."

She came around and gently put her arms around him, resting her face lightly against the gauze wrapped around his chest, afraid to hug him too tightly. "Thank you for making it all look legal. I think I'm beginning to want this baby, John, if only because of the looks on their faces, knowing how they would look at the poor thing if they knew the truth."

He grasped the back of her neck, and she could feel his strength returning. A restless desire was beginning to stir deep inside her, a desire to know the unique pleasure she'd experienced that one night in his arms.

"You *will* love this baby," he said. He placed both arms around her. "I'll help you through it all, Tess. We'll show them. And they'll all have their own bitter pill to swallow when they find out the truth about El Paso's most illustrious citizen." His grip tightened, and she knew John Hawkins was not going to be happy until Jim Caldwell paid for what he'd done.

Chapter Twenty-One

Tess set a cup of coffee in front of Captain Booth, gave another to Ken. They both sat at the kitchen table with John, and their talk made her nervous. It had been six weeks since John was shot. He was healed enough to think about revenge, but physically he was far from full strength. Captain Booth was a short, wiry man who sported a large mustache. His shaggy sandy-colored hair hung to his shoulders, and he wore a buckskin shirt. There was a scar on his left cheek that showed through his beard.

"You say you know who did this, Hawk," Booth was saying. "You have to tell me what's going on."

John glanced at Tess as she sat down. She looked extra pretty today in that green dress she wore, something she'd made for herself that was gathered under her breasts in such a way that a person would hardly know she was carrying. He hated the thought of her getting involved in this mess, possibly having to testify against Jim Caldwell.

He turned his attention back to Captain Booth. "I'll tell you, but you won't believe it. Either way, you have to keep completely quiet about it. Don't even tell any of the other

Rangers—not yet. Without the right proof, it wouldn't be any use."

Booth shook his head. "And how do you plan to get this proof? I've had enough surprises from you, Hawk. I don't want any more of your stunts, and I don't want you doing this alone. You've already nearly got yourself killed. Let me and the other Rangers help this time."

John glanced at Ken.

"He's right, Hawk," Ken told him. "I ain't told him nothin', but this is somethin' you can't do alone. It's too big."

"Part of it I *have* to do alone." John looked back at Booth. "I have to go to Mexico."

Tess closed her eyes. He would ride away again, possibly for weeks, months, possibly forever.

"You know we're not supposed to stick our noses into Mexico," Booth answered.

"And you know, Captain, that we do it all the time. This time I'm not going in order to try to arrest someone down there. I'm only going to get information, find out who in Mexico has been buying stolen cattle." He leaned closer. "From Jim Caldwell."

Booth's eyebrows shot up in surprise. "Caldwell!"

"I told you you wouldn't believe it." John leaned back in his chair. "Now you know why we have to lay low on this until I get the proof I need. If you doubt Caldwell's involvement, maybe my wife can convince you otherwise. I asked her to sit in on this so she can tell you in her own words what she knows."

Booth frowned, looking at Tess. He still had not gotten over the shock that John Hawkins had married, and a lovely thing she was. One thing he hoped was that this woman would have a calming affect on John, keep him from pulling the wild, risky stunts that kept him in trouble. "What in the world do you know about all of this, Mrs. Hawkins?"

Tess sipped some coffee from one of only six ceramic mugs she owned. She had had to restock all her homemaking supplies after the fire, and still needed many things. "I suppose I should have gone straight to you in the first place," she answered. "I just . . . I could hardly believe it, and I knew that without real proof, people would have laughed me off. In fact, they would probably have railroaded me right out of town." She took a deep breath for courage, folding her hands in her lap as she spoke, telling Captain Booth what she had seen and heard. The man shook his head in wonder.

"If I hadn't already seen the worst in men, I couldn't believe it. But men come out here, see how big the land is, how little law there is, and they think they can make up their own rules and get away with anything." He finished his coffee. "You're right, Hawk. This calls for damn good evidence."

John glanced at Tess. He knew she didn't want him to go away, but he had no choice. "I figured I'd go into Mexico," he told Booth, "see if I can work my way into any group of cattlemen down there who deal with Jim Caldwell or Casey Dunlap. I'll find out where they meet, try to set something up so Rangers can be there and catch them red-handed. We don't have to be concerned with the Mexicans. They can go their own way. All we need is to catch Dunlap selling stolen cattle. He's Caldwell's top man. He might spill what he knows about Caldwell just to try to keep from hanging."

"Trouble is, you think it's Dunlap that shot you," Ken spoke up. "It ain't gonna be easy not puttin' a bullet in the man yourself."

Hatred sparked in John's dark eyes. "No, it won't." He looked at Booth. "I have a strong suspicion it was Dunlap, but I might never be able to prove it. If I can get him put away and pin the rustling on Caldwell, that will be satisfaction enough. Any cattle stolen over the winter will most likely be taken into Mexico, before spring roundups. They'll want to get them out of Texas as fast as they can. Caldwell will know he doesn't dare sell rebranded cattle anyplace in Texas right now. That's why I think Mexico is the place to get the information I need."

Booth sighed. "Well, then, you do what you have to do. I don't aim to have another one of my men back-shot. There's no more low-down act on this earth than that."

Tess felt the disappointment growing in her heart. John would go away again.

"I'll get a message to you whenever and however I can," John told Booth. He rose, and Tess hated the thought of seeing him strap on a gun again. "You have to remember not to say a word to Sheriff Higgins about what I'm up to. Tell him I've gone north, not south, if he asks. When I send a message, it will give you only a place and time—no names. I won't even sign my own name."

Booth also rose. "Thanks for the coffee, ma'am, and for being brave enough to tell us what you know. I suppose you realize you'll have to do without your husband again for a while, but I suspect when he gets back, you'll be taking our best man away from us. Ken says you plan to settle on your father's farm."

Tess looked at John. They had a lot to talk about. Would this put an end to their plans? "Yes. John will go into ranching himself." She looked back at Booth. "I would like to rebuild there. My father would have liked that."

"Well, with John Hawkins running the place, I don't reckon you'll have to worry much about raiders."

The memory of Abel hiding under the bed flashed into Tess's thoughts. "No, I certainly won't have to worry about that."

The men talked a little more, and finally Booth shook John's hand. "Good to see you up and healing," he told him. "Just don't go into this if you aren't ready physically."

"I think I'm about ready." John walked with both men to the front door, then turned to look at Tess as they left. She stood in the archway between the kitchen and parlor, looking rather forlorn. "I'll come back in one piece this time, and it will be over," he told her.

"I hope you're right."

John threw the bolt on the door, then walked closer. "I'll try to get back before the baby is born."

She felt a pain in the pit of her stomach. "I'm afraid for you, John."

He reached out and pulled her into his arms. There had been no chance to make love yet, through all his healing. He had watched her closely, had seen the honest love in her eyes. She had faithfully nursed him, bathed him, fed him, read to him, never complaining. He kissed her hair. "Come to bed with me, Tess. No more sleeping out here. It isn't necessary."

She rested her head against his chest. "It's . . . broad daylight."

"Doesn't matter. This is one thing we haven't talked about . . . one thing we know still needs doing."

A charge of passion moved through her as his hands trailed lightly over her back. "I'm not . . . quite so slender right now. My waist has grown."

"You don't really think that matters, do you? There's nothing much prettier to a man than when his woman is carrying his child; and that's what this is . . . our child. Don't ever forget that."

She looked up at him. "Can't you let someone else go to Mexico?"

He shook his head. "You know I have to do this or never feel satisfied."

She moved her hands along his strong forearm. "I will miss you as I've never missed you before. The first time . . . was different."

"I know."

"You left angry. I'm sorry about that."

"I wasn't angry. Just disappointed."

"I won't ever let you leave that way again. I've never felt this way about another man, not the young man I thought I loved back in San Antonio and never about Abel. The whole town thinks I'm crazy, but I don't care." She met his eyes. "I love you, John Hawkins. This time I can say it with no reservations."

It still didn't seem real to Tess that she was married to this wild, sometimes ruthless man, but when his full lips met her mouth, the reality of it hit her. She really did love him. This would not be like that first time. This was not just a duty or an experiment, nor just so he could legally claim her as his wife. This was sheer desire, total need, aching passion. It had lain buried deep inside through his sickness, had stubbornly refused to surface even when he was better, for she still wrestled with the right and wrong of it . . . until now . . . until his delicious kiss immediately erased all her former doubts and inhibitions.

She returned the kiss with groaning desire, the true woman in her coming to full life. She had not expected this to happen in the middle of the morning. Yet she realized this was just the kind of thing to always expect from John Hawkins. He never did anything by the rules, not even making love.

She felt embarrassed, nervous, on fire, as he led her into the bedroom. Just like that first time, he was immediately in full control. He pulled back the covers and sat her down on the bed, then knelt in front of her and began unbuttoning the front of her dress. She closed her eyes, touching his hair. "I'll have to make the bed all over again now."

He eased the dress off her shoulders, down her arms. "Not if we stay in it all day."

Tess blushed. "We can't do that."

"Why not? Is there some law against it?"

She smiled as he began unlacing her camisole. "At least let me . . ."

He pulled the camisole open, exposing her full breasts. He leaned forward and kissed at a taut nipple. "Let you what?" he asked, moving to her other breast.

She sucked in her breath at the surprising ecstasy of feeling him gently taste her breasts. "I'm . . . This is hard for me . . . in daylight like this. Let me finish undressing myself and get under the covers."

His lips moved down to her belly, kissing gently. "All

right." He kept kissing at her belly, laying her back and slowly inching dress and slips over her hips, bringing her drawers along.

"John . . ." This was not what she'd just asked him. She was going to make him turn around and let her get under the covers. He straightened up on his knees and pulled everything off, so that she again lay there in only her open camisole and shoes and stockings. "This isn't what I meant." She pulled a blanket over her nakedness while he pulled off her shoes and stockings.

From then on she knew it was useless to argue. She lay still while he stood up and removed his shirt, his socks, which was all he wore on his feet. He pulled off his denim pants, and she closed her eyes when he took off his long johns. How strange that she had bathed this man many times, yet now she was embarrassed to look at his nakedness. This was entirely different. This was not John the injured man. This was just John, her husband, the man who wanted his woman.

She felt his hands run under the blanket then, along her thighs. He moved up onto the bed beside her, gently probing places only John Hawkins had touched so beautifully. He made her want to open up to him, and whatever he was doing to her, it made her return his kisses with wanton desire. His hair hung down around her face, as though to shroud her sight from their nakedness, making it easier for her to allow him to take the blanket away. His long locks brushed gently across her face and neck as he moved down again, tasting her breasts, her belly, tickling her stomach as he moved farther down to kiss her thighs, kiss at the hairs that hid secret places.

His fingers worked magic, and the urgent, almost painful desire ripple through her, moving out to every nerve end until an explosive desire tore through her, making her want a man as she had never wanted a man before. And that man had to be John Hawkins.

She dug her fingers into his shoulders. "Hawk," she whispered. It was all she could think of to say. For some reason he was Hawk now, wild, demanding, unbridled, lawless. "Hawk . . ."

Quickly his lips were at her breasts again, her throat, her mouth; deep, probing kisses. They lay crosswise on the bed, and she felt her head moving to the edge. He moved between her legs, and his huge hardness was pressing against her.

"You're mine now, Tess Hawkins, this time completely. Tell me you love me."

She could hardly find her voice, it was so hard to catch her breath. "You know . . . I do. I love you, Hawk."

"Look me in the eyes when you say it."

She opened her eyes. Never had she felt so bold and daring, so on fire, so brazen . . . or so sure. "I love you." She gasped then, when he moved inside her in one quick thrust. He began a rhythmic, rocking motion that sent her somewhere beyond reality. In moments her head hung over the side of the bed, and she lay in naked splendor beneath him, not caring that he looked upon that nakedness. It was all right. This was her husband, and he loved her.

John raised up and grasped her hips, pushing deep. He'd been with his share of women, but none had given him this kind of pleasure. The first time he'd made love to Tess, it had been wonderously beautiful for him. But it was not like this. This time he saw true love and want in her blue eyes. This time she was giving all of herself to him, heart and soul, not just her body. This time it was for her own pleasure as well as his. She was more woman than he ever thought he would end up taking for a wife. He had hardly even given thought to marriage until meeting Tess Carey. And when she had this baby, they would truly be family.

His life surged into her, and he held her tight against himself until the throbbing finally ceased. He came down beside her then, pulling her close, moving to lie lengthwise on the bed and pulling covers over them.

"I don't want you to go," she said, snuggling into his shoulder.

"I have to do this, Tess."

"I don't know what I'd do if you never came back."

"I'll come back."

"What about the baby? I want you here when it's born. You have to help me learn to love it, John."

"You won't need any help. The minute you put him or her to your breast, you'll love it. I already love it." He ran a big hand over her stomach. "And I love you. I've never loved a woman like I love you."

He moved on top of her again, and she suspected he'd really meant it when he'd said they would stay in bed all day.

Morning broke cold and still. Tess realized her nose was cold. It was nearing the end of December now, and although the temperature seldom got this low in these parts, they were having a cold spell. She moved against John, thinking how the past week had gone by much too quickly. He was leaving today.

She ran her hand over his solid chest, noticing how white her skin was against his. She kissed the scar left from where a bullet had nearly killed him. Surely God wouldn't turn around and take him from her now. Surely he would come back safe and sound.

He sighed deeply and turned to her. Nothing needed to be said. They could feel it. He didn't want to leave. She didn't want him to go. Yet he would tell her goodbye today. They had to make love once more.

How many times had they done this since that wonderful day they'd lain in bed together nearly all day? She could no longer remember. Every day. Every night. They could not get enough of each other. John Hawkins was a man with big appetites, including a healthy hunger for sex with the woman he loved. Tess didn't mind. He had awakened an equal hunger in her she never knew she was capable of feeling.

This time they needed no preliminaries. This time they simply had to be united once more, expressing their love in the most sincere way a man and woman could express such a thing. This time she simply opened herself to him and welcomed him inside. He slid into her gently, slowly, teasing her, wanting to stretch it out for as long as possible.

He knew every inch of her now, had tasted and touched every part of her. He owned her as no other man had ever owned her. She would never belong to another man quite this way. When John Hawkins laid claim to something, there was no doubting his right to possession. And woe be to the man who might try to take that possession from him or try to harm that possession. Never had she felt so safe and contented. They moved in gentle rhythm, each fully knowing the other's every need now, every movement.

Their lovemaking reminded her of beautiful music. Ecstasy. That was the only word for it. Symphonic ecstasy, their hands, lips, tongues, hot skin, privates, all the instruments that played together. She had heard such music only once in her life, at a concert when she was a little girl. She had never forgotten, and making love with John Hawkins brought back the beauty of it. He had taught her there was no shame in this. He had taken away the horror of Chino, the disappointment of Abel. He had awakened her to the true meaning of love, and of lovemaking.

They moved quietly under the covers, and soon his life again surged into her. She had no doubt that if she were not already with child, he would have made her pregnant by now. She suspected she would be having quite a big family as long as John Hawkins was in her bed. The child in her belly now would have plenty of brothers and sisters.

John settled beside her, stroking her hair. "When I get back, I'll get started out at the ranch and we'll live a normal life, I promise."

"I believe you." She kissed his chest. "I'll pray for you. And don't say God won't listen. You're as good as any man out there in the streets, a far better man than Jim Caldwell, for all his spouting about civilizing Texas and bringing in more churches."

"Whatever you say." He kissed her gently. "I have to get up or I'll end up spending the day here in bed again."

"I don't mind."

He studied her red hair, which lay in a thick tumble against the pillow. "God, you're beautiful, Tess Hawkins."

She ran her fingers over his finely chisled face, the square jaw, high cheekbones, deep-set eyes. "And if men can be beautiful, you are the most beautiful man I've ever seen. The other women only pretend to be shocked by you or to disapprove of you because of your dark skin and Indian looks. Deep inside they are as moved by the way you look as I am. They're all jealous of me, you know."

He grinned. "You think so?" He kissed her nose.

"I'm sure of it."

He laughed and rolled over, sitting up. "I doubt it. Half of them think I ought to be hanged."

"Well, before long they'll know the truth, who the *real* bad guy is."

He pulled on some long johns. "I hope so." He stood up and put on a shirt. "It's cold. You stay there while I stoke up the heating stove and the cooking stove. I'll put on some water so we can wash. Soon as I eat some breakfast, I'll have to leave, Tess."

Her heart fell at the words. "Then I'll take my time making breakfast."

He turned and met her eyes. "I'm sorry."

"I know." Her eyes teared. "Come back to me, John."

"I always have and I always will."

A tear slipped down her cheek. How strange that an act of horror had brought them together, and now if it meant never knowing John Hawkins, she would not change what had happened. As he left the room, Tess shivered into the blankets, immediately colder just because he was gone from the bed. It was going to be hard sleeping alone after this.

Chapter Twenty-Two

This was taking too much time. John lit another cigarette, waiting for Don Emiliano Cordera. The man lived
like a king here in Camargo. Here, it seemed, men were
either peasants, or very wealthy. Don Emiliano was wealthy.
His sprawling stucco home sat in the middle of thousands
of acres he claimed for himself, and thousands of cattle
grazed on his land.

"Señor Hawkins, I am told." A short, wiry Mexican
entered the room, wearing a white, ruffled shirt and snug-
fitting black pants. His black leather boots reached his
knees, and his thick, gray hair lay in slick waves away from
his face. A neat mustache graced his upper lip, and he
smiled as he put out his hand. *"Buenos días, señor."*

John set his cigarette in an ashtray and put out his hand.
"Buenos días. And you are Don Emiliano Cordera?" He
towered over the man, but Cordera stood so erect and
proud that it made him seem taller than he really was.

"Sí. Bienvenido! Sit down, Señor Hawkins. I will have one
of my servants bring you something to drink. I have some
fine wine." He picked up a small bell and jingled it, as he
sat down himself on a black leather sofa. John sat, a small

table between him and the man, in a leather chair that matched the sofa.

"Wine sounds just fine. You have a beautiful spread here, Señor Cordera."

"Ah, yes, my father spent many years building this *ranchero*. We survived the French occupation and Maximilian, and under Porfirio Díaz, men like myself have never been so prosperous."

"So I see." And how many of Díaz's enemies have you helped capture and murder or put in jail? John wanted to ask. Everyone in the States knew Porfirio Díaz ruled like a dictator here in Mexico. Those who supported him did well. Those who did not sometimes disappeared and were never heard from again. But he was not here to argue Mexican politics. He hated this small talk and would rather get to the point, but it was dangerous to offend a wealthy Mexican in his own country, which was probably exactly what he would end up doing. Still, he had no choice left. Cordera was his last hope of getting the information he wanted and getting back to Tess before she had that baby. God he missed her, ached for her. "Do you have sons, Don Emiliano? Children who will one day inherit all of this?"

"*Sí*, I have four sons," the man answered proudly. "All are grown and are much help to me already. Two are married, and I have five grandchildren now!"

John smiled and nodded. "I hope I can say the same someday. I am only recently married. My wife is expecting a child at any time now."

"Ah, it must be hard for you not to be near her. Why are you three hundred miles away, *señor*? Perhaps it is farther? It is almost three hundred miles from here to the Rio Grande. And, my men tell me, you are one of those—what are they called?—*mariscals*?"

"Not a marshal. Texas Ranger."

"*Ah, sí.*"

John watched the change in Cordera's eyes as he looked him over. Texas Rangers were not welcome in Mexico.

The servant girl brought in a tray with two wineglasses, along with a bottle of chilled wine, and set them on the small table. Cordera picked up the bottle and dismissed her.

"You see?" He held up the bottle. "It is cold! I have men whose job is to bring ice from the Sierra Madres. If none can be found there, they must go into the mountains of New Mexico and bring it all the way back here. Did you know that if you pack ice in straw, it can last for weeks?" The man poured two glasses of wine.

"Yes, I know," John answered, thinking how nice it must be to be so wealthy you could pay men to do nothing but make trips into the mountains to collect ice. He took the glass of wine Cordera held out to him.

"So, *señor*, tell me what business a Texas Ranger has here on Ranchero de Plata? Do you know the meaning of *plata?*"

John sipped the wine. It was indeed delicious and cool. "Silver," he answered.

"*Sí.* That is what started all of this. My father owned a silver mine in the Sierra Madres. Now it belongs to the government, but I was paid much money for it."

In return for what? John wondered. Mexico's current government didn't help its citizens without getting something in return. He only nodded. "Good for you. By the way, you speak good English."

"*Sí.* I hired an American to teach me. You have no trouble understanding me?" Cordera studied the handsome, obviously Indian man who sat across from him, suspicious, curious. The big man looked like someone who knew how to handle himself. He knew the reputation of the Texas Rangers, didn't like having one here on his *ranchero*. Texas Rangers had no business anyplace but in Texas, but this man looked to him like someone who didn't care about rules. That kind of man was the most dangerous. "Do you speak Spanish, *señor?*"

John nodded, thinking what a braggart Don Cordera

was. This was a powerful, proud man. He would have to be very careful. *"Sí. Yo lo comprehendo."*

"Bueno. I suppose a Texas Ranger must know the language."

"You can't live in Texas without knowing Spanish."

Cordera laughed. "Texas should still be a part of Mexico, you know. But, what is done is done. I suppose it cannot be changed now. So, again I ask, what is a Texas Ranger doing so far from where he is supposed to be?"

John took another sip of wine and leaned back in the leather chair. "I'm a man who gets to the point, Señor Cordera. When I am through telling you why I'm here, you have every right to bring in your men and have me thrown off the place. I have no power here. I know that. I came to ask your help. Others tell me that although you rule with an iron fist, you're an honest and fair man. I am counting on that."

Cordera sipped more wine himself. He'd met a few Rangers over the years, didn't like their arrogance or the fact that sometimes they came into Mexico after men wanted back in the States. Those things were supposed to be left up to the Mexican government. But this Ranger, there was something about him he liked, an honesty in those dark eyes, a daring, straightforward approach. "And how would my honesty and fairness help you, *señor*? I am harboring no American outlaws here. Nor have I broken any American laws."

John leaned forward, resting his elbows on his knees. "Maybe you *think* you haven't broken any laws. But I'm afraid it's possible you have. You might have some information that could be useful to me, Don Cordera, and frankly, I have no place else to turn. I have been talking to people and asking questions for weeks, and the answers finally led me here. In a *cantina* in town, one of your men told me he thinks you do business sometimes with an American rancher named Jim Caldwell. Is that true?"

Cordera weighed the question and sipped more wine before answering. *"Sí. Es cierto. Por qué?"*

John sighed, praying he'd done the right thing by coming here. "As I said, Señor Cordero, I have no power here and no plans to make trouble for you. Down here that would be impossible for an American. I ask this next question only because I am desperate for some information. And I ask that you be honest with me."

Cordera's eyes narrowed with suspicion. "It is as others told you, *señor*. I am a honest man."

John nodded. "Then tell me. Are you aware that Jim Caldwell deals in stolen cattle? Has he ever sent cattle down here with the brands burned off?"

Cordera stiffened, and he slowly set his wineglass on the table. "I have seen brands burned off. But it matters little to me how Señor Caldwell gets his cattle. It is not my business."

"Isn't it? Does your new *presidente* know you deal in stolen cattle from America?" John watched Cordera squirm a little.

"Porfirio Díaz cares little how I come by my cattle, *señor*." Anger began to move into Cordera's dark eyes as he leaned forward to rest his elbows on his knees. "And I do not take lightly that you seem to be trying to threaten me in my own home. I will remind you I have many men, and you are only one man." He looked John over carefully. "My instinct tells me you are good at what you do. You would not go down easy, *señor*, but however good you are with that fine gun you wear, one man cannot fight thirty and remain alive."

The open, though obviously fake, friendly attitude was gone. John could see he was facing the real Don Cordera now. That was good. He would rather know a man was being truthful. Still, he had already crossed the danger line. He might never leave this *ranchero* if he wasn't careful. He drank a little more wine and set his own glass aside.

"I am not a fool, Señor Cordera. Of course I know better than to insult or threaten you on your own land. I am not trying to do either. To put it bluntly, I am desperate for some information, and you are my last hope." John felt a little relief when Cordera's eyebrows arched in surprise and some of the fury in his eyes changed to curiosity and pride.

"Your last hope, *señor,* should be that I do not have you shot. Tell me, *por favor,* what this information is that you need, and how you think *I* can help you. In fact, I am curious to know *why* I should help you."

John rose, walking to stand in front of a stone fireplace. He looked around the room. "Señor Cordera, Jim Caldwell is very much like you up there in Texas. He owns a big ranch, has a lot of men working under him, has money and power. But there is one big difference. I am guessing that if you did decide to shoot a man, you would stand him up and let him see what's coming, maybe even give him a chance to defend himself, just like you're giving me a chance to explain myself now. You wouldn't shoot him in the back from a distance and run off. I guess what I am saying is I believe you are an honorable man. Jim Caldwell has no honor."

Cordera frowned and stood up himself. "In the back? And who did this Jim Caldwell have shot in the back?"

John rested his hand on his gun. "Me. The only trouble is, I lived."

Cordera folded his arms, looking John over. "And how do you know it was Señor Caldwell?"

"Believe me, I know. I also know Jim Caldwell has been dealing in stolen cattle. But with a man as rich and powerful as he is, I have to have solid proof. I have to catch him or his men in the act." John walked behind the leather chair he'd been sitting in and braced his hands against the back of it. He'd been in the saddle for weeks, and his rib still ached off and on. It was hurting him right now, but he was trying to ignore the pain. "I'll spell it out for you, *mi amigo.* The Texas Rangers have considerable power of their own, and the proper people know where I am. If you have me shot, Mexico will have more trouble and attention from the States than it's ever had before, and your *presidente* wouldn't like that. That's not a threat. It's just a fact. Since he is more of a dictator than a president, I don't think Señor Díaz wants our government getting involved down here. Even if you don't have me shot, that could still happen due to the simple fact that you are dealing with stolen American cattle. Now maybe you weren't even sure they were stolen, but they are, and we aim to put a stop to it and prove that Jim Caldwell is behind a good deal of the cattle rustling that has been taking place in west Texas."

He picked up his wineglass and drank down what was left.

"Go on, *señor.*"

John set down the glass again. "Surely you are wealthy enough that if you never buy another steer from Jim Caldwell, it won't affect your *ranchero.* I know you get the cattle a little cheaper because they're stolen, or maybe you didn't know why. But I suspect you can afford to buy your cattle the legal way, and perhaps you would make a fine impression on Díaz if you helped me in this. I know your *presidente* would just as soon shoot an American as look at him, but at the same time I think he would rather not have any more trouble with his northern friends than necessary. How long do you think you would be able to keep all of this from being taken away from you, if you are the cause of the American government getting involved in this? Our government hates Díaz. You and I both know he's nothing more than a dictator. He could turn on you at any time. Help me now, and I promise you that if Mexico has another revolution—and you know damn well how easily that could happen—and if that revolution threatens you and your fine sons and this beautiful *ranchero,* I will personally see to it that you get some help. You get a message to the Rangers, and we'll do what we can to support honest Mexican citizens like yourself against dictatorship." He grinned then. "And you know the kind of fighters we Texans are."

The look of deep worry on Cordera's face eased slightly at the last statement, and the man could not hold back a smile of his own. "And you Texans know the kind of fighters we Mexicans are, no?"

John nodded. "So, why fight each other? Why not work together against the wrong that's done on both sides? The time has to come when we must face the fact that we are neighbors, whether we like it or not, and we have to get along. You're a smart man. Who do you think is the better ally? The American government? Or Porfirio Díaz? Men like you can support Díaz all you want, but you also know he could decide at any time to seize what is yours. For all you know he is already plotting a way to do just that. He doesn't like any one man becoming too wealthy and powerful. A man like you could be a threat to his power in case of a revolution. You know he's had other opponents shot. Who is to say when he will decide *you* are his enemy rather than his friend? If it comes to that, we can help you take shelter in Texas, save your family."

Cordera rubbed at his mustache and turned away, pacing for a few quiet seconds. "It is true you would help me if I needed it? If my family should have to flee Mexico, you would give us shelter?"

"It's true. I'll make sure all the proper people are aware of your situation, and of the fact that you helped us . . . if you decide to do so. If not, all I can do is go back to Texas empty-handed and find some other way to prove Jim Caldwell is the bastard I believe he is. Trouble is, that might still end up involving you, in a much more public way, and Díaz would not like that. Do it my way, and we can keep this very quiet here in Mexico and keep attention, especially Díaz's attention, away from you." John could only pray his threat of Díaz taking the man's land from him would work. He knew the only way to get anything out of a powerful *don* like Cordera was to stir up the man's distrust of Mexico's dictatorial *presidente*—make the man worry about losing everything he owned.

Cordera paced again, then walked back to the sofa and sat down. He opened a gold container of cigars and handed one to John. "Sit back down and smoke with me," he said. "Tell me your plan."

John smelled victory. He came around to the sofa and

sat down, taking the cigar and letting Cordera light it for him with one of several long matches lying on the marble table. *"Gracias."* He puffed on the cigar for a moment. "There is a man who works for Caldwell. I believe he is a ringleader in the rustling," he told Cordera then, as the man lit his own cigar. "His name is Casey Dunlap."

Cordero slowly nodded. "Ah, yes, Señor Dunlap. I know him well, but I do not much like him. He sells me the cattle, but I can see in his eyes that he does not like Mexicans. You, *señor,* have respect for us. I can tell, even though you are obviously Indian. Mexicans and American Indians do not get along so well, you know."

John grinned. "Well, I'm not a *Texas* Indian. I'm not Apache or Comanche. Maybe that helps."

Both men laughed lightly. "So, *señor,* I am listening. What is it you would have me do?"

John could already see Dunlap and Caldwell standing on a hanging scaffold. He could not keep the fires of victory from burning through his gaze as he answered Cordera. "All you have to do is make the same plans with Caldwell you always make, meet him or Dunlap or whoever it is you meet, except that Texas Rangers will be waiting with you. The most important thing is something in writing. Do you have anything like that?"

Cordera hesitated. "I hope this is not a trick, *señor.* I am not accustomed to trusting Americans."

"Nor am I accustomed to trusting Mexicans. But I am trusting you, Don Emiliano."

Cordera studied John's eyes intently. "I have a letter, informing me the cattle I ordered for this spring will be delivered in two more weeks, at a canyon on the northern end of the Conchos River. It is signed by Señor Caldwell."

John could not help smiling as he breathed a deep sigh of relief. "Give me that letter. It's the best piece of proof we could have. Once we capture the men and the stolen cattle, there will be no way out for Caldwell." He stood up, almost wanting to shout with joy. Soon! Soon he could go home to Tess. He could almost feel her in his arms.

* * *

This was unlike any pain Tess had ever known. Right now she hated this baby for what it was doing to her, hated Chino for causing this. She even hated John, for not being with her. He'd promised to come back before the baby was born, but the baby was coming early. That made matters even worse. Even at full term, others would have thought the child was coming early.

The gossip would be heavy, but somehow she and John would get through it. The trouble was, she had to get over being angry with John, and she had to learn to love this baby.

She gripped the rails at the head of the bed, unable to keep from crying out with another gripping pain. It tore through her insides like witch's claws, a pain so intense and so deep that it terrified her. She'd always known childbirth was painful, but she had not expected this. The worst part was that Dr. Sanders could not be here. He was thirty miles away taking care of some kind of emergency. His wife had come in his place. Mary had assisted her husband with other births, and she'd assured Tess she knew what to do, but she was young and had never had a child of her own yet. How could she understand this? Louise Jeffers had agreed to help. Tess had wanted Jenny there, but Louise and Mary had insisted she was not needed. They didn't understand that she *was* needed, not for physical help, but a kind of moral support only Jenny could give her, something these women did not understand.

"How much longer?" she groaned, lying in a bath of sweat. It was early April, and the weather was unusually hot.

"It's hard to say, dear," Mary told her. "I don't think things are quite ready, but I can tell the baby is properly positioned. The first one always takes longer, but I assure you, this should be an uncomplicated birth. I just hope the baby will be all right, since it's coming rather early."

"Has . . . to be," Tess moaned. "John . . . so wants it."

But did *she* want it? This baby had done nothing but totally alter her life and make her fat and sick and uncomfortable, and now it was causing her ungodly pain. Would it look like Chino? Would it grow up to be a horrible person like Chino?

What a foolish thought. It would be raised in a loving home, with a man who planned to be the best father he could be. But would he—or she—know a mother's love? Up to now she'd been determined to love the baby fully, had told herself she must not blame the child for its beginnings. She'd promised John she would love it, but John wasn't here to see what she was going through. How could you love something that brought this much pain, especially when you didn't want it in the first place? The only good thing this baby had brought her was a man she'd learned to love more than she'd ever thought possible. But the fact remained, that man was not this baby's father. It was Chino, the hated Chino. She could see him raping her, *feel* him raping her. It had been vicious and painful, and now the product of that rape was bringing more pain.

She screamed when the agony grew even deeper this time. She began to lose touch with reality, hardly aware of where she was or with whom. This had been going on for hours, endless hours.

Was that Jenny hovering over her? "How much ... longer?" she screamed. "Make it come! Make it come!"

"We can't force it to come," someone told her. "It has to happen naturally, Tess."

"Noooo. No more!" Tess curled up on her side. "Get John. What if he dies, Jenny? What if Casey Dunlap ... kills him?"

Louise frowned, looking at Mary. What was she talking about? "Casey Dunlap?"

"He ... shot him. I ... heard. Why did John ... have to go after him? He'll ... get killed. I should have told. He didn't ... have to go after them, Jenny."

"What on earth is she talking about?" Mary asked Louise.

"I don't know." Louise leaned closer. "What could you have told, Tess?"

Tess cried out with another pain. They were much closer together now, seemingly endless. When would it stop? She felt engulfed in terror, bathed in agony. John. Where was John? He should be here. She hated him for not being here. "John," she moaned. "Get John. He'll . . . never catch them. Nobody knows Caldwell . . . is a cattle thief. I . . . heard. I heard. I can tell them the . . . truth. You tell them, Jenny. Go to . . . the Army. Tell them . . . what I know. I don't want John to die."

"She's delirious," Mary commented.

"Apparently," Louise returned, wondering at the strange comments. *Was* she delirious? Where was John Hawkins? What had been so important that it had taken him away so long he couldn't be with his wife now when she was having their baby? She looked at Mary. "What do you suppose she means by her comments about Harriet's husband? And Casey Dunlap? Isn't he Jim Caldwell's top man?"

"Yes." Mary leaned over Tess. "What do you want Jenny to tell the Army, Tess? What has Mr. Caldwell done?"

Tess screamed with the black pain, lost in it, hating it and everyone who had caused it. She hated Jim Caldwell, too, and Casey Dunlap. It was their fault John couldn't be here.

"Thieves," she groaned. "Rustlers. I know."

Mary's eyes widened when she looked at Louise. "What in God's name is she saying?"

Louise shook her head. "I think you're right. I think she's delirious." She checked Tess. "The baby is coming." She began ordering Tess to push now, to take deep breaths and push. She looked over at Mary as Tess screamed and strained and cried. "Don't say anything about what you heard, Mary. Let me handle this."

"How? What will you do?"

"I'm not sure. I'd better talk to Harriet. Just don't say

one word to any one, not even your husband. Promise me that. She's probably just hallucinating."

Mary nodded. "I promise."

"Bring the hot water and some more clean towels," Louise said.

Mary left the room, and Louise leaned over Tess. "What is it you know, Tess Hawkins?" she asked softly. None of it made sense, but she probably owed it to Harriet, as a friend, to tell her what Tess had said in her delirium. It was true she could be fantasizing, but pain sometimes had a way of forcing people to spill the truth. What *was* the truth? Surely it wasn't what Tess had just said about Jim Caldwell!

Things became frantic then as the baby suddenly came very fast. There was no more time to wonder about what Tess had said. There was only time for pushing and pulling and forcing out afterbirth, cleaning membrane away from the baby's face and mouth, forcing out that first cry. It was a boy, a very strong, healthy, full-term boy. It didn't seem possible this could be John Hawkins's baby, but then Tess *had* admitted she'd lain in sin with the man after her abduction, and there was no mistaking the child had Indian blood. He had a full shock of black hair, and his skin was a reddish brown color. His eyes remained closed, but there was no doubt they would be black, too.

Louise cleaned up Tess while Mary worked to bathe and wrap the furiously screaming baby.

"My gosh, he's strong," Mary commented. The baby kicked and squalled, making little fists with his tiny hands, stiffening against every move Mary made to get a diaper on him and a blanket around him. She walked with him while Louise finished with Tess, hoping the child would quiet down once he was in his mother's arms. Finally a still-dazed Tess was ready, and Mary leaned over her. "Here is your son, Tess. He's beautiful and healthy. You should be very proud, as I am sure your husband will be when he sees him." She laid the baby into the crook of Tess's arm.

Tess was only vaguely aware at first, wondered where the

crying came from. She soon realized it was right beside her. A baby. *Her* baby! She struggled to get back to reality, turned to look at the tiny bit of life that lay beside her . . . tiny . . . yet plenty big for a newborn. He was crying and sucking at his fist.

He's hungry," Mary said. "Let me help you feed him. It takes a little practice at first. Do you feel up to it?"

Up to it? This bastard child of Chino's wanted to feed at her breast! Oh, God, she had no feelings for him! God forgive her! John had said that once the baby fed at her breast, she would love him. She *had* to love him! She'd promised John. But where *was* John? What if he got himself killed and never came back? How could she love this child then?

Louise propped some pillows behind her and Mary helped her open her gown, washed her breast and gently massaged it, helped her position the baby to find his mark. It hurt at first. Of course it hurt. This was *Chino's* child! Oh, God, she didn't want it! She didn't . . .

The pain was gone now, but the sudden pull at her breast had brought her further into reality. She looked down at the perfectly formed bit of life feeding at her breast. His little fist curled up against the white of her skin. Dark . . . so dark. Like John. Yes, he *could* be John's, couldn't he? Somehow she had to learn to love this baby. Maybe . . . maybe it was possible. But she couldn't do it alone. She needed John.

"Dear God, bring him home," she whispered.

Chapter Twenty-Three

Tess sat down wearily in the rocker presented to her by Louise and Rachael and the other members of the quilting club. Louise's husband, who had built Tess's little house, had made the rocker by hand, as well as the lovely cradle in which her new son now slept. The gifts had been a pleasant surprise, as had the food some of the women had sent over. Louise and Mary had taken turns the first few days helping care for the baby until Tess was well enough to do it herself. She appreciated the help, not just because the birth had been difficult and had left her weak, but because she had so much to learn about caring for a baby. A job made harder by her mixed emotions over the baby.

She sat looking into the cradle at her feet, leaned forward to rest her elbows on her knees and study her new son. He was eight days old now, and she still had not named him. She wanted John to do that. He was a sweet child, had cried very little since that first squalling after he was born, and he slept almost constantly between feedings. What kept her most tired was the feedings themselves, for the baby had quite an appetite, demanding more milk every three hours, and she could tell he had already put on a little weight.

Did she love him? Of course. Every mother loved her baby, didn't she? She closed her eyes and leaned back, feeling horrible at having to admit she was not sure. If only she could stop thinking about the child's father. When he fed at her breast she sometimes had flashes of Chino, grabbing and biting at her there. Once she even tore the baby away from his feeding and made him cry. Her heart nearly broke now at the memory, and since then she had forced herself to see only the baby, the innocent baby. The child was perfect, handsome, healthy, alert. Already she could make him grin when she touched his chin and talked to him. His dark eyes were bright and watchful, his little hands strong.

John was going to love this son of his . . . probably more than she did. That wasn't right. The boy wasn't even of his own blood. How strange that a man who could be as mean and violent and seemingly uncaring as John Hawkins could love this little baby more than his own mother loved him. Her guilt weighed on her, and she let the tears come again.

"I won't," she sobbed. "I won't allow myself to feel this way. This is my son. *My* son. He's so innocent." She leaned down and took him out of the cradle, wrapping him tight and holding him close to her breast. She rocked him, kissed the fine, black hairs on his still-soft head. "I will learn to love you, my sweet baby," she whispered.

If only John were here. He would help her through this. Just seeing him with the baby would help. What was she going to do if he never came back? She would have to raise this child alone . . . Chino's child. "Stop it," she told herself. "You have to forget him." She kissed the baby again, and just as she was about to put the still-sleeping child back into his cradle, someone knocked at the door.

She quickly wiped at her tears and blinked rapidly to try to erase the signs of crying. New mothers were not supposed to cry. They were supposed to be deliriously happy. She kept the baby in the crook of her arm and went to the door, surprised when she opened it to see Harriet Caldwell standing before her. The woman's buggy was at the hitching post outside, a hired hand standing beside it. "Harriet! I'm—"

"Surprised?" The woman looked her over. "You look very nice, Tess, not at all the weary, bedraggled new mother."

Tess smiled. "I assure you I *am* weary and bedraggled." She stepped aside. "Please come in. It's turned so cold again, and I don't want the baby to get a chill." As Harriet stepped inside, Tess noticed she was holding a wrapped package. She closed the door. "The weather is crazy. Hot one day, cold the next."

"Yes, it can be quite unpredictable this time of year."

Tess watched the woman curiously. What on earth was she doing here? "This is actually the first day I have truly done my hair up right and put on a decent dress instead of a gown and robe. I was happy to discover this dress fit me. I was worried I would never get my old waistline back."

"Well, dear, we all suffer a slight change in our girlish shapes after having babies. It's a fact of life." Harriet, wearing a dark brown taffeta dress, dark brown gloves, a fur cape, and a matching fur hat, turned to look at her, holding the regal pose she always displayed. The billowing, cascading ruffles at the back of her dress made swishing sounds as she walked over to the sofa. "May I sit down?"

"Of course!" Tess caught something different about her, a small hint of . . . what was it? Apology? Worry? Apprehension? She could not quite name it, but something was different.

"Come and sit beside me and let me study that new baby. I am told he is just the most perfect baby ever born, according to Louise."

The comment brought a wave of pride to Tess's heart that she had not yet felt for the baby. She walked over and sat down beside Harriet who reached over and pulled the blanket farther away from him, studying the round face, the perfect little nose, the pretty mouth. His dark skin showed not a blemish.

"I have to oil his hair a little," Tess explained, "to keep it under control. It seems to always want to stick up in every direction."

Harriet smiled. "Well, obviously it will someday be just like his father's. And he will probably be as big and strong. With John Hawkins for a father, he will probably be a pistol to raise."

"He probably will be," Tess replied, *because his father was the notorious—No. John* was his father. She must always remember that. "I am so glad you decided to come and see him," she said. "If you would like to hold him, I'll go and make us some tea, or I can put him back in his cradle."

"Why don't you put him in his cradle, dear? I have a gift for the baby, and we need to talk. If you think he will sleep for a while longer, we can go into the kitchen together and talk there."

"Certainly." Puzzled, Tess rose and laid the baby back in his cradle. Harriet followed her into the kitchen, and Tess set two cups on the table. She filled a tea strainer with tea leaves taken from a can on the table, then set it in one of the cups. "I already have hot water." She poured some into the cup. "I will let you brew yours first."

"Well, while I am doing that, you can open this gift." Harriet laid the package beside the other cup, and Tess sat down, pulling away the string and the brown paper in which it was wrapped. Inside was a knitted baby blanket in lovely colors of blue and yellow, pink and white.

"This is lovely! Did you make this yourself?"

"I most certainly did. Made it in four days."

"My goodness! I have to admit, in spite of my talent for sewing, I have never been good at knitting. Thank you so much, Harriet. This is so . . . unexpected. I know you have never approved of my marriage or even believed—"

"That doesn't matter right now," Harriet interrupted. She took the tea strainer from her cup and laid it in Tess's.

"Those leaves are probably still strong enough to brew your own cup."

Tess studied her eyes. There was that look again, an almost pleading look. She rose and poured hot water into her cup, then set the kettle back on the stove. "Is it too warm in here for you? The house is so small, when I keep the cookstove hot, it warms the whole place."

"I am fine." Harriet removed her cape and hung it over the back of the chair. "I will tell you point-blank, Tess, that I did want to see the baby and give you the gift. But there is a more important reason for my visit."

Tess slowly dunked the tea strainer up and down as she studied the woman's usually cold gray eyes. She was shocked to see Harriet looked almost ready to cry. "What is that, Harriet?"

Harriet took a deep breath as though for courage. "Louise told me something that disturbs me greatly. I have said nothing yet to my husband. I wanted to talk to you first."

Tess frowned, feeling a hint of alarm. Said nothing to her husband? "What do you mean?" She moved a bowl of sugar closer. "Here is some sweetener for your tea."

Harriet spooned a little of the sugar into the cup and took a sip of the tea. "Louise told me in strict confidence. She promised me that Mary would also keep what she heard to herself. They both decided I should be told, that perhaps I should come and talk to you about it."

Tess spooned some sugar into her own cup. "About what?"

"About . . . something you said when you were delirious with pain from the birth."

My God! Tess thought. What on earth had she said? Had she put John in more danger? She slowly stirred the sugar. "Go on."

"Well, you said . . . you said what if Casey Dunlap kills your husband? What would you do alone with a baby?"

Tess frowned, struggling to pretend surprise and innocence. "I . . . can't imagine why I would say that."

"Can't you?"

Tess was surprised that Harriet looked ready to cry.

"You also said that Casey Dunlap was the one who shot John Hawkins. Not only that, you said John had gone after Dunlap, but that he didn't have to do that. You said you knew the truth yourself, that you had seen . . . something, heard something." The woman blinked back tears and looked down at her teacup. "You said my husband was a cattle thief, and that your husband was out to prove it . . . that you knew the truth. You apparently thought you were talking to that tramp, Jenny Simms. You called her by name, told her to go get the Army and have them go help John."

Tess closed her eyes and sipped some of her own tea for courage. "I . . . had no idea I'd said those things."

Harriet sniffed. "Thank God I know I can trust Louise and Mary. I understand that you probably would have said nothing if not for the pain and your missing your husband and needing him. That is not the point. The point is pain often forces the truth out of people. I want the truth, Tess Hawkins. What made you say those things? What is it you think you know?"

Tess struggled to think straight. If she told the truth, the woman would go straight to her husband, which could set off a chain of events that could foil whatever John was doing to capture Dunlap and Caldwell. Still, even if she said nothing, Harriet realized something was wrong and would probably go to her husband anyway. She met Harriet's eyes, saw the pain there. "First tell me where your husband is right now."

Harriet frowned. "He is out on spring roundup. Casey Dunlap is his best man, but he is gone right now, out buying more cattle, so I am told."

Out stealing more cattle, more likely, Tess thought. "I'm sorry, Harriet. I can't tell you everything. It could endanger my own husband. When he gets back from wherever he's gone, the truth will be known. Please be assured that anything I might know has never been told to another soul except John and his partner. I had no idea I had said anything in my pain. I'm sorry."

"Sorry?" Harriet rose. "I am not here to protect Jim. I am here to protect myself. I need to know the truth, Tess. I have . . . suspected something myself for a long time." She faced Tess. "You might as well know my husband and I have disagreed on some of his tactics for a while. I am well aware that he has bullied neighbors into selling out to him, that he tried to do so with your own father." She held her chin proudly, standing stiff and erect. "When I married Jim Caldwell, it was because it was expected of me. We came from neighboring plantations, wealth marrying wealth. Jim has never been an easy man to live with, but he could provide for me in the way to which I was accustomed. You have to understand he is himself a proud man, Tess. He lost everything in the war, as did my own family. It devastated him. When Colonel Bass offered this free land here in Texas, he was overjoyed to be able to start over. He learned the cattle business from the bottom up. The only thing he'd known before that was cotton, and, of course, we still grow some of that. But it was cattle that boomed after the war, and my husband took advantage of that. His one driving goal was to rebuild the empire he'd lost in Virginia, be just as wealthy again. What worried me was it became an obsession for him."

She turned away, folding her arms. "I was raised to appreciate and enjoy the finest things in life, Tess. I will admit that. I wanted it all back just as much as my husband did. The only difference is, I would never deceive someone, deliberately hurt someone or steal from someone to get what I wanted. That is the God's truth. If my husband has been doing those things, I am not so sure I can remain living with him. He dreams of talking our sons into coming out here and becoming cattle barons themselves, but they choose to stay in Virginia where they have lives and families of their own. They never got along well with their rather bullying father." She sighed deeply, her voice shaky with emotion. "I miss my sons. I want to know if you think my husband is going to be found guilty of cattle rustling. That is a hanging offense, as you know. I need to know what you know. If my husband is a cattle thief ... possibly a murderer ... I intend to leave El Paso, go back home to Virginia. I still have family there, and they have rebuilt a reasonably decent life. My parents are dead, but I have two sisters and a brother there ... and my sons. I have wanted to go back for a long time, but Jim never could find the time. He was too busy rebuilding his little empire here." She faced Tess again. "Please tell me what you know, Tess."

The woman's story astounded Tess. "I ... had no idea about your personal problems, Harriet."

"And it is not easy for me to share them with anyone, least of all you, after the way I have treated you. I want you to understand that part of the reason I seem so ... so aloof and demanding ... is my own way of covering up the hurt." The woman blinked back tears. "I was raised to be proud and honest and dignified, taught that certain things were proper and other things were not. One of the "proper" things was that a woman was a good and faithful wife to her husband ... whether she loved him or not." She turned away. "I can tolerate a lot of things, Tess, but I cannot tolerate a husband who would murder and steal. Is that what my husband has done?"

Tess sighed, rubbing her hand across her forehead. "I don't know about murder, Harriet. I ... overheard him in his study one night, talking with Casey Dunlap and Sheriff Higgins." She told Harriet all of it, praying she was not ruining John's plans by doing so. "Jim Caldwell might not have pulled the trigger himself, but I have no doubt he would dearly like to see my husband dead. Personally, I believe Casey Dunlap shot him. But we might never be able to prove that. One thing John *does* want to prove is that ... that your husband is behind a good deal of the cattle rustling that has taken place in west Texas. He was strangely upset when my husband caught and killed Derrek Briggs and his gang." She blinked back her own tears.

"I'm sorry, Harriet. If John gets the evidence he is after and this whole thing comes to court, I will have to testify to what I heard. There is no doubt in my mind your husband has been rustling cattle, probably selling them in Mexico, where it would be easier. I couldn't go to the Rangers with my story because Jim Caldwell is too highly respected in these parts. No one would have believed me without definite proof, and I knew your husband was too smart to leave any evidence anyplace on his own land, namely the stolen cattle. He has to be caught some other way, and that is what John is trying to do."

She met Harriet's gaze, seeing the deep hurt in the woman's eyes.

"You don't have to leave El Paso. Your women friends won't desert you, Harriet. Most of the women in these parts have been through their own hells of one kind or another. I . . . I discovered something about my own first husband that devastated me. He was a complete coward when the farm was raided. He hid under the bed while I fought off those Comancheros all alone. He never even came out to help when they set the house on fire and dragged me off. I guess that is part of the reason John Hawkins became so easy to love. He was all courage and daring. He made me feel so safe."

Harriet slowly nodded, a tear slipping down her cheek. "This land has a way of making men ruthless, Tess. But it was the war that made my husband ruthless. When you send a ruthless, desperate man into a land where there is basically no law but those he sets for himself, you end up with a man who hardly knows right from wrong anymore. The fact that the Indian situation was much worse when we first came here only made matters worse. It hardened him even more. I hardly know the man now, but then, in many ways I never did." She quickly wiped at another tear.

"What will you do?"

Harriet took a deep breath. "I will leave."

"He'll want to know why."

"And I will tell him. I just won't tell him how I know."

She took her fur cape from the chair. "Will you testify against him?"

Tess stood up. "If I am asked, I won't have any choice."

Harriet nodded, hooking the front of the cape. "I understand. And I won't blame you. I thought about begging you not to, but I have a feeling he will be found out anyway. And men like my husband can't keep running Texas. He calls those like your own husband violent and uncivilized, but his own behavior is no different." She picked up her gloves. "I just don't know how I will explain this to our sons, or what I will do with the ranch. I suppose I will have to hire an attorney and sell the place."

"You don't know yet what will happen, Harriet."

"I do know." Harriet turned and walked around the table to the kitchen archway. "I will think of you often, Tess Hawkins."

Tess walked a little closer. "And I will remember you and pray for you, Harriet." She walked the woman to the door, and Harriet stopped and glanced at the cradle. The baby's little hands were flailing about, one foot sticking up in the air where it had come out from under the blanket. He was making tiny gurgling noises. She looked at Tess.

"I am considered a wealthy woman, Tess. But you are wealthy in your own way. You have a strength I never had, and great courage and daring, just like the man you married. He isn't really the father, is he?"

The remark startled Tess, but it was spoken calmly, and with surprising sympathy. Tess studied Harriet for several silent seconds. "No. A woman often simply does what she must."

Harriet smiled sadly. "Yes, she does. I hope you have at least learned to love the man."

Such curious questions. "I love him very much. And John loves me."

"Then you are a lucky woman. I never did learn to love my husband, and I am not so sure he ever did love me." She turned and opened the door. "Don't worry. I will keep your little secret."

She walked out, and Tess went to the doorway. She watched Harriet climb into the buggy. "Goodbye, Harriet," she said softly. She waved, but the other woman did not look back.

Chapter Twenty-Four

"There they are!" John watched the herd of cattle snaking its way along the Conchos. "Eight men. There are only eight men." He could taste victory, feel Tess in his arms.

"I'll be damned," Ken muttered. "All this time I still couldn't hardly believe it. I mean I did, but you know . . . Jim Caldwell, of all people. I don't reckon we'll be lucky enough to see him down there."

"Hell, no. He's home pretending to be a good citizen of Texas. But you can bet Casey Dunlap is down there!"

They could hear whistles and calls now as the rustlers urged the cattle to keep moving.

"You just remember we *need* Dunlap," Ken warned.

John felt on fire with hatred and revenge. "I'll remember." He had ridden from Camargo to Juárez to wire Fort Bliss, telling Captain Booth to send help to Fire Canyon at the northern end of the Conchos. Thank God he'd gotten the information he needed early enough to have time to make the long trip back to Juárez and to the Conchos before Dunlap arrived. If he had not come to Mexico early in the winter, he never would have found the information he needed in time. The long ride to Juárez had been tiring. He'd ridden practically night and day, and he'd had to board Sundance at Juárez and rent another horse, after nearly riding Sundance to death.

He was still weak himself, and his ribs were hurting. He wondered if he would always have this pain whenever he strained himself physically; but right now he knew the pain was worth what he was seeing.

"This is the real prize, Ken," he said quietly.

Both men watched the procession from a cluster of boulders on the hillside along the river. Their horses were tied a few yards below the hill out of sight, where four other Rangers waited.

"I have the letter I told you about, signed by Caldwell himself," John said. "But Dunlap is our real key. I'll finally have the proof I need to nail Jim Caldwell!"

Ken spit a wad of tobacco at a grasshopper. "You've been workin' on this a long time. You must be anxious to get home to that wife of yours." Both men waited for the men and cattle to move farther into the canyon.

"She must have had the baby by now," John commented. "I promised her I'd be back before that happened."

"Oh, I expect she'll forgive you."

"I don't know. It's going to be hard on her, considering the circumstances."

"A baby is a baby. All women love babies. Don't matter where they come from or even if they ain't the most perfect baby they ever seen."

"Yeah, well I'll still feel better when I'm with her. Let's go."

They both remained crouched as they moved back down to their horses.

"Remember, Dunlap is the one with the snakeskin boots," John reminded the other four men. "A couple of you know him by sight. He's tall and thin, and I expect he'll be riding at the front of the others. Be careful who you shoot at. Much as I'd like to slice his heart out myself, we've got to take Dunlap alive."

"Them ain't words I ever thought I'd hear *you* say," Ken returned.

The others grinned and mounted their horses. "We'll watch out for Dunlap," one of them told John. "He's all yours, Hawk."

They headed for the north end of the canyon, where they would chase the rustlers toward the south end. Ken and John would be waiting for them. There would be no room for escape.

Ken and John headed south and waited behind thick underbrush as the outfit of men and cattle gradually came their way. After several long, anxious minutes, both men pulled out their rifles and moved out from behind cover, still on horseback. They leveled their Winchesters at the men who approached.

"Dunlap!" John had the man in his rifle sight, and it was a struggle to keep from pulling the trigger. "Hold it right there!" he shouted. "Texas Rangers! You're under arrest!"

There was a temporary look of shock on the men's faces, and Dunlap let out a string of filthy expletives while guns were pulled and men whirled their horses. They began shooting in every direction, quickly aware that more Rangers were riding hard toward them from the north end of the canyon. Horses whinnied and cattle bellowed and began to stampede from the noises of gunshots magnified by the echoing canyon walls. Three of the men headed back north, and five, including Dunlap, charged south, shooting at Ken and John as they tried to get past them. Ken shot down two of them, but John felt helpless. He could so easily blast Casey Dunlap out of the saddle, and he dearly wanted to do just that. But he had to keep him alive. He hated to do it, but he shot the man's horse instead, depending on Ken to take care of the other two. His only goal was taking Dunlap alive.

Dunlap's galloping horse tumbled headfirst, its hind quarters flipping up into the air and throwing Dunlap to the ground. John charged his horse up to Dunlap, who had lost his handgun in the fall. His eyes were wide with a mixture of surprise and fright, and he turned to run, looking frantically for his gun. Seconds later someone tackled him to the ground, and he already knew who it was. John Hawkins. His heart pounded with fright. He had no doubt Hawkins knew he was the one who'd shot him. The Ranger would be out for blood, and everyone knew what that meant.

He rolled over, landing hard blows into John's face, wondering somewhere in the back of his mind why the man didn't just shoot him.

John jerked him to his feet, hatred and vengeance overflowing in his soul as he returned the punches, throwing vicious blows to Dunlap's midsection, his face. Kill! He so dearly wanted to kill him! "You back-shooting bastard!" he growled, landing more blows.

In spite of his bony frame, Dunlap was tough and did not go down easily. One hard blow finally landed him on his back, but as John reached down to jerk him up again, Dunlap kicked hard at John's ribs, delighted to see he had apparently found a weak spot. John doubled over and stumbled.

Quickly Dunlap jumped up and grabbed John's six-gun from its holster, cocked it, but before he could fire, a shot rang out, and he screamed with the horrible pain in his right knee and crumpled to the ground.

John wiped sweat and blood and dirt from his face. He was on his knees, still grasping his ribs when he heard the shot, saw Dunlap rolling on the ground and screaming, holding his knee. He saw his own gun lying on the ground, then looked up to see Ken standing there.

"You've saved my ass enough times. I figured it was time I returned the favor," Ken said.

They exchanged a look of mutual understanding and appreciation. "Thanks," John told him. "The bastard kicked me right in the spot where I was wounded." He grabbed up his gun, looked at the still groaning Dunlap, who had both hands wrapped around his knee. He looked

back at Ken, and Ken nodded. Ignoring his own pain, John
walked over and placed a foot on Dunlap's chest, pressing
hard to hold him down. He cocked his gun and aimed it
at the man's face.

"I want the truth, Dunlap, or I'll shoot out the other
knee!"

"Goddamn it, help me! My knee! Jesus, my knee!"

"How about *both* knees!"

"You son-of-a-bitchin' half-breed bastard," Dunlap
cursed. "Why don't you just . . . shoot me! Everybody knows
. . . you always kill your man. You're no better . . . than a
murdering outlaw!"

John pushed harder with his foot, making it harder for
Dunlap to breathe. "Here's how it is, Dunlap. There's
nothing I would like better than to kill you . . . slowly.
But I need you alive. You're going to tell the truth about
shooting me in the *back!* And you're going to tell the truth
about Jim Caldwell! And until Ken and I both hear you
say it, you're going to suffer more and more, understand?
I won't mind a bit shooting out your other knee, and I'll
by-God do it! I'll shoot off your fingers one by one if I
have to! You won't die, Dunlap, but you'll by-God *wish* you
were dead! You know I'll do it, you back-shooting bastard,
so start talking! You're the one who shot me, aren't you!"

Dunlap struggled to breathe. He knew Hawkins would
do exactly what he threatened to do. He'd hang anyway,
but for now he couldn't stand the pain. "I . . . shot you . . .
you stinking breed!" he answered through gritted teeth.

John leaned down and placed the barrel of his six-gun
hard against one of Dunlap's eyes.

"John! We need him alive!" Ken reminded him. "You'll
get to watch him hang."

John literally trembled with a need to pull the trigger.
"And what about Caldwell? These cattle are *stolen*, aren't
they? You've burned off the brands, and you were going
to sell them to Emiliano Cordera, right? Jim Caldwell is
behind the whole thing. He's been doing this for three or
four years now. True?"

Dunlap curled onto his side, grabbing his knee again. "How . . . did you find out . . . about Cordera?"

John knelt down and grabbed hold of the man's hair, jerking his head back. "That doesn't matter. I want to hear you tell me it's *true!*" John growled.

A panting, sweating Dunlap grimaced as he answered. "It's true."

John kept hold of Dunlap's hair and rammed his six-gun against the man's throat. "You're going to testify to that in court, Dunlap! You nail Caldwell for us, and I just might be able to get you sent to prison instead of hanged! God knows how bad I'd like to see your neck stretched, but I'd rather see Caldwell put out of business! You cooperate, and you just might live!" He put his gun away and jerked Dunlap to his feet. The man screamed bloody murder with the pain in his knee, but John pushed and shoved, finally getting Dunlap into the saddle on another man's horse. Ken was examining that man, one he'd shot.

"He's dead," he told John. He looked around. "I wounded the other three. We've got men to bury and wounds to tend, and we've got cattle to round up. We need to take them back with us, show the burned-off brands."

"We have enough men for all of that," John answered, still glaring at Dunlap.

One of the other Rangers rode up to them. "We have one dead Ranger," he said. "One dead and one wounded rustler."

"What the hell are you doing arresting us in Mexico!" Dunlap screamed. "You . . . can't do that!"

"Texas Rangers can do anything they want," John answered.

"Like hell! This is . . . false arrest! You'll be in trouble on this one, Hawkins!"

John picked up a rock and walked over to the man. "Well, then, when we get you and these cattle across the Rio Grande, I guess we'll have to officially arrest you all over again, won't we?" With that he slammed the rock against the man's already-shattered knee, enjoying his screams of pain. "That's for shooting me in the back, you stinking coward, and for costing the life of a Texas Ranger here today!" He threw down the rock and ordered three of the rangers to go round up the cattle. "One of you help the wounded and guard them. Ken and I will start digging to bury the dead. We have too far to go to try to take them back with us."

As the others headed out, Ken faced John, wiping sweat from his eyes with his shirtsleeve. "Good job, Hawk."

John winced rubbing at his ribs again. "Thanks for saving my rear."

"All in a day's work."

John managed a smile. "Yeah." His dark eyes showed an affection he'd never allowed to show before. "I'll miss working with you, Ken. You come visit me and Tess often, you hear?"

Ken nodded. "Actually, you were right a few months back when you said I was gettin' too old for this. Maybe you could use a ranch hand once you get settled."

Their gaze held in mutual understanding. "I probably could at that. I'll be sure to come to you first."

Ken nodded. "I'm glad for you, Hawk." He looked around. "And glad this mess is over with."

John looked over at a groaning Casey Dunlap. "Yeah. So am I. So am I."

Tess laid the baby in his cradle, setting it beside the bed. She wanted to keep him close so that she heard any little fussing he might make. She started to take off her robe to go to bed when she heard someone knock at the back door. She frowned, wondering who would come so late, but her heartbeat quickened when she realized it was probably John. He was back!

She retied her robe and hurried to the door, flinging it open, but to her surprise and sudden terror it was Jim Caldwell who barged inside, closing the door behind him.

Tess quickly moved around to the other side of the table. "How dare you walk right in here!" she said.

"And how dare *you* destroy my life!" he growled.

She grasped the top of her robe, pulling it tighter around her throat. "What are you talking about?"

"You know goddamn well what I'm talking about, you bitch! You *know* something! I don't know what it is or how you know it, but you drove my wife away! She *left* me today. Thirty years of marriage, and she's gone! The worst part is, she accused me of cattle rustling, even said I probably did business with Comancheros! I'm a law-abiding citizen of Texas, trying to—"

"Don't tell me about being law-abiding!" Tess interrupted. "My husband was *back*-shot, right after paying a visit to your ranch!"

"That had nothing to do with me! I want to know what kind of *lies* you've been spreading about me, woman!"

"I haven't been spreading any lies. I've said nothing to anyone but your wife, and *she* came to *me* asking questions! Our conversation went no further. So how would you know about it? Harriet promised not to tell anyone she had come to see me."

"She didn't have to tell me." Caldwell began moving around the table. "The man who drove her here told me where she'd been two days ago. It was after that Harriet started acting strangely. Yesterday she packed her bags and told me exactly why she was going back to Virginia. She caught the train just an hour ago. How in hell am I supposed to face my sons with the bullshit she's going to be telling them about their father?"

Tess moved toward the archway, trying to think. Did she need to defend herself physically? "Anything you might have to explain to your sons is your *own* fault, Mr. Caldwell! What do you expect me to do about it? Why are you even here?"

"I want to know what you told my wife, and *why!*"

Tess could see his fists were clenched. "What difference would it make?" She moved toward the heating stove in a corner of the parlor. She had no gun in the house. The only weapon she could think of was the poker.

"It makes a difference to *me!*"

Tess looked at him defiantly. "I hope you realize what John Hawkins will do to you if he finds out you barged in here uninvited and threatened me!"

"I don't give a damn what John Hawkins thinks! I can take care of him anytime I want! Something tells me *you're* the key to all of this."

Tess frowned. She thought she heard a noise outside. What was going on? "I am no longer needed to put your neck in a noose, Jim Caldwell! You've done that to yourself. If you had not been so intent on owning everything you could put your hands on, and bringing in more money in any way you could, even if it came to rustling cattle, you wouldn't be in this mess!"

He stepped even closer, in a threatening posture. Tess reached behind her, feeling for the poker. "I'm asking you again, what is it you know? What did you tell my wife?"

Tess's heart pounded so hard it hurt. The baby! What about the baby! She had to keep his attention away from her little boy. The man looked demented. He might do anything for vengeance. "I told her the *truth*—something I heard one night at your house. You were having a meeting, with Sheriff Higgins and your foreman, Casey Dunlap! I heard you wish John Hawkins *dead*"—she sneered—"and I heard you talking about stealing cattle! I know, Mr. Caldwell, and it won't be long before the whole town knows! But that won't be because of anything I've said. I never told a soul but John! He is out there somewhere right now getting all the evidence he needs. It will do you no good to threaten or harm me."

"You'd be surprised the power I have, missy, the people I control! Nobody in this town will believe I've ever done such things, or that I had anything to do with shooting your husband. Believe me, if it *had* been me, I'd have *finished* the job, and killed his partner, too! I've got plenty of men who can find John Hawkins and make sure he never gets back here with any evidence. And *you!* You are going to keep your mouth *shut!* In fact, I'll shut it *for* you!"

"You've lost your mind," Tess answered. She grasped the poker and swung it, but a strong hand grabbed her arm and wrenched the poker away. Struck by a hard blow to the left side of her face, she was aware of stumbling over a low table and landing on the floor. Something hit her on the head. Then everything went black, yet she could hear a crashing sound, heard Caldwell shout to someone outside.

"Light it," he said. "I've got the lamp in here."

She heard a strange whooshing, smelled smoke. Smoke! Was she dreaming? Imagining? Why couldn't she move? The smell grew stronger. Still she couldn't move. All consciousness left her then, for how long she couldn't be sure. When she came to she was aware of heat, bright flames, more smoke.

Fire! Never would she forget another fire, the old house back in Georgia in flames, her little brother screaming for help. She could see her mother running inside to save him, never to come out again. Flames everywhere! Everywhere! Coming out every window, every crack and crevice. Her mother and little brother inside. They were screaming . . . screaming! She struggled to rise. She had to help them. She looked around the smoke-filled room, able only to get to her knees. Where was she? Was she inside that burning house? She could hear crying. Was it her brother? Maybe it was the cabin at the farm. Comancheros! They were burning her out again!

Who was that crying? A baby! *Her* baby! This was her house, and this was real. The baby . . . fire! Smoke! Jim Caldwell had set her house on fire and planned on her and her baby burning up. What a terrible revenge against John! She couldn't let him come home to this. And she could not let her baby die this horrible way!

She could feel heat now as she kept her head low where there was the least smoke. The baby was crying harder. If he kept it up, he would inhale too much smoke. He could die just from that. What kind of man would do a thing like this to a woman and child! She looked around, getting her bearings from the furniture, knowing if she stayed to the right of the sofa and crawled straight forward, she would reach the bedroom doorway. Struggling against the pain in her head and flashes of blackness, she moved on hands and knees toward the bedroom, and the sounds of her crying baby.

She knew then. She knew how much she loved her son. If she had to crawl through flames to save him, she would do it. She scrambled faster. She could see the door jamb, see the rocker panels of the cradle. The baby's crying was mixed with coughing now. "Dear God," she muttered. "Save us!" She felt for the cradle, found it, reached inside. Weeping with joy, she took out the baby and held him close, so happy to feel him moving and kicking, to hear his sputtering cry. She quickly untied her robe and wrapped him inside it, hoping to shield him from more smoke.

She had to struggle against her own panic and tears then. Flames licked at all the walls of the house. How was she going to get out? She thought she heard noises outside, shouting, the clanging of the fire bell; but she knew from what she saw that the house was already too far gone for anyone to save it. She had grown to love this place where she had truly made love to John Hawkins for the first time, where this precious little baby boy had been born, this helpless creature who depended completely on his mother for sustenance and love. All she had managed to rebuild from her shattered life was here, and it was going up in flames . . . again. She remembered the noise outside, remembered Caldwell calling out to someone. That someone had set fires all around the house to prevent any escape. Jim Caldwell expected her and her son to go up in flames, but she would not let him win! Never!

She crouched, ducking her head and running into the kitchen, stumbling into the table. Keeping the baby close with one hand, she kept to the floor again, crawled to the back door. It was engulfed in flames. Yes, it was apparent that Caldwell had had help in this. A fire from one oil lamp could not have spread so quickly, and she did not doubt it was Sam Higgins who had set fire to the outside walls. The house was just far enough out of town that no one would have seen the flames soon enough to help her.

Memories of her mother's horrible fate gave her the courage she needed to overcome her greatest fear. It would be so easy to curl up and let the smoke take her, then the flames. But the baby. The baby did not deserve this, nor did John deserve to come home to find both of them dead. But how was she to get out? She would have to reach into the flaming door to open it. Terror began to engulf her. "Mama!" she wept. "Help me."

She heard a crashing sound then, and she looked up to see the flames at the door were no longer there. The door had fallen outward, as though her mother had heard her cry for help and had knocked it over for her. The frame was still burning, but the opening was a way out. In spite of her bare feet, Tess took what she knew was her only chance. She ran through the opening, felt the horrible heat on her feet and ankles, felt people grabbing her, someone beating at her legs and feet.

"The baby! She's got the baby!" Whose voice was that? Mary Sanders?

"I think they're all right," someone else said. That sounded like Dr. Sanders. "Her head is bleeding." Someone turned her over, and she could see everything was lit up by the flames. "Look at her face," Sanders said then. "It's bruised, almost like she was hit."

"Maybe it was outlaws that did this."

Higgins! That was Sam Higgins's voice!

"Caldwell," she shouted. "Jim Caldwell! He . . . tried to kill me! Don't let . . . Higgins near me! He . . . helped!"

"The woman must be delirious," she heard Higgins say.

"No! Find Caldwell! Find Caldwell," she screamed. "Don't let him get away . . . until my husband gets back. He'll . . . tell you! Jim Caldwell knows that I know . . . he's

a cattle thief. A murderer! He . . . tried to kill me and my
baby! John will . . . prove it! Please! Find Caldwell! Hold
him until . . . John gets here. And stop . . . Higgins! Don't
let him . . . near me!''

"What's this all about, Higgins?" someone asked.

"The woman's mad. Everybody knows it," Higgins
answered. "You gonna listen to a raving, terrified woman
who's never been right since she was abused by Comancheros? She doesn't know her own mind. She would never
have married John Hawkins if she wasn't a lunatic."

"I believe her," a woman said.

Louise! It was Louise. "Harriet Caldwell got on the train
this morning and went back East to her family there. She's
left her husband, and she came to tell me why before she
left. She didn't want to watch him hang."

"Hang!" someone shouted.

Someone else lifted Tess. "Let's get her to my office.
Her feet and legs are burned," she heard Doc Sanders
say.

"I've got her," the man holding her answered. She recognized the voice of Harold Jeffers, Louise's husband. He
was a big, strong man.

"My baby," Tess wept.

"I have the baby, Tess," Louise told her. "He's fine."

"Nobody is touching me!" Tess heard Sam Higgins saying. "First one who tries gets shot!"

Someone carried her off, amid shouts of "Get him!"
A lot of yelling and scuffling followed. She looked over
Harold's shoulder to see a pile of men beating on someone,
most likely Sheriff Higgins. Beyond that, she saw her little
house in a ball of flames. If she had been left inside two
minutes longer, she never would have escaped, and she
had no doubt it was her mother's spirit that had saved her.

She hardly felt the pain in her feet and legs as someone
laid her on a cot inside Doc Jeffers's place. All she could
think about was the baby. She begged to hold him, and
Louise laid him in her arms. She was more fully conscious
now, and she studied the boy. Untouched! He was still

perfect and unburned, but his face showed smudges from smoke. He coughed a little, looked up at her with his big, dark eyes . . . and grinned.

"My sweet, beautiful, precious little boy." She wept, pulling him close. "I love you." She kissed his fuzzy head. "I do so love you."

Chapter Twenty-Five

"I hope all three of them hang! If they don't, I'll kill them with my bare hands!"

Tess stirred awake from the first deep sleep she'd had since the fire. That had been three days ago, and this was the first time the pain of her burns had subsided enough to let her rest. She scooted to a sitting position just as John came walking into the spare bedroom where Mary and the doctor had put her in the big, rambling house they used partly as a hospital.

John's big frame seemed to fill the small room, not just in size but also because of the air of power and anger about him. It was obvious he was fresh off the trail, his clothes dusty, his face showing a several days' growth of beard, his shirt stained with sweat. "John! You're finally back. Thank God!"

He threw his hat on the bed and grabbed a wooden chair, planting it beside the bed. "And I'm damn sorry, Tess! I should have been with you. How bad is it?" He reached out and took hold of her hands.

"Dr. Sanders says it's only superficial burns. I ran over the flames so fast they didn't have a chance to burn deep.

I won't have any scars, and today the burns don't even hurt."

He looked down at her bare feet and legs, wincing at the dark red spots. "Damn!" He squeezed her hands tightly. "When we wired Booth from Fort Stockton, he wired back the news about the baby and also the fire. I told Ken to take care of things and left. I rode day and night to get here as fast as I could."

"It's all right, John. The fire . . ." Her eyes started to tear at the memory of not wanting or loving her baby at first. "It was the best thing that could have happened. It made me realize . . ." She smiled through quivering lips. "I love him so much, John. I didn't know it until the fire, when I thought he might die from the smoke and flames . . . when I was afraid I wouldn't be able to reach him— save him."

He rubbed the back of her hands with his thumbs. "I told you you'd love him." He leaned down and kissed the back of one hand. "Where is he? I want to see my son."

"He's right over there in that little bed, with pillows all around him. I wanted him in the room with me so I could hear if he cried. I wanted him in this bed with me, but at first I was in so much pain I was too restless and it kept him awake."

John rose and walked around to the small cot where the baby lay. "He's awake," he said, grinning. He pulled the blankets away and studied the boy. "My God," he said, "he's perfect. He's going to be a handsome boy, Tess." He leaned down and carefully picked him up. "I wish I wasn't so dirty. I didn't even want to take the time for a bath. I just wanted to see you and this baby, to see with my own eyes you were both all right." He held the child gingerly in the crook of his arm, supporting almost the entire backside of the infant with one big hand. "He's so tiny."

"Not really. He's big for only three weeks old."

John grinned, coming back around and sitting in the

chair. He gently laid the baby on the bed beside Tess, and she could see the love and wonder in his eyes.

"You're a father, John Hawkins. I haven't named him yet. I wanted to let you name him."

He leaned closer, letting the baby grab one of his fingers. "He's strong."

"And just look at him. No one would ever know he wasn't—"

"We'll never refer to that again." John met her eyes. "He *is* mine, Tess. He looks like mine, and he *is* mine. We both have pasts we would rather forget. It starts right here. Right now."

She pulled the baby closer against her, scooting down and kissing his velvety cheek. "What do you want to call him?"

John sighed, thinking a moment. "How about Texas?"

She raised her eyebrows in surprise. *"Texas?"*

"Sure. All the way here I thought about it, and it was Texas that brought us together, and Texas is where we're staying. Texas Randall Hawkins. That's really not a bad name. Out here the name Tex fits. Randall, of course, is Ken's last name."

Tess smiled, toying with the baby's tiny chin. "What do you think, Tex? Is that a proper name for such a tiny, sweet, innocent baby?"

John laughed lightly. "He won't always be tiny, sweet, and innocent."

Tess met his eyes. "With you for a father? I suppose not." She laughed herself. "I can just hear what Jenny will say when I tell her. She's crazy about the baby. She'll say, 'That sounds just like something John Hawkins would name a kid.'"

They laughed, both knowing more and more what they wanted . . . needed . . . as soon as she was well enough. Tess reached out for his hand. "I'm so glad you're all right. I was getting so worried. What happened, John? Did you get the proof you needed?"

He squeezed her hand, fires of victory in his eyes. "More

than enough. I found one of Caldwell's biggest buyers in Mexico and talked the man into helping me. I have a letter signed by Caldwell himself. And we caught Casey Dunlap herding stolen cattle into Mexico."

She watched him carefully. "You didn't kill Dunlap?"

He pulled his hand away, afraid he'd squeeze too hard in his anger. He rose and walked to a window. "Oh, it was sorely tempting, but we needed him alive to testify to what Caldwell had been up to, except now there is twice the reason to hang the man—for trying to kill you and the baby. If he doesn't hang—"

"He'll hang, John. How could they not hang him, *and* Higgins and Dunlap. It's over now. We can put the past behind us, just like you said. You *will* quit the Rangers now, won't you?"

He sighed. "I will." He turned to face her. "We lost a lot in that fire, but we still have a little money left. We'll manage somehow. I'll start building a house out on the farm, and a barn. Some of the other ranchers have already offered to give me a few head of cattle to start with, just for what I've done to stop the rustling. And when we get big enough, Ken said he'd quit the Rangers and come work for us."

Tess thought how well he fit Texas. She studied the gun on his hip, remembered how he'd rescued her. "Lord knows we'll be safe out there against outlaws and Indians with you around. My husband won't be hiding under a bed if we're attacked."

He grinned, seeming a little embarrassed.

"You look so tired, John. You aren't really fully recovered from your own wound. That trip must have been hard on you."

He sighed, rubbing at his rib near the wound. "Actually I got in a little tussle with Dunlap. Took a good kick. That's the first time a man ever put me down quite that way, but the wound—there wasn't anything I could do about it. If not for Ken, I'd probably be dead. Dunlap was ready to shoot me." He sat back down. "Ken's been wanting to pay me back for saving his hide a couple of times. He finally got the chance."

Her eyes teared again. "Thank God.

Their gazes held, so much more to say, feelings so intense. John thought how beautiful her hair looked all tangled and a tumble against the pillow. He wished it looked that way because he'd just made love to her. "You all right? I mean . . . the birth and all. How bad was it?"

She sighed. "Bad. It took nearly a full day. I do have to say I cursed you a few times for not being there."

He leaned back. "I'm damn sorry, Tess."

She gently stroked the baby's soft cheek with the back of her fingers. "What you accomplished was more important."

"How in hell did Jim Caldwell know you had any idea what he was up to? I take it that's the reason he was at the house."

"It's a long story, John. Thank God the citizens got together and captured him before he could get away. Some of his own men actually helped turn him in." The baby started to fuss. "Why don't you go get cleaned up while I feed your hungry son? Get us a room somewhere so we can truly be alone. We have so much more to talk about, so much planning to do."

He leaned forward, taking her hand again. "You'll probably have to testify, you know. We can't truly settle in until Caldwell's trial is over. We might have to travel all the way to Austin or Fort Worth, but we can take the train."

"I'm not afraid to testify. I just want it over with, so we can both live a normal, and I hope peaceful life." She smiled. "And have more babies." The baby cried harder, and she turned on her side, unbuttoning the flannel gown she wore. Little Tex eagerly sought his nourishment, sucking away, his tiny fingers digging into the white of her breast. "He really is a lot like you," she commented teasingly.

"I think I'm jealous," John said with a smile. He leaned over them both, kissing her cheek, her breast, the baby's cheek. "I've never seen a prettier sight," he told her. "I've never had something so wonderful to come home to." He gently smoothed back some of Tess's hair. "Thank you for giving me a family, Tess Hawkins. Not long ago I never even considered such a thing could be possible."

"And I never knew what it was like to be loved the way you can love a woman, or that I could love this baby so much. He's ours, John, just like you said. Who would ever have thought the way we met would lead to this?"

John watched little Tex, astounded at the turn his life had taken. He straightened, putting on his hat. "I'll get us that room." He walked to the door. "I love you, Tess." He looked back at her, realizing he meant the words more deeply than ever before.

"And I love you, John Hawkins." How wonderful to be able to say it with true meaning.

John left, and Tess closed her eyes, thanking God he was back and unhurt. She could hear him talking in the other room, heard raised voices as he walked outside. The whole town was in an uproar, many of El Paso's citizens ready to hang Caldwell, Higgins, and Dunlap on the spot, or so Mary had been telling her.

One thing was certain. John Hawkins knew how to smell out trouble and kick it out into the open. He'd done it again, and this time he'd brought his man in alive. The Texas Rangers were losing a good man, but he was hers now, and they weren't getting him back.

Birds sang sweetly, and Tess breathed deeply of the warm morning air. Three-month-old Texas still slept soundly in the small bed Harold Jeffers had made for him, with special wooden sides to keep the baby from falling out of it. The bed had been presented by the townspeople for John's work in finding the true culprit behind a good deal of the cattle rustling in the area. They had also volunteered to come here to the farm and help raise a barn and house.

They had worked incredibly fast. The barn was finished,

and John was out there right now with a stallion he'd captured a few days ago. Chickens pecked away at feed Tess had scattered for them earlier, more wild horses grazed in a fenced area, and cattle grazed farther out in a field. Tess stood on the porch of their new house, which still needed some finish work, but was livable.

She had never felt more content. The horrible past was truly behind her, and she was a far different woman than the Tess who'd been abducted a year ago.

John was a good father, much more attentive and helpful than she ever dreamed a man like that could be. He'd taken to ranching as easily as breathing, and he fit right in out here.

Jim Caldwell and Casey Dunlap would be hanged in Austin. Sam Higgins was in prison for several years. Tess often prayed for Harriet, understanding how the woman must be suffering. No one in El Paso had heard from her. The Caldwell ranch was up for sale, the transaction being handled for Harriet by a local land agent. John intended to buy part of it.

Tess never dreamed life could be so perfect, and it struck her only then that it had been exactly one year this month that her farm was attacked and burned. She'd been dragged off, to later be rescued by the mysterious and violent John Hawkins. Little did she know then the kind of man he really was. The thought spurred her to walk across the yard to the barn, which still smelled like fresh lumber.

"Whoa, boy."

The words came from John, who was working with the stallion in a double-wide stall. Tess noticed he'd managed to get a rope bridle over its ears and into its mouth. The horse was a beautiful animal, coal black, and wild . . . wild like Texas, wild like John Hawkins could be at times. "That stallion reminds me of you," she said, walking closer. The stall gate was open, and the horse whinnied and reared. Tess held her breath while John hung on to the rope.

"Stay back," he told her.

Tess watched him, first stern and commanding, then talking gently in Spanish to the horse. The stallion finally calmed down.

"I'll be riding him within a week," he told her. "But mostly I'll just graze him and use him for stud service."

She thought how John fit this kind of work, seemed to love it. Because of the heat he wore only his denim pants and weathered boots today. He was shirtless, and she watched the muscles of his arms, shoulders, and back as he worked with the fiercely strong horse, man against beast, both stallions, both wild, both loving freedom yet willing to be tamed. John gently removed the bridle, then slipped out and shut the stall gate.

"Let's just hope he doesn't kick it down," he told her. He walked to a bucket of water and drank some, then took the ladle and poured some over his hands. "And how does that horse remind you of me?" he asked, taking down a towel to dry his hands.

"I think you know," she answered. "He's strong and sleek, beautiful and wild."

He looked at her and grinned. "Now you're embarrassing me, Mrs. Hawkins."

"You love it."

"Do I?" He walked closer, pulling her into his arms. "I know that I love *you*."

She reached around his neck. "It's been a year, John, since we met. A whole year."

He kissed her hair. "I thought about that myself this morning. One year ago I was a restless, wild Texas Ranger who didn't care if he lived or died, and who thought he had no real happiness in his future, certainly not love."

"And I was a married woman who . . ." Her smile faded as she studied his dark eyes. "Who never really knew what it meant to be married."

He leaned down and met her mouth, then swung her up into his arms and walked into a stall with her. She let out a little scream when he tossed her into the hay. "John! What are you doing?"

"This is a brand new stall, fresh, clean hay, never had a horse in it yet."

She watched him come toward her. "John Hawkins! It's ten o'clock in the morning! I have chores. The baby will wake up from his morning nap anytime, and . . . and someone could come."

"Let them come. This is our land, our house, our barn, and you're my woman. I want my woman."

"Here? Now?"

He crouched over her, pushing up her dress. "Here. Now."

She put her hands against his chest. "John—"

He answered with a searching kiss, deep, lingering, demanding. He moved his lips to her neck.

"John, we can't—"

"Yes, we can. We can do anything we want."

She felt her drawers being slipped down, felt straw against her bare bottom. "John Hawkins, I thought you were becoming more civilized."

"I am. Look around you. We have a home, a baby, a ranch. Isn't that civilized enough for you?"

"You know what I mean." She drew in her breath when he yanked the drawers completely off and moved between her legs.

"I know exactly what you mean. I guess you'll never civilize that part of me, except that I won't ever share it with any other woman but you."

She thought about Jenny, all the prostitutes to whom he'd probably given great pleasure. The thought of it brought her secret jealousy to a boil again. "You'd better not," she told him.

"Why would I need to? I am married to the prettiest redhead in Texas." With that he slid into her almost unexpectedly. Tess closed her eyes and sucked in her breath with the pleasure of it. He pushed deeper, and she found herself meeting his rhythmic thrusts with wanton eagerness. This was like him, unbridled, spontaneous. She was instantly lost in his kisses and caresses, his exotic, intimate invasion. There was nothing left to say, and she had no protest left in her.

Outside, on a rise overlooking the farm, a small band of Mexican bandits sat studying the ranch, the horses, and cattle.

"I say we take the cattle, see if there is a woman down there and see what else might be valuable to us," one of them said.

Their leader shook his head. "I was asking around in Juárez. They say the Texas Ranger called John Hawkins lives here." He looked at the first man who had spoken. "Do you wish to ride against John Hawkins? Try to take his woman?"

The first man frowned, studied the ranch a moment longer. "We will go somewhere else."

The leader grinned and turned his horse. They rode away, leaving the ranch, its horses and cattle—and John Hawkins's woman—behind.

FROM THE AUTHOR . . .

I hope you have enjoyed my story. For information about the many other books I have written, send a self-addressed, stamped envelope (letter-size, please—9½″ × 4¼″) to my attention at 6013 North Coloma Road, Coloma, Michigan 49038. I will send you a newsletter and bookmark. Or you can visit my home page at http://www.parrett.net/~bittner. Thank you!